Praise for Shelley Noble

"With *The Colony Club*, Shell[...] of trailblazing heroines. Daisy's [...]'s determination combine in a [...] n and construction of the first [...] e uncertain times, this book is [...] .e broad shoulders of those courageous women who have gone before us."

—Alix Rickloff, author of *The Last Light over Oslo*

On *The Tiffany Girls*

"*The Tiffany Girls* is a richly detailed and impeccably researched story of art and friendship. Shelley Noble has crafted an intimate view of the professional and personal lives of the incredible women who brought Tiffany glass to life. A beautiful novel!"

—Chanel Cleeton, *New York Times* bestselling author of *The Cuban Heiress*

"Under Noble's deft hand, Grace, Clara, and Emilie come vividly to life in turn-of-the-century New York City in her new novel, *The Tiffany Girls*. I couldn't help but root for the trio of heroines as they strived to become artists in their own right through their work for Louis Comfort Tiffany, renowned master of stained glass. Readers will revel in the fascinating and lavish details and never look at a Tiffany lamp the same way again. An immersive, wonderful read!"

—Heather Webb, *USA Today* bestselling author of *Strangers in the Night*

"This story is beautifully written, and as rich, colorful, and breathtaking as Tiffany glass."

—Lecia Cornwall, author of *That Summer in Berlin*

"A fascinating look into the art world, and the working conditions of women, at the dawn of the twentieth century. A sweeping cast of characters, comprised of both historical figures and fictional ones alike, brings the high-stakes word of the Tiffany glassworks to life in vivid detail. Richly researched and utterly captivating, a must-read for fans of turn-of-the-century historical fiction."

—Aimie K. Runyan, bestselling author of
The School for German Brides and *A Bakery in Paris*

"*The Tiffany Girls* sparkles with as much light, hope, and wonder as Mr. Tiffany's stained-glass creations."

—Kaia Alderson, author of *Sisters in Arms*

"A historical fiction of bold new beginnings and the creative courage of three women artists who forged their careers at Tiffany's glassworks."

—Tessa Arlen, *USA Today* bestselling author
of *In Royal Service to the Queen*

"An inspiring friendship tale of talented female artists and their search for independence in a world that wasn't too keen on female autonomy."

—Eliza Knight, *USA Today* bestselling
author of *Starring Adele Astaire*

"Rich with finely wrought detail, *The Tiffany Girls* is the moving, little-known story of the women who worked as artists making glorious glassworks for Tiffany, their struggles, heartaches, and triumphs. Not to be missed!"

—Christine Wells, author of *One Woman's War*

Also by Shelley Noble

Historical Standalones
The Tiffany Girls

Beach Reads
Picture Perfect Autumn
Summer Island
Imagine Summer
Lucky's Beach
A Beach Wish
Lighthouse Beach
The Beach at Painter's Cove
Forever Beach
Whisper Beach
Christmas at Whisper Beach
Breakwater Bay
Newport Dreams
A Newport Christmas Wedding
Stargazey Point
Stargazey Nights
Beach Colors
Holidays at Crescent Cove

Historical Mysteries
A Secret Never Told
A Resolution at Midnight
Tell Me No Lies
Ask Me No Questions

THE
COLONY CLUB

A Novel

Shelley Noble

WILLIAM MORROW
An Imprint of HarperCollins*Publishers*

THE COLONY CLUB. Copyright © 2024 by Freydont Noble LLC. All rights reserved. Printed in the United States of America. No part of this book may be used or reproduced in any manner whatsoever without written permission except in the case of brief quotations embodied in critical articles and reviews. For information, address HarperCollins Publishers, 195 Broadway, New York, NY 10007.

HarperCollins books may be purchased for educational, business, or sales promotional use. For information, please email the Special Markets Department at SPsales@harpercollins.com.

FIRST EDITION

Interior text design by Diahann Sturge-Campbell

Library of Congress Cataloging-in-Publication Data has been applied for.

ISBN 978-0-06-325248-6

24 25 26 27 28 LBC 5 4 3 2 1

To my family with love

"It's such an honor to meet you, Mrs. Harriman."

Daisy Harriman roused herself from her usual afternoon bask in the sun and reluctantly turned from the window. She loved this room overlooking the garden and filled with sunlight. The sun was kind to old bones, and hers had been around for a good ninety-two years.

She smiled across at the eager young journalist who sat perched on the edge of the chintz armchair, her notepad and pencil held at the ready, part Emily Post, part Jacob Riis. So enthusiastic, so energetic and determined. And for a moment, Daisy was that young woman, with all the world before her. But that was behind her now. Daisy and other like-minded women had forced their way into their rightful place in the twentieth century. A new generation would carry on from here.

"How does it feel to be the first-ever recipient of President Kennedy's Citation of Merit award?"

They both looked at the wall where the framed certificate hung in a place of honor. Citation of Merit for Distinguished Service to Florence Jaffray Hurst Harriman. *Daisy was proud to have done her small part. Bordie would have been amused, and proud, but neither her husband nor her daughter, Ethel, had lived to see it. She was quite alone now.*

And yet never quite alone: she had been one of many

and they were still with her in spirit, if not in life. No, never quite alone.

"You've had such an astounding career," the journalist, whose name was Meg, continued. "Social reformer, union organizer, politician, diplomat. And to think that you began accomplishing all these things before women even had the right to vote."

She made it sound like ancient history, Daisy thought, and yet it seemed not so long ago when she and the ladies of the Colony Club first marched in support of the women garment workers, fought for the purity of food, for decent housing for the poor—for the right to vote. Her stint as Minister to Norway under Roosevelt during the war that changed the world seemed like yesterday.

"You were a young society matron living comfortably in New York City. You could so easily have been content with that life, donating to various causes from the comfort of your home. And yet you chose to lead. You took to the streets to protest the inequities of society. Risked your reputation and your physical safety to inaugurate change. You even barely escaped the German occupation of Norway with your life when you were minister there.

"You have served as an inspiration to so many. Can you tell me . . ."

"Yes?"

"What inspired you to step out of your secure life and throw yourself into the causes that would change the landscape of American culture forever?"

Daisy chuckled. "Oh, dear, did I do all that? Well, if you must know, it all began one summer, when I couldn't get a room at the Waldorf . . ."

CHAPTER 1

August 1902
Newport, Rhode Island

Florence Jaffray Hurst Harriman swept into the drawing room, the lace under her trumpet skirt swishing ominously. "It's absolutely outrageous," she announced, coming to a stop equidistant between the two wing chairs where her husband, Borden Harriman, and their friend Charles MacDonald, who was visiting Newport for the month, were both nose deep in their respective evening papers.

Bordie was the first to look up. He smiled indulgently at his wife.

Daisy recognized that look, but at the moment she was in no mood to be indulged. "You'd think we were living in the Middle Ages and not 1902," she continued, since neither one of the men seemed inclined to ask her what she was upset about. "It's the twentieth century, for heaven's sake."

"What is it, my dear?" Bordie asked.

"I need to go down to the city for a day or two to run a few errands that I didn't have time to do before we left for Newport, and since the townhouse is being renovated, I don't have any place to stay. I just had Miss Gleason call the Waldorf to reserve a room and they refused her. Even though she told them it was for me. The concierge said they did not cater to unaccompanied ladies, no matter who they were. The very idea. I have a good mind—"

Bordie broke in before she could continue. "Well, why don't you stay with one of your friends? I'm sure Anne Morgan would be glad to have you. Maybe the both of you could travel down and have a nice afternoon of shopping and errands and such and stay at her house overnight."

"Anne is on the Continent and everyone else is in Newport."

"Have Bordie drive you down," Charles suggested. "You can both stay at the Waldorf."

Bordie put down his paper. "I have no intention of returning to Manhattan; I just arrived in Newport yesterday evening. And I'm certainly not staying at the Waldorf or any other hotel if I can possibly help it."

Daisy huffed out her exasperation. "That's because *you* don't have to. *You* can stay at the Union Club, or the Princeton Club, or any of your many clubs and be as comfortable as if you were in your own home, which, I might remind you, is covered in tarps, construction dust, and heaven knows what else."

"She's got you there," added Charles, earning him a sour look from Bordie.

"I suppose I could stay at the YMCA, but Miss Gleason might balk. Private secretaries do not stay at the Y."

"And neither do the wives of bankers," Bordie retorted.

"If I had a club to go to, which I don't, I'd certainly stay—" She broke off. "Oh, Bordie, you're a genius."

Bordie, who had just returned to his paper, put it down again. "I shudder to think . . ." he began.

"A club," Daisy exclaimed. "Women should have a club of their own. Just like the men do. A place where we can stay overnight, have parcels delivered, write letters, make telephone calls, enjoy dinner . . . that's exactly what we need. How clever of you to suggest it.

"I think I'll telephone Kate Brice; I bet she'll be interested. Hmm, and Alva Belmont. And Maud Bull, and Emmie . . ."

Bordie laughed. "That's quite a bevy for an afternoon of errands."

"Sounds more like a tea party," Charles agreed.

"Oh, no," Daisy said. "Not a party, a meeting. We're going to establish a women's club. I don't know why I didn't think of it before." Daisy whisked out of the room, calling for her secretary and leaving the two men, their papers forgotten, staring after her and no doubt wondering what on earth Daisy was up to now.

DAISY WAS UP early the next morning, making lists of prospective members of the club. Her mind raced ahead as she imagined all the comforts and efficiency a club would bring to so many of them. After all, while the men were running banks and railroads and corporations, women kept houses with numerous staffs and children running smoothly, along with organizing all of their philanthropic endeavors. It was only fair that these entrepreneurs of society should have a club of their own.

As soon as Miss Gleason arrived, Daisy put her to work on the next week's schedule and went upstairs to fetch her hat.

An hour later, almost the acceptable hour for morning calls, Daisy took the carriage down to the Astors' Beaulieu cottage, where Kate Brice was still abed.

"I'm so sorry, did I wake you?" Daisy asked, bustling into the boudoir and smiling at a bleary-eyed Kate.

"Not at all," Kate said on a yawn and pushed herself up to rest against a mound of pillows. "Have you breakfasted? Coffee?"

Daisy's smile broadened. Leave it to Kate to rise to any occasion, any time. Friendly and persuasive, Kate could always be counted on to do her bit.

"I've had a glorious idea," Daisy said, sitting on the edge of the satin coverlet.

While the maid brought and poured coffee, Daisy explained, "Only a germ of an idea, but a club, just for women."

Kate's eyebrows lifted. "A club?"

"Yes, for women, but run in the same manner as the men's clubs."

"Cigars and port?" asked Kate, only slightly tongue in cheek.

"Certainly . . . Well, perhaps not cigars. But that's not what I mean. Only that it would operate along the same order as the men's clubs."

"And what do you know of the operations of men's clubs?"

"Well, I imagine they're run on the same basis as any good hotel, or household, for that matter. And though they may be the secret bastions of the male creatures, one can imagine. Here's my plan . . ."

Less than an hour later, Daisy and Kate, hastily coiffed and dressed in a blue silk gingham frock, were driving along Bellevue Avenue on their way to the first of several morning calls.

Four calls later, they were climbing back into the carriage.

"Three interested and one undecided," said Daisy. "But Adelaide Gibson never decides anything without picking it to death first. She'll come around. Shall we have lunch at Bailey's Beach?"

"Yes, indeed," Kate said enthusiastically.

The private beach club of the Newport elite was doing a robust noontime trade. And Daisy and Kate, who had gained enthusiasm with each stop, managed to snag two more society dames interested in hearing about the proposed club.

Appetites appeased and energy restored, they began a series of afternoon visits, and by the last call, Daisy had issued at least a dozen invitations to tea the following Thursday.

She dropped Kate off at Beaulieu and had the carriage return home.

"Not bad for a day's work," Daisy said, stripping off her gloves and depositing her hat with the waiting parlormaid, before striding into the parlor to find Bordie and Charles sitting in exactly the same places as she'd left them the night before.

"Back from the city already?" Bordie asked, not really think-ing. It would have been nigh impossible to get to the city and back again in one day, much less accomplish errands while there. For an intelligent man, he could sometimes . . .

"Yes, dear." Daisy left them to their papers and hurried to her office, where Miss Gleason was also seated in the same place where Daisy had left her that morning. However, unlike the men, Miss Gleason had organized Daisy's week, tallied the weekly expenses, and separated the mail into neat stacks to be perused, answered, or handed back to Miss Gleason for their reply.

And Daisy thought, as she had many times, that, underap-preciated though they might be, women's efficiency and good sense was the glue that held a well-run organization together. It just made her more optimistic about the idea of a place where women could go to exchange ideas with like-minded women.

She'd barely sat down at her desk when the first RSVP ar-rived.

Dear Daisy, I'm sorry to have to decline your lovely invitation for tea. Mr. Starrett has put his foot down. He says that the place for a women's club is in her home. He was most ada-mant that I have nothing to do with such a venture. I wish you the best of luck with your club idea and I hope to see you at the Havemeyer soiree on Friday.

Well, she should have expected something like that. But no matter, there were plenty of society ladies who knew how to circumvent their husband's reactionary views about a woman's place in society.

She tossed the note into the trash basket. "Kate Brice and I made the rounds today. All in all, it was a fruitful enterprise, though we did receive several 'My husband wouldn't approve.' Lord, if we waited for our husbands to approve, we wouldn't even get dinner on the table. At least I have a slightly enlightened husband in Mr. Harriman."

Not being married herself, Miss Gleason wisely held her peace.

"And Eben Rollins Morse, who happened to be home at Villa Rosa, actually said, 'Women shouldn't have clubs—they'll only use them as addresses for clandestine letters.' Which makes one wonder what actually goes on in men's clubs."

Daisy pushed away from her writing desk and walked over to the fireplace, its unused grate covered with a floral fire screen for the summer.

"It seems like for every woman who shows interest in a new idea, there are ten men telling us we can't or shouldn't, or ridiculing the very idea of women meeting on their own to carry on conversations that aren't about fashion or children."

She adjusted a pair of Dresden swans on the mantel and turned back to Miss Gleason.

"Women have every right to a place of their own where they can relax and discuss whatever they care to. I have every hope of succeeding."

But by the time the first meeting of the women's club assembled in her parlor the following week, six ladies had found it necessary to beg off. Only two of them made the excuse of prior engagements. The others had been dissuaded from participating by their husbands.

Those who attended were quite enthusiastic and, over tea cakes and watercress sandwiches, they tossed around ideas as easily as a badminton cock on a sunny afternoon. Miss Gleason was enlisted to take minutes, and it quickly became evident to Daisy that it wouldn't be long before she would need to hire a separate secretary for "the club," as she'd begun to think of it.

Everyone had questions.

"When will we meet? We're all so busy with the season between September and the new year."

"Which is exactly why we need a place to relax during our busy days out," Daisy answered.

"*Where* will we meet?" asked Maud Bull.

"Depends on how many members we attract."

"Thirty? Maybe forty?" asked Emmie Winthrop, rather wide-eyed.

"A hundred at least," said Daisy, "or it won't be a club."

"Well, it all depends on what we offer. What will we do at the meetings?"

"We'll have various speakers of interest," Daisy explained. "Concerts, readings, talks on current events . . . We can hold receptions, tea parties, whatever we want. But first and foremost, it will have rooms for members to stay overnight when visiting the city." Daisy's remark activated a pregnant pause.

"Without our husbands?"

"Yes," said Daisy, "that's the whole point."

"Absolutely. Only the essentials," Kate quipped. "No husbands. But a room for one's maid, of course."

"Kate, really," said Lillian Stevens. "My Albert . . . Well, I just don't know. Besides, I never travel without him."

"That's just the point. Now you will be able to."

"Let's cross that bridge when we come to it," said Mary Dick, who was older than the others but already had experience in forming working girls clubs. "Remember why you're starting this club."

"Because Daisy couldn't get a room at the Waldorf." Helen Barney sighed. "Though why she would want to . . ."

"That was just the tinder that inspired me to create a place where we can be ourselves, luncheon among ourselves, focus on issues that matter to us—"

"And the country," interjected Alva Belmont.

"Definitely," Daisy agreed. "Situations that reach beyond us but that we should have a voice in."

Lillian groaned audibly. "Not women's suffrage again."

"Why not?" snapped Alva Belmont, who had declared herself a suffragist long before most of them had ever heard of the word. "Just because you're satisfied to let your husband make decisions for you . . ."

That raised a few eyebrows since Alva was on her second husband, having divorced William K.Vanderbilt five years before to marry his friend Oliver Belmont.

"Most of us know our—"

"Ladies, ladies." Daisy's voice broke over their heads. "This is just why we need such a club; a place to discuss ideas in the open, express our opinions—respectfully, of course—and perhaps learn to think in different ways. Discuss, debate, then go out and act."

"Yes," agreed Anne Morgan in her serious voice. "And we must have a gymnasium with a running track. Strong mind in a strong body."

Maud Bull raised her hand. "I second that. No more having to reserve time with Mr. Keenan and his gymnasium. It's so lowering."

Several of the ladies groaned.

"Yes," said Kate Brice. "If we must exercise, let us have a club where we can get it over with and then go downstairs to lunch." She reached for another cucumber sandwich.

Emmie Winthrop sighed. "I just want somewhere to play lawn tennis without having to take the carriage all the way out to Queens."

"Tennis? But where will we ever find such a space? Even if we rented out a whole floor of some building."

"We could rent one of the meeting rooms at the Plaza," suggested Maud.

"For tennis? We'll need someone's ballroom," said Emmie.

"Well, you're not playing tennis in my ballroom."

"No, no," Daisy assured them. "We'll need a space for that, and for lectures and concerts, and . . ."

"The roof of one of the hotels," Emmie suggested, clearly enamored with the idea. "Perhaps the Plaza."

"If you think I'm going to chase your serves down eight flights of stairs, think again," said Kate.

"Bridge," said Maud.

"Bridge? What bridge?"

Maud rolled her eyes, clearly forgetting her manners. "The card game."

"No gambli—"

"And debates," added Alva, cutting off further conversation about card games or tennis.

"And concerts and edifying lectures." Lillian jutted out her chin and glared at Alva.

"Good heavens," exclaimed Margaret Norrie. "We'll need an entire *building* to accommodate such things. Even the Princeton Club doesn't have all these things."

"Which is all the more reason why the first New York women's club should," said Daisy. It was a daunting prospect. She hadn't really gotten that far in her imaginings. No further than a nice sitting room with writing desks and a comfortable well-appointed bedroom and bath, where she could awaken in comfort, refreshed and ready to face the day. Suddenly her mind was snowballing with new possibilities and the enormity of the potential that lay before them. Not just a place of refuge, but where they would have a voice, make a difference in the world around them. A real difference.

"If we want to attract members," said Mary Dick, the voice of experience, "we should think of a name. Having a name makes it stick in the mind. Besides, we can't just keep calling it *the club*. People will get the wrong idea. It leaves the mind to wander in undesirable directions, imagine all sorts of inappropriate things."

But as with most things among the ladies, they all had suggestions, but agreement on what that name should be was much harder to come by.

"The City Club, for when we're in town."

"Already taken by the men."

"Town Club?"

No one was very enthusiastic about that one.

"The Liberty Club!" exclaimed Helen. "Because while we're there, we'll be free."

They considered that for a few minutes.

"Too political sounding," Lillian pointed out.

Alva pursed her lips, but left what she was thinking to the others' imaginations.

The afternoon flew by. The tea cakes and sandwiches disappeared and the sherry magically appeared. They made plans to meet again when they all returned to the city, but just before they adjourned, Margaret Norrie called out, "The Colony Club, because we're like the original colonists, but where they explored a new land and made it their home, the club will be the home of new ideas, new associations, and progress."

They all agreed that it was the perfect name and reluctantly departed just in time to rush home to prepare themselves for dining or a ball or a concert or any of the other possibilities Newport offered its summer residents.

When the door finally closed behind the last departure, Daisy breathed a sigh of relief. "It's invigorating to see such enthusiasm, don't you think?"

Miss Gleason nodded but kept writing in her notebook. She had filled more than a few pages since tea was served.

"The Colony Club. It's turning into more than a modest little brownstone where we could stay overnight, entertain a few friends, and have some lunch."

"Indeed," said the still-writing Miss Gleason.

"But what we didn't discuss at all is how are we to finance the club."

"True," agreed Miss Gleason.

"What we need is a planning committee."

"So you are not dissuaded?"

"Heavens, no. The women of Manhattan want a women's club, and they shall have it."

April 18, 1963
Washington, D.C.

"Mrs. Harriman?"

Daisy pulled her mind from the past and gazed at the still-enthusiastic-looking young reporter.

"What happened next?"

Daisy smiled ruefully. "Sadly, not much at first.

"Little did I know that it would take almost two years before we actually broke ground. It may seem like a long time these days, but back then we were busy with our regular social obligations, and trips to Europe, and our summer estates. We did manage to form a steering committee. And secure the financing, thanks to Anne Morgan, who convinced her father, J. P., to form a men's advisory board, who provided the funds for a new clubhouse."

Daisy leaned over and patted the journalist's hand. "Don't look so surprised. In those days, enlisting men was really the only way to get large sums of money. But not to worry, we had no intention of letting them rule the Colony Club.

"We began holding meetings at members' houses or rented assembly rooms, but at last we bought property on Madison Avenue, and the Colony Club was truly born."

January 1903
Manhattan

Well, we did it." Daisy shivered and pulled her mink coat more tightly around her. She wasn't cold; she was excited and just a little daunted as she and Anne Morgan stood on the sidewalk across the street from 120–124 Madison Avenue, the site that would become the Colony Club.

She'd signed the papers that morning at the bank, with the newly appointed treasurer, Anne Morgan, and Bordie and J. P. in attendance to give the two women credence. Anne had handed over a check for $400,000.

Daisy, who had utmost faith in the club, had nonetheless quaked in her fur-lined winter boots as the check changed hands. There was no going back now, even if they wanted to, which none of them did.

Now Anne stood at Daisy's side on the sidewalk, both fairly humming with excitement and a sense of amazement and pride.

Passersby hurried around them, anxious to get out of the biting cold. If they did slow down, they must have wondered what possessed two ladies swathed in mink and sable from head to toe to be standing still as statues in the middle of pedestrian traffic.

"Hooray for us," said Anne in her husky voice. "Now let's go inform the others. They must be beside themselves with anticipation." She raised her hand and motioned to her carriage, which immediately pulled up next to the curb. The foot warmers inside were welcome even after a mere few minutes standing in the cold.

The carriage rattled forward, and in a few minutes the two women were entering Daisy's row house, where forty committee members of the Colony Club were waiting in the newly decorated ballroom.

Forty, thought Daisy, and growing daily. Miss Gleason was doing double duty as secretary, and even though she was incredibly efficient, Daisy hated to impose on her for much longer. The Colony Club might be foremost on Daisy's mind, but she did have other duties and responsibilities to attend to.

A huge cry of hurrah rose up as they entered the ballroom; fervent applause followed, only dying out when Daisy, as the duly elected president, walked to the front and pounded a gavel on the speaker's podium.

"This meeting of the Colony Club will now come to order."

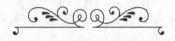

CHAPTER 2

March 1904
Manhattan

Nora Bromley sat at the polished wooden table, her chin propped in her hand as she watched the world grow dark outside the library window. She was one of the last students to leave the New York School of Applied Design for Women each day. And though the school was commonly referred to as NYSAD, Nora thought it was an unfair acronym. There was nothing sad about the school.

It was the best thing that had ever happened to her and she spent every moment she could within its high-ceilinged rooms. A haven of learning cloistered away from the noise and the distractions of the outside world. And, especially in March, the cold.

She'd finished her last tutoring assignment an hour before. The school had helped her set up sessions with several girls who needed a little extra help in the architecture division and who could afford individual attention. Nora received a small stipend, and they let her use the library late to study. Nora was one of the poorer students, just managing to eke out the tuition fees with the money her father had left for just this purpose.

Money that should have gone to her brother, Jimmy.

Nora drew her attention back to the page she'd been reading. She'd have just enough time to finish this chapter before they locked the school for the night.

She'd already begun to steel herself for the frigid streets out-

THE COLONY CLUB   17

side after spending hours in the silence and warmth of the library when the door clicked open behind her. The guard was early tonight.

She turned the page and read faster, even as she rose and began to gather her things.

"Ah, I thought it might be you burning the midnight oil."

Not the night guard, but Professor Gerhardt.

"Professor." Nora turned to face him. "I was just finishing this chapter on the new techniques in storied buildings."

"Excellent, excellent."

Professor Gerhardt was a tall man, extremely thin, whose height-to-frame ratio, he often joked, was an architectural miracle.

"I've been meaning to talk to you . . ."

Nora swallowed and pulled herself up to her full height. Still, she barely reached his top vest button.

"I'm sure you are aware of the competition coming up before the end of term."

"Yes, sir." How could anyone not be? There was a fifty-dollar prize for first place and twenty-five dollars for second. Plus their entries would be adjudicated by a panel of esteemed architects. A good showing could go a long way toward a promising career.

"And have you a design you plan to enter?"

"I do have something I've been working on."

"Good, good. I don't have to tell you what will be expected of a winning design. You always do impeccable work." He hesitated. "May I ask, are you planning to continue your work in architecture once you graduate?"

"Of course, sir. What else would I do?"

He smiled down at her, the lens of his pince-nez catching the light.

"Many of our young ladies opt for marriage—not that you can't do both, mind you . . . under the right circumstances."

"Meaning if she marries another architect. One who allows her to work by his side."

And most often takes credit for her work, Nora thought.

"As you say. It's a difficult field, but there are successful female architects. It takes determination and an iron will."

"I understand. But I will be an architect." She'd promised. "In fact, I've been studying different firms where I might obtain a position as a draftsman. At least, an apprenticeship."

"That's just the right attitude. And of course when the time comes, the school will help you enter the job market as we do with all our promising students."

"Thank you."

"I hope I haven't dissuaded you. I believe you could have a bright future ahead of you."

Nora smiled. "You haven't deterred me in the least."

"Excellent, excellent. Now finish up here before you get locked in for the night. And bundle up well. It's bitterly cold outside. Good night."

Nora watched him leave, thinking this wouldn't be the worst place to spend the night. Warm and quiet and more space than she could ever use. But she quickly finished reading her chapter and reluctantly headed downstairs to face the elements and the two-block walk to the Parker Hotel for Young Working Women, where she shared a room with two other girls.

She tucked her head inside her coat collar and bent into the wind. Her ears hurt from the cold but she refused to tie her scarf around her head. It reminded her too much of the poor souls who had been their neighbors on Perry Street.

The Parker was a narrow, four-story brick building, too large to be a boardinghouse, but not large enough to offer the amenities of a real hotel. In fact, it had nothing much to recommend it but cheap rooms and adequate fire escapes that ran down the facade like black scars. Nora hurried inside and stood shivering in the entrance hall long enough to take off her mittens. Knowing she wouldn't be receiving any mail, she ignored the bored desk boy and trudged up three flights to the room she shared with two other working girls, Inez, a mannequin at Bonwit Teller, and Lucy, a fancy goods finisher at Macy's.

The climb warmed her a bit, but as soon as she opened the door to her room, she felt the draft seeping under the one window. The room was dark. She groped for the electric lamp, which gradually lit to reveal just what she'd expected. A mess. Stockings drying over the radiator, clothes strewn about the floor. There were dirty dishes in the sink that was to be used only for washing faces and hands, not cooking; three beds, only one made; stacks of magazines that had fallen over and fanned across the threadbare braided rug.

The small drawing table that sat at the end of Nora's bed was holding not her latest renderings but an empty ginger beer bottle and several glasses.

She gathered everything up, dropped the items down next to the sink of dishes, and scrubbed off the desktop. When it was thoroughly dry, she pushed it up against the wall and stuffed a towel into the cracks between the window and the sill. It was still cold, but a lot better. She shimmied her portable drawing board out from under her bed and balanced it on top of the table, pulled over a wooden chair, and sat down with her back to the room.

Only then did she unroll the drawing, her latest depiction of the idea she was working on for the competition. She carefully placed the box of pencils and straightedges to the side, then took a few moments to frown at her work. It was still in its initial stages, though there had already been several attempts. This sketch was at least closer to what she could see in her head. But she hadn't managed to transfer it perfectly to lines and arcs and angles.

Maybe she was trying for too much, but if she did manage

to win the prize, she wanted to win it with this, her dream of a hospital for tuberculosis patients. She could see it in her mind's eye; a place with light and sun and clean fresh air, surrounded by trees. A place where Jimmy would have been cured.

But this was all wrong. If she situated the rooms so that everyone got light, it made it hard for the staff to move from one to the other. She drummed her fingers on the drawing board. Unless she . . . She took her gum eraser and attacked the last wing she'd just drawn. *An octagon*, she reminded herself. A central staff desk, with wings radiating in a half circle from it . . . Her pencil began to fly just getting the ideas down; she'd do measurements and ratios once the drawing set. And an atrium large enough for the light to reach the floor. It would save on electricity—because her hospital would have electricity. The Romans had seen the efficacy of natural light, so she must be on the right track. It was important not to be so forward-thinking that she failed to incorporate the successes of the past.

Soon the pairs of hose, the crusted dishes, the faint smell of tinned sardines, even the cold faded away as she lost herself in her design, just as she had in the days when she sat on the floor watching as Jimmy copied the fantastic castles from the book that Grandpapa Bromley had brought over from the Old Country. Their father, coming in from his work at the tailor's shop, would look over their shoulders and say, "Castles in the air, eh?" not attempting to hide his pride in his son's talents.

Jimmy would be the first Bromley to go to school. A fine college, maybe.

Jimmy would smile up at him, grasping the bit of pencil in his thin hand, and say, "No, Papa, it's for us to live in. I'll build it for you and Mama." And their father would smile and turn away before they could see his eyes glisten with unshed tears.

Now it was up to Nora.

They'd kept Jimmy's sketches in a little wooden box, which they hid under the bed. Drawings on any scrounged scrap of paper, small and large, torn or crumpled, that came their way. Nora had those scraps of paper still, though she no longer had her older brother.

Tuberculosis, they'd said, and she held his hand until Jimmy had gone on to his castles in the air without her.

It was after midnight when Nora turned out the light and climbed into bed. She pulled the covers up to her ears, and lay listening while the wind howled and rattled the window like an angry collections agent.

Inez and Lucy came traipsing in some time later, giggling and shushing each other to be quiet and only making more noise for their efforts. Nora had made sure her supplies and clothes were safely stored away before she'd gone to bed, so she pretended to be asleep until the other two finally called it a night.

Perhaps when she got a job, she would be able to send money to her sister, Louise, and still afford a room at the Y for herself. A room all her own, where she could have a place for all her things and wouldn't have to worry about them when she was away. *A room of her own.* It sounded like heaven, she thought, as she finally slipped into sleep.

ELSIE DE WOLFE smiled at the audience, taking in the orchestra before lifting her chin to bestow her radiant thank-yous upon the balcony, even though they were faceless from this distance. Lastly, she nodded to the private boxes, then dipped into her well-practiced curtsy, lingering for a moment before stepping back as the next actress took her turn.

Her smile fully in control, Elsie listened carefully to see if the applause was louder than hers had been. Not that it really mattered. Mr. Thomas had written the play for the leading man, and for Lionel Barrymore in particular, who was a popular draw. It didn't leave much for the actresses to do. It was, Elsie decided, a fact that she and other actresses often had to put up with.

And they called actresses divas.

Actors could be twice as demanding and usually got what they wanted. It was the way of the world.

And if Elsie had been rather passed over in the reviews—not that Elsie cared about that—it was her part that was to blame.

Still, it was hard to keep smiling when the crowd roared to life, applauding and stamping their feet as Lionel stepped forward, knowing he was in command of the moment, the reason they had come. The rest of the actors might as well be salt shakers. And as Elsie stood next to Drina in her drab costume, Elsie knew at least there she outshone them all. Her costume had been made in Paris. She'd had it designed for the part and shipped to New York before the opening. If she had to play second fiddle to the star, at least she would do it in haute couture.

No one outshone Elsie de Wolfe's look onstage.

Lionel finally stepped back from his bow and gestured to stage right, where Augustus Thomas, the playwright, was waiting to take his bow.

He strode onto the stage; clasped his hands as he bowed.

She supposed she should be glad that *The Other Girl* had proved to be a resounding success. In spite of the initial tepid reviews, the Criterion Theatre had been filled night after night with enthusiastic theatergoers. They roared with laughter at the cracks and hijinks, gasped at the physical comedy, and whistled and applauded enthusiastically at the last curtain.

Charles Frohman, who was producing the play, intended to keep it running until June. Which meant Elsie would have to postpone her trip to France and meet Bessie there later.

The curtain finally closed on the last act, and the cast relaxed on cue, all except Lionel, who was still riding high on his applause. He clapped Augustus Thomas on the shoulder, joked with the stage manager as he made his final exit for the evening. He would have friends waiting in his dressing room, fans waiting at the stage door, more friends and fans waiting at whatever restaurant he was dining at that evening.

Elsie replaced the bouquet the actresses were presented with after each performance on the prop table. They would be collected and transferred to refrigeration to be used again the following evening. Did anyone ever guess that after the first few nights, the flowers lavished on the ladies night after night were actually repeats?

She headed to her dressing room, delicate, graceful, reminding herself to not let down until the door closed behind her and she was alone with her dresser, a girl named Clovis, of all things, who spoke with a lisp when she spoke at all.

Just as well; Elsie didn't want to hear what she might say. She turned her back to the girl and let her undo her gown. A gown she'd paid for herself.

Clovis helped her into her dressing gown of black silk, embroidered with giant white peonies, and hurried away with the costume. Elsie sat at her dressing table, reaching for the cold cream without even having to look, watching her face in the mirror for any sign of defeat, of failure, of . . .

There was a knock at the door. *Friends. Fans.* Elsie put down the cold cream. How silly she had been. She was a star, beloved, and on her way to the top. She straightened her shoulders, smiled at her image in the mirror, and called out, "*Mes amis. Entrez, s'il vous plait.*"

"THAT WAS DELIGHTFUL," said Daisy as the curtain lowered on the evening's performance of *The Other Girl*. She'd suggested the play because Bessie Marbury's companion, Elsie de Wolfe, was starring in it. They were both members of the Colony Club and had waxed enthusiastic about the play that had just opened at the Criterion Theatre.

Daisy had enjoyed it immensely, her thoughts rarely straying to her plans for the Colony Club as they had at the opera last week. Even Caruso hadn't been able to keep her mind from churning over ways to push the construction of the clubhouse along. It seemed to occupy her mind constantly these days.

"Lionel Barrymore certainly knows how to entertain," said Bordie, perusing his program.

"He does," Daisy agreed.

"And your friend Elsie was quite lovely."

"She was," Daisy said distractedly. She'd just caught sight of Bessie in the orchestra talking to two gentlemen, one of whom was Charles Frohman, the producer of the play. Probably making another deal; Bessie never lost a chance to mix business with pleasure.

"Though I must say . . ." Bordie continued, "she didn't have much of a part; actually—"

"No," Daisy agreed, preempting him from stating the obvious. Elsie might be the best-dressed actress on the Rialto, but her acting was less than inspiring. At least with Bessie as her agent, she shouldn't have trouble continuing to get parts.

"You seem distracted, my dear. You're not still stewing over what James Barclay said during the intermission, are you?"

"About how the building site for the clubhouse is still lying empty for over a year after acquiring the property? I haven't given it a thought."

Bordie chuckled and helped her into her coat, a lovely green velvet with a mink collar that he'd given her for Christmas. "Of course you haven't."

"But if one more person comments on the slow progress of the building . . . Well, they just don't understand the difficulties of getting a good architect."

"Stanford White turn you down?"

Daisy adjusted her collar. "It's not that he's turned us down; he just puts us off."

"He didn't look well the last time I saw him. Everyone is saying . . ." Bordie's next words faded away. Bessie was headed backstage, Frohman and the other gentleman following in her wake as if she were the star of the evening and they had just signed on the dotted line.

As soon as the door closed behind the trio, Daisy turned to Bordie. "The ladies have decided they want Stanford White and Stanford White they shall have."

And first thing Monday morning she would pay a call on Bessie Marbury. If anyone could clinch the deal, it was Bessie.

CHAPTER 3

Sunday was supposed to be a day of rest, Nora thought despondently. For Inez and Lucy, it meant church, where they dutifully carried their prayer books but were really on the lookout for respectable young men with futures. Which Nora thought silly since they spent Friday and Saturday nights with the boys from the boardinghouse next door, who were fun and spirited and much too forward for Nora's taste. Not that she was a prude, as she was continually having to remind them. But she had obligations.

So on every Sunday instead of resting, Nora, dressed in her version of Sunday best, made the trip out to Brooklyn to have Sunday dinner with her family, what was left of it.

Tiny flakes of snow greeted her at the sidewalk when she stepped out of the Parker's front door. She sighed, and, tucking her head against the cold, she walked as fast as she could toward the trolley stop. She climbed in with other shivering passengers and began the long ride down to the bridge where she would get on another trolley, and then another to Flatbush in Brooklyn, and eventually make it to her sister's apartment.

The wind across the East River buffeted the car and rattled the tracks as they made their slow way across the bridge. Nora crossed her arms and hunkered down, wondering if the new underground railroads—if they ever finished them—would be heated. Now *that* would be a luxury.

Her teeth were chattering and her feet were numb by the time she climbed off the last trolley. It was snowing in earnest and she slipped and slid all the way down Flatbush Avenue toward Louise and her husband Donner's apartment. Donner worked at the Havemeyer sugar refinery, where he made a large enough salary for Louise to stay at home to take care of their baby.

When Papa died, he made Louise promise to take care of Mama and Rina until Nora finished her architectural training and could get a job to help. Nora hadn't waited to graduate but immediately started turning over every spare penny she earned from her tutoring. The effort was just resented by her ever-resentful older sister.

The apartment was on the first floor of a brick building and had its own kitchen and water laid on. Nora brushed the snow off her shoulders and scarf, straightened up, and knocked on the door.

She heard Donner's deep voice yell for someone to open it.

The door swung open.

"Nora!" Rina exclaimed as if Nora didn't come every Sunday to share a meal, even though her presence just increased Louise's resentment. But Nora did it for Mama and Rina.

"Shut the door!" Louise ordered, wiping her hands on her apron and not coming closer than the doorway to the kitchen. "Heat isn't free."

Nora slipped inside, and Rina practically threw herself against the door in her hurry to close it.

Louise immediately disappeared back into the kitchen. Nora said hello to Donner, though his head didn't appear from behind his copy of the *New York Journal*. She knew Mama wouldn't come out of her bedroom when Donner was at home, and though Nora longed to go see Mama, it was bound to bend her sister's nose out of shape if she didn't see Louise first.

She was standing at the stove stirring a big pot of stew, which Nora knew would consist mainly of carrots and potatoes, most of what little meat there was going to Donner. They could easily afford meat. There was no reason to be so stingy. The room was steamy and the window foggy. At least it had a window, something their Lower East Side apartment had lacked.

Resigning herself to being ignored, Nora pulled out her handkerchief, untied it, and let the coins it held drop onto the table. Louise, with the ears of a fox, turned at the sound.

She took one look at the meager pile, sighed mightily, and came over to scoop the coins into her hand. "Is this all?"

"Yes, some of my tutees didn't return to school after the holidays."

"Holidays," Louise scoffed.

"There will be more next time." At least Nora hoped there would be. Not that it would make any difference to her sister. Sometimes Nora thought Louise just enjoyed acting miserable.

"There had better be. We have another baby on the way."

Nora glanced at her sister's flat stomach. "Congratulations."

"Another mouth to feed." Louise carried the money over to the cupboard and poured it into an earthenware jar she kept on the shelf.

"One more semester and I'll graduate. I should be able to get an architectural or drafting job that will pay more. Then things will get better, I promise."

Louise picked up her spoon. "Promises are what got us in this lousy situation in the first place."

Nora glanced quickly at the doorway. "Shh. Do you want Mama to hear you? She gave us everything she could; now it's our time. We promised Papa."

"Easy for you to say. You got everything you wanted."

"I didn't want Jimmy to die. Or Papa, either." Nora knew she should just shut up. It was the same argument they always had. And anything Nora said would just make it worse.

"Can I do something to help?"

"You can set the table."

And that was the last time it was mentioned, though it sat

between them, hovering over the stewpot on the table like a black cloud. Everyone concentrated on eating. Mama praised the stew, and Rina would make a face at Nora whenever she was sure Louise wasn't watching.

It was the same every Sunday. Donner would leave the table as soon as his bowl was empty. Mama insisted on doing the washing up. Louise went off to tend to the baby, and Nora and her sister Rina crept off to the small bedroom Rina shared with their mother for some quiet conversation.

"I hate her," Rina said as soon as they were sitting on the one narrow bed, hardly large enough for one person, much less two.

"Hush, it's hard on her. The extra responsibility."

"Pooh, Mama cooks and cleans and takes care of the baby. She dusts and does the mending. If she were getting paid, we could afford to get our own apartment."

"No, you couldn't. And you wouldn't want Mama going back to cleaning other people's houses, getting chilblains and painful joints, would you?"

Rina huffed out a sigh. "No. But I could help her."

"Neither one of you is going to do that. You're going to finish school, then we'll look for a good position for you."

Rina flopped back on the bed. "Maybe I'll meet a rich handsome stranger and marry him, then I'll build a big house for all of us to live in, 'cept not Louise and Donner."

"You just concentrate on your math and forget about rich strangers. How is math going?"

"Okay? It's hard, though. I don't see why you got all the math in your head and I got none at all."

"You have plenty of math in your head. You just need to use it. Let me see your homework."

Rina rolled off the bed, slumped over to where Mama's old sewing machine was wedged in between a dresser and the wall, and returned with a notebook of figures. "Okay, look . . ." Rina slid closer to her and a few minutes later, Mama came in to see two dark heads deep in study.

She was holding Nora's coat and scarf. "It's snowing hard— you'd better get back to town before it clogs up the tracks."

"But we haven't had any chance for a visit," Nora protested.

"We'll visit next week, now you get going. It's dangerous in the snow."

Nora took her coat. "I'll try to get here earlier next week. If it's nice we can go for a walk."

"Yes," Mama said, putting the scarf over Nora's head and tying it under her chin. Nora gritted her teeth, but she didn't pull it away.

Mama and Rina walked her to the door. Donner was nowhere to be seen. Nora called out her thank-yous, but, getting no response, she hugged Mama and Rina and slipped out into the weather.

The snow had turned icy and it stung Nora's cheeks. All thoughts of removing the headscarf fled and she hurried down the street, eyes focused on the ground so she wouldn't slip and fall.

The trolley was crowded and Nora just managed to find a seat. They rattled across the bridge toward Manhattan, Nora's teeth chattering with its rhythm.

When they neared the city, she slipped the scarf off her head.

It was dark, but the snow had abated when she wearily climbed the steps to her room. She dreaded coming back here almost as much as she dreaded going to visit her family. But there was the prospect of a position only a few months on the horizon. Not just an internship, but as a draftsman or architect with a decent salary. She would make good on her promise. She owed her family everything and she would realize the trust Papa had placed in her to take care of them.

Maybe when she had a job she could get an apartment. Mama

and Rina could come live with her. But she had to find a good job first. And there was the contest . . .

ON MONDAY JUST before noon, Daisy took the carriage down to Irving Place.

The day was sunny, but there was still snow in patches on the ground, and she was glad she'd worn her fur coat and muff.

She was suddenly feeling more optimistic. A year ago she'd had the idea of convincing Bessie Marbury and her protégée and partner, Elsie de Wolfe, to join the club's planning board. She had not been disappointed. They'd both been invaluable members of the organization's committee.

Bessie had embraced the idea and run with it, as Bessie often did. As one of the most formidable theatrical agents in New York—perhaps the world—with clients like George Bernard Shaw, Victorien Sardou, and Georges Feydeau, she had clout in places that Daisy and her set didn't. She knew how to organize, fundraise, and arm-twist with the best of them. And Elsie, with her dramatic allure and acquaintances in the theater world, added just the right amount of glamour.

When the carriage came to a stop in front of the brick-face corner brownstone a few minutes after noon, Daisy hesitated only momentarily before stepping down.

If it had been up to her, she would have made a morning call, but Bessie, a thoroughly organized and busy professional woman, only allowed social calls at noon. Though Daisy suspected this had more to do with long nights at the theater and the amount of spirits consumed at their Sunday salon, which attracted some of the world's most estimable, and often infamous, artists, actors, and writers.

She hoped she wasn't imposing on Bessie's time. One didn't like to take advantage of one's friends, and she had already asked a lot of the industrious Bessie.

Of course, knowing Bessie, she would have just said so out-right and saved Daisy a fruitless visit. Though she had to admit no visit with Bessie and Elsie was ever entirely fruitless. Life was always an adventure at "the bachelors' house."

Bessie answered the door herself.

Daisy was momentarily taken aback. Seeing Bessie was always a bit of a shock. A mature women ostensibly in her late forties, though no one knew for certain, short and heavyset with a face that even the most generous would not call comely, she presented a formidable figure. Today she was swathed in a chocolate-and-gold brocade tea gown that seemed to magnify her girth. Daisy often thought that Bessie cultivated her oversized figure as well as her personality as a tool of power.

Elisabeth Marbury had the figure and the personality to wrangle men into doing her bidding.

"My dear Daisy, come in."

"I hope I'm not too early."

"Not at all. Is this about the club, perchance?"

Daisy smiled ruefully. "It does seem that I have a one-track mind, but really the site has been lying razed for months now, as James Barclay reminded me at the theater this weekend. Our lack of progress appears to be a running joke at various men's clubs around town. And we still haven't gotten a firm answer from Stanford on whether he will design it."

"Hmmph. James Barclay." Bessie waved the banker and his attitudes away with a flick of her wrist and a jangle of bracelets.

"I shouldn't worry," she said, while the maid took Daisy's coat and muff. She motioned Daisy through the foyer. "But let's dis-cuss it over a glass of sherry. You don't mind, do you? If I had my way, tea would be banned from morning and afternoon calls al-together. If Anne Morgan is to have her track, and Emmie Win-throp her tennis courts and a swimming pool, I must insist on having a full working bar."

Daisy laughed. "I don't think you'll find too much objection to that. If we're discreet. We do have a couple of members who belong to the Temperance League."

"The more fools they."

She led Daisy past the dining room, and Daisy paused as she always did just to peek inside. The once-dark wallpaper and ponderous dining furniture had been transformed by Elsie into a bright uncluttered space, furnished with white table and chairs, green-and-white surrounds, and a white ceiling that created an invitation to enjoy.

"I never pass this room without thinking I'm walking into a garden," Daisy said. "If I can ever get Bordie to give up his dark wainscoting and morose leather chairs, I will definitely consult Elsie."

"She has transformed the whole place into a display of light and color," Bessie said as they continued across the hall to the parlor. "No more stodgy, overcrowded Victorian rooms for us."

"How does she find the time?"

"Oh, she loves it. She's always had an impeccable sense of color and proportion. And she loves poking about antique shops and markets to find just the thing she thinks will be perfect for some space or other, not caring a whit if it's authentic or a copy. I don't see it, but I'm happy that she's found something relaxing away from the demands of the theater. I sometimes wonder . . ."

"But do have a seat, Daisy. Elsie is around here somewhere." She sat ponderously in her "visiting" chair, which her friends called the Throne, for its heavily carved and ornate Baroque construction, and rang for refreshments.

Daisy sat on a parlor chair opposite Bessie and next to a gold Moroccan-print chaise longue.

"Have the ladies changed their minds again?" Bessie asked. "I've been so busy these last few weeks I've hardly spoken to a soul outside of the theater business."

"Oh, no. They want Stanford White. It's just about the only thing they all agree on. But he still hasn't signed. I know he's busy, but the club needs his artistry and his reputation if we are to be taken seriously in this endeavor."

"And you shall have him," Bessie said. "So worry no more about that."

A moment later, Elsie, wearing a flowing yellow tea gown of the latest Paris fashion, wafted into the room, accompanied by her two French bulldogs, Faustina and Fauvette, who were in turn followed by a maid carrying a decanter of sherry and plates of sandwiches and sweets.

"Daisy," Elsie crooned. "Bessie said you were coming. It's been ages." She glided over to take Daisy's fingertips in hers, then wafted over to the chaise longue, where she stretched gracefully into a pose—a cloud of floating meringue next to Bessie's bread pudding.

"Now, Daisy," Bessie said, as soon as the sherry was poured and the plates passed. "Tell us what else is on the agenda."

"First and foremost, we need to get Stanford's signature. I want to break ground on the clubhouse before everyone leaves for the Continent, after which it will be impossible to get anything toward a permanent clubhouse decided. We can't just keep moving our meetings, lectures, and concerts from one place to another like a group of vagabonds. The lecture on Renaissance tapestries at Sarah Hewitt's ballroom was so crowded I was afraid people might start succumbing to the lack of air. Several ladies mentioned it and asked when I thought we would be in our new home.

"The membership has grown so quickly that it's hard to keep up with accommodating them all. I'm thinking about hiring an assembly room for the duration. There's one only two doors down from the construction site that would be convenient for keeping an eye on things . . . when we finally have something to keep an eye on."

"Ah," Bessie said. "An excellent idea."

"I'll bring it up at the next board meeting. I doubt if we'll have any arguments on that."

Bessie laughed. "With this group of ladies? Lord, they can argue over whether grass is green and the sky is blue."

Daisy sighed. "I try to think of it as active minds at work. And they're all depending on me to steer us through these preparatory days. But I can't do that until we have an architect."

"Well, never mind," said Bessie. "Perhaps it slipped his mind. He's already quite busy between the Grand Central competition, the Madison Square church, and the Payne Whitney mansion, new digs for the newlyweds. They say Helen is impatient to take up residence."

"And so are we," said Daisy. "Helen doesn't have to deal with forty women all with their own ideals in mind. She'll tell him exactly what she wants and he'll run off to Europe on a buying trip and heaven knows when we'll see him again.

"We need an answer. And we need him to get started. Even without his other obligations, it will take at least a year for him to draw the plans and hire the crews and begin construction, another year to complete the exterior, interiors, and furnishings. That will be the end of 1906 if all goes to schedule."

"And it will, Daisy," Bessie said and drained her second glass of sherry. "We shall have the most prominent club in the city with a running track, a tennis court, a pool, and a bar. Alva will even get a place to debate women's suffrage. You just leave Stanny to me."

"Thank you," Daisy said, feeling slightly more optimistic.

"Not at all. Another glass of sherry?"

Daisy left a half hour later much reassured and feeling a warm glow from the sherry. She had every reason to think they would soon have Stanford White signed on to the club. No one ever held out against Bessie for long.

"DAISY SEEMS NERVOUS," Elsie said as Bessie returned from seeing Daisy off. "Is there a problem with Stanny?" Elsie poured herself another glass of sherry and inspected the sandwiches, looking for one that didn't contain meat.

"No more than the usual," Bessie said. "But he's not a young thing anymore. I'm afraid his lifestyle is catching up to him. But he'll sign. He can't afford not to."

Elsie turned, a crustless egg-and-tomato triangle held daintily in her fingers. "Because the rumors are true? He's close to broke?"

Bessie barked out a laugh. "Lord, Stanny has been close to broke for . . . I don't know how long. It's his health in combination with the pressures of staying one step ahead of his creditors and his clients that worries me. He has to take every commission he can, especially ones that pay well, and the Colony Club is able to do just that. Though perhaps I'll give him a little nudge. We'll all be leaving town soon."

Elsie sighed and slumped back on the chaise, managing not to spill her sandwich or her sherry. "Everyone but me."

"Never you mind. A successful play is vastly more important than a few extra weeks in Versailles."

Elsie took a bite of the sandwich. Sometimes she wondered if Bessie was just humoring her. Elsie didn't need cosseting. She needed success. Only last year she'd been the star of a Frohman play, *Cynthia*, only to fall into a supporting role in a mediocre play that had been written as a vehicle for Lionel Barrymore and where she had to share what was left over with her sister-in-law, of all people.

This wasn't acceptable. She stood and walked over to the fireplace; took a Ming porcelain dog from the mantel. "I was wrong. I don't like the way this looks after all."

CHAPTER 4

April 1904

As the end of term and the architecture competition neared, Nora took to staying late at school, not in the library as she usually did, but in one of the classrooms that had been left open for those working toward competition entries. There were only four of them who had taken advantage of the offer. Most of the girls preferred to work at home, away from curious eyes.

Nora had given up trying to do any work in her room. She needed space for her rendering, which she would complete in watercolor. She was a decent colorist, but attempting detailed work when you were surrounded by drying underclothes and giggling roommates was nigh impossible.

So here she was, wishing she had packed a sandwich and frowning at the sketch before her. It seemed like every time she found a solution to one problem, another one sprang up to replace it. She knew the scheme of her building was sound. Her rendering of the facade was forward-thinking, tempered by a sense of tranquility and caring.

But architecture was more than a pretty facade. Every aspect, area-to-ceiling-height ratio, width of halls and traffic flow, heating and ventilation, kitchen-to-dining-room distance, accessibility . . . The devil was in the details. All aspects had to fit like a jigsaw puzzle to reveal the building of the future—hopefully, the near future.

Nora had no illusions about the difficult road that lay ahead.

She had gotten a taste of it at the night classes she'd taken down at Cooper Union to augment her mechanical drawing and engineering skills, something she hadn't shared with her family. Even though the classes themselves were free, Louise would never understand the need for extra schooling, even if Nora explained the advancement and knowledge these courses would bring her and the additional pay she could earn. To Louise, it would be just one more thing that Nora had that the rest of them didn't.

Nora didn't understand Louise's bitterness. She had always wanted a family, babies, a nice apartment. She was on her way to achieving that. She'd never even wanted to go to school. Ever. And she still wasn't happy. Maybe it was having to house Mama and Rina. If she was in her place, Nora would like to think she would be happy to keep them safe. But then Nora had never longed for "a family of her own"; she already had all the family she ever wanted, and if Papa and Jimmy had lived, she would be staying with them still.

She shook herself to banish her morbid thoughts. One should only think positive thoughts when doing what one loved.

Moving her work to the school had been a good thing. She was already too often annoyed at her roommates' noise and giddiness. She didn't resent them. She was glad they were enjoying their lives. She just wished they'd do it a little less loudly and with a lot more neatness. A little annoyance was acceptable, but a lot of annoyance she was afraid led to bitterness. And that was a place she refused to go.

"Don't worry, Jimmy," she whispered to the drawing before her. "I will build you the most glorious hospital. And then a school for children like we dreamed of. And apartments where the windows shine with sunlight. Just wait and see—"

"Nora! You're mumbling to yourself again."

Nora looked up from her drawing board. "Sorry."

"Oh, I don't mind." Doris Lasky wiggled her mechanical pencil at Nora. "Just wondered if you were having trouble with your drawing."

"Just the usual." Nora couldn't very well confess to talking to ghosts.

They smiled across the room at each other and went back to their work. The other two girls in the room didn't even look up.

Nora pressed her hands to her back and stretched. She was stiff everywhere; even her fingers were tired. That was enough for today. Diagramming the air ducts and vents could wait until tomorrow when her mind was fresh and focused.

She began packing up her things, carefully covering her work with a muslin sheet, lest one of the other girls was inclined to peek. Silly, really. It wasn't like they would steal each other's ideas. They all had submitted their preliminary plans for acceptance into the competition. She knew that Doris was submitting a cottage design; hers was among several house plans of various sizes and complexities. Verity Klimpt was designing some kind of memorial; there was at least one school, a bank, and several office buildings.

As far as Nora knew, hers was the only hospital.

They were told before submission that they wouldn't be judged against each other, but on how successfully they completed their vision. They all listened and nodded as that announcement was made. Not one of them believed it, except maybe Doris, dear thing. You got ahead in life by being better than the others in your field. It was just how the world worked. And if you were female . . .

At the School of Applied Design for Women, they worked in a somewhat rarefied atmosphere. Of course there were jealousies and a bit of backstabbing, but nothing compared—Nora knew—to what they'd face when they tried to enter a profession dominated by men. She'd had a taste of it already at Cooper Union. The hard looks, the snide comments in the name of fun, the dismissive sighs when she ventured to ask a question of the professor.

It hadn't been easy to keep her temper and just concentrate on learning everything. The courses had expanded her knowledge of drawing immensely and given her a little taste of what she would face in the future. It would be tough, but she would be tougher. She was determined to succeed. For so long, she'd been impatient to make a start when it seemed like she'd never get there.

And then suddenly, her chance was here.

DAISY SLIPPED HER arms into the spring coat Bordie was holding out for her. His hat and gloves were on the foyer table and he was trying to look patient.

"I hope I haven't made us late. I don't want to miss the awards presentation, but there's so much to do before we leave for London."

"Please don't say you're going to try to hold a groundbreaking ceremony before the ship sails."

Daisy laughed. "Heavens, no. We thought about it, but we had a ribbon-cutting ceremony when we bought the property, and look how long it's taken us to get a plan. I think we all were a little superstitious about celebrating too early again."

"Understandable." Bordie took his hat and gloves and offered her his arm. "Shall we go?"

The ride across town to the School of Applied Design for Women was made in companionable silence, or so Daisy thought until Bordie asked, "Why are you so pensive tonight?"

"Am I?"

"If you're worried about being in Europe while White comes up with the designs, don't be. He does know his way around buildings."

"It's not Stanford that I'm worried about, not exactly. It's the ladies—they never can agree on anything, except that we should have a club."

Bordie laughed. "Fortunately for both you and White, they'll all be out of town, too. Now tell me again, this is an architecture award?"

"Yes, you missed the wallpaper exhibit last month when you were in Boston. There are two cash prizes and several special mentions. All will be an aid in acquiring a professional position. One day women architects—"

"Yes, I know, dear, but let's just concentrate on the architect you've got for now."

"I don't envy any woman trying to break into architecture, or doing anything unusual for that matter. Today the *Post* printed that our club women"—Daisy's eyes rolled upward, a combination of disgust and trying to remember the exact words— "'lacking in their scholarly equipment still feel they must dabble in affairs of politics and business when they would do better to keep an eye on the monthly household expenses.' How dare they?"

"You shouldn't be wasting your time reading that yellow press."

"I didn't, but Alva did. She was incensed."

"Alva is always incensed over something."

"True, and I do think the article might have taken a swipe at women's suffrage."

"Ah, that explains it." Bordie sighed. "Who's giving the speeches tonight?"

"I'm sure whoever it is will be brief. Everyone in attendance is on their way to dinner or the theater. And yes, it will be crowded and overheated, but as patrons, it's our duty to attend, not to mention an honor to be invited."

"Yes, dear," he said, clearly resigned to a couple hours of boredom. Bordie was a numbers man through and through. *Rational* was his middle name. He appreciated art and a good dinner. He was a philanthropist as long as it didn't require too many personal appearances.

As contributors to the school, they were among the invited guests for their year-end competition for best architectural designs. Daisy was proud to be a supporter of the school. Mrs. Hopkins's original idea for a design school had blossomed into a well-established three-year program with almost four hundred female students.

"Tonight's competition, besides the monetary prizes, will hopefully launch several young women into a career in building."

"Yes, dear," he repeated docilely.

"Do not twinkle those eyes at me, Bordie. I'm quite serious. And besides, aren't you interested in what the young women have designed?"

"Actually, I am."

A few minutes later, they arrived at the school.

"I think it's so wonderful that they have an architecture program here," Daisy said as they rode the elevator up to the exhibition room. "There are only a handful of programs for women in colleges and most of them are unaffordable. But that will change. It would have been wonderful to have a female design the club, but there aren't many to choose from." She glanced at her husband. "What are you smiling at?"

"Just wondering if the world will ever catch up with you."

The elevator let them off outside the exhibition hall, where they deposited coats and hats and entered a large room where, in addition to the architectural entries, designs of wallpaper, carpets, book covers, and more were also displayed.

Daisy stopped just inside the door and peered into the crowd. Most of the guests were, like Daisy and Bordie, dressed for whatever event they would attend after the awards had been presented.

Daisy spotted Bessie conversing with Anne Morgan and steered Bordie toward them.

"I told you I'd bag him for you," Bessie said good-naturedly as Daisy reached them.

Daisy glanced around, hoping no one had overheard. No matter how much she was around Bessie, she never quite got used to her blunt manner.

"Is he here tonight?"

"Just arrived a few minutes ago. He's over there, talking to Professor Gerhardt, the head of the department. Though I think the professor was more interested in meeting Elsie than talking about the state of architecture."

Elsie was indeed holding court with several men. Dressed in shimmering peacock blue and silver, she was like a wisp among the more staid matrons in the room.

"I'm surprised she could make it," Daisy said. "Doesn't she have a performance tonight?"

"Oh, she's gotten very adept at whisking in at hour call. She was never one to sit at home and 'rest' before a show. I expect they'll make their way over to us before long. Anne and I just arrived ourselves and we were about to take a closer look at the entries. I have no doubt there will be some real talent on display this evening."

Bordie nodded to the ladies and slipped off to join several of the other husbands by the punch bowl, which he would soon learn was not spiked with anything but perhaps soda water.

Daisy, Bessie, and Anne made their way through the crowd to look at the exhibits. Bessie had been right. There was real talent here.

The first few were designs for domiciles: two cottages, a brownstone, and a manse of classic proportions. They admired a school and two landscaped parks before stopping at a watercolor depiction of a hospital.

"Impressive," said Bessie.

"Unusual," Anne added.

More than impressive, thought Daisy. It was not just a hospital, but a sanctuary and retreat for tuberculosis patients. That was a subject she'd been aware of for quite some time. She'd studied the dire situations of TB patients and the lack of adequate facilities for treatment. Most sanitariums were little more than a waiting room for . . . But this. With its precise pen-and-ink lines and the watercolor wash of greenery, none of which was tall enough to block out the sun, it radiated good health. And hope.

They passed on to a modern steel-and-concrete high-rise, more houses, a train station, another school, and a memorial statue.

All were more than adequately portrayed. But Daisy wondered just how many of them would actually continue with the profession once they had graduated from school.

They paused by the row of young women, looking very much like schoolgirls, nervous and uncomfortable.

"Excellent job, ladies," Bessie said to the group in general.

Anne nodded. "Very nice."

"Which one of you is the designer of the hospital?" Daisy asked.

One of the girls nudged the one next to her forward. "I-I am."

"I very much like your idea of all the rooms accessing natural light. I'm glad you recognized the necessity of fresh air and ventilation to the sufferer. I hope you continue in your studies. It's something we must address if we're going to cure this dreadful disease."

The girl, small and dark, just stared at her. She would have to get over that shyness if she was going to survive among all those aggressive male architects.

"What is your name?" Daisy continued.

"Nora, Nora Bromley."

"Well, Miss Bromley, I look forward to seeing your building grace the city one day." Daisy turned to the others. "You all have done yourselves and your school proud. We wish you the best of luck."

They would need more than luck, Daisy thought as she, Bessie, and Anne rejoined the crowd. She wasn't under any illusions about the chances of most of them becoming actual architects. Some would accept jobs as either draftsmen or tracers; one or two might marry a fellow architect and work in his shadow for the rest of her career until too many children called her away from even that. The others would return home and resume their normal lives as if they hadn't learned a new craft at all.

"Ah," Bessie said. "Here's Stanny making his way toward us."

Stanford White. Tall, charming, with eye-catching red hair and a mustache, Stanny, as his intimate friends called him, was a dashing man about town. He also had a reputation that had never been fully explained to Daisy. She only knew Bordie, though an admirer of his talent, didn't care overmuch for his company. The reasons why, when Daisy pushed him, were vague.

No matter. The rest of society admired and respected him. He was responsible for the most spectacular mansions in Manhattan, Newport, Long Island. He'd designed Madison Square Garden, the Washington Square Arch, and, with his associates, McKim and Mead, won the Pennsylvania Station contract. Churches, office buildings, and almost every important club in the city bore his name. The Players club, the Union Club, the Metropolitan Club, the Harmonie Club, the Century Association. And now, the Colony Club.

It was actually happening.

"So delightful to see you," Daisy said.

"The delight is all mine." Stanford bowed slightly as he took her hand in his, not quite a handshake, not close enough to kiss. Still, it sent a slight shiver up Daisy's spine. The man certainly did have charisma. But Daisy didn't much care about that. What she cared about was getting construction started in a timely fashion.

"We await your designs with great anticipation."

He smiled, another slight nod. "And they will be waiting for you when you return from Newport at the end of summer."

"I realize we did take rather a long time to decide exactly what our needs were," Daisy admitted.

"It's a lady's prerogative to change her mind," he answered with his usual charm.

"And when there are forty of us . . ."

He laughed. "Indeed."

"Have you taken a look at the exhibit tonight?" Bessie asked, deftly changing the conversation. "Lots of talent."

"Yes, I've noticed," Stanford said, casting his gaze briefly in the direction of the display wall. "Too bad they're all women. I've got so many projects going on that I could use an extra draftsman or two. They're dropping like flies. No stamina, this last lot."

"And do you not think any of these women would be adequate to do the job?" Anne asked quietly.

Bessie blinked; Daisy cut a glance toward the usually timid Anne. For such a robust, energetic young woman, she was extremely shy, and that she would question Stanford White was surprising.

Stanford chuckled. "You won't catch me out there, Miss Morgan. I think that most of these women are capable of acceptable drafting. One or two are outstanding. It's their penchant for getting married and quitting that holds most firms back from hiring them."

"Ha," Bessie scoffed. "Quitting even faster than the male draftsmen who realize it's hard work for little pay and move on to more lucrative professions? You were just complaining about not being able to keep them."

"Touché, my dear Bessie. Even so, my partners are dead set against hiring women. Charles Mead would have a fit to even see one in the drafting room." Stanford glanced again at the exhibition wall. "Though I must say, there are one or two, if they were men . . ."

"If who were men?" asked Elsie, gliding up to the group.

"These girl architects," Bessie said.

"From what I've seen of them," Elsie said, "any of them could could do very well against their male counterparts."

"And I, of course, bow to your succinct insight," Stanford said gravely.

"Well, it's true," Elsie said playfully.

If she'd had a fan, she would have rapped his knuckles with it, Daisy thought. Sometimes it was hard to tell when Elsie was acting and when she wasn't. It might have turned into a clever badinage if they hadn't been interrupted by the arrival of Bordie, who nodded to Stanford before saying the judges were going to be examining the entries any minute if they wanted to get a good view.

"Excuse me, ladies, the headmaster, Professor Gerhardt, is beckoning." Stanford moved away.

The others hurried to find places near the front of the exhibit to await the judging.

CHAPTER 5

That was nice, what that lady said," Doris whispered to Nora. They were standing along the wall with the other competition entrants, trying not to fidget and feeling very much on display even though the crush of invited guests was ignoring them completely.

"I guess," Nora whispered back. "But what could a rich society lady possibly know about 'this dreadful disease,' or care about it, for that matter?"

"Rich ladies are always doing good works."

"You mean, they get their husbands to send money."

"That doesn't sound like you, Nora. Their money gets things done. It supports this school. It will build your hospital."

"Sorry. You're right. I'm just nervous; it's making me cross. She was nice." And Nora had stood there like a half-wit instead of thanking her. How would she ever attract clients if she couldn't talk to them? She was an embarrassment to the school.

Nora looked over the room, trying to find the woman who had spoken to her, but it was a sea of finery; she'd never been around this many rich people in her life.

Men in black evening suits, women dressed in silks and lace, feathers and tiaras perched on their heads at various angles. Nora had spent the first half hour mentally measuring the angles of feathers to heads and calculating how many hatpins it took to prevent them from falling just to calm her nerves. She tried to see them as people. But they were like exotic beings as far from Nora as they could possibly be.

And yet they supported her school. Cared about curing tu-berculosis, if the woman was to be believed. People who might eventually hire her to design their homes.

The school's teachers moved among the guests, nodding and smiling, sometimes stopping to chat, as if it were a normal after-noon instead of a life-changing night for two students at least. And a rite of passage for thirty-eight more. Nora thought maybe she should have spent more time learning how to behave in so-ciety.

"Have you ever seen so much finery in your life?" Doris whis-pered in Nora's ear.

"Never."

"Do you think those are real diamonds and pearls?"

"Of course," said Lydia Rhodes, who stood at Nora's other side. "And the emeralds and rubies, they're all real."

"Like she would know," said Verity Klimpt from Doris's far side.

Lydia nudged Nora to the side to get a better look at the invited guests. "Look over there, I'm sure that's Alva Vanderbilt . . . well, Alva Belmont now. She divorced . . . Oh, wait. Is that . . . ? It is." She let out a little squeal; they immediately shushed her. "That's Elsie de Wolfe."

"Where?" Verity asked, stretching on tiptoe.

"Over there in that smashing dark-blue-and-silver gown. She always wears the latest fashion. I'm sure it's a Worth."

"She looks like a starry night," said Doris on a sigh.

"Who is Elsie de Wolfe?" Nora asked, curiosity momentarily replacing her jitters.

All three girls looked at her in shock.

"How can you not know Elsie de Wolfe?" asked Lydia. "She's a famous actress."

Nora looked over the crowd. How could Lydia tell one spar-kling guest from the next?

"Over there, standing with the lady who complimented you and the tall man with red hair."

As Nora caught sight of the lady's gown, the man walked away and joined Professor Gerhardt.

Suddenly there was a rustle through the crowd of guests and the professor presented the three judges. Miss Alice Hands, a graduate of the school and one of the few working female architects in the city; Mr. Lord, from the architectural firm of Lord and Hewlett—Nora had sent her curriculum vitae to them—who sometimes lectured at the school; and the redheaded man.

Mr. Stanford White.

A ripple of surprise rolled through the line of students. Stanford White was the most sought-after architect in New York. A word from him . . . And he was judging their work. Nora's knees began to quake.

The judges started at the far end of the wall, stopping before each entry, occasionally nodding or talking briefly among themselves before moving on to the next.

Nora's thudding heart was just one of many. Not all of the girls who entered designs needed the prize money, but the awards would be an added distinction to their letters of introduction. Nora needed the money as much as the honor. Fifty or twenty-five dollars would change everything. She had already decided to give half of her winnings to her sister to help with the housing and feeding of their mother and younger sister. The rest she would save toward an apartment for the three of them, if she won.

She slowly crossed her fingers, hiding them in the folds of her skirt.

Doris's shoulders straightened when the judges reached her "English Country Cottage" and slumped again when they passed without stopping overlong before it.

"Do you think they liked it?" Doris whispered.

Nora could feel her tension as if it were her own.

"I'm sure they did," Nora answered.

The judges stopped at the next rendering, a stark, seven-story, stone-and-steel "American Insurance Building," by Lydia Rhodes.

"Just like her heart," Doris whispered.

Lydia stood aloof, poised and confident, knowing that if all else failed, her father would secure her success in life.

Most of the girls disliked her, but Nora envied her desperately. Not for her uncaring heart, but for the comfort she took for granted, something that Nora would never enjoy no matter how successful she might become.

One by one, the designs were inspected and judged, the students' culmination of three years' work. With each move, one more student sagged with relief that it was over, while the others still waiting to be judged became wound more tightly than before.

A tile-roofed colonnade, an industrial warehouse, a marble archway, several mansions, a general store from a girl who had traveled all the way from Ohio to study.

Two-thirds of the way down, the judges stopped at Nora's "Hospital for Tuberculosis Patients."

Doris slipped her hand into Nora's. "I hope you win."

Nora squeezed her hand back. So did she. Both of them could really use the prize money. Doris was saving her money to go to California to further her studies. And the money would keep Louise off Nora's back for at least a couple of months. Long enough to find a decent-paying job as a draftsman.

Nora's hospital design wasn't as grand or as large as some of the other designs. And not at all like the overwhelming edifices that one usually equated with hospitals. It was only three floors tall with courtyards and solaria, housing all but the severest cases on the ground floor, where the rooms opened onto lawns and gardens, and, most of all . . . onto fresh air.

Nora had managed to capture all of this in her watercolor

rendering. And though not particularly interested in landscaping, Nora knew that architects were also responsible for the surroundings as well as the interior designs of the buildings. She was proficient in both.

The panel seemed to be spending an inordinate amount of time in front of her rendering, but she couldn't tell if they approved or not. Her entry was detailed and accurate. She'd checked her dimensions at least twenty times. And even though Nora would rather be doing mechanical renderings of beams, footings, and lintels, she knew she was an excellent watercolorist.

Professor Gerhardt had said her color treatments breathed life into her designs.

Nora just hoped they got her a job.

She'd sent out letters of introduction. Several of the professors had given her recommendations. She'd had two appointments for interviews for junior draftsman. One had turned out to be an unpaid internship. The other paid so little that Professor Gerhardt and Professor Lehmann of Linear Drawing had both advised her to turn them both down. How could they expect anyone to live on those kinds of wages? She suspected they assumed she had other means of income—a father or a husband.

She tried not to let her confidence slip. It had only been two appointments. Her professors were certain she would find a suitable position.

Nora prayed they were right.

It seemed to take forever for the judges to reach the end of the exhibit, where they paused long enough to make a final perusal of the wall. Then they exited the room to talk among themselves and decide the winners.

The line of would-be architects breathed a communal sigh. The guests went back to their conversations or took second looks at the exhibit. Time slowed to a crawl for the nervous entrants.

Even so Nora was surprised when the door opened and the

judges returned. The room quieted while Professor Gerhardt announced several special mentions. Doris's cottage was one of them.

In the cover of polite pause, Nora was the one to take Doris's hand. "Congratulations."

"Second place . . . Verity Klimpt's 'Soldiers Park.'"

Nora caught Lydia's eye. Surely it was now between the two of them. Lydia smiled as if she already knew the verdict of the panel.

Nora lifted her chin, proud and determined, even though it cost her dearly. She'd done her best work and if she left the design school without a prize or even a mention, she could still hold her head high.

And suddenly, Doris was nudging her forward. Professor Gerhardt was clapping and smiling at her. Everyone was applauding, even Lydia Rhodes.

"You won!" Doris gave her a more forceful nudge and Nora went as if in a dream to accept her first-place prize.

Nora didn't know whether to laugh or cry, so she did neither. Just accepted her award and the many congratulations, her medallion clutched in one hand and the prize money in the other. She'd won first place—fifty dollars. *Fifty dollars.* It was like a miracle in the Bible. She hadn't dared let herself dream that she would actually win first.

She wished Papa and Jimmy could be here to see her triumph . . . but if Jimmy were here, she wouldn't be. She bit her lip to keep it from quivering. *I did it, Jimmy. I did it, Papa.*

She would tell Mama and Rina all about it tonight. She'd promised to come out as soon as the presentations were over. They had been so sure she would win.

Then she was gathered into the line of girls, Nora and Verity holding their awards at the center. The startling flash of a camera and then everyone was dispersing.

Nora started to follow them, but saw Professor Gerhardt walking toward her. He was accompanied by Stanford White. Nora looked wildly around. They couldn't be headed for her, but the other girls had already left.

Mr. White was a tall man, taller than she'd thought, with red hair and a bushy red mustache. And older than she'd imagined him. Stanford White, the pinnacle of architecture in New York.

Professor Gerhardt lifted one long finger. "Miss Bromley, a moment, please."

Nora sucked in her breath so hard she almost choked.

"I want you to meet an associate of mine. Mr. Stanford White."

"Congratulations," Mr. White said, not looking at Nora but past her shoulder to her hospital. "Very impressive renderings. Very calming to skittish clients. A woman's touch. Yes. An interesting idea."

Nora managed a thank-you, but she doubted if Mr. White was even listening. Then he turned without warning to pin her with bright blue eyes. "How's your mechanical drawing?"

"Excellent," the professor interjected. "We sent her down to Cooper Union for advanced drafting classes."

"Mmm, a little dab of a girl." Mr. White glanced past Nora to Lydia's insurance building. "Then, larger isn't always better."

"As well as an impeccable artist," Professor Gerhardt added.

"I can see that." He looked down at Nora. "I may have need of some additional renderings of several buildings I'm currently working on. Piecemeal work, paid by the assignment. Bring your portfolio to my office Monday morning and I'll take a look. Technical schemata and client watercolor examples, like your exhibit tonight. If they're acceptable, I may have some work for you. Eight o'clock. Fifth floor. The professor will give you the address. Don't be late."

He nodded to the professor. "Gerhardt. Nice bit of talent here tonight. Good evening." Both Nora and the professor watched as he strode away.

"Well," said Professor Gerhardt. "I'd say it's been a banner evening for Miss Nora Bromley. McKim, Mead, and White is a plum training ground for young architects, even as an independent artisan."

Nora fought for words. "I don't know how to thank you."

"It wasn't my doing," the professor said. "And you don't have the job yet. Be sure to pick out your neatest work, though you always do neat work."

"I will, and I meant thank you for everything you've taught me, for all of you at the school."

"You are quite welcome. But you understand, even if he does take you on, you'll have to subsidize it with other work. But do a good job for White and the news will spread. They may even take you on full time. That would be something. To begin in McKim, Mead, and White, the pressure to produce quickly and cleanly will be intense, but the payoff could be great."

"I'm up to the task."

"I'm certain you are. You'll have a bright start and I believe if you persist, you will go far." He pursed his lips. "I must say, I'm surprised that he made such an overture. McKim, Mead, and White has never employed a woman as a draftsman. Your conduct must be impeccable," the professor said. "You must be determined."

"I am determined," Nora said.

"And not be daunted when others get the better opportunities."

"I'm still determined, sir."

"It won't be easy, so tell me now if you are absolutely certain you intend to continue in architecture as a profession."

Nora frowned. Of course she would continue. "I do intend to. I won't fail. I can't."

Both of the professor's thin eyebrows lifted. "Courage is easy before the battle, my dear."

"I won't give up, Professor."

"Good. But you will have to be better than the rest. You need more study, but you can get that by paying attention, eyes and ears always open. You're representing all of us, so keep a professional demeanor at all times and give them no cause to regret hiring you."

"I won't."

"Good. We're all very proud of you. Now go join your friends and celebrate. The real work begins next week."

There would be no celebrating with friends tonight, Nora thought. She had to catch the trolley for the journey across the river to Brooklyn. Mama and Rina would be waiting to hear about the contest and Louise would want whatever money she could get out of it.

So with her medal and money stuffed deep into her pockets, she bid her professor good night and started across Twenty-third Street to the trolley stop.

It was after nine o'clock when Nora finally reached Louise's apartment. She was tired and hungry and hoped Louise would offer her something to eat. She'd been too nervous to eat during the day and too much in a hurry to catch the trolley to stop even for a cup of tea.

She was just walking up the sidewalk to the apartment when the front door banged open and Rina came flying out.

Nora laughed for the first time today, then she saw Rina's face in the light of the streetlamp.

Her euphoria died there on the sidewalk. "What is it? Is Mama unwell?"

"No!" cried Rina, her round cheeks wet with tears. "She says I have to leave school and go to work in the factory."

"What is this nonsense? Mama would never say such a thing."

"Not Mama. Louise. She says we're too expensive. But I can't. I can't quit school. I promised Papa."

They had all promised Papa, but not all were as keen at keeping his wishes. Nora huffed out a sigh. "Don't worry, Rina. You will not leave school, and I will tell Louise that."

Rina, only thirteen, with thick dark curls, long lashes, and more height than Nora, was already a beauty. With an education, she would do well in the world. But first Nora would have to unruffle Louise's feathers. She was fairly certain the money in her pocket would go a long way toward doing that.

"Let me come live with you. I can sleep on the floor. I won't be a nuisance. l won't eat hardly anything."

"Silly, how would you get to school every day from across the river?"

"I could go to school there."

Nora eased Rina away. "Listen, little one. Soon I hope to be able to get you and Mama and me our own apartment, but it is still a time away. Try to be patient and learn your lessons and your manners, and for heaven's sake, put a hankie to your nose. It's running. "

Rina fumbled in her skirt pocket for her hankie.

"That's better. Now dry your tears before we go inside. You don't want anyone, especially Louise, to see you when you're not at your finest."

"You sound like Mama," Rina said and slipped her arm through Nora's.

"Good," said Nora. Hopefully her own manners, the ones Mama had drummed into her impatient head, would stand them all in good stead. She would need them. She was to present herself at McKim, Mead, and White on Monday. She would have to remember to show them her finest, too.

A rush of anticipation and abject fear coursed through her. But first she must deal with her older sister.

"Scoot now," she whispered to Rina as soon as they were inside, "and tell Mama I'll be in shortly."

Rina ran off and Nora stepped into the kitchen.

"Well, you're late enough, " Louise said, casting Nora a quick look over her shoulder.

"Tonight was the awards presentation. I told you."

"And I suppose Rina has been telling tales of how meanly she's treated here."

"Not at all."

Nora had had years to accustom herself to her older sister's brusque manner. Louise had been bitter ever since Nora could remember.

Nora understood part of it. When their brother, Jimmy, became ill with tuberculosis, Louise, as the oldest, had had to go to work to help their parents take care of the younger two girls.

They'd lived in a crowded, but decent, tenement building. Mama cleaned houses and took in finishing work from the tailor's shop to help support the family, while also keeping their apartment clean and neat. Papa had been diligent about saving money so that his only son would get a higher education. The first in the family. Jimmy, as it turned out, had not lived long enough to graduate from the tenement school.

When he died, Papa had refused to spend any of his tuition money and decreed that Nora would take Jimmy's place at school.

Louise had resented them all since that day, but especially she resented Nora.

Nora didn't blame her. Nora had gotten her heart's desire. And Louise was forced to put her own life on the back burner.

Now at last, Nora would prove to them that she was fulfilling her part of the promise.

"Where is Donner this evening?" Nora asked.

"Working the night shift. Why?"

"No reason, just being polite."

"Ha!" Louise turned around, flinging soap suds from the wooden spoon she was holding. "Oh, bother," she said and snatched up a towel to sop up the spill. "I suppose you think you're better than us because you get to go to posh awards presentations while my husband works his fingers to the bone, just to put a roof over our heads. He didn't bargain for having the whole family sponge off us."

"I'm sure he didn't, but the family doesn't sponge off you. I give you every free penny I have. And I'll send more once I begin earning a steady paycheck."

"When-when-when. You mean *if*. Who ever heard of a woman working as an architect? A complete waste."

"Or I could move in here and live with you," said Nora just to irritate her sister. No way would she subject herself to that situation.

"Don't you dare threaten me."

Now it began; the inevitable accusations, devolving into miserable tears. But Nora was too exhausted to care. She'd worked nonstop, graduated, had a potential job—fingers crossed. She wanted her family to be happy for her; she could be celebrating with her friends instead of making the journey out here only to face the habitual recriminations from her sister.

"Let's not fight. I only came to give you this. Not only did I attend an awards program this evening, but I had a design entered in it . . ."

Louise snorted and went back to washing her dishes.

"I won fif—twenty-five dollars." Nora reached in her pocket, extracted half of her prize money, and laid it on the oilskin tablecloth. She'd slip Rina a little extra for her and Mama and make her promise not to tell Louise. Nora would keep the rest. She could always turn it over later if it was really needed.

Louise's mouth dropped open, then she lunged and snatched it off the table.

"Where did you get this?"

"I won it for my design. It's yours for Mama and Rina's room and board. But I expect you to make it last," Nora said, drawing herself up to her full five feet, two inches. Even bent over the table, Louise seemed to tower over her, at least in Nora's mind.

But she'd learned long ago not to appear weak. Not to Louise, not to anyone.

"No more threats of sending Rina to the factory. No skimping on food or any other of Mama's needs. Now I'll just say a quick hello to Mama and leave you in peace."

Nora, Rina, and their mother spent a cozy hour sitting in the parlor while Nora quietly told them about the competition and all the fancy people who were there. About winning, but not about the money. Mama would have insisted on Nora keeping it all for herself. As it was, she had never told them how much of her paltry income she ceded to Louise each week.

She did tell them about the meeting with Mr. White. "But don't say anything until I know for sure," she whispered. "I don't want to get Louise's hopes up." Or face her recriminations if it didn't pan out.

She asked about Rina's schoolwork and laughed quietly at her mimicry of one of her teachers, careful not to awaken the sleeping baby in the next room. Louise broke down enough to bring in a tea tray, but didn't stay.

Mama looked sadly at her retreating figure. "It has been hard on her."

"I know, Mama. Things will be different soon."

When it was time to leave, they both followed her to the door. Nora called out a goodbye to Louise. She didn't expect an answer, she didn't get one.

And feeling a little deflated, she took her leave. She was just a few steps down the sidewalk when she heard footsteps behind her. She whirled around.

"Rina!"

"Here." Rina pushed a brown wrapped parcel at her. "Mama made it. She was going to wait for your birthday, but she says wear it to your meeting with Mr. White with her love."

Nora took the parcel. Hugged her sister and watched until she was safely back in the building. Then she waved goodbye and turned her back on the two solitary figures standing at the first-floor window.

CHAPTER 6

Nora spent the weekend organizing her best work with a variety of mechanical schemata and detailed cross sections. On Monday, she awoke hours before her appointment with Mr. White. Double-checked her case for the third time, making certain she had included all aspects of her education: facades, detail drawings, floor plans drawn to scale, electrical and plumbing installations. Of course, on any actual projects there would be electricians and plumbers, but it was necessary for architects to have a functional knowledge of these subjects and she didn't want Mr. White to have any reservations about hiring her.

The architectural firm of McKim, Mead, and White was located at Fifth Avenue and Twenty-first Street, only three blocks from where she lived. *Three long avenue blocks*, she reminded herself. She planned to leave early so she wouldn't have to rush and appear disheveled and out of breath when she arrived.

She paced back and forth in the narrow space between the beds until it was time to dress, which she did at the last minute, taking special care not to wrinkle the tucks on the shirtwaist Mama had made. With the addition of a straw boater that Nora had to borrow from Inez, and feeling very professional, she went downstairs.

She reached her destination early and, deciding that it did no harm to be more than punctual, she took the elevator upstairs to the fifth-floor drafting room. Stood outside to take a fortifying breath, and, touching the rows of tiny pleating down the front of her blouse for good luck, she opened the door.

She was in an anteroom. A bespectacled clerk looked up from his desk; his eyes widened and he shot out of his chair.

"May I help you?"

"I'm here to see Mr. White. He's expecting me."

He took in her outfit and her person and his expression changed as if he'd just bitten into something nasty. "Really?"

"Yes, really."

He sat back down, sprawling slightly. "What would this be about, then? You planning on building a mansion?"

"Several, if necessary, but my interest is in larger edifices." Nora gave him a fulminating look. And when he didn't react, she continued, "I'm here on business."

He barked out a laugh and leaned forward. "How the mighty have fallen." He shook his head. "If I were you, I'd keep my business where it belongs."

Nora gritted her teeth, corralling her indignation.

"My business," she said stiffly, "is in this portfolio and is with Mr. White."

"Give us a look, then." The glint in his eye sent a chill up Nora's spine. She'd seen plenty of those looks when she still lived on the Lower East Side.

And from her jangle of nerves and desire to impress rose an anger she hadn't felt in a long time. She pushed it down. She would have plenty of time for anger—after she got the job.

"I don't know what you're implying"—though she did; she just didn't understand why he would think such a thing, since she was respectable to a tee—"but I have architectural plans in this case that I'm bringing for Mr. White's perusal."

A flicker of doubt passed across the man's face, then wariness. "I guess I could—"

A door opened and another young man strode in. He was tall, but not so tall as to be intimidating, with long legs and arms whose shirtsleeves were rolled up almost to his elbows. "Kendricks, I forgot to tell you that Mr. White is expecting a—" He saw Nora and stopped. She could see his Adam's apple bobble as he swallowed.

"I beg your pardon." He hastily tried to roll down his sleeves, a hopeless proposition since he had taken off his cuff links and the cuffs flopped around his wrists.

"You must be Miss Bromley. I must apologize. I . . ."

"You mean she really is an architect?"

"Yes, Kendricks, she is."

Nora could tell that he was holding back his opinion of the clerk, which he surely would have given, if Nora hadn't been present. She liked him already.

The clerk bolted up, ramrod straight, crimson suffusing his cheeks. "Sorry for the misunderstanding, miss."

Casting him a last dagger look, the newcomer turned back to Nora. "I'm George Douglas, Miss Bromley. If you'll come this way, Mr. White is expecting you."

He ushered her through the door and into a wide hallway. "It's just down here." They walked side by side in silence for several feet until Mr. Douglas said, "Please forgive your introduction to the firm. We don't get very many, um, visitors here. We usually see our clients in their own homes or offices and, um . . ."

"You don't normally employ women," Nora finished for him.

Mr. Douglas's step faltered.

"N-no. Of course not. I mean . . ."

"Of any kind."

"Uh, this is Mr. White's office." He opened the door.

Nora took a deep breath and stepped inside.

The room was smaller than she expected. Mr. White sat at a large desk, his chin resting on his shirt collar, his shoulders slumped, and looking a little worse for wear than the last time she'd seen him. His suit was wrinkled, his face seemed swollen, and there were heavy bags under his eyes. Nora had seen that look many times back in the old neighborhood. Men who worked too hard during the days and drank and gamed too hard through the nights. This did not bode well.

Mr. Douglas shifted uncomfortably. "Miss Bromley to see you, sir."

Mr. White didn't raise his head, merely opened his eyelids enough to squint at her from beneath his full eyebrows. Then he pushed himself upright, said, "Hospital," and motioned for her to sit down in the chair across from him.

"Have you brought your portfolio?" he asked, tugging once at the lapel of his jacket, suddenly all business.

"I have it here," Nora said.

Mr. Douglas appeared at her side. "May I?"

Nora handed him the portfolio, which he opened, then carefully laid her drawings on the desk before Mr. White.

"Ah, yes," White said, lifting up her copy of the hospital watercolor to the light.

Beside him, Mr. Douglas's eyebrows arched slightly.

Nora held her breath.

White put down the first rendering and picked up a second, the floor plan of the first floor. He patted the other papers on his desk and found a magnifying glass, which he used to compare the drawing to the inset of specs.

Nora found herself mesmerized by the mustache that spread across his upper lip and tilted up at each end as if it wished to fly off his face.

A couple of grunts, a crook of his finger, and Mr. Douglas stepped forward to look more closely at her work.

Mr. White lifted the hospital floor plan out of the way to uncover several interiors of various mansions she'd done as exercises in art class.

One page followed the next, the two men occasionally exchanging looks in some kind of silent communication.

Nora knew the exact moment when White made his decision.

He straightened up and stretched back against his chair. Mr. Douglas took a deferential step back.

"Not bad," White said. "Where do you work?"

The question startled her.

"Your studio," Mr. Douglas explained. "What studio do you work from?"

"Oh, I use the ones at the school. When they're open."

"And when they're closed?" asked Mr. White.

"I—" She glanced quickly at Mr. Douglas. What should she tell them? Not that she worked at a table among dirty dishes and laundry.

Mr. Douglas frowned, then leaned over and said something in Mr. White's ear.

"Are you crazy? Charlie would have my head. Yours, too, dammit."

Mr. Douglas straightened up. "Mr. White, may I suggest?" He tilted his head toward the office door.

"What? Oh, certainly, my boy." White stood.

"Miss Bromley, would you please excuse us for a moment?" Mr. Douglas was already ushering White toward the door.

Nora watched them out of the corner of her eye as they left the room.

Mr. White limped slightly, his steps uneven as if he were in pain or had the weight of the world on his shoulders. Mr. Douglas waited for him to exit, then followed him out.

They stopped just outside the door; Nora could see their shadows beyond the frosted glass.

Nora strained her ears to hear what they were saying. She couldn't make out the words, just knew the conversation quickly became more insistent; Mr. Douglas's voice strident on occasion, and Mr. White's answers gruff. She briefly considered sneaking over to the door and putting her ear to the glass, but didn't dare take the chance of getting caught. So she sat, picking at her nails while her fate was being settled without her.

It seemed an eternity before the two men returned. Mr. White stood for a moment, looking down at Nora, then continued around his desk to settle heavily behind it.

"Mr. Douglas has convinced me to give you a try. You'll be given a desk in the drafting room temporarily and several assignments. If your work is as exact and detailed as those you've presented and you can get the job done quickly and efficiently, we'll see about finding someplace to put you permanently."

She was half aware of Mr. Douglas wincing, but Nora didn't care. She'd do anything to get this job. Well, almost anything.

"George here will give you your first assignment. Let him know when you've completed it and I'll take a look." His fingers brushed the air as if he were flicking lint off a coat.

Then his eyes closed and his chin dipped once again to his chest.

"If you'll come with me." Mr. Douglas quickly gathered up her designs and returned them to her case.

Nora said a quiet thank-you, to which Mr. White didn't respond, and she hurried after Mr. Douglas.

It wasn't until they were in the hallway that Nora stopped and turned to face him. He was a nice-looking man, with blond hair slicked down on either side of a center part.

"Am I . . ." She couldn't get the rest out.

"On trial."

Nora shivered.

"You're our first female draftsman—drafts woman? I'm not certain what the others' reactions will be. Don't you know anyone with space for you in their studio?"

Nora shook her head. She didn't know anyone who even had their own studio.

"Just keep your head down and do your work until we can, um, find somewhere to put you."

Nora nodded and looked at the floor.

Beside her, Mr. Douglas chuckled; she twisted her head enough to see him.

"I didn't mean literally, exactly. I meant just mind your own business, but it's not a bad idea. We have no other women working here, except the secretaries down on the fourth floor. McKim and Mead are dead set against women in the drafting room. They think they will only distract the male draftsmen. So don't distract."

"I won't."

"We're stretched thin and losing draftsmen faster than we can replace them. You wouldn't be here except for your detail work and watercolors."

"They won't know I'm there," Nora assured him and tried to make herself invisible.

"I doubt that." He gave her a quick smile that lit up his serious face. It was gone before she could appreciate more than that he had nice, straight teeth.

He started walking again. "You'll be paid by the piece."

"Hopefully better than the shirtwaist factory girls," Nora mumbled.

He cast a glance over his shoulder. "Better than that, but not by much."

Nora, appalled that she'd actually said it out loud, ran to catch up.

"If you work out, you'll have all the work you can handle and they might put you on salary. Come on.

"This is my office," he said, stopping at another door to her right. He opened it and waited for her to go inside. It was practically the same size as Mr. White's, though whereas Mr. White's had a window overlooking the street, Mr. Douglas's had no window, just walls covered in sketches and diagrams, overlapping at the edges, pinned at awkward angles. Stacks of plans and sketches balanced precariously on top of a metal filing cabinet, a drafting table was wedged into the corner next to an easel. It was a wonder he could find space to draw.

"Pardon the disarray. Mr. White's private office is on the sixth floor and I take a lot of work up there. I'll just get you started . . ."

While he riffled through several sheets of paper, Nora perused a design that was pinned on the easel. It wasn't a building she'd ever seen in New York. But it was certainly interesting.

"Aha," he said and brought out several pieces of paper.

"Where is this building?" Nora asked, pointing to the high-rising structure.

"Still in my head, unfortunately." He quickly turned the easel around and placed the papers on top of another pile of papers.

"Here is a rough sketch for a set of columns. They need to be drawn precisely to scale. Also with a cross section of the capitals. They're not standard Doric, so check your measurements. Can you handle it?"

Nora took the papers, compared them. It looked like straight-forward copy work. "Yes."

"When you're finished, you'll bring them back here. Understand?"

"Yes."

"Then if they pass muster, I'll give you another assignment, and if that passes, I'll take them in to Mr. White, and if he deems them to his liking"—he paused to give her another infinitesimal smile—"which I'm sure will be the case, I'll take you down and set you up with the business department. You will be working solely for Mr. White, but paid through our offices."

Nora's eyebrows rose.

"Oh, it's very common. He has a whole cadre of artists and artisans working on projects; that's why he assumed you had a studio to work out of. But as it is . . . we'll find you a place here temporarily. Come on, let's get you settled."

"I like it—your building," she said and followed him out the door.

The drafting room was at the end of the hallway through a pair of double doors. Mr. Douglas stopped before going inside. "I just realized. Were you told to bring your drawing implements with you?"

"Yes."

"Well, where are they?" he asked, his eyes flitting to her case and back.

"In my pockets."

"Your pockets?"

"Yes." She pulled out a ruler to show him. "My mother made special pockets. That way I always have my hands free."

"Ha, how clever. Ready?"

Nora nodded.

But he hesitated. "A word of advice? Watch your back; the waters are infested."

Before Nora could react, he opened the door to the drafting room.

It was huge and filled with rows of drafting tables, each occupied by a man, head bent over his work.

Mr. Douglas cleared his throat. "Gentlemen."

Those nearest him looked up, their eyes darting from him to Nora, their mouths slowly going slack. Gradually, in a wave across the room, they all looked up. At seeing Nora, expressions slowly changed from attention, to annoyance, to apprehension, to shock.

"This is Miss Bromley; she will be taking Mr. Firth's place. That is all."

He motioned Nora to follow him. Not only Nora but scores of other eyes followed him down the first three rows of desks, then behind the last row until he reached the very back corner and a shallow alcove where one lone desk was partially separated from the others.

"It's like it was made for you," Mr. Douglas said.

Or a leper, thought Nora.

"We just pushed it out of the way to make more room, but I think you'll be more comfortable here with a little space to yourself."

And a window, thought Nora.

"Thank you," Nora managed. She'd noticed several empty drafting tables in their trek to the outskirts of the room. He didn't need to put her almost out of sight. But she wouldn't hold it against him. Actually, she looked forward to the solitude . . . and the window.

"Paper sheets are in those shelves over there, size and thread marked on each shelf, tracing at the top, then down the scale to the bottom." He indicated the cabinet, which was a good ten feet long and filled with compact shelves that reached above her head. Fortunately, she spied the rolling library ladder, stationed at one end.

". . . Correct size and paper type is denoted on the top-left corner of the sketches you've been given." Mr. Douglas turned the paper on her desk so that he could point. His fingers were long and graceful and Nora had to blink a couple of times to concentrate on the numbers scribbled on the corner of her column rendering.

"When you finish, bring your work directly to my office."

He nodded and turned to face the room. Some fifty-odd heads snapped back to their drawing boards. Mr. Douglas left the room, and Nora took up the tools of her new life.

As soon as the door closed, heads began to turn her way again. She quickly relieved one pocket of pencil, straightedge, protractor, and magnifying glass. From the other, she extricated a small sketch pad and a pouch that contained a pen, a small bottle of ink, and her best erasers. She spread the pencil and erasers neatly in the trough at the bottom of the drafting board and placed the rest on the narrow shelf below.

Then, trying to ignore the curiosity of the others, she carried her sketch over to the paper shelf. She didn't miss the snort from one of the men as she passed by. No matter; she wasn't in the least intimidated. That was one thing growing up on the Lower East Side had taught her. How to ignore taunts and slurs and roving hands. A few snorts and catcalls might make her uncomfortable, but were nothing to her.

She chose her paper slowly, methodically. She carried it back to her desk, ignoring the "Why aren't you home having babies?" question from the second desk in the last row. She didn't look back; she wouldn't give him the satisfaction. She'd have plenty of time to put the face to the words. Her desk was behind them all.

She spread out the paper, sat down, and adjusted the angle of the table. Then she just studied her first assignment before she even picked up her pencil.

A rough sketch of a Doric column, with an inset of a cross section of the capital. Simple enough. Still, she studied it closely. Used the magnifying glass to read the scrawled numbers in the corner and found what she suspected.

Though all Doric columns followed the same basic silhouette, architects constantly adapted the form. The ratio of this cornice frieze and architrave indicated that it would be bearing weight of some magnitude.

She moved the sketch to the side close enough for easy reference and got out her straightedge.

For the next hour, Nora graphed and measured, plotting out points and angles, and finally crafted the column with precision. Then she moved on to the cross section of the capital.

When it was done, she wrote the specs in a ruled-off box in

the corner, and sat back to consider her work. It had taken her longer than usual, but she'd been extra careful and she was satisfied. She rolled up the design and carried it to the door and into the hall.

She could hear the immediate buzz of conversation as the door closed behind her.

Nora sighed. If they just kept it to whispering, everything would be fine. In the few classes she'd taken at the Cooper Union night school, the men had been more vocal and a few of them had been downright nasty. Night school at Cooper Union was free and attracted all kinds, and those were the only courses open to women.

She wondered briefly if any of those men were now working in the room she had just left.

No matter. She knocked quietly on the door to Mr. Douglas's office. He was sitting at his drafting board, but quickly stood up and, sticking his pencil behind his ear, came to meet her.

"Finished already?"

Nora's stomach did a flip and a flop. Had nerves made her rush too much? Had she missed anything? She held out the rendering.

Mr. Douglas took it over to the easel and tacked it on top of his building.

Nora held her breath and didn't let it go until Mr. Douglas whooshed out his.

He looked up at the wall clock, wrote something in a blue ledger book, and handed her another design.

"Think you can make a good start on this before lunch?"

"Lunch?" She barely squeaked out the word. She would actually get time for lunch? Not that she had brought a lunch.

"We usually take a half hour around one. If Mr. White approves this, I'll take you down to the business office to get you put on the books then. That should still give you a few minutes to . . ." He breathed out a laugh. "I was going to say wolf down a sandwich, but that doesn't sound very civilized, does it?"

Nora shook her head. "You don't have to watch your language around me. Just try to think of me as one of the men."

Mr. Douglas's lip twitched. "I'll take that under advisement. Now, about this next design. It's a facade for one of the secondary entrances for the Pennsylvania Station."

"The new station?" A tiny thrill ran through her. This was something special indeed. "Yes."

He frowned slightly. "Yes, what?"

"Yes, I can get a good start on this before lunch."

"Oh, right. Specs in the corner as always." He nodded.

Nora stood for a moment. Was she dismissed?

Another slight frown. It made his eyebrows dip.

"Is there something else, Miss Bromley?"

"No. Is that all, Mr. Douglas?"

He laughed. "Yes, of course. We'll figure this out. Carry on, Miss Bromley."

She slipped out of the office. She just hoped that things weren't always going to be so awkward whenever she had to deal with one of the men.

She returned to her desk and spread out the sketch. Chose the paper from the paper shelf, and returned to her seat to comments of "Is she still here?" A groan, and a couple of snickers.

But it was the loud snort from desk number two that should have warned her. She positioned her ruler and her compass, but when she reached for her mechanical pencil, it wasn't where she'd left it.

She looked carefully along the trough, thinking maybe she'd been distracted and not paid attention. But it wasn't there.

Felt along the shelf beneath. No pencil. She tried not to panic; she had a spare, but they were expensive items. She glanced up to find others secretly snatching glances at her. She stood, looked carefully on the floor around her stool, beneath her drafting table; there was no pencil, but she had already begun to suspect what had really happened to it.

It had been a favorite ploy of the male students at Cooper Union. Steal things, move them just enough to make her wonder. She had thought these working draftsmen would be a little more mature. Obviously not. She'd give them a chance to return it. She had another in her second pocket. She'd learned to always carry a second and a third pencil for just such mishaps. She reached into her pocket and pulled out her second pencil, glanced up and caught several men watching her. She waggled the pencil at them, gave them a tight smile, and started work on the station entrance.

She was still drafting when she began to notice men leaning back, stretching, taking bags out from under their desks and heading for the door. Lunchtime. There were only a few stragglers left when she looked up to see Mr. Douglas standing over her.

She started.

"Sorry, I didn't want to surprise you and cause your pencil to slip."

"Fortunately, I was just rechecking my dimensions."

"It looks good."

She looked up at him. She felt like smiling, like singing, that a professional architect, and one definitely higher up in the order than any of the men who sat at the now empty desks around her, would compliment her.

"If you're finished with that, we'll drop it off in my office and I'll take you down to the business office."

She hesitated, wanting to ask whether that meant she was hired or if they would no longer need her services and were paying for the work she'd done. She didn't know how to ask.

"May I?" he asked, indicating the rendering.

She nodded and rolled up her drawing, and Mr. Douglas

stepped back, waiting for her to rise. She slipped off her stool, quickly gathered all her tools, and crammed them back into her pockets.

"No need for that. You're hired. Didn't I make that clear? Sorry, I don't usually deal with business stuff. He liked your work. You're hired for special projects. You can keep the desk until you or we find a suitable studio for you to join. And you can leave your tools here."

She smiled, but still slipped the rest of her things into her pockets. She wouldn't tell him why she found it necessary to carry her implements with her. That would really make her life impossible; not only would it create more antagonism among her coworkers, but it might make Mr. White rethink hiring her.

She would bide her time, then deal with them in her own way. But not yet.

She and Mr. Douglas took the elevator down to the fourth floor and into a large office where three women were busy typing. He stopped at the center desk and introduced her to Miss Higgins, a buxom woman whose auburn hair was pulled back severely from her face, making her appear older than she probably was. Rows of ledgers labeled with numbers and letters were lined up on a bookcase behind her.

Miss Higgins wrote down her name, then handed her several sheets of paper and pointed her to a small writing table in the corner where she could fill them out.

Mr. Douglas followed Nora over. "If you're all set, I'll get back to work. Can you get yourself back upstairs . . ." He pulled out a pocket watch and consulted it. "By two o'clock?"

"Of course, thank you."

But instead of leaving, he looked back at Miss Higgins."Perhaps, Miss Higgins, you could show Miss Bromley where the ladies, um . . ."

"Take their lunch? Of course, Mr. Douglas."

He nodded sharply and left the office. His departure was followed by a round of tittering from the other two typists in the office.

"Girls," Miss Higgins said sharply, but she was fighting a smile. "When you finish filling out those forms, Miss Bromley, we'll show you the ladies' lunchroom and the other, more necessary facilities. This is Miss Walker and Miss Smith. In the lunchroom or after work hours, we're Sadie, Lavinia, and Higgie."

Not having brought her lunch, Nora used the facilities and took the elevator back upstairs.

Men were beginning to drift back in from their lunch. Nora saw a large piece of paper on her drafting table and hurried toward it, wondering if it was a new assignment and if it had been sabotaged while she was out. It was intact. She read the specs, then selected the paper and began to work.

At six o'clock, the other draftsmen began packing up. Nora was hurriedly completing the corner specs on another set of columns when Mr. Douglas strode across the floor toward her desk. "Did you get those finished?"

"Yes, sir."

He winced, but looked over her shoulder. "Good. Can I take them?" Not waiting for her answer, he rolled them up and was almost to the door when he turned.

"Bromley, same time tomorrow." And he was gone.

Nora broke into a grin at the closed door. He'd called her Bromley. Not Miss Bromley, just Bromley. She was already one of the guys.

And though her back ached, her neck was stiff, and a blister was developing on her index finger, she made her way home, walking on air.

CHAPTER 7

April 18, 1963
Washington, D.C.

"With Stanford White signed, we thought our biggest
obstacle was behind us." Daisy smiled, remembering her
enthusiastic naïve self. "We now, as we saw it, only needed
to decide on the look of the new club. Over the months
we had accrued quite a list of things we absolutely had to
have, but hadn't quite decided on the overall style of the
clubhouse. We readily eschewed the Beaux Arts style and
the Italianate. Then someone suggested that since we were
the Colony Club, we should use the early colonial style as
our inspiration. Everyone readily agreed, and since we had
more enthusiasm than knowledge of what that entailed,
we invited Stanford to enlighten us. The dear man was
patience itself, explaining why certain things wouldn't work,
why others would be out of scale, then had to explain what
scale was. He came to several meetings armed with books
and renderings and proceeded to give us all lessons in
architecture.

"And at last we had an idea of what the clubhouse would
look like. A few weeks later, it was with relieved minds
that Bordie and I and Bessie and the Morgans left for the
Continent, knowing that with our clubhouse in Stanford's
capable hands, we could enjoy ourselves completely that

summer, confident that when we returned, things would be
moving apace.

  "It was good to get away. London and Paris are always
stimulating, but even more so this trip. It seemed wherever
I went, advances in social issues and politics greeted us.
Whomever I met, whether at one of Bordie's functions or in
society, conversation invariably circled back to the Colony
Club . . ."

May 1904

Daisy sat perched on the Queen Anne chair in Worth's private showroom, trying not to glance at the copy of *Le Temps* that she'd managed to snag at the news vendor that morning before climbing into a taxi to the rue de la Paix. From what she could glean from a quick glance at the headlines, France had just instituted a law limiting workdays for children to ten hours or less. She was anxious to learn more. There was a move to make similar laws back in the States.

"And this, madam, is one of our most elegant new designs, *et le couleur c'est parfaite* for madam's flawless complexion."

Daisy put aside her thoughts on child labor to give the modiste her full attention. Social issues were important, but a new wardrobe for the season was a must.

Another mannequin paraded before her, graceful and smiling, and who probably would never come close to being able to afford any of the gowns she wore daily.

"It's beautiful," Daisy said. "And I do adore that burgundy velvet." The mannequin turned to reveal a demi-train that pooled into clouds behind her. The modiste was right. It would look lovely with her complexion. And with the new fur coat Bordie had insisted she buy just the other day, it would be divine.

She and Bordie never wanted for money. And, though appearances would suggest otherwise, they always lived within budget. Still, she sometimes wondered if she spent less, she could do more for those who really needed it.

It was one of the few altercations she and Bordie ever had. And she had to admit the dear man did have a point. Having money opened doors to more money, and if you used it properly, you could do much more than dropping a coin in the Salvation Army kettle.

The mannequin wafted away, only to be replaced by another, and another. A visiting dress of champagne satin finished with a jacket of sable brown. A tea gown of green with ruffles of Valenciennes lace. Quite lovely, but Daisy also wanted to have a look at the Poiret salon. Bessie's tea gowns, though an oddity on Bessie, might be just the thing for a prominent banker's wife at her leisure. And Daisy was certain Bordie would agree.

She chose three gowns and made an appointment for fittings the following day. On her way out, she ran into Anne Morgan.

"Ah, we meet again," Anne said.

"We do seem to be on the same schedule," Daisy said. They'd spent much time on the ship over with Anne and her father and his mistress. And with both parties staying at the Bishop when they were in London, they'd often dined together.

"Yes, another day being poked and prodded into shape," Anne said, sounding rueful. She was a substantial, muscular young lady, as much a challenge to the dressmaker as she was to her father. The former deftly stuffing her into the latest fashions, and the latter still holding out hope that his daughter would marry well. As yet, Anne, who was already thirty, refused to fit into society's expectations.

"Will you be at the Rothschilds' dinner this evening?" Anne asked, barely repressing a sigh.

"Indeed. Bordie says the Minister of Labor will be there. I was just reading about the new law passed here in France. Ten-hour workdays for children. I know it's a topic you're also interested in."

"Yes, I am. Now if only we could pass something half as enlightened in the States."

"Perhaps he will have some tips on how to go about it. And if he does, I'll gladly pass them on to our own government. Now I must run. I'm meeting Bordie for lunch and you don't want to keep the modiste waiting."

ELSIE STOOD ON the deck of SS *L'Aquitaine*, imagining herself as the figurehead on the prow of an ancient ship as she searched the horizon for a sign of land. Even after five days at sea, the closing night of *The Other Girl* still lingered in her gestures, her voice, her mannerisms.

Funny how you could absorb a character so fully that it was difficult to come back to yourself. Though perhaps if her true self had been given more time to develop . . . But with rehearsals and performances and touring, she never seemed to be where or who she wanted to be.

As it was, she was only happy with Bessie in their little Villa Trianon, where Elsie could remake the rooms into songs of light and air. *Surroundings that soared past the Victorian blanket of melancholy* . . . There she was, doing it again. Acting for the stars above.

She was impatient to be reunited with Bessie. She had so many ideas for redecorating the villa. She liked decorating, though she'd never had an art lesson in her life. Buying and designing made her feel vibrant in a way that theater no longer did.

She'd been acting for more years than she cared to consider, and though Frohman's latest play had garnered excellent reviews and was a box-office success, it hadn't done much to further Elsie's career. Her chance at stardom was narrowing, her light eclipsing, her life diminishing to no more than one defined by the proscenium.

But not in Versailles at their petite retreat. There she felt whole, hopeful, and safe.

She could hardly wait to get there, tear out what was left of the old, search the markets and antique stores for beautiful things to surround her. Beauty, she must have beauty, and comfort and light.

A WEEK WENT by, then two, then three, and not one of Nora's fellow draftsmen had bothered to introduce themselves. They'd merely snickered each time she left the room, or made snide comments about why Mr. White had hired her. A few showed outright hostility.

She started arriving early every morning and staying late each evening. It wasn't that she was trying to impress, but merely to protect herself. One morning she'd arrived to find her stool missing and spent the morning standing at her desk, until someone took pity on her while she was downstairs on her break and returned it. The next week, her drafting table had been turned on its side. Two of the draftsmen had helped her to right it.

Day after day, a few associates took every opportunity to make her life in the drafting room miserable. If she went to use the facilities, when she returned, her work would be misplaced. At least no one had gone so far as to actually steal or destroy her things, not since her pencil on that first day.

She took to carrying her pencils and straightedges in her pockets every time she left her desk, even if it was just to get more paper from across the room.

At first her every move was commented on: "Apple polisher,"

"Goody Two-shoes," and some of the more lurid suggestions on how she got the job. It was hard to think that these educated men could be so coarse. They sounded more like the Lower East Side derelicts she'd always avoided on her walks to and from school. Then she would remember Professor Gerhardt's advice on how to get on. So she got on.

After a month of keeping her head down as Mr. Douglas had suggested, doing meticulous work, and spending lunchtime with the working girls on the fourth floor and not even trying to be accepted by her fellow draftsmen, they slowly began to ignore her.

For the most part.

There were still a handful of vocal antagonists, led by Collin Nast, the man who sat at the second drafting desk in the last row. Her nemesis. He'd been insulting from the first and always made some scurrilous comment every time she passed by.

Mr. White made no mention of moving her to another location. She wasn't certain that he even remembered she was there.

When the secretaries asked her how work was going as they ate their lunches in a room barely larger than a cloak room, Nora just sighed and rolled her eyes.

"Are they still stealing your pencils when you're not looking?"

"Yes—not as bad as at first, but yesterday someone shoved the pieces I was working on off my drafting table. They said it was the wind. The window wasn't even open. One edge got bent, but I managed to trim it so it didn't show. I'm getting a little fed up."

"You're not going to quit?" Lavinia asked, her eyes wide. A tall, slender girl, she spent much of lunchtime every day painting and repairing her nails.

"Never," Nora said. "Just let them try to drive me away."

"That's our girl," said Sadie, a curly-haired blonde who had the accolade of being the fastest typist of the three. "At least we hardly ever have to deal with the men. Except for Higgie. She's the one stuck with their excuses and complaints. Isn't that right, Higgie?"

Higgie, who had just walked in with her lunchbox, arched both eyebrows. "What did I miss?"

"Isn't it true that you're the one always having to put up with the men's complaints?"

"Well," said Higgie, "if you mean they're always late, always broke, sloppy as all get-out, and have no clue as to how things actually get done in an office . . ."

"Unappreciated is what we are," added Lavinia.

"At least they have to be nice to us if they expect to get their paychecks. And it's better than standing on your feet all day at the stores," Sadie said. "The girl I room with has to soak her feet like an old woman every night. Her back is already giving out and she hasn't even found a husband yet."

"Well, I don't want a husband," Lavinia said. "I want my own money and to be able to keep it, even if I have to work for it."

"How about you, Nora?"

"Me? I have to work, and I want to be an architect."

"Do you think they'll ever accept you?"

Nora shrugged. "If they don't, I'll leave them in my dust." She frowned. "I don't even care if they accept me or not if they would just stop trying to sabotage me."

"You should make a plan," said Lavinia, rubbing her hands together like a music hall villain.

"To do what? I was told not to be a distraction. Calling any attention to myself will be fatal for my career. I don't dare make waves; even the bosses don't want me there."

"And we don't want to do anything that would jeopardize Nora's position," Higgie said.

"I don't even think Mr. McKim and Mr. Mead know I'm there," Nora said. "I've never seen them come into the drafting room."

"But Mr. White does," said Lavinia. "And he's the real cheese.

He's very dashing, but he does have a reputation," she added, looking at the others.

"Lavinia, don't tell tales," said Higgie, sounding more like Miss Higgins of the business office.

NORA SETTLED INTO work, managing to ignore most of the taunts and practical jokes. But that was before someone poured her ink on her stool and she ruined her skirt by not seeing it before she sat down.

She took one look at the back of her skirt and considered throttling Collin Nast where he sat smirking at his drafting table. *Don't distract*, she warned herself, and took measured steps to the door and into the elevator. Once downstairs, she dropped all pretense of composure and burst into the fourth-floor office.

"Look what they did!" she exclaimed, trying to look over her shoulder to see the black stain on the seat of her next-to-best skirt.

The other girls hovered around.

"This isn't fair. They've ruined your skirt. You should tell."

"Absolutely not," Higgie said. "You'd be sacked for certain. Just try to bear it; they'll lose interest if you ignore them enough."

"My professor warned me. I expected not to be accepted, but outright sabotage . . ." Nora sighed. "It's hard to understand."

"Not really," Higgie said, gathering up her lunch things. "It's a matter of fear. You've upset their complacency, what they think of as a man's sphere. They're afraid of you, Nora Bromley. Go back upstairs and make them quake."

"But how?"

"You'll think of something."

"Yay," exclaimed Sadie.

"But watch your back," added Lavinia.

"By all means," added Higgie. "And try a solution of milk and salt on the stain."

The next day, instead of lunching with the secretaries, Nora took her sandwich and followed several of the men down the hall and into a nice-sized room with several long rectangular tables and straight-backed chairs. The talk had been lively, until she walked in and looked around with what she hoped was a bland expression, because God knew her knees were knocking. She spied an empty place halfway down the table between two men who worked on the far side of the room and sat down between them. She didn't try to look at them, just calmly ate her sandwich while conversation died around her.

She forced down every bite, though it scraped her throat like sandpaper every time she swallowed. When she was finished, she neatly folded the paper it had been wrapped in and pushed her chair away. She just caught the malicious glint in Mr. Nast's eye.

"Gentlemen, as much as I'd rather enjoy my lunch elsewhere, until my things stop disappearing, my workspace being molested, and all items that have been stolen are returned, I feel it necessary to spend as much time as possible on the fifth floor, even during lunch, just to keep an eye on you." She nodded slightly and, with an effort not to look in Nast's direction, she walked out of the room—

And right into George Douglas, carrying several rolls of plans under one arm.

She stumbled back. Had he heard her little speech? She was supposed to not be distracting. Had she overstepped? Of course she had, but what was she supposed to do, have her things stolen every time she left her desk? She'd be broke from replacing them before the summer was out.

"Mr. Douglas, did you need to see me?"

"I did, and it was more than worth it."

That flummoxed her. "I'm sorry?"

"Oh, don't be. Tell me what's been going on in the drafting room."

Three draftsmen stepped out of the lunchroom, cast suspicious looks at the two of them, then hurried away.

That's all she needed, the men thinking she'd ratted them out. "Nothing. Nothing's going on," she said, loud enough for the departing men to hear her and hopefully pass it on to the others. "I really need to get back to work. If you don't need me."

He shook his head.

She didn't wait for anything else, just hurried down the hall to the elevator.

So much for her triumph. The appearance of George Douglas might have created just the opposite effect of what she intended.

She didn't breathe easily until she'd reached the business office to give Lavinia, Sadie, and Higgie an update.

They were waiting for her.

"Well?" asked Lavinia. "Where were you during lunch?"

"I was dining with the gentlemen upstairs."

"They invited you?"

"Heavens, no. I spent last night thinking of things they would really hate. And boy, as soon as I walked in, you could have heard a pin drop. We all ate in total quiet until I left."

"Famous!" cried Sadie.

"It would have been, but as I was making my exit, I ran smack-dab into Mr. White's assistant; he ruined it all. He was standing outside the door and asked me what was going on."

"*Men*," Sadie exclaimed with such furor that the others laughed.

"Now I'm afraid they'll think I told on them, but I didn't."

"Well," said Higgie, "if this doesn't work, we'll come up with plan B."

"Thanks," Nora said. "I'd better wash my hands and get back to work before they start dismantling my desk."

When Nora returned to the fifth floor, she was surprised to find everyone silent and hard at work. She had just made it to the back of the room when she found out why.

"So now you're not just a little slut, but a rat to boot," said Collin Nast, jumping up from his stool to bar her way.

"I'm neither, but you're a bully and it's not necessary. I'm not in competition with you."

"Lucky for Nast," came a voice from someone close by, though no one even lifted their head.

Collin Nast snapped around, studied the people behind them, then turned back to Nora. "Why don't you go home where you belong instead of taking the job of a man who needs to support his family? What did you have to do to get White to give you this job? Are you still doing it?" He pouted his lips with what Nora thought might be meant to be a pucker for a kiss, but it just made her want to punch him.

Nora bit her tongue to keep from snapping back, *Then who will support my family?* She knew you couldn't fight with bullies; they always won. But you couldn't retreat or they would just get worse.

"Nast, give it a rest." It was a draftsman who sat several tables away slightly in front of Nora's desk, and one of the few men who acknowledged her in any form that wasn't derogatory. He was fair-haired with a round baby face and was just the kind of person a bully would pick on. Nora appreciated his attempt to intercede, but she could fight her own battles and didn't want him to bear the brunt of Nast's bad temper.

"Oh," said Nast. "I'm afraid this must be yours." He held up a wooden protractor.

For a moment no one moved, then one by one, heads turned toward Collin Nast. Nora felt her pockets—how could she have missed it? She'd been so careful to always take everything with her.

"It must have fallen off your desk; you should be more careful with your implements." He took a piece of the protractor in each hand. It had been broken right down the center.

He didn't bother to hide his satisfied smirk. It made Nora want to do bodily harm. And she knew she was more than capable of doing it, but it would cost her her job and she wouldn't give him the satisfaction.

Screwing up every bit of her self-control, she expended a huge sigh; she took the pieces of the protractor from him and held them up for the room to see, while slowly breaking into a smile.

"I guess I'll be joining you for lunch again tomorrow."

There was an audible groan. Nora didn't react, just turned away and began pulling the rest of her tools from her pockets and returning them to the tool trough. A process that was becoming very irksome.

She was already dreading lunch tomorrow. She would so much rather be eating with the girls downstairs. But the men had declared war and she would have to rise to the occasion . . . somehow.

A minute later she was bent over her work, trying to create and complete an arch with a broken protractor, when another protractor appeared before her face.

"I have an extra." It was the baby-faced guy from down the row. "I'm Fergus Finnegan, by the way."

"Nice to meet you, Mr. Finnegan."

"Just call me Fergus."

"Fergus."

She took the protractor from him with thanks and then bent back over her work, hiding her smile, hoping she'd just seen the first crack in their armor.

CHAPTER 8

Summer 1904
Manhattan

With summer, heat descended on the city. It seemed to Nora that even the nights refused to cool, which made the following day even more unbearable. The streets were sticky and smelled of rotting food and horse manure. Even leaving for work before the sun rose over the skyline left Nora's collars soaked with perspiration by the time she reached the drafting room. Her lightweight spring skirts felt more like the heaviest wool rather than gabardine.

At McKim, Mead, and White, the draftsmen were coming in earlier to spend more time in the controlled environs of the drafting room. After all, you couldn't have sweat dripping off noses and onto newly drawn plans.

Mr. White was rarely seen and Nora finally learned from the girls downstairs that he intended to spend most of the summer in Europe buying furnishings for the Payne Whitney mansion. She had studied the periods of art and their furnishings as part of her curriculum, but the only real experience she had with "decor" was the lumpy and sagging sofas of their old apartment on Perry Street or the infrequent student trips to the museum.

Besides, these days, more and more people were furnishing their houses from catalogues and furniture stores, or going to dealers who had inventories of such things. That was fine by her. She'd just concentrate on the building proper.

With the bosses away, either on buying trips for clients or in Newport or Long Island for the social season, the business was being run mostly by George and several other senior architects. And while they were going about their suddenly burgeoning responsibilities, the others found time to linger over lunch, engage in a bit of horseplay, and think up new ways to harass Nora.

The one silver lining was that she got to spend longer lunches downstairs with the three secretaries and even met some other girls who worked at the bank on the first floor.

Her treks out to Brooklyn for Sunday meals were even more debilitating. Fully pregnant now, Louise had sunk into a vile temper from which she refused to emerge. Their mother had taken over all of the cleaning, cooking, and seeing to Little Don, as well as looking after Rina, Louise, and Donner, who Rina informed Nora was usually away from home all day and came in late reeking of gin.

Nora promised her she was saving money to move them out.

"Mama won't leave her now. I don't think Louise can manage alone."

On Nora's next visit, she took fruit and sausage and a bag of hard candy. But instead of assuaging Louise's temper, she'd just made things worse.

Mama decided it would be best to discontinue Sunday lunch until Louise had delivered and recovered. Rina argued, but Mama insisted. "As soon as the baby is born, things will go back to normal."

Nora missed the two of them, but she felt relieved to be able to concentrate on her work. And without Louise hounding her for her pay, Nora was able to save extra money with an eye to the future.

Summer finally loosened its grip on the city in September.

One morning just as they were settling down to various projects, Mr. White burst into the room.

"Bromley!"

Nora bolted from her stool in pure reflex. Everyone else stared at Mr. White, who stood feet apart, glowering ominously. He looked tired. He turned on his heel, not waiting for an answer, and limped out of the room.

Any attempts at a welcome died on the lips of the draftsmen, who merely returned to their work.

Nora scooped up her current sketches and hurried after him, wondering if she'd done something wrong. How could he know anything unless George Douglas had complained about her? But why would he?

She slipped into the hallway to find Mr. Douglas waiting for her.

"What is it?" she asked, trying not to sound alarmed.

"No idea. He just came in like a whirlwind. I heard him yell 'Bromley' from my office, so I came out to see what was going on."

"Did you tell him about my forays into the gentlemen's lunchroom?" It was the only thing that she thought might get her in trouble.

"Of course not, and I won't unless you ask me to. You seem to be handling yourself quite nicely on your own."

"Thanks."

"Come on, I'll walk you down." He started off without her, a lapse in manners that she could only attribute to his surprise at Mr. White's unexpected appearance in the drafting room.

And that was when she realized she'd left all her drawing implements behind. God only knew what would be their fate. But she didn't dare go back.

Mr. Douglas rapped on Mr. White's door, then opened it and stood back for her to enter. *Now* he remembered his manners. Or was too chicken to lead the way.

Mr. White was leaning over his desk, a roll of art paper spread out on the top and held down at the corners by various objects that must have been within reach.

He made an impatient gesture for them to approach. Mr. Douglas had to nudge Nora forward.

"Did you get those specs on the Madison Square church finished?"

"Yes, sir, I turned them in to Mr. Douglas a week ago."

He glanced up at Mr. Douglas.

"Indeed she did. They were excellent. I started her on the Grand Central Terminal concourse."

"Well, take her off it."

"I don't quite—"

"I need her on something else. Mrs. Harriman and her club ladies are back and they want to see the designs for their club."

Nora had heard he was designing a clubhouse for some society ladies, though Nora couldn't imagine them sitting around drinking brandy and smoking cigars like she'd heard the men did. She stifled a giggle at the vision it conjured.

"They want to see the completed design. I have the floor plans here somewhere. I've completed enough to give them an idea. But they won't understand anything without a presentation painting.

"I don't have time to do it. I've just barely returned from Europe, where I picked up some beauties for the Payne Whitney House. It will take another couple of buying trips; there is still a lot of house to furnish and Mrs. Whitney is anxious for it to be completed." He shook his head as if he couldn't believe the vagaries of women wanting a habitable home for their family. "And I'm due in Sheepshead day after tomorrow."

"The races, sir?"

"As always."

He paused to rummage through the stacks of art paper on his

desk, then looked behind him at a chest with renderings thrown haphazardly across the surface.

Mr. Douglas stepped forward to intercede before he made a total mess of things.

"I believe we filed those floor plans before you left for the Continent in May."

"Right, so we did." White looked around the office.

Mr. Douglas reached past him, pulled open an oversized drawer, and lifted out a large cardboard folder.

"Voilà, eh, George?"

"Yes, sir."

"Spread 'em out on the desk. Bromley, come take a look."

She stepped forward, still at a loss as to what was expected of her, and watched as Mr. Douglas lifted out a sketch of the facade of a building, mainly pen-and-ink with several changes made in pencil: circles, arrows, scratch-throughs, and scribbled notes.

"Nice Federal facade, brick face, not red, but rose and gray in this pattern"—he rummaged through some smaller papers, found one—"*this* pattern, headers facing out."

Nora longed for a pencil to take notes, but Mr. White plowed ahead.

". . . and these windows . . ." He paused to pick up a mechanical pencil and made some adjustments, then used the pencil to point at each fixture as he explained them. "They're two stories high, assembly room in front, gymnasium behind, but you don't have to worry about that now. Balcony. I have a sketch here of the original balcony that it's patterned after." Before he could turn and search for the sketch, it appeared before his face. He took it from Mr. Douglas. "So across the front . . ." He put up his hands, palms facing out, then opened them like a curtain. "Delicate, ladylike, while complementing the brick, the two enhancing each other, portraying longevity, strength, without being ponderous. See where I'm going?"

Nora nodded. She was imagining it in situ, finished, a delicate but sturdy work of art.

"Dormers across the roof; the detailed dimensions are listed somewhere. George will find them for you. Can you do it? By tomorrow."

"Tomorrow, sir?" interjected Mr. Douglas.

"It's their regular meeting day. They've rented a temporary meeting place two doors down from the construction site. Probably meaning to keep an eye on the progress. So, George, make sure they aren't continuously sticking their lovely noses into the actual construction and making suggestions. Now, can you do it?"

"Yes, sir. I'll—" Nora stopped herself before she continued with "I'll try." She *would* do it. She would do anything to prove her worth. He would have no excuses for giving her work to someone else. Even if it meant . . . working on a ladies' club.

"But what about the Grand Central designs?" George Douglas frowned in confusion; they'd obviously discussed assignments at some point since his return.

"I'll put Nast on it. Or Finnegan, he's adequate."

"He actually has some good ideas, sir."

"Fine, though I could do with fewer ideas and more grunt work. Oh, pardon me, Bromley. Forgot you were here."

He patted her shoulder and rested his hand there for a long second, before Mr. Douglas cleared his throat and his hand moved away.

"I'm counting on you. The ladies were impressed by your design school sketch. I should have thought of this before. Make it feminine, calming, comfortable, so they won't change their minds again. God, those women have an opinion about everything. Not sure I should be abetting them in this club idea, but . . ." He shrugged as if to say, *What can you do?* "If you have any questions, ask Douglas; he's in charge."

Nora looked at George Douglas; his expression said this was news to him.

"I'll need it by tomorrow morning for their noon luncheon meeting."

"There's only one thing, sir," Nora said.

"What?" The word was imperious, and both men turned to stare at her as if she'd spouted blasphemy.

"I don't have watercolors with me. Or even own ones good enough for a presentation rendering."

"Oh, that's all. George, get her what she needs. And take these away. Get her an easel or some such. Tomorrow morning, Bromley."

"Yes, sir."

Mr. Douglas quickly rolled up the sketches and ushered her out the door. It had barely closed behind them when he said, "*Can* you do it?"

Nora finally took a deep breath. "I'll have to. But I'll have to stay late."

"Fine. Just get the night watchman to lock up after you leave. I'd stay, but I have a night class tonight."

"A course in architecture?"

"Actually, I'm studying business at Columbia."

"You're not giving up architecture?"

"Far from it, but one should be prepared for the future."

"Oh." They'd reached his office and she followed him inside. A bit of rummaging and he brought out a wooden box of paints and another of brushes, which he inspected before handing them to her. "I think they're usable. I try to farm out the watercolor renderings. Design and mechanical drawing is my forte, if I have one. I like the geometry of it all."

He took her back to the drafting room, where their entrance caused bald-faced curiosity. And after Mr. Douglas deposited the watercolors at her drafting table, dragged over an additional stand so that she could spread out her paints, and brought her an easel to prop the original facade sketch on, their curiosity was unmistakable.

Mr. Douglas, who seemed unaware of the attention he was causing, found several jars that he filled with water from a sink that was located in a closet that Nora had never noticed before.

Then he nodded to her and left the room.

Nora sat down and, determined not to give the others the satisfaction of her notice, she began organizing her supplies on the extra table.

She took a long time to study the sketch of the facade, trying to absorb what Mr. White felt when he designed it. That wasn't hard to do, even where the original had been hastily drawn over where she supposed he—and the ladies—had changed their minds about what they wanted.

The capitals of the Corinthian columns had been redrawn to take on a smaller profile, a note and an arrow pointing toward the balcony with *S Car* written beside it. She looked through the subsidiary sketches and found the original balcony he'd taken the design from, an existing home in Charleston. Its delicate ironwork would be a nice juxtaposition against the columns, dormers, and brick.

When at last she felt she "saw" the design, from the overall feeling of the whole to the nuances of the details, she got out her straightedge and other implements and began to transfer the original drawing to a new sketch. After meticulous gridding, measuring, adjusting, and double-checking, she had a pencil drawing that precisely recorded the original and was of a quality of which anyone would be proud.

She stretched her back, rolled her head, trying to loosen her tense neck muscles, and realized she had missed lunch. Well, she wouldn't leave her drawing until it was finished and deposited on Mr. White's or Mr. Douglas's desk.

She was taking no chances on sabotage today.

But she did walk around, forcing the circulation back into her legs and limbering up her fingers, never venturing far from her workspace and never taking her eyes off her work.

Then she went back to turn the pencil sketch into a color rendering.

Watercolor was like an old friend. And though she'd been away from it for a while, when she picked up the brush, it was like she'd never put it down.

She only left her desk long enough to change the water, and even then she hurried. Occasionally, she became aware of someone walking close by, slowing down. Curious, perhaps? That was fine as long as they didn't get too close.

The afternoon wore on, and soon the other draftsmen began to pack up and leave for the evening. Nora was just finishing a little clean-up detailing. She would have to wait until it dried before adding the pen-and-ink delineations.

"Wow, that's some rendering." It was Fergus, and he was studying the watercolor on her drafting table. "Well done."

Once Fergus had broken the ice, a couple of others wandered over to peer over his shoulder.

"Now, fellas," Fergus said, "let the lady work. Give her room."

The other men stepped back, but one even complimented her color choice. Fergus winked at her and turned away, only to run into Mr. Nast, who for some reason had chosen that exact time to walk past.

"Watch what you're doing, Finnegan. I came to see what you're all gawking at. Is Bromley showing you her Florodora act?"

He leaned over; the little group swayed forward against his weight.

"Hey, watch it, Nast!"

"What-ho?" Nast grabbed Fergus's shoulder, shoving him

against one of the other men, who staggered forward and fell against the desk. The water jar bobbled.

Nora and Fergus both made a grab for it, but it was too late. The jar tipped, then fell over, splashing water over Nora's drafting table and over her almost-finished rendering, before rolling off the table and crashing to the floor.

Nora froze, not even attempting to try to save the drawing. They all watched, helpless, as the delicate shades ran into each other and then off the page.

Fergus grabbed the rendering and tried to shake the water off, but only managed to spray paint over the rest of them. The colors that were left on the paper merged into a muddy mess.

Fergus turned on Nast. "You did that on purpose."

"Me?" Nast said. "It was Dolan here that knocked over the water."

"Because you pushed me," said the man, nursing his side.

"It was your clumsiness," Nast said. He turned and walked away.

Dolan lunged for him and the two men went down.

So much for not causing a diversion.

Her painting was destroyed, the men were fighting, and she would be fired tomorrow for certain. She couldn't even cry; the pain and sense of betrayal she felt was much deeper than tears.

The two fighters were soon broken up and Nast returned to his drafting table as if nothing had happened.

Dolan stood, brushing himself off. "I'm so sorry. It was Nast's doing. I would never do anything to undermine another architect's work."

Nora nodded, she couldn't speak. Her work, her dreams, lay in a puddle on the drafting-room floor.

"What are you going to do?" Dolan asked sympathetically.

Nora shook her head. "By tomorrow morning?"

"He needs it that soon?" Fergus asked.

Nora nodded.

"But that could take hours," Dolan said.

"So she'd better get started," Fergus said. "Dolan, get some clean water. Allaby, get a rag and let's clean up this mess."

Several other men joined in and made short work of it. Nast didn't even look to see what they were doing, just bent over his work, and Nora wondered how he could not feel the flame of anger that burned in her eyes.

"Is there anything else we can do?" Fergus asked.

Nora shook her head. "But thank you. I'll just sit here a bit."

Gradually they all left for the day, some glancing her way out of curiosity, some with a sympathetic look or nod. Fergus paused as he passed her desk, gave her an encouraging nod, then joined the others.

And when the workroom was empty but for her, Nora laid out a fresh sheet of paper and began again.

CHAPTER 9

Someone was shaking her. Nora forced her eyes open, blinked furiously against the sunlight. She'd overslept! She was going to be late for work. She bolted upright. And slowly realized she was at her drafting table at the McKim, Mead, and White offices.

"Have you been here all night?"

"What?" She looked up, blinked again. George Douglas stood over her, looking as bright as a new penny.

And she came fully awake. "My—" She looked frantically around and found her watercolor of the Colony Club tacked to the easel, safe and sound. She slumped in relief, then, realizing the state she must be in, attempted to smooth her skirt while quickly tucking a stray strand of hair behind her ear.

He glanced past her at the water jar and the ruined watercolor still lying on the floor.

"What happened?"

Nora shrugged. She was too tired to think. The sun had already been rising when she put the final touches to the women's Colony Club facade. She tried to shift in front of the destroyed version, but she was too late. He reached past her and lifted up the discarded first attempt.

His mouth tightened.

"What time is it?" she asked.

"Just past seven o'clock," he said, without taking his eyes off the rendering he was holding. "I came in early to check over the floor plans for the club before today's meeting. What happened here?"

"I wasn't satisfied with the first one so I did it over again."

"So you poured water over it and threw it on the floor?"

She shook her head while her mouth searched for an excuse.

"It was an accident."

"What kind of accident?"

"Just an accident. What do you think of the second one?" She tried to pull the ruined one from his grasp, but he held tight.

He lowered the drawing but didn't let go while he studied the new rendering. "Stanford will be pleased. He was right about you. Just the right amount of femininity to be inviting."

"That's a good thing?"

"Yes."

"Good. What shall I start on next?"

"You should go home and get some sleep."

"I'm fine. I'll just go downstairs and tidy up, if you will—if you will take my rendering to your office." She began gathering her pencils and other implements together.

"Don't think I don't know what has been going on here. I've wanted to intervene before, but you were handling things just fine on your own."

When? How? He only came to the drafting room to pick things up, drop others off, occasionally giving an encouraging word or a suggestion to one of the draftsmen.

"But a word from you and I'll put a stop to it."

She grabbed his sleeve. "Please, no. Everything is fine. I can handle everything here. I've learned so much already. Please, I don't want to jeopardize my position here."

The outer door opened and Nora took the opportunity to snatch the ruined drawing from his hands and stick it quickly under her desk.

Fergus Finnegan strode in.

"Back so early?" Seeing George Douglas, he stopped midstride. "Oh, uh, good morning."

"You're early, Finnegan."

"Just wanted to catch up on some work before it got crowded."

"Hmmm." George's eyes narrowed.

Fergus cut a concerned look toward Nora.

Nora shook her head, casting pleading eyes to Fergus.

"Seems there was an accident to her first rendering," George said.

Fergus snorted. "Weren't no accident. Some of the guys—"

"I should have put paid to several of them already."

"No. Please. I can't be a distraction. I want to be an architect."

George Douglas almost smiled. "And so you shall be. But neither I nor Mr. White will tolerate sabotage in this firm. Fergus, you can pass the word around—discreetly."

"My pleasure."

"If you're finished with this one," Douglas nodded toward the new rendering, "I'll take it away to be mounted."

Nora nodded.

"Nice work, Bromley."

"Thank you."

Nora held her breath until he had unpinned the rendering and carried it to the door. Fergus didn't move until the door closed behind him. "Gads! Were you here all night?"

"Yes, and I fell asleep, and of all mornings, *he* comes in early."

"Well, at least it was the Golden Boy's assistant. When the GB himself comes in early, it's only to go directly upstairs to his private office to sleep it off."

"Does that happen often?" Nora asked, momentarily distracted.

Fergus shrugged. "Don't know what I'm saying. Forget it."

Nora was curious, but she didn't even want to think about gossiping on the job. That would cause huge problems. "Would you mind my things while I go downstairs to freshen up?"

"Sure." Fergus crossed his arms and stood stiff-legged in front of her desk. "Don't you worry, Miss Bromley. Your stuff is safe with me."

"Thanks, but Fergus?"

"Yeah?"

"Could you just call me Bromley like you do the other guys?"

"Sure thing, Miss—Sure thing, Bromley."

And feeling much better, Nora hurried downstairs to make herself presentable.

"GOOD HEAVENS, NORA, if we didn't know better, we'd think you were out carousing all night."

Nora looked quickly to make sure the three secretaries were the only ones around and then sank into an extra chair. "I never left. The 'boys' ruined the design I was working on and since it was due today, I had to finish it. Then I fell asleep and George Douglas found me like this." She gestured to her paint-stained and rumpled clothes. "I was sure I was going to be fired."

"George wouldn't do that. He's a sweetheart," said Sadie, and sighed at her typewriter.

"Like you would know," Lavinia said. "He's all business all the time. Alas."

"I came to see if one of you has a comb I could use."

"You're going back upstairs?" Lavinia asked.

Nora nodded. "Anything to keep this position."

"Well, you're going to need more than a comb," Higgie said. "When was the last time you ate?"

Nora shrugged. "Breakfast yesterday?" she guessed.

"Honestly, you can't compete if you're not taking care of yourself. Sadie, go down to the lunchroom and make some coffee." Higgie reached into her desk drawer. "Here." She thrust out a package wrapped in brown paper. "It's just cheese and bread, but it will keep you going until you can go out for lunch."

Lavinia handed Nora a comb.

"Thank you. I'll be back in two shakes." Nora stood, but her back twitched and her knees felt like cement. Sleeping bent over your desk after spending the day working bent over your desk was bound to have some drawbacks.

She hobbled away to the lavatory, where she splashed water on her face and fixed the worst of her hair, then took a closer look in the mirror over the sink and sighed. Her eyes were puffy and she looked pale. She retucked her shirtwaist into her skirt and smoothed her hands down the front, which had taken most of the spill and would probably never be completely clean again.

It would have to do. But as soon as she got a little ahead, she was going to refurbish her wardrobe. And ask her mother for advice about getting out stains.

DAISY SET OUT from Thirty-eighth Street in good time to make the meeting. In fact, she'd left early. Even though the Morgans' residence was only a couple of blocks away, she wanted to have time to swing by the building site on her way.

It was something she did whenever she got the chance. It seemed to be an interminably long process, though Bordie assured her that "these things take time" and progress looked steady to him. She took him at his word, though she still wished they would hurry.

She'd been appalled when she first saw the depth of the hole they'd had to dig in order to accommodate the swimming pool and other facilities that would be housed in the basement. Swimming underground. It was still something she couldn't quite imagine.

She had to consciously not worry about how the pool would be kept clean and free from leaks and bacteria and a million other things that she didn't understand and couldn't help if she did.

And today it did look like they had made progress; there seemed to be more steel beams than before. *Steel.* Stanford had assured them the club would include all the most modern advances in construction as well as interior conveniences. Electricity throughout, fireproofing, the most advanced system of heating and proper ventilation. Important things, to be sure. Still, she couldn't help wishing they would move a little faster.

Today Stanford was presenting the final facade and floor plans to the board and the building committee. The operative word being *final*. Fingers crossed that any additional changes by members would be minimal today.

Daisy had shown a good deal of patience while the ladies fought for additions and modifications, but today she planned on pushing through all but the most egregious deficiencies of the plans.

She didn't expect there to be any. Stanford had proven himself through some of the architectural gems of the city and throughout the country. She had no doubt the Colony Club would be one of them.

Today's meeting was being held at the Morgan mansion. It was an auspicious place to finalize the design with McKim, Mead, and White, who'd also designed J. P.'s expanded library next door. Which, she reminded herself, had been under construction for at least two years and still wasn't finished.

Stanford had promised the club would be ready by the end of next year. Daisy would just have to trust in that.

Anne met Daisy at the door.

"It's so exciting. Come in. Bessie is already here. She brought Elsie." Anne bustled her into J. P.'s personal library, a large room that would soon be replaced by the building next door that would eventually contain his entire collection of books, drawings, maps, and manuscripts.

At the far end of the room, two rows of chairs were arranged in a semicircle in front of a long mahogany table and two easels large enough to almost hide the beautiful Florentine fireplace behind them.

Bessie, dressed in a tailored houndstooth suit, held court with Sarah Hewitt and several other women gathered around a tea table covered with urns and cakes and delicate china. Next to her, Elsie, petite and graceful as always, cast her gaze around the room, no doubt thinking of ways to bring the rather somber furnishings of the Morgans' library into the modern period.

Sometimes Daisy thought Elsie had missed her true calling.

"Elsie, so glad you could make it," Daisy said. "I thought you might already be in rehearsal."

"We start next week. The play opens the second week of December."

"Alas," Sarah said. "I've been trying to tempt Elsie into helping me decorate my morning room for ages, but she's always being whisked off to the bright lights of the theater."

"Nonsense," Elsie said. "I'll have plenty of time to do both." She sighed sweetly. "Arranging rooms actually gives me more energy for the theater."

Several other women entered and Anne excused herself to greet them.

She returned almost immediately with Helen Barney and Kate Brice, carrying an edition of the *Sun*. "Now they're accusing us of smoking and drinking, and we don't yet have a building to smoke in even if we wanted to."

"That's not all," said Mary Dick, from where she was sitting on a small sofa talking with Mrs. Perkins, one of the established elders of many women's charitable organizations. "The anti-smoking group already sent us a pledge to sign to forbid smoking in the clubhouse. I wrote them back politely saying that since we as yet didn't have a clubhouse, it would be premature of us to sign anything at this time."

"And so it continues," said Sarah. "I don't know what all the fuss is about. You'd think we were planning to walk naked down Fifth Avenue."

"For the Easter Parade, delicious," squealed Kate, and cast Daisy such a mischievous look, it was hard not to smile. But this was serious. The idea of a club was purely innocuous as far as Daisy could see, and yet it had managed to threaten the male order, the church leaders, the moral pontificators—and their wives.

Kate Brice threw up her hands. "My pastor actually stopped me after services and strongly advised me to put away the notion of belonging, because . . ." She lowered her voice and said in a creaky imitation of the pastor, "'If women are bored with their home life, perhaps they are not aware of their duties to their husbands and their children.' Well," said Kate. "A less-refined woman would have kicked him in the shins. I merely asked him in my meekest voice, 'Oh, is that why men go to their clubs? To shirk their responsibilities?' I beat a hasty retreat before he said anything more that would tempt me to tell him exactly what I thought of his wrong-headed ideas."

"That's all fine for you," said Emmie Winthrop. "But it's serious that so many people are upset."

"Yes," Daisy said, stepping in to curb the argument, one they seemed to have in some form or another every time they met, whether for a luncheon or a concert or a political lecture. "All the more reason for getting our clubhouse built and occupied. Once they see for themselves that it is a . . . a . . ."

"Den of iniquity?" suggested Bessie, straight-faced.

"A place for the betterment of ourselves and consequently for the betterment of society and our families, they will come around."

Bessie hmphed. "I doubt it. You know what they say about horses and water."

"Where is Stanny?" Elsie said. "I long to see what he has planned."

"And so you shall," said Anne, looking toward the door, where the butler was about to announce their guest of honor.

Daisy was always taken a bit aback whenever she saw him. Large and vivid. With fiery hair and a mustache that announced his entrance into any room. He was followed by two of the Morgans' liveried servants carrying several cardboard tubes and a large rectangular shape covered in oilcloth that had to be the rendering of the club.

Conversation stopped altogether for a split second, then Anne moved forward to greet him. While Stanford made his way around the room, conversing with each group of women, Anne directed the servants to the front of the room, where they immediately set the rectangle on one of the easels and the tubes on the table before discreetly moving to the side, waiting in case they were needed again.

"Hmmph," Bessie said. "You'd best call the meeting to order or they'll keep him chatting all afternoon. He's a busy man."

"I was just thinking that," Daisy agreed, though she'd been more concerned with her own curiosity than Stanford's plans for the afternoon.

Daisy took her place at the front of the room and rapped her gavel sharply on the table. She'd learned almost immediately that a weak gavel was no better than a whisper to a room full of ladies enjoying themselves.

"Ladies," Daisy announced. "Please be seated." For once the members didn't dawdle, but quickly took their seats and turned expectant faces toward Stanford White and the covered painting behind him.

"Please welcome Mr. White, who has so graciously taken time away from his work to be with us today." She paused briefly to let that soak in.

Enthusiastic applause, dulled only by the tea gloves worn by the participants.

Daisy ceded the floor to Stanford. He needed no introduction. They'd been waiting for him with bated breath for the last two years or more.

As Daisy sat at the end of the first row, Stanford said, "It's wonderful to see you ladies looking so fine. The halls of Newport and Long Island must be dimmed in sadness now that you've returned to the city."

Titters, sighs, all the usual responses to his inimitable charm.

Daisy smiled and thought, *Just get to it, please.*

"Ladies, I offer you . . ." He whisked the cover off the rendering with the flourish of a magician. "The Colony Club."

CHAPTER 10

Whatever Fergus had said in Nora's absence, there was a lot less tension in the drafting room when she returned, except perhaps from Mr. Nast, who still seemed determined to make her life miserable. But she could deal with him. And now she knew she at least had one friend in Fergus. Along with being accepted by Dolan, Allaby, and a few others, things were looking up.

George Douglas assigned her some detail work that kept Nora busy for most of the morning and into the afternoon. She assumed Mr. White had taken the rendering to the ladies' meeting, but so far she hadn't heard him return. It was an honor to be chosen for such an important part of the procedure, but what if they didn't like what they saw?

What if they hated it? Would he blame her? She'd done her best, under the circumstances.

She ordered herself to stop worrying, and almost had, when the door banged open and Mr. White, carrying several rolls of floor plans and limping painfully, lurched into the room.

After a brief, surprised look, all the men went hurriedly back to work. Nora did, too. It was obvious he was in a thunderous mood. And Nora was afraid it was because of her.

As he made his way across the room, Nora became aware of George Douglas running in behind him. Nora sat immobile as the two men converged on her.

"Bromley!" White bellowed in a miasma of gin.

Nora suspected everyone in the room must have jumped.

White pulled the top off the tube, dumped the rolls of floor plans onto her drafting table, and shoved the tube at George.

"Now they want a place for their dogs to lounge while they're lunching. A dog lounge. You're a woman, you figure out a place to put them."

Nora was so astonished, her concerns about her presentation drawing fled.

He reached into his breast pocket and pulled out several sheets of paper that he riffled through, then shoved one of them at her. "Give 'em a dog house, make it appealing, add it to the plan, then bring it to my office. I penciled in the dimensions. George, I need you. I'm dining with the Payne Whitneys, and I—" He took George's arm and propelled him toward the doorway, leaving Nora helpless to even ask if the ladies had liked the presentation.

Then a high-pitched "Arf, arf" hit her ears. She didn't have to guess where it came from.

She bolted off her stool and strode over to Nast. "What is wrong with you? What do you have against women in architecture? We hold a pen as you do, roll our paper the same way, can take perfect measurements, perhaps even more fastidiously than men. We want to join you in architecture, not take your jobs, if that's what you're worried about. We just want to work."

Sit down and shut up. This "distraction" would get her fired for sure.

She held her ground as her hopes for her future came crashing down around her. But if she was going to be fired, she would go down standing up for herself. Nast had deigned to turn his head just enough to see her without really having to face her. She took a step toward him and peered over his shoulder.

"And if you question my ability, I can tell you—that arch you've just drawn? You miscalculated the angle of the arc by at least six degrees and it will probably collapse if built."

She didn't wait for his reaction, which would undoubtedly be rude, but went back to her desk to figure out what the needs of a dog lounge would be.

She kept her head down, arranging the various papers White had left with her.

And heard, "Bravo, Bromley," whispered from a nearby desk. She didn't look up to see who had said it.

She found the scrawled dimensions, followed by a note *under 8 lbs*, which she assumed was the size of the dogs allowed. That made things a bit easier and would be in line with the dimensions given.

Unfortunately, Nora's only firsthand knowledge of dogs were the mangy half-starved curs that roamed the streets of the Lower East Side, rummaging in garbage cans and fighting each other for the spoils. Dogs who would attack people if they got too close. The people she knew didn't have pampered dogs with special rooms where they could "lounge."

Why would they even bring their dogs to the club just to sit in a room until they were picked up again? Why not just leave them at home? Didn't they have servants to look after their pets?

Not her concern, Nora reminded herself. It wasn't the dogs' fault. She tried to conjure up her brother's castles in the air. She would make such a place for dogs. A safe place large enough for them to play, an area for food and water. And for the beds that had been scrawled on the spec sheet, she pictured soft pillowed couches where sleep was a comfort, and not a lapse in your will to survive. And a special place for them to do their business away from dainty slippers and trailing hems.

And like the days spent watching her brother draw, the anger, fear, and hunger dropped away and her imagination took off. In a matter of minutes she had carved out a space from a basement cloakroom, near an exit. Then for good measure, she took out her borrowed watercolors and made a quick presentation sketch of the interior. And found that she was quite pleased with the results.

Not that it was real architecture, more like a flight of fancy. But hopefully it was what they wanted and she'd get paid for her bit of nonsense.

While the watercolors dried, she spent the time looking over the other floor plans of the ladies' club. There was a swimming pool in the basement. Now there was something she'd like to see. And not only a swimming pool, but dressing rooms, sitting rooms, a steam room, and Turkish baths; a hydropathic room and massage, manicure, and hairdressing rooms. Nora had never heard of half those things.

The first floor held the usual first-floor areas: parlor, coat-room, office, lounging room, reading room, and something called a strangers room. What on earth would they use that for?

The second floor was two stories high and divided in half by a gymnasium in back and an assembly room in front with lounging and dressing rooms in the middle.

Nora smiled, trying to imagine the ladies changing out of their feathers and jewels and into the bloomers worn by the "new women" in their craze for exercise. Walking to and from work was enough exercise for Nora, and running for the trolley or away from the gangs of urchins that used to torment her was more exercise than she ever cared to do as a hobby.

There was a floor to house the workers and one at the top for restaurants and guest bedrooms. The ladies would have every-thing they needed, right here in one place.

She had to admit, she'd like to see what it looked like finished. Draftsmen never saw the fruits of their labor. Even architects rarely visited their sites. The actual building was turned over to a foreman, who directed the construction crews, plumbers, and electricians.

This digression from her actual work was interrupted by the

entrance of George Douglas, who called out the names of six men and motioned them out of the room. Fergus, the odious Mr. Nast, and four others she hadn't met in all her months of inhabiting the same room followed Mr. Douglas out.

Mr. Allaby, whose desk was nearby, slumped in his seat.

"Psst," Nora hissed to get his attention.

He turned.

"What's going on?"

"I think he's choosing the men to work on the final plans for the Grand Central Terminal contest. They're choosing the winner in a few weeks."

"Oh." The new train station would link New York to the north, south, and west. That would be something to work on. She glanced at her painting of the dog room and felt disappointment wash over her. *You're a woman, you figure out a place to put them* . . . Mr. White's words came back to her like an indictment. Was that all she'd been hired for? Doing the work that no one else wanted?

The men returned a few minutes later with worksheets.

Mr. Nast paused before sitting down. "How's the doggie room coming? Guess you won't be taking our jobs after all." He wiggled his spec sheet at her. "We'll be busy on the Grand Central Terminal project. Arf, arf."

He sat down.

Nora tried to tamp down the anger that was threatening to erupt. She'd already gone too far today. She gritted her teeth, clenched her fists beneath the drafting table, and willed her painting to dry faster. She couldn't even escape down to the secretaries' office to spill out her feelings. She didn't dare leave all these plans and drawings. It would be a total disaster if something happened to them now.

When the paper was dry enough to move, she slowly rolled up all the plans and returned them to the case. Then, for once leaving her paintbrushes and paints out—let them destroy company property if they would—she carried her watercolor and plans to show to Mr. White.

As soon as the drafting room door closed behind her and she was alone in the empty hall, she growled and stamped her foot. She should be on the Grand Central team. She hadn't been here as long as most of the others, but she was as good as they were, better than some of those chosen.

Raised voices coming from down the hall—Mr. White's office—stopped her next outburst. Mr. White was arguing with someone. Perhaps this was not the time to interrupt him. She knocked on George Douglas's office door. There was no answer. Maybe he was the one Mr. White was arguing with.

She took a few steps closer.

"None of the work on the church is finished, the Payne Whitney commission is hanging over my head, and now the Colony Club with forty women who can't make up their minds."

A loud bang made Nora jump. Just a fist banging on a desk. Mr. White? Mr. Douglas would never dare. She shouldn't be listening. She told herself to hurry away before she got caught out, but she couldn't make herself move.

"I've had to sign everything over to my wife, rent out the house, all her incessant demands. This will drive me to bedlam!"

Nora crept a little closer.

"Sir, keep your voice down; do you want the whole world to know?"

"Hell, the whole world knows; they just choose not to see. I've had to sign my losses over to the firm. I'm living on a goddamned contract. And now someone is following me."

"Following you? Surely not."

"I've seen them, more than once."

"Okay. I'll look into it, but you must calm yourself. Try to get some rest. I can take care of things here."

"God save me from this pestilence."

Nora stepped back, trying to free herself from the paralysis that had overcome her. *Go back to the drafting room.* Pretend she'd never been here. Were the others aware of the troubled waters that surrounded them? She certainly wouldn't tell. All she wanted was to forget everything she'd heard.

But the door opened suddenly and Nora didn't have time to retreat.

For an earth-stopping moment George Douglas stared at her, his emotions boring into her with a precision that held her pinned like a plan to an easel. He closed the door behind him.

"What did you hear?"

"N-nothing. Mr. White wanted to see these. He said to bring them to him when I finished. I'm finished," she said quickly and hoped her words weren't prophetic. "Take them." She thrust the plans and watercolor at him. No way was she going into that office after what she'd just heard. She didn't care if George Douglas thought she was a nosy parker. She didn't want to know any more than she'd already heard. She didn't want to know even that much. She wanted to think of Mr. White as a great architectural talent, a genius, not some broken man on the edge of hysteria—and ruin.

George took everything and Nora didn't miss that his hands were shaking slightly. "Thank you, Miss Bromley," he said stiffly. "I'll, uh . . ." He lifted the drawings just as "Is that Bromley out there?" rumbled through the door.

Nora and George looked at each other.

"I guess he wants to see you."

Nora swallowed. A few minutes ago, she had been ready to read him the riot act for leaving her off the Grand Central team, now her knees were quaking at what she might find inside that office.

George led the way.

"Well, what do you have for me?" White asked before they'd

actually gotten inside. Mr. Douglas nudged her ahead, shut the door, and carried her plans to the desk before Nora could answer.

White, who had been standing at the window, returned to his desk and spread out the floor plan, placed her detailed watercolor to the side. His head snapped from one to the other, comparing, analyzing, and . . . eons ticked by while Nora stood in the middle of the office and watched her future play out before her.

"Well, come tell me what you did here."

Nora jerked forward and went to stand beside him.

"I thought the best place to accommodate the, um, dogs, would be to take space from this cloakroom and from the area next to it, since this doesn't appear to be a retaining wall."

White stiffly lowered himself into his chair. He picked up her watercolor with its silly cushions and dog runs and food stations.

Nora was suddenly embarrassed. What had possessed her to think that this piece of whimsy would be acceptable to anyone? Castles in the air, she'd told herself, but dream castles for dogs didn't pay. Bricks and mortar did.

"I . . ."

"I knew you'd come through, Bromley." White tapped his finger on the page. "It's a doggie harem. They'll love it. George, she can assist you on the clubhouse project. Free me up to take care of this, uh, other." He nodded sharply. "I knew I saw something in you, Bromley.

"As soon as some walls are up, she can set up over at the construction site. Be close to the project."

George froze mid-gesture as he reached for the plans. Nora opened her mouth to protest, but no words came. He was moving her off all the other projects *and* out of the drafting room.

"But what about the Grand Central project? And Penn Station. I was working on the concourse," Nora blurted out. She heard her words, not believing she'd dared to say them out loud. And quailed at his coming reaction.

But White merely waved his fingers as if flicking off water. "I'll give it to Nast or Finnegan or somebody out there."

"But—"

"If that's all . . ." George's voice broke in from behind her. He took her elbow and propelled her out the door.

They were halfway back to the drafting room when she pulled away. "But I don't want to work on that silly clubhouse for rich ladies and their pampered dogs. I want to do something meaningful. Projects like a railroad that will carry people all over the country."

George huffed out a sigh. Took her elbow again, guided her into his office, and shut the door.

"Now listen."

"No, you listen." Nora stopped as a new realization hit her. "You're in charge of the ladies' club?"

"Yes."

"Why? You should be working on the railroad commission, not the likes of Nast. He can't even—" She broke off. You couldn't squeal on your fellow draftsmen, even if you didn't like them, even if it was true.

"Because I volunteered."

"What? Why on earth would you volunteer for that when you could be working on something much more important?"

"Because he needs someone to do it. He's overworked and . . . not in the best of health. And if you're thinking this is some kind of demotion, think again."

"Shouldn't you be more concerned for your own career than a sense of loyalty? Aren't you afraid they'll push you aside if you don't fight?"

"Not particularly."

"That's because you're not a woman."

His eyebrows popped into two arcs. "Not the last time I looked—" His cheeks flamed. "I mean . . ."

"What?"

"Nothing. Those guys might get ahead faster, but not in the long run. Bromley, have you ever worked on a construction site? Even been on one?"

"Professor Gerhardt took us to see one during class, but the foreman wouldn't let us get too close." She was still annoyed about that. "He was afraid we'd get mussed." She rolled her eyes.

George laughed. "Well, here's your chance." He grew serious. "Do you know most architects don't bother acquainting themselves with the day-to-day construction of their designs? Of course they have other things to do. But it's amazing what you learn about form and function, as well as the mechanics of balance and strength, watching a project being built.

"I could have assisted him on the Grand Central project, except that it's not signed yet; there are other companies vying for the job. But this club is a reality, using state-of-the-art materials, things that you don't normally come across in typical house or building plans. Picture it. A swimming pool in the basement. The system for getting water in and out is a major undertaking; the ventilation will use the latest designs. Think about it.

"The Colony Club will be a comfortable, beautiful environment, safe and modern and lasting. So what if it's feminine and a bit frivolous; it will be supported by a foundation of steel. Literally."

"But what will you do? What will I do?"

"Well, I'll check on the site regularly; make certain that they're following the architect's instructions, make adjustments when problems come up. You will oversee the project, keep everything on schedule and work out any problems that arise when I'm gone. I'm guessing that you'll also do some detail work. The brick pattern alone will keep you busy. It's unusual and will need to be precisely drawn so they don't start cutting corners.

"We'll spend a lot of time going between here and the site.

But if you keep your eyes and ears open, you'll be amazed at the knowledge you can gain. Knowledge that will inform your craft. I think being on-site is necessary to truly understand a building, to appreciate architecture as a whole." He shrugged. "Besides, I like it. You understand?"

"I don't know. I've never thought about it before." She'd been too busy juggling her family's needs, her schoolwork, and trying to carve out a place for herself in a field that didn't want her.

"I promise, Bromley. It might not be as exciting as a big splashy project, but the learning opportunity will be invaluable."

"You're beginning to sound like you're selling me a Banbury tale."

He laughed. A clear-bell kind of laugh, and she smiled in spite of her inner turmoil.

"I would never do that," he said. "It's against my nature."

"Does Mr. White never go to a site?"

"Not as much anymore—he has a bad hip, and he has other commissions taking his time. It's a constant juggling act; when he starts a new building, he's still designing the interiors for an earlier project, and he also spends a lot of time in Europe buying interior decor and furnishings for others. It's a constant drain on his stamina.

"Even though he isn't a hands-on architect, I've learned a tremendous amount from him. By spending more time on-site now, when I decide to go out on my own, I'll be more prepared than any of those guys out there who never leave the drafting room.

"Didn't mean to ramble on. So are you convinced?"

"I guess."

"Well, that's a start."

CHAPTER 11

As the days went by Nora doggedly drew detail after detail for the women's club, at first meticulously rendering the intricate design of the facade's brickwork, then tracing details of the heating ducts. Nearby, Nast, Dolan, and Fergus were busily finishing details for the Grand Central project before the final judging. Everyone was optimistic that they would win the contract and the entire drafting room buzzed with anticipation. Grand Central would be their largest contract since the Pennsylvania Station, which was still under construction years after its inauguration.

George was away from the office much of the time.

Sometimes Nora would arrive at work to find plans already placed on her desk with written explanations or instructions, which she would complete and leave in his office to be collected whenever he made an appearance.

Rarely did they connect in person beyond a few hurried instructions before he dashed off again.

As the day to announce the winner of the Grand Central competition drew near, tensions were running especially high. Nora had been the brunt of an inordinate amount of hostility when one afternoon, George appeared in the doorway and shouted, "Bromley, my office," and disappeared again.

He sounded so much like Mr. White that Nora cringed. She was willing to be barked at by Mr. White, but not by George Douglas.

She rolled up the plan she'd just finished, shoved her writing implements into her pockets, and, her chin held high, went to see what he wanted.

George was standing at his drawing table, braced on his hands and mumbling to himself. Nora drew herself up, put the plans on the desk behind him none too gently, and was about to remonstrate with him about snapping at her from across the room when he turned.

He was neatly dressed in a tweed suit, but there was a smear of plaster across his cheek and the shoulder of his jacket. He winced when he reached for the plans.

She lost her train of thought. Her annoyance turned to a kind of anger. Not at him but *for* him.

"What happened to you?"

He looked down and tried to brush the plaster dust from his jacket with one hand. The other arm he held close to his side.

"Just a little accident."

"A little accident? What if it had been a big accident? You're an architect. You're not trained to do construction. It's dangerous. Obviously."

"Nah, I'm careful. Usually."

But Nora didn't want to hear excuses. "You should be working on the Grand Central project. Instead, you're banished to this silly women's club."

He looked at her curiously. "Do you know how many men—uh, people—it takes to construct a building from a few sheets of paper? How many workers have to be coordinated, and kept on budget and on deadline?"

"That's why they hire a foreman," she retorted.

"Yes, but for an architect, being on-site is an irreplaceable opportunity to make certain that things are proceeding to plan."

"But you have carpenters and welders and electricians to do those things."

"Yes, but they're forever trying to save money and stretch out the time and will cut corners if you don't keep tabs on them. They don't have the same responsibility to the building as the architect."

"I think it's a waste of your talents."

"So do a lot of others, only . . ."

"Only what?"

"Only I didn't expect you to be one of them."

She stared at him. "I—I'm not. It's just—"

"Then don't judge it until you try it. You came here to be an architect, start by doing what needs to be done." He reached for her plans, unrolled them, nodded a couple of times. "These look fine. Gotta run." He rolled them up, reached for his overcoat, winced as he shrugged into it, and was out the door before she could react or apologize or anything.

She didn't leave right away. Just stood where he'd left her. And gradually her indignation melted into ruefulness. He hadn't given her a chance to explain.

He should be designing his own buildings, like the one on the easel. She moved closer to look at the drawings on his wall. A row of what must be apartment buildings, with sleek, unadorned lines, big plain windows. Not at all like Mr. White's designs.

George seemed to be Mr. White's right-hand man. Had his loyalty made him offer to take over the ladies' club? Did Mr. White depend on him, or did he just use that loyalty to get George to do the jobs he didn't want?

ELSIE WATCHED WARILY as three burly workmen maneuvered the Louis Seize armoire through the door of Sarah Hewitt's sitting room. "Careful now. Watch out for the edge." She'd promised Sarah she'd fully redecorate the room even though she was appearing in the Pinero play *The Wife Without a Smile*, at the Criterion Theatre.

The men carried the armoire across the room to settle it between two bay windows.

Elsie fluttered her hand. "A little more to the right. Stop. Yes, that's it."

"Ah," sighed Sara, peeking in the doorway. "Elsie, you make even directing movers look graceful."

Elsie motioned her friend into the room. "Do I?" Of course she was graceful, everything she did had an innate grace. Her acting, her dancing, her life, her interiors. She had learned from an early age that if you're not born beautiful—she'd been an ugly child—you must be graceful, surround yourself with beauty, and from that beauty will spring your own. It had worked so far.

She nodded dismissal to the workmen and waited for Sarah to join her.

Sarah took her elbow and squeezed it affectionately. "I just love it. Thank you so much for agreeing to humor me. Ever since the first day I saw what you did with Irving Place, I knew you would understand exactly what I wanted."

"Louis Seize does show off these new textiles wonderfully," Elsie agreed. "And I say if it was good enough for Marie Antoinette, it's good enough for us."

Sarah laughed delightedly. "I agree."

"Actually, I have a couple of smaller pieces that I'm storing in the hall of Irving Place that I think would go perfectly with the unicorns tapestry. I'll have them brought over. Bessie is threatening to rent a storage room since she swears she can't take a step anywhere in the house without stumbling over some newly purchased objet d'art."

"Poor Bessie. Well, you'll just have to find more places to design, won't you? It's so rare to find someone who understands the importance of decorative arts in our lives. My sister, Eleanor, and I work diligently toward expanding Papa's museum at Cooper

Union. We're already stuffed to the rafters; we'll never have the space to properly display the textiles that Anne's father donated.

"I wish you could design the entire Cooper Union Museum just like this to see the textiles in situ, as it were. I'm hoping when the club opens, it will reserve a little gallery space for the decorative arts."

Sarah sighed. "I know acting is your first love, but if you ever get tired of working nights and touring all over the country, I bet you could do just what you're doing for me . . . for others."

"You mean become a professional decorator?" asked Elsie. "I don't think there is such a thing."

"Well, there should be," Sarah said half-apologetically.

"Actually, Bessie has mentioned it. I sometimes wonder if it wouldn't be better to—" Elsie broke off. "Oh well, a subject for another day. Now let me tell you what I have planned for that little alcove over there." They both turned their attention to the niche in the far wall, the subject of Elsie's future being deftly turned.

Elsie wasn't quite ready to contemplate life after acting. A tiny thread of her still clung to the notion that the *next* play would be the one that would catapult her to success. God knew it wouldn't be this one.

The Wife Without a Smile was turning out to be a bit of a dog. Rehearsals had been hilarious. But Elsie was afraid it was one of those cases where the participants enjoyed themselves more than the audience would. Pinero had written some excellent plays; unfortunately, this was not one of them.

"Do you have time for tea? Please say you do. I can have our chauffeur drive you straight to the theater."

"Why not?" Elsie said more enthusiastically than she felt. "I think I can squeeze past the stage door guard just before hour call." God knew she played opposite some actors who rushed in every night just in time to slap on some grease paint and stride onstage reeking of their last drink. Elsie de Wolfe traipsing in at hour call reeking of Earl Grey wouldn't raise an eyebrow.

NORA DIDN'T USUALLY heed the newspapers, except for headlines shouted by the corner newsboy. Still, she knew exactly when the draftsmen learned they had lost the Grand Central contract. It had been awarded to the firm of Reed and Stem, experienced railroad designers, and the commission had decided on their utilitarian design.

Like a fast-moving storm, the atmosphere changed in the drafting room. Hands that had been busy with railroad details were now idle. The men who had been assigned exclusively to the contest waited to see what they would be assigned next.

Nora felt their disappointment. She had hoped to be assigned to the station once she finished with the ladies' club.

Mr. White had been out of town when the decision was announced. For days after, he didn't make an appearance. When he did return a week later, he merely looked in on the drafting room before holing up in his private office upstairs for another few days.

When he finally reemerged, he acted as if nothing had happened. He strode into the drafting room, sheets of paper dangling from his hands, then paused to peruse the room, almost as if he were counting heads. They'd lost several draftsmen already that fall: two had quit, one had been fired, and another had just stopped showing up for work. There was speculation that losing the contract meant that more draftsmen would be let go.

Nora held her breath; she guessed most of the others did, too.

His gaze alighted on Nora, blinked as if he was surprised to see her. She lowered her head and tried to be invisible.

Footsteps echoed across the wooden floor. Several sheets of design paper appeared on the desk before her.

"See what you can make of these." Mr. White leaned past her

to point at the page. "The basement ventilation conduits have to be adjusted to accommodate the additional room as well as circumventing the cantilevers of the running track. And without having to change the plumbing, or losing any more space from the other rooms. Damn dogs. Find a way to make this work, then bring it to my office."

Nora nodded without looking up. "Yes, sir."

Only after he'd walked away did she look up to find Nast, Dolan, and Fergus all looking back at her. Dolan smiled, Fergus gave her a thumbs-up, and Nast sneered. Nothing had changed in the drafting room.

It took her several hours to find a plan that might work. She was a little out of her depth in the area of ventilation. When she had come up with the best she could do without consulting the plumbing contractor, she rolled up her drawing and carried it to the office.

Nora's knock had grown more confident over the months. Even so, it went unanswered. She knocked again, then opened the door just a crack. He was standing at the window, his hands clasped behind his back as he stared outside.

And her heart broke just a little to imagine the disappointment he must be feeling to be passed over in favor of another firm.

"Mr. White?" she said quietly. "I've brought the ventilation specs."

He turned toward her and she stepped back involuntarily. She'd expected a contemplative, disappointed man. Or perhaps a stoically philosophical man. After all, he did have more work that would keep him busy.

But the intensity that rolled off him was staggering. Whatever he was feeling, she couldn't guess, but it was powerful and frenetic. And her thoughts shot back to the conversation she'd overheard just a few weeks before. Had losing this contract been the last straw?

She took another step back at the force of his emotion. "What?"

Nora forced herself to put the plans on his desk. "The Colony Club ventilation changes."

"Ah. Yes." He walked over to his desk and sat down to peruse them.

Like the others, she'd been disappointed about the lost contract, but it wasn't until she saw him sitting at his desk that it really hit her. Where the giant rendering of the Grand Central Terminal had hung behind him, there was now only a blank wall. Mr. White seemed smaller in the absence of all that magnificent inspiration.

Which was ridiculous. He wouldn't let losing a contest get him down. There would be other bigger and more profound projects for years to come. Maybe even a hospital. And she would make herself so indispensable that she would someday, like George Douglas, become the right-hand man to the greatest architect in the world.

She watched closely as his index finger moved from the drawing to the spec box and back again.

Finally he looked up. "Take them over to George at the site. Make sure he gets them and they don't sit around somewhere until the foreman remembers that he was supposed to act on them. Miss Higgins will give you cab fare."

It took a moment for his order to sink in. When it did, it shattered her momentary glimpse into the future.

"Well?"

They hired messenger boys to deliver plans and goods among the various projects. She'd never once heard of a draftsman being asked to deliver plans somewhere. And now, after the months of being ridiculed, then ostracized and ignored by the majority of her coworkers, while throwing herself into a project she didn't care about, Nora was being demoted to errand boy?

She bristled, but bit back her retort, remembering Professor Gerhardt's warnings that she'd have to work harder and be better than the rest. It was unfair. But it was the state of the world.

"Perhaps sooner than later?" Mr. White suggested.

Nora started. "Yes, sir. Right away."

She picked up the plans, carried them to the door. She'd made it this far, further than most women. She would do what she had to do to succeed. She'd been working solely on a building without ever being curious as to its location. Surely that wasn't the way it should be. George had decried architects who didn't bother to go to the site of their designs. Well, now she would see hers.

She opened the door, then turned back again. "Please, sir, where is the Colony Club?"

HOW COULD SHE not know where the club was? Nora thought as she waited for the trolley to come. She'd only asked Higgie for trolley fare because she was too embarrassed to tell them she'd never ridden in a cab and she wasn't sure that the driver wouldn't try to cheat her by driving around in circles.

Higgie merely raised her eyebrows, muttered something about cheapskates, and handed her twenty cents out of the petty cash tin. "Get some hot tea to warm yourself when you get there. The weather's turned cold this year."

Nora thanked her and set off for the trolley stop that would take her up Madison Avenue to the site. By the time she disembarked at Thirty-first Street, she was frozen to her bones. She'd already bought a new skirt and two shirtwaists that had been on sale with a bit of her new salary. The rest she'd carefully squirreled away in the women's section of the bank downstairs from McKim, Mead, and White.

But if she had any extra after the next paycheck she would

buy a heavier shawl to wear over her shoulders. And maybe next year if all went well, a new winter coat.

When the trolly let her off, she stood on the sidewalk across from the Colony Club, just taking in the sight. She recognized the pattern of the brick. Lord knew she had worked on it enough. A soft rose color, it was unique in that the pattern was made up of smooth sides against rough headers. According to Fergus, it had gotten derisive reviews in the newspapers. Well, pooh on the reviews. The brickwork was precise and elegant.

She crossed the street and stopped in the open doorway, peered inside at a maze of wood and steel, a skeleton of the building, the foundation on which everything would stand.

Nora sucked in a breath and stepped over the threshold. A thrill ran through her. She was standing on a construction site, surrounded by steel and concrete and sawdust. The first real building she had worked on. No matter it was a women's club. It was also her building. *Her building.*

This was where she belonged. *We're here, Jimmy. We're actually here.*

She took a cautious step inside. The floor held. Of course it did. She took another, and another, as the sounds of construction echoed from inside.

She walked toward the sound, past a temporary shed where tools were stored and another small structure that looked like the foreman's office. Down a hallway with weight-bearing walls of steel and brick into an open area filled with ladders, saw-horses, and scaffolding.

No one seemed to notice her and she didn't see George Douglas anywhere, so she wandered across the floor past steel beams that rose like a geometric forest above the first floor. Past rectangular cutouts for windows that would someday be filled with glass panes.

"Hey, you!" A heavyset man hurried toward her, breaking her reverie. "Excuse me, miss, you can't be in here. Step away from that opening. This is a working construction site and a dangerous place for young ladies."

"I came to see Mr. Douglas."

"If you'll leave your name, I'll tell him you were here. But you can't stay."

Yes, she could. And she would. She had every right to be here. This was just like the first day she'd come to McKim, Mead, and White and some man tried to prevent her from entering. She had breached that bastion already. Earned her place in the drafting room. Now she would have to earn it once again.

"I have something for him. Where is he, please?"

"He had to run an errand, but the foreman is here and I'll make sure he gets whatever it is."

"I was told to give it directly to Mr. Douglas. I have changes for the ventilation ducts and he needs to see them immediately," Nora insisted.

"Again? They just finished rerouting them to avoid the running track cantilevers. A running track for society ladies, dumbest thing I ever heard of. If they wanna run, they can stay home and run after their children. That should keep 'em busy."

"Nonetheless, *I* need to leave these plans."

"You just leave those here and I'll be sure he gets 'em when he gets back." He was already nudging her toward the door. "I'm sure if he has questions we can figure it out or he can take it up with Mr. White."

"Mr. White gave specific orders. I'll just wait and he can take it up with me."

"You?" The word exploded like an accusation.

"I drew the specs. I think I can best explain any questions about them."

"Sure you did. Now run along with you."

"Where's the foreman?"

"He's up there." He pointed to a scaffolding that rose almost to the ceiling.

"Oh, good. I'd like to introduce myself."

The man groaned. "I'll call him down, if that'll satisfy you."

Nora shook her head. "No need. Hold this for a minute."

"Huh?" he said as he grasped the tube automatically.

She untied her shawl and threw it over a nearby sawhorse. And tossed her coat after it. In one deft move, she stuffed the hem of her skirt into her waistband, snatched the tube of plans from him, and tucked it under her chin. Before he realized what she was doing, she'd swung herself up to the first rung of the scaffolding.

"Miss, stop! You can't do that."

"Sure I can. I'll show you." She was out of reach before he even moved to stop her.

CHAPTER 12

Daisy looked over their newly rented assembly hall. With large windows in front and four oak double doors opening into a large foyer, it would work well for meetings, concerts, and even the occasional ball. They would use one of the two office spaces for a coat check and the other as a repository for minutes and plans until they could be transferred to the permanent building just two doors up the avenue. This had been a good idea.

Especially seeing the number of members in attendance today to hear Mrs. Florence Kelley speak on the importance of the new child labor laws. Daisy had been determined to book the forceful and persuasive Mrs. Kelley ever since she'd heard her speak at the New York Child Labor Committee at Carnegie Hall a few weeks before.

She'd held the audience spellbound as she enlightened them on the plight of working children throughout the country, and especially on their own doorsteps in the city.

"Just across the river," Mrs. Kelley continued, "New Jersey has done much to relieve children of this burden, but we are woefully behind in following their lead. With your and others' support, the New York Child Labor Committee can make those inadequacies change.

"The army of child laborers is increasing daily, from the fields to the mines, to right here in the sweatshops and factories of the city—our city—of New York. Nearly every state either has failed to pass protective laws or ignored the ones already in force. And our state is among the most culpable.

"Between the lack of education, poor diet, and poverty, what future will these poor souls have, with their learning nonexistent, their creativity ignored, their bodies and minds stunted from work and fatigue and meager diets? Caught between the greed of the factories and the need and sometimes selfishness of their parents. They must have someone to fight for them. More compassion, yes, but we also need to act.

"I urge you to join us in spreading the truth of this situation. Thank you."

The hall erupted into enthusiastic applause.

Daisy was one of the most enthusiastic. She'd already considered forming a subcommittee on the subject.

As she made her way to the podium to thank Mrs. Kelley, more than one member stopped her long enough to express their concern or their surprise at the prevalence of child labor. And their determination to make a change.

"And so young," cried Emmie Winthrop, her eyes swimming in tears. "The poor lambs."

"Action, not tears, Emmie," Alva said, taking her arm.

Daisy smiled and kept moving to the front of the hall. Anne Morgan had an interest in child labor conditions. She would talk to her about forming a committee. Which would probably get the club more bad press. Honestly, you couldn't win. One minute the newspapers and clergy were throwing out outrageous accusations that the club would create lazy, indolent wives and mothers, destroy family values, and undermine morality. In the next, they were warning the women to stay out of politics and progress. It was infuriating. It was also a challenge.

"Thank you for such an informative program," Daisy said, extricating Mrs. Kelley from a knot of enthusiastic questioners.

"It was my pleasure. I must say I had no idea your group would be so well conversant in the plight of children in the workplace. Such interest and intelligent questions."

"We strive to keep ourselves well-informed and active in bettering our society," Daisy assured her. She had been a little concerned about presenting such a depressing subject, considering they were approaching Christmas. But with the monthly luncheon concert scheduled for next Tuesday, the rehearsals for the Christmas tableaux vivant in aid of the St. Anne's Home for Girls, and an evening of holiday poetry and songs by the Aid Society children's choir the following week, what better time to bring attention to those children who had little to celebrate in their lives.

Several more ladies stopped Daisy and Mrs. Kelley on their way to the foyer to show their appreciation before pulling their coats closer and hurrying out into the cold.

Anne greeted them at the door. She was holding Mrs. Kelley's wool coat. "To avoid the crush of the cloakroom. You must come back and report on your progress when we get our permanent clubhouse. The conditions of workers in general and children in particular are a concern of mine," Anne said matter-of-factly. "And Mrs. Harriman has been instrumental in convincing the authorities to reduce the hours they are made to work."

"Indeed?"

"Yes," Daisy said. "We'll be organizing plans to do more. I was introduced to the Parisian bill to limit hours this past summer, where they instituted a ten-hour workday for children. The Colony Club will push for even shorter hours and for the law to enforce the existing age limit of fourteen. No child should grow up under the circumstances you have just described."

"No, they shouldn't," said Mrs. Kelley, pulling on well-worn leather gloves. "But many have no choice. They are often the breadwinners of their families, as hard as it is to believe."

"Like those poor newsboys," said Mary Dick, coming up to join the conversation.

"At least the boys have boardinghouses where they can get

a bed and warm food," Anne said. "But it isn't nearly enough. Thank you very much for your enlightening talk."

"It was my pleasure. But I must run. I look forward to establishing a continuing relationship with the Colony Club. We women hold an untapped source of power to change things. And we must use it. Good day."

"I must run, too," said Lillian. "Alva has offered me a ride home. I suppose I'll have to hear her rattle on about women voting. But I'm interested if you form a child labor committee."

"Thank you, we will be," Daisy said, but Lillian was already hurrying out the door.

"Count me in, too," Anne continued.

"I'm tapping you to organize it, if you will."

"Certainly. And I'm sure there will be interest. Since we decided to rent the assembly hall for the duration, our attendance has soared. I'll be glad when the permanent building is finished. But for now I would be thankful for a cup of tea."

"Well, if you can forgo tea for a few more minutes, Bessie and I have been promised a quick tour of the construction site, if you'd like to accompany us. Stanford has put his assistant, Mr. Douglas, in charge of overseeing the site. Thank heavens. He's promised to meet us here—ah, this must be he arriving now."

They watched as a tall blond-haired young man navigated his way through the departing women. He was quite good-looking and several of the ladies glanced his way as they passed.

Daisy waved. He nodded and stepped off to one side to wait for her.

Daisy and Anne quickly retrieved their coats, pulled Bessie from a group of gesticulating women, and met Mr. Douglas at the door.

"Mrs. Harriman?" he asked and introduced himself. "Shall we?" He ushered the three ladies out the door for the short walk to the building site.

Shelley Noble

On the way, he explained the conditions they would find. "But don't be alarmed—when all the pieces are together and it's painted and furnished, you will have the most beautiful clubhouse in the city."

Charming and with a glib tongue, thought Daisy.

They were indeed only two doors away, and often their talks and meetings had been interrupted by the distant sound of construction.

"Now please stay close to me. A construction site can be quite dangerous. This will be the front entrance," he continued, leading them through a heavy temporary doorway beneath a steel lintel and down what appeared to be a hallway.

"On your left are temporary structures we use for storage and a site office."

"An office?" Daisy asked. "Do you have heat?" It was freezing inside the building. How could they possibly get any work done?

"No, the electricity won't be laid on until near completion and any open flame would be a fire hazard."

"Your fingers must freeze to your pencils," Bessie quipped.

"It can be a bit nippy," he agreed and flashed Bessie a charming smile.

They entered the main floor, and he explained where the offices, library, tearoom, and such would go, even though now it was just a maze of beams and crossbeams.

"Is it hard to imagine the end result?" he asked suddenly. "I can see it. Plenty of light through the large windows, enough places for everyone to enjoy." As he described the various features, the others followed his gaze, and soon Daisy felt as if she could see it, too.

"We're standing just above the swimming pool," George said. "Unfortunately, access to it now is very limited. On the floor above us, the gymnasium and track are already in progress."

"Can we see it?" Anne asked.

"I'm afraid not today. There's only the ramp to that floor, and it is too dangerous for visitors just quite yet."

Daisy could believe it. They had stopped near a tall scaffolding of pipes and platforms that rose to the ceiling. It didn't look sturdy enough to hold brawny men like the one hurrying toward them.

"Mr. George," he huffed and scowled beneath a full beard and bushy eyebrows. "Pardon, ladies, but there's someone to see you. Had something for you. I said I'd take them, but she wouldn't take no for an answer, insisted on waiting."

"She?" asked George.

"A little spit of a thing."

"That would be Miss Bromley," George said. "Where is she?"

The man pointed up to the scaffolding. "Up there. Took off before I could stop her. Climbed it like a regular monkey."

"Good heavens," George said, looking up the scaffolding.

Daisy, Bessie, and Anne looked up, too.

"Bromley!" he yelled.

Nothing happened for a long moment, then slowly a petite little face appeared over the edge high above them. Daisy bit back a gasp.

"Oh, good, you're back," she answered in a melodic, assured voice.

"What the—What are you doing up there?"

"I've got some reconfiguration plans for you. I'll be right down."

They all watched, speechless, as one foot with stockings in full view swung over the side and found purchase on the first rung of pipe. Daisy held her breath as the scaffolding swayed. Then the second foot followed and the girl descended as easily as if it had been a stepladder. She jumped to the floor, turned, and, seeing four people staring back at her, exclaimed, "Oh," and tugged at the waistband of her skirt. The hem of her skirt promptly fell down to the floor.

Bessie clapped her hands together. "Brava, my dear. That's the best entrance I've seen in years."

The girl smoothed her skirt, touched her hair. She was petite and fine-boned and looked too frail to be capable of that athletic climb. But perhaps what Daisy mistook for frailty was merely sinew. And good for her.

She was shivering, not from fright or embarrassment, Daisy thought, but from the cold. She looked around, saw the threadbare coat lying over a wooden contraption. She lifted it off the wooden bar and gave it a brisk shake before handing it to the girl. "Put this on before you catch your death. Your lips are absolutely blue."

She did as she was told, all the while looking warily at George Douglas. While she fumbled with the buttons with no doubt numb fingers, Daisy had to stop herself from doing them up for her.

George didn't look any too pleased, but he turned his smile on the other three and said smoothly, "Ladies, may I present Miss Bromley, our newest . . . uh . . ." He seemed to fumble for a word. "Draftsman and, uh, member of the architectural firm."

Daisy and the others smiled back.

"And an expert climber into the bargain," Daisy said.

Miss Bromley cut an apprehensive look at George, and Daisy quickly added, "An asset to any architectural firm, I'm certain."

The girl didn't react, didn't relax or smile, but just stood there thrumming with energy.

"I think she's marvelous," Anne said.

Skittish as a colt, Daisy thought. Would she be in trouble for her feat of derring-do? Then Daisy recognized her. Small stature, the sharp, quick eyes. "Aren't you one of the girls from the School of Applied Design? We were at the end-of-year awards ceremony. The tuberculosis hospital," she exclaimed. "You took first place."

"Yes, ma'am."

"That's right," Bessie said. "I told Stanny he should snap a few of you up. Looks like he took my suggestion."

"And now you're working on our clubhouse," Daisy said. "We're delighted to have a woman on the team. That will make it even more special."

"I'll add my brava to that," Anne said.

For a brief moment an emotion flickered across the girl's face, not relief or pride, but curiosity. Now what on earth could that mean?

"Well, we won't take any more of your time, Mr. Douglas. Thank you for our tour. We can see that our clubhouse is in good hands."

"Of course it is," said Bessie, "but I'm ready for a glass of sherry. Nice meeting you, Miss Bromley, George. Come along, ladies."

He showed them back to the entrance and saw them safely to the sidewalk.

Bessie shook her finger at him as soon as they were outside. "George, you'll all have pneumonia before the interior walls go up. Are you really bivouacking in the office for the duration?"

"It's more efficient if I'm on-site."

"Well, go get yourself some tea. And take that girl with you. Her lips were absolutely blue. Ladies, shall we? But I suggest something a little more spirituous since none of us will be climbing anything more today until we climb into bed. And, George, do what I tell you," she repeated before she hurried the other two women down the sidewalk.

NORA HADN'T MOVED while George saw the three women out. She hadn't been aware of the cold while she'd been up on the scaffolding talking with Mr. Wojcik.

She also hadn't been aware of her own tawdriness until she was standing before those women in their fancy hats and fur-collared overcoats. What must they think, her skirt hiked up, her blouse wrinkled, her hair mussed? She knew what her mother would say.

She licked her fingers and pushed her fallen tresses behind her ears just as George Douglas returned.

She immediately started in with her explanation, hoping it would allay any anger.

"Mr. White sent me over to give you the new specs for the . . ." She looked around.

"They're up here!" came a voice from the scaffolding.

Nora let out a relieved breath; she'd forgotten about them while she'd been experiencing architecture firsthand. "You weren't here, but I was told the foreman, Mr. Wojcik, was, so I went up to give them to him. And I asked what he was doing and he was kind enough to show me how the cantilevers were used to support the cornices, and explained the difference between the—But you already know that. But I didn't, so he took me through the steps of how they were installed. So much faster than reading about it and trying to figure it out on your own. I guess I lost track of time and—"

"Bromley, stop babbling."

Nora snapped her mouth shut. "Am I in trouble?"

"No, but you could have been—"

His next words were cut off as Mr. Wojcik himself climbed down the scaffolding and hurried toward them, carrying the tube of plans. "Don't go yellin' at the girl, George. She's brighter than most of the men working this job."

He handed Nora the plans. "You come back any time, miss. We'll be installing the gymnasium running track next week. Now that's a real good example of cantilever construction." He turned to George. "But she needs better shoes."

And a split skirt, Nora thought, like the ones the bicyclists wore. She'd hate to ask more of Mama, but perhaps she could redo one of Nora's old skirts to fit. She still had her sewing machine from her days doing piecework.

"And . . ." Mr. Wojcik bent closer to George and lowered his voice. "Some long johns if she's gonna spend much time here. The poor mite's half frozen."

George cut a look toward Nora and blushed.

"I'll, um, have Miss Higgins take care of the necessities," he said. "But for the moment, Bromley—"

"Yes?"

"I've been instructed by the ladies to take you to tea. They're afraid working here will give you pneumonia. And they may be right." He took the plans from her. "C'mon, then." He strode toward the door.

Nora snatched her shawl from the sawhorse and threw a quick thank-you over her shoulder to Mr. Wojcik.

"I should really get back to the office," Nora said, hurrying after him.

"Not until you explain these, as you said you must. And since I'm not standing here another minute in the cold, you'll have to explain it to me over a—a cup of tea."

"I can explain it here. It will only take a minute. Mr. White just wasn't sure what version we were on."

Mr. Douglas shook his head. "Neither am I. Look, I've been out here most of the day. I need something warm if I'm supposed to concentrate on this latest change. So, tea. There's a little place right around the corner where we have lunch sometimes. And don't worry, it's my treat."

"I can pay," Nora bit back. What was she saying? She needed every penny.

He slowed. "Don't argue. The place is respectable. And . . ." He grinned. "So am I." He slipped her hand into the crook of his arm.

It felt strange walking down the street in the company of a young man, her fingers touching the wool of his coat. She wanted to dig them into the warmth it offered. The thought of a cup of tea in a warm place suddenly sounded wonderful. And it would sustain her for the trolley ride back to the office.

The café was around the corner and half a block west, small and comfortably warm. A portly rosy-cheeked woman wearing an apron greeted them. "Well, Mr. George, this is a surprise."

"Good afternoon, Mrs. Tova, this is a . . . colleague of mine, Miss Bromley."

"Ah, a colleague, and much prettier than Mr. Wojcik. Sit yourselves down and I'll bring something nice for you."

She hurried away. Mr. Douglas pulled out a chair for Nora and she somehow sat down without tripping over her own numb feet. What a day; there would be so much to tell Rina next time they met.

Mr. Douglas sat down across the small table from her.

Nora kept her head down, suddenly feeling more awkward than usual. She heard him open the tube, slip out the plans, and spread them out.

She twisted in her seat to see better since she was viewing the plans upside down.

He realized that and moved them so they could both see. They were in full discussion, any awkwardness of the situation forgotten, when Mrs. Tova returned with tea, sandwiches, and little cakes.

Nora's mouth dropped open. They hadn't ordered all this. How would she ever repay Mr. Douglas for this generosity?

Mrs. Tova set everything on the table. "We close in about forty minutes and I didn't want all this to go to waste. You don't have to eat anything you don't want."

She put two heavy mugs of steaming tea on the table while Mr. Douglas returned the plans to the carrying tube. Nora immediately wrapped her fingers around her mug to warm them.

"Wonderful, Mrs. Tova. We'll be glad to help you out."

Mrs. Tova chuckled and bustled away.

Mr. Douglas looked over at Nora. "Eat up. You wouldn't want to hurt her feelings." He took a plate and piled it high with food and placed it in front of Nora.

"But Mr. Douglas . . ."

"And would you mind calling me George? Mr. Douglas reminds me of my father—he's nice enough in his way, but . . ." He shook his head in a way that made Nora laugh.

"So, Bromley," he said, looking over the plate of sustenance. "Where did you learn to climb like that? Did you used to live in the country?"

"I've never been to the country," she admitted.

"No?"

"I've been to Brooklyn."

"Ah. And is that where you learned your feats of daring?"

Was he making fun of her? Did she really want to confess that until today this was the farthest north in Manhattan she'd ever been? Well, she wasn't ashamed of her background.

"No, I learned it on the fire escapes of Perry Street running from boys who would take my lunch pail."

He stopped, a sandwich inches from his mouth. "Oh, I'm sorry."

"Well, don't be," Nora said, the sandwich turning to sand in her mouth. "My family is respectable. My father was a good tailor, before he died. My mother and two sisters live in Brooklyn and . . ." She put her sandwich down. Her eyes suddenly threatening to fill with tears. *And my brother should be here, not me.*

"I didn't mean that. I just meant that I'd never bothered to ask you about yourself before. Very ill-mannered of me."

Nora shook her head.

"Eat, or you'll hurt Mrs. Tova's feelings."

She picked up the sandwich. "Were those ladies today members of the club?"

"Huh? Oh, yeah. Mrs. Harriman. She's the president. The

heavyset lady is Miss Marbury, a big theatrical agent, and Miss Morgan is J. P.'s daughter."

"I've heard of him. The banker."

"Right."

"Do you know them?"

"Only acquainted because of the building. Way above my touch."

"Why do they need a club?"

"I don't know. Men have clubs, I guess they wanted one, too."

"But dog rooms and running tracks; it all seems silly."

"Maybe, but it keeps us employed."

"Can I come back to the site?"

"Of course. We're both going to be stuck on this project for a while. Does this mean you're coming over to my way of thinking?"

"Maybe. Mr. Wojcik told me such fascinating things . . ."

The rest of the sandwiches and cakes and a second mug of tea were quickly taken care of as they talked about architecture and building sites, and after a thankful farewell to Mrs. Tova, they were again on the street.

And Nora realized she had been gone for hours. Panic nearly knocked her off-balance. "I shouldn't have been gone so long. I have to . . . They'll wonder where I am." Not thinking, she started off down the street toward the trolley stop.

"Hey." George caught up to her. "Where are you going?"

"To the trolley."

"They sent you on the trolley? Cheapskates. Learn to stand up for yourself, Bromley. It's the only way, or they'll walk all over you. Come along."

"Where are we going?"

"To the office, but the taxi stand is this way."

CHAPTER 13

As fall turned into winter, Nora and Rina began meeting at a tea shop near the Flatbush trolley stop where Nora was able to slip her a bit of money while they caught up on the news. Mama never came; she was afraid to leave Louise alone.

Rina was impatient to move away. "It's impossible there. Donner hardly makes an appearance except to eat food Mama has cooked, complain, and sleep. Louise is either moping in her room or yelling at Mama or bursting into tears for no reason. Mama has moved the new baby into our room. I've tried to help, but Mama makes me go to school every day, and I do, but I feel bad. I don't want to be a burden to anyone." Rina hung her head. "But I am."

Nora reached across the tea table to take her hand. "You're not. Who even gave you that idea?"

"Louise. She called me a moocher and an ungrateful—a word Mama said I wasn't allowed to say. I hate Louise. I know I shouldn't. Mama says it's not her fault. She just has the baby dismals. It's something that happens to some women, and we should be patient with her. But it's hard to do. Louise was mean enough before she had babies. Ugh. I'm never having babies."

Nora laughed, but she was worried. Papa had said they were to take care of Mama, not have Mama take care of them.

She'd been carefully squirreling her money away in the bank—but there was still nowhere enough to get an apartment, much less support Mama and Rina.

But she was invited for Christmas dinner, and for a moment

the memory of Christmas on Perry Street rose in her mind. Maybe Louise would be better by then and they could be a family again.

That would be a blessing, though it would mean dipping into her savings to buy presents for them all.

Fortunately, Higgie took money from petty cash for Nora to buy work boots and long underwear, which she did, gratefully. When she brought them in along with the receipt, the secretaries insisted she model them before leaving for the site.

They huddled around the washroom door, waiting for Nora's "I'm ready." Then they crammed through the door to see.

Lavinia burst out laughing. "I'll never look at a man the same way again."

"Lavinia," scolded Sadie, then she too broke out laughing, clutching her stomach. "Oh, you make my sides ache."

"Well, I think they're very functional," Higgie said. She fought for a moment, then she gave in and laughed with the others.

Mortified, Nora stood on tiptoe to look at herself in the mirror. Slowly a smile crept over her face. They might be funny-looking, and she had to admit they were. But they were more. Even more than warm, they were a symbol. She was a serious working architect, gaining respect in the drafting room as well as the construction site, and she'd wear her union suit with pride.

She spent the next two weeks clomping around the site in her heavy work boots, admired indulgently by Mr. Wojcik, as she learned firsthand how mechanical drawings turned into actual structures, sometimes working with him and sometimes bent over plans with George Douglas as they pushed to keep everything on schedule.

"The ladies want to be able to have their first meeting in a year and a half," George said.

Nora blinked. "That's only eighteen months."

"We're in good shape now. It's important to stay that way. Progress in increments. That's how to get to the end in a timely way."

She learned how the circular track was supported and slowly became a convert—not to the idea of rich ladies dressed in bloomers huffing around in circles, but how a track could be used as indoor rehabilitation for patients and the elderly when the weather outside was inhospitable. And she began making notes of her own in the back of her construction notebook.

In the basement, the marble swimming pool stood empty. At one end, framing marked the dressing rooms, lounges, hair salons, even her dog lounge. Pipes denoting steam rooms, lavatories, and something called a hydropathic room appeared like apparitions in the dark.

On the first and second floors, walls went up; plasterers moved from floor to floor. There were still floors above them to do, but downstairs was beginning to look like a building.

Time flew by. Nora spent most mornings in the drafting room, drawing details of cornices and alcoves for the Payne Whitney mansion on Seventy-ninth Street. (Though Nora couldn't imagine who would want to live all the way up there.) After a quick lunch with the secretaries, she'd don her union suit and boots and take the trolley to work on the Colony Club.

One morning Nora woke up to freshly fallen snow; the bedroom window was surfaced by sheets of ice. Out on the street, swags of greenery appeared, wrapped around each lamppost.

Christmas was on its way.

A few days later, George assembled the workmen for an announcement. They would be taking Christmas week off; they would begin laying the fourth and fifth floors first thing in the New Year.

A hooray went up among the men.

But not from Nora. A week without work would mean no pay for her. And she had presents to buy.

SINCE THE DAY Daisy had visited the building site with Anne and Bessie, she hadn't had much time to worry about the building's progress. Mr. Douglas had assured them they were on schedule to finish by the fall of 1906, and she took him at his word.

Her mind and attention turned to the holidays. Since they planned to spend Christmas at Uplands, their home in Mount Kisco, she and Miss Gleason had been doing double duty scheduling town events and away-events while reserving adequate time for the most important event of all—shopping.

Daisy could have easily relegated the task to Miss Gleason, or had representatives of Bonwit Teller and FAO Schwarz visit her at home, but she thrived on the energy of the holidays: the bustle of the shoppers, the ringing of the Salvation Army bells—she always made certain that she had coins at the ready to add to their kettle. And finding the perfect gift for the people she loved.

Daisy wasn't frivolous, but she did believe in delighting people with special gifts. Like giving Miss Gleason a paid week off to visit her family plus a handsome mohair scarf that Daisy hoped she would love.

A pair of cuff links from Gorham's for Bordie as well as a desk set designed specially by Louis C. Tiffany.

A Dorothy Dollhouse for Ethel, who had already received quite more presents than she needed since she had just celebrated her eighth birthday two weeks before.

Miss Gleason stayed to see them all off, then closed up the house for the few days they would be gone before departing to spend Christmas week with her family.

Daisy pulled the carriage robe around Ethel, and the girl snuggled close to her and was soon asleep. Daisy dozed herself to the rocking of the carriage as they made their way out into the countryside. Bordie would come up by train in time for Christmas Eve. Until then, Daisy would enjoy arranging poinsettias and holly on tables and mantels, overseeing the hanging of pine swags over the doors. And cozying up to the fire at night and dreaming of a world where no child would be forced to work fourteen hours a day; where food was pure and not adulterated with bacteria and worse. And every family had a decent home and food upon the table.

She knew the futility of thinking the world would ever become a perfect place. But there was so much that could be done. So she would sit watching the flames, a glass of hot cider at her elbow and a novel that she meant to read but which lay unopened on her lap, and dreamed of things she could accomplish, beginning with the club that would give voice to thinking women.

THE WEEK BEFORE Christmas, Inez got engaged to one of the men from next door and moved out. Nora had barely breathed a sigh of relief before Connie, who worked with Lucy at Macy's, moved in. Having the third girl was good for Nora's purse, but worse for daily living since Connie came with several suitcases and was even messier than Inez had been.

Fortunately, Nora was kept busy at work. Then the day before Christmas, the entire firm shut down for the holidays.

She packed up her drawing implements, took her purse from the shelf below her desk, and, after wishing Fergus and a few of the other men a merry Christmas, she went downstairs to collect her week's pay and give her good wishes to the secretaries.

They were all in a festive mood, excitedly looking forward to spending time with family and friends. And they were all in a hurry to get away.

Nora hadn't even bought presents for her family yet. She hurried down the street to Madison Square, where she knew vendors would be selling things cheaper as the night wore on.

The park was crowded; she wasn't the only one to have left presents to the last minute. The sidewalks were lined with carts and tables piled high with everything imaginable. She walked by a rack of picture postcards watched over by a man with a wooden leg; a young girl hawking hot corn as her mother manned the charcoal fire. She paused by a table stacked with embroidered handkerchiefs where an old woman wielded her needle with gnarled fingers as if she was afraid she might run out of wares. She had plenty, but in a moment of pity, Nora bought two and was rewarded with a toothless smile.

Unfortunately, Nora's moment of charity quickly succumbed to the cloud of melancholy she'd been fighting all day. The secretaries were so excited; Mr. Wojcik was looking forward to the week with his wife and children. Everyone, except Nora, was excited about the holidays. She hadn't even seen George for the last several days because Mr. White needed him elsewhere. Never had a chance to wish either of them a merry Christmas. Mr. White had left days before the rest of them.

Everywhere, shoppers searched for bargains, while sellers tried to make a living. The atmosphere was festive and yet a little desperate. And Nora thought about her dog lounge and just how silly it was when so many people needed so much.

A heady aroma of roasting chestnuts hit her with memories of the past: strolling through Tompkins Square Park on a day much like this, Mama and Papa and Nora, Jimmy, and little Rina running along on chubby legs trying to see everything at once. Papa had splurged and they'd shared a bag of chestnuts hot in their mittened hands. But that was before Jimmy had become ill, before Papa lost his spirit.

Nora kept walking, the aroma drifting away along with her memories.

At the next stall she bought a felt beret for Rina and a shawl for Mama. It was a bit dear, but it was just the color to bring out the rose in Mama's cheeks, something that Nora hadn't seen in the last few years. Farther along, she found a wooden horse on a pull string for Louise's little one, and a crocheted cap for the baby. A chamois tobacco pouch for Donner and a scarf for Louise.

And she still had pennies to spare from the money she had set aside. She was tempted to return to the chestnut seller but when she got there she couldn't bring herself to stop.

She spent the evening alone, since Lucy and Connie were both out. She ate a roll with some sardines and carefully cleaned up after herself, not that anyone would notice. And spent the rest of the evening carefully wrapping her packages in brown paper and string.

The next day she started out early for Brooklyn, her canvas bag filled with gifts. It was cold and overcast and people rushed down the frigid streets, heads bent and huddled against the wind, intent on getting to where they were going as fast as possible. Nora was excited, too, and yet filled with trepidation of what the day would bring.

The trolley to the bridge was crowded and except for worrying about her packages being crushed, Nora welcomed the human wall against the wind. Crossing the bridge, she forgot about the cold as her anticipation and anxiety took over. She hadn't seen her mama or anyone but Rina for the last few months. She had no idea of what to expect. Would she be welcomed? Would Louise be as sour as ever?

Nora's shoulders slumped; she wondered what Higgie and the secretaries were doing. What George was doing. She missed them. Christmas week stretched empty before her. She would work on her hospital and the other designs she'd neglected lately.

By the time the third trolley let her off near Louise and Donner's apartment, Nora was shaking with cold and anxiety, making it hard to think merry Christmas thoughts. But she must, for

Rina and Mama's sakes. She strode down the street singing "Silent Night" under her breath as if it were a march, not a lullaby.

Rina opened the door before she'd finished knocking. Her dark hair was braided into a coronet on the crown of her head, and she was wearing a dress that had been let out and made over and refreshed with a red ribbon. Nora was wearing the same dress she'd worn last Christmas.

"Come in." Rina took Nora's mittened hand and pulled her through the door. Mama appeared from the kitchen at the same moment.

Nora extricated herself from Rina's grip, thrust the bag of presents at her, and ran to throw herself in her mother's outstretched arms.

"Ach, you are cold," Mama said as she began to unbutton Nora's coat. "Come into the kitchen where it's warm." She trundled Nora through the doorway and to a chair at the table.

"How are you, Mama? I haven't seen you in so long."

"Too long." Her mother handed her a cup of hot bouillon. "But Louise is a little better now, and soon we can go back to being a family."

Nora clasped the hot cup with both hands. She'd been feeling sorry for herself for being shunned by her family; she hadn't thought about how her mother must feel.

"I'll try to be nicer to her today."

"You are always nice, but there is something I want to talk to you about before the others come."

"Yes, Mama?" Nora put down her cup, preparing herself for whatever might come.

"Rina says you've been giving Louise money."

"I've just been giving Rina a little spending money when we meet."

Her mother, tiny like her daughter, turned her steely dark eyes on Nora. "Before that. You have been working while you go to school and giving the money to Louise to support Rina and me. No more of that."

"But I want to help."

"Then attend to your work. And Rina is to attend to her schoolwork. No more talk about running away and working or moving into the city to live with you." Her mother had been leaning over the table, but she straightened now and turned her gaze on the doorway. "Rina?"

It took only a few seconds before Rina's head appeared around the jamb followed by the rest of her.

"I'm sorry, Nora. I know I wasn't supposed to tell. But I got so angry one night, my tongue ran away with me."

"Not your fault," Nora assured her and held out her arm for Rina to come stand by her chair. "I shouldn't have told you to keep such a secret. I'm sorry, Mama. But I wanted Louise and Donner to treat you better than they do."

"You leave your sister and her husband to me," Mama said. "I'm not angry. But there was no need to do that. It was Louise's promise to your father and she made it of her own free will. Besides, we earn our keep."

Her words were like a slap. That they should have come to this. "I also made a promise. To work really hard and save my money." She winced when she thought of the meager presents she had carried from Manhattan. "Mama, I'm saving for a home for you, Rina, and me. A proper home. But it will take a little time."

"Ah, like your brother, rest in peace, dreaming of castles in the air."

"No, Mama, I was thinking maybe an apartment in Chelsea."

It took a moment for her mother to relent, and the smile that transformed her face filled Nora with all the warmth that the bouillon hadn't managed.

Rina flung her arms around Nora. "I'll study hard. I promise."

"Now, enough of this," said Mama. "You girls set the table, dinner is almost ready. And as soon as Donner comes home . . ."

"From the pub," Rina finished and received a sharp look from Mama.

When Donner arrived a few minutes later, Louise came in holding Little Don by the hand. There was no sign of the baby.

Mama blessed the food and they all ate, a somber repast, and Nora wondered if they would ever laugh as a family again.

As soon as the pudding was served and their plates were scraped clean, Little Don announced, "Pwesents," and they all— except Donner—went into the parlor to sit around the little tree that sat atop the bureau and leaned slightly under the weight of handmade doilies and paper chains.

They passed out presents. Rina exclaimed over her beret. Mama exclaimed over her shawl. Little Don waddled over to Nora's chair and stood on tiptoe to give her a kiss, then carried his new horse away to the opposite corner where he engaged in a serious conversation with the wooden toy.

"And this is for you, Louise." Nora held out the parcel. Louise looked at it, and for a moment Nora was afraid she would refuse to take it.

But at last she did, opening it with excruciating slowness. Looked at the scarf inside while Mama and Rina craned their necks to see.

"It's lovely," Mama enthused.

Louise looked up; for a moment her eyes held Nora's. "Thank you." Her hands closed around the package and she burst into tears. She sprang from her chair and ran into her bedroom.

They all stared at the closed door.

"She hated it," Nora said. "I thought . . ."

"No, no. It isn't your fault. She's just stuck in the dismals and can't rouse herself. She's getting better. It just takes her unex-pected sometimes."

"Maybe she's sorry for being so mean to Nora and then getting such a nice present from her."

"Rina," Nora and Mama said together.

"Well, she should be."

After that, they retired to Mama and Rina's bedroom, which now also contained a crib and Louise's new baby. Nora gritted her teeth. The baby was sleeping and Nora leaned over to put the cap she'd bought on the blanket. "She's very quiet," Nora said.

"Except when you're trying to sleep," Rina said, and Mama pinched her cheek.

Nora left an hour later, armed with leftover meat, a loaf of Mama's Christmas bread, and a new split skirt that Mama had recut and sewn together in a matter of minutes while they talked in low tones and sang, "lully lula, thou little tiny child," in small quiet voices. Even the baby, waking briefly, cooed before closing her eyes again.

People were still about and the trolley was crowded. It hadn't been a bad Christmas Day. Maybe by next year Louise would be free of her dismals and they could be happy again.

ELSIE WATCHED FROM the door as Bessie was helped into Anne's carriage, which would take them to the train station. The two were off to Boston for a week of festivities. Elsie was glad they were going even though it was lowering to know that while she was here performing in the least-successful play of the season, they would be wining and dining and having a wonderful time.

She tried not to begrudge their interest in each other. It was Christmas, after all. A time for comfort and joy. The festive mood was everywhere—except in the Criterion Theatre. *The Wife Without a Smile* had been a huge hit in London. How could it be failing so singularly in Manhattan?

God, she was doomed. Elsie shut the door and went back

inside to fetch her coat and face another humiliating evening at the theater.

And to make matters worse, after all the advance notices, she'd been entirely ignored in the reviews. Or course, her part *was* totally ignorable. She should be at the pinnacle of her career. She was not meant for a predictable career in theater. She was made for a meteoric rise and untrammeled success.

Elsie de Wolfe refused to be merely competent.

But first she had to face another night, another five nights, actually—rumor had it that the play would close New Year's Eve. *Good riddance*, she thought, but she was afraid even that wouldn't save her from this looming darkness.

She swooped into the theater like she did every night, dressed in her designer gown, bravely hiding behind a facade of graciousness and success, just to change into her designer costume that she'd ordered and paid for herself. Parts and plays and fading careers aside, there was no reason she should appear in any way a frump.

She carefully applied makeup, cleared her mind of superfluous thoughts, and concentrated on her character. Kept in character while Clovis pinned her tiara of cloth roses to her hair. Then spent a moment regarding herself in the makeup mirror.

She wasn't that old; besides, she and Bessie had each decided to shave off several years at the beginning of the season.

The call boy knocked. "Five minutes, Miss de Wolfe."

She took a deep breath, rose to the occasion, and hurried to the stage.

And hurried off again almost three hours later. But no matter how quickly she walked, the memory of the lackluster applause followed her down the hall. The applause that had died before the final curtain finished closing.

One down, four more to go. Was this to be her swan song? An ignominious end in a tepid play by a great playwright?

She needed a plan. Perhaps a new direction altogether. Her interior designing had received good reviews. Sarah Hewitt had been ecstatic with the changes Elsie had made to her sitting room. But one couldn't exactly make a living from giving a friend good advice. And she couldn't go on depending on Bessie, financially or emotionally, for the times when she was between plays, especially not when J. P. Morgan's daughter was always just a stretch of Bessie's fingertips away.

It was time to act, just perhaps not on the stage. Elsie refused to play supporting actress or second fiddle to Anne or anyone else.

By closing night she was beside herself with agitation. She felt the future closing in and she still didn't have a plan.

She was almost glad when the final, final curtain dropped on that albatross, and she exclaimed dramatically, "It can go to the pigs," her voice cracking to punctuate her delivery and to keep her moans of disappointment from escaping. Everyone expected Elsie to be dramatic, and she didn't let them down on closing night. But she wasn't acting. Tonight she meant it. Those were the last words she would ever speak in the theater.

Her life and career had reached their nadirs. Only a deep dark abyss of her denied dreams lay ahead.

She changed into her latest Paris creation. Wrapped a fur stole about her shoulders and swept out of the theater. An automobile awaited her. The chauffeur opened the door and she slid inside. She was headed to Rector's, where she would laugh and celebrate and drink champagne to welcome the new year, while she tried to figure out a way to live through this, the darkest period of her life.

CHAPTER 14

April 18, 1963
Washington, D.C.

"The drive back to Manhattan after Christmas was bittersweet
as always. The beauty and serenity of the house and grounds
were always reviving, and it was especially gratifying that year
because the weather was accommodating for Ethel and her
new pony. She was becoming a very good rider and I looked
forward to the many times we would ride together.

"Mr. Harriman had gone back to town the day after
because bank holidays never lasted for long. Ethel and I
took the carriage a day later. Of course Ethel, exhausted by
new toys and the fresh air and her pony, fell asleep before
we even reached the road to town."

Sitting here in the sunroom, Daisy could almost feel the
soft weight of Ethel sleeping against her, see the brightness
of the snow-covered fields through the carriage windows,
the copse of evergreens standing like friendly sentinels
along the way. Such a long time ago . . .

Daisy roused herself. "But I digress. Of course I was
looking forward to my return to the city and the New Year's
Eve festivities. And there was much to arrange for the first
Colony Club meeting of the year.

"So I knew something was up when I was paid a morning
call by Bessie Marbury and Sarah Hewitt—together, the very
next day. Not a coincidental arrival of friends. One was a

busy theatrical agent, the other a busy curator of the Cooper Hewitt decorative arts museum. And knowing that Bessie never made morning calls, I surmised that something was afoot. I immediately rang for tea and hurried to join them in the morning room."

January 1905

"We've been thinking . . ." Bessie began as soon as Daisy entered the morning room and greetings had been exchanged. "Well, actually we have a proposal."

"Indeed," said Daisy, and sat down to hear what it was.

"Not to put too fine a point on it, Stanny is overextended."

Daisy stifled a groan; this could not be good news.

"I just saw him the other night. Helen Whitney is pestering him to finish their house. Well, who can blame her? It's been three years with no end in sight. But the point is, he's promised to finish it by next year." Bessie scoffed. "Not much hope in that, I'm afraid."

"And what about the Colony Club?" Daisy asked, alarm creeping into her voice.

"I think we need to consider appointing someone else to finish the interiors and furnishings."

"I agree," added Sarah.

For a moment Daisy just stared at the other two, while her mind conjured the bedlam that such an announcement would cause.

"But he's also contracted to us."

"Yes," said Bessie. "And if you want to wait and see, we'll most likely have to postpone the opening for another year."

". . . or so," Sarah put in.

"No. Absolutely not. The ladies have been good sports, but they want and need a clubhouse. A lot of money has been invested in its success. And the Princeton Club will be dancing with glee if we don't open. Not to mention the newspapers. No. We have made a promise and I, for one, intend to keep it. Though at the moment I don't see how. Do you?"

"Actually, I do. I suggest we hire Elsie in his stead."

Daisy was certain her mouth dropped open. Had Bessie lost her mind? A stupid question. Bessie never lost her mind. "Elsie? But she's an actress." Which was possibly the least useful response she could have had.

"Yes, and a decent one. But she has an eye and sensibility that is wasted in the theater. Her sense of proportion is unerring. *And* she would create a vastly more feminine interior than Stanny, genius that he is, with his love of objets d'art and European history. Think of it. It would be like having our little Irving Place house—"

"And my sitting room," Sarah added, "for the entire clubhouse."

"That does sound wonderful," Daisy agreed. "But there is also a vast difference between changing the look of a few rooms and coming up with a unity for five floors."

"True, but I believe Elsie can do it. And so does Stanny."

"So he's in on this, too?" Daisy gave Bessie a direct look.

"I didn't put him up to the idea," Bessie said innocently, which was a dead giveaway.

"We'll have to put it to a vote," Daisy said.

"Naturally," agreed Bessie. "As house committee chairwoman, I'll call a meeting of the building committee an hour before the regularly scheduled luncheon meeting next week and kill two birds with one stone."

Daisy thought there would be more carnage than a couple of birds when the other hundred-odd members found out that their decor would be the responsibility of an amateur. Daisy shuddered. "And you think you can convince all twelve of the committee members to hire Elsie?"

"My dear, selling talent is my business. And I would never try to sell one that wasn't up to the task."

That was certainly true; Bessie was the biggest agent in the theater.

"It's a very forward-thinking idea," Bessie continued. "Not only to have a female architect working on the structure, but now the possibility of a female decorator. The Colony Club will indeed be a women's club."

"I'm convinced," said Daisy. "If we can get the committee on board, I'll present it to the members at large."

"I'll do better than that," said Bessie. "I'll have Stanny come and ratify it."

"There's only one thing," Sarah said.

"And what is that?"

Bessie cleared her throat. "We haven't told Elsie yet."

ELSIE SAT IN the dark of her boudoir, the shades drawn, the shadows of her recent purchase, a plaster cast of *The Three Graces*, literally turned to stone at her feet as they danced together for eternity. The epitome of exuberance in the antiques store this morning . . . now stolid and inanimate as the ghosts at Miss Havisham's wedding.

She was feeling morose. No, morose was such a mediocre emotion; morose didn't take any energy or imagination to actualize. No, Elsie de Wolfe was feeling . . . tragic.

She'd tried to be more than the mediocre actress she was in dread of becoming. But stardom eluded her; she could feel opportunity slipping from her grasp.

She wrapped her arms around her waist, the silk of her tea gown cool and sleek. She raised one arm, then the other, felt the silk of her favorite pagoda-style sleeves slip down to her shoulders, and heard the front door click open. She dropped her arms. Her sleeves fell back into place.

She quickly turned on lamps and lifted the shade. Glanced at her reflection in the mirror. Rolled her shoulders back, pasting a smile where she felt none. But needs must. It was all well and good to feel tragic, but not for Bessie.

She faltered for a moment. She'd never had to pretend in front of Bessie before. Not until Anne Morgan had become a permanent fixture in their household. Her sudden need to pretend now rolled around in her mind like wine turned to vinegar on the tongue. Somehow she would have to learn to live with Anne's intrusion into their life.

"Elsie, dear? Where are you?"

"Coming." Elsie took a second to fluff her hair, then turned and stubbed her toe on the Graces.

Biting back a cry of pain, she eased around the statuary, then stepped to the side to avoid another recent purchase. She was getting more and more requests to help furnish the rooms of her friends, and she'd started buying things that caught her eye and bringing them home. They lined the hallway and flowed over to the bedroom. Bessie had complained just this morning that if she was going to continue decorating for others she would have to get an office.

Elsie had forcefully lifted her spirits by the time she floated into the foyer to meet Bessie, who had just tossed her fur-trimmed coat to the parlormaid.

"Where on earth have you been?" Elsie asked. Bessie never left the house before one, not even for Elsie. Elsie just hoped it wasn't because of Anne.

Bessie was dressed in one of her business suits and a black felt hat that she was hastily unpinning.

"Paying a morning call on Daisy Harriman." The hat went the way of the fur-trimmed coat.

"Oh?"

"Yes, come into the dining room. I need my lunch if I'm to get any work done today."

Elsie's throat tightened. She didn't think she could eat a bite. But she followed Bessie into the room. Usually the sunny decor made her feel hopeful. It had been one of her early ideas, getting rid of the dark and stodgy past and bringing in light and fun.

Bessie took her place at the head of the table and when Elsie moved to sit at her usual spot, Bessie patted the chair beside her. "Come sit with me. There's something I want to discuss."

If Elsie had ever suffered from stage fright, it was now. What could they have to discuss except two things that Elsie dreaded, Anne Morgan and Elsie's career. But she smiled with desperate affection and took a seat to Bessie's left.

They waited while the maid served deviled ham and toast points and a pot of hot coffee, which she left on a warmer in front of Bessie.

"You're not eating," Bessie said.

"Not much of an appetite today," Elsie said, and sighed before she could stop it.

"Don't let it get to you, my dear," Bessie said, helping herself to the ham. "Plays, even the good ones, sometimes fall victim to a fickle public."

Elsie waved a graceful hand. It took a conscious effort when she really felt like clawing the air in frustration.

She appreciated Bessie's support, especially since she was fully aware that Bessie didn't think all that much of her acting abilities. She was known as the best-dressed actor on the Rialto, not the best actor, no matter how expensively she was costumed.

"It isn't just the play."

"I know."

"Oh, Bessie," Elsie cried, dropping all pretense. "What shall I do to get out of this awful pit?"

Bessie got that look she assumed when she was about to deliver a home thrust. Elsie steeled herself for the inevitable.

"I know, my dear, that you long for a larger destiny. But have you ever thought that, perhaps, your grand inspiration lies not in the theater, but elsewhere? In doing something that utilizes your special gifts?"

Elsie, even in her most selfish moments—and she had to confess, there were many—couldn't pretend to see how Bessie could save her, or if she even deserved to be saved.

"Just think," Bessie continued. She looked around at the white and green that Elsie had chosen to replace the deadly, dark Victorian malaise that had been their dining room. "Your eye for synthesis. Your instinctual sense that sees decor as it should be used, a combination of color, proportion, and comfort.

"These are all special gifts. Look . . ." She gestured toward the Ching vase that held the flowers Elsie had brought home from the theater and arranged. "A nondescript vase, a bunch of theater flowers become a kaleidoscope of color and shape in your hands.

"There's an opportunity here, my dear. If you'd but grasp it."

Elsie winced, not at Bessie's words, but at the words she didn't say: *Before it's too late.* And she loved Bessie all the more for it. Many others would have let her die on the vine and simply forget she ever grew. But not Bessie.

Elsie didn't want to abuse Bessie's belief in her. And she couldn't continue to lean on her. She had to change things now, while she still had Bessie's affection, even though she had to face the fact that she would now have to share it with Anne.

"And look how you transformed Trianon. And Sarah's sitting

room; it's remarkable, everyone says so. A perfect métier for your talent."

"Become an interior decorator?" Elsie asked. How did one even go about doing that?

"Not just a decorator. *The* decorator. You could change the course of furnishings for the whole country. Become America's first female interior decorator. A woman consulting women in their own domains."

The first female interior decorator. Bessie's words exploded in Elsie's mind, swelled and blossomed into a bright future.

She could do it. So what if she didn't know one architectural period from another, and couldn't draw. She could hire people. Have an atelier of different artists to do that. She would go on buying trips, searching the haunts and habitudes of Europe for just the right piece of furniture, paintings, statues for her clients. Just like Stanny and the other architects did. She would transform interiors, convince her clients to leave the dreary past and embrace an uncluttered and light future.

"But . . . how would I get started?" She had already redone rooms for several friends to universal applause. She'd have them spread the word, subtly of course, to others.

"Well, Sarah was at Daisy's this morning and we all agreed that you have a remarkable talent for home decoration. And Sarah and your other friends would certainly spread the word."

Elsie hesitated. She'd have cards made up, and then . . .

"I'm certain you will be a resounding success," Bessie said, pouring herself another cup of coffee. "Especially when word gets out that you are designing the interior of the Colony Club."

Elsie's life flashed before her.

"The Colony Club? But that's Stanny's commission."

"He's all for it. That's why I visited Daisy this morning. It has to be approved by the club members, of course, but I don't see any problems."

The Colony Club. Was this the final death knell of her acting career? She would begin a new career. Like doing a play with no one in the cue box. Could she do it? She could. There was room to excel in decorating. She could see it now—the appointments with prominent New Yorkers, booked months in advance. No more late nights at the theater. No more tours and bad hotels, no more long train rides to small towns in the Midwest. Instead she would be paid to sail to the capitals of Europe.

But could she make a living at it? She would need to get backers, like for a play production. Have them put up some seed money. It would take a lot of work . . . But suddenly she could see it, her creations, unfettered by others' interpretations, and she felt the undeniable rush of power as the curtain opened on her new and glorious future.

"I'll do it."

"Good—now the first thing to be done is to inform the ladies, then rent you an office and a storage space."

DAISY DIDN'T KNOW how Bessie managed it, but all twelve members of the house committee were in their seats when Daisy walked into the assembly hall. There was an expectant air about the group and Daisy wondered how much Bessie had already told them about the new plan.

She quickly divested herself of her winter coat and took her place as president on the dais next to Bessie, chairwoman of the committee.

Bessie was quick to call the meeting to order. After all, there were bound to be questions and arguments and they had a luncheon to attend.

Bessie was clever that way. The tight timing limited the amount of fractious behavior Daisy anticipated. No one would want to miss the bill of fare.

Conversations quieted on the first gavel strike.

"Welcome to the first official meeting of the Colony Club of 1905," Bessie said. "And as such, I have only one item to submit to you today."

There were looks, Daisy noticed. But no one said a word.

"Mrs. Harriman and I have been keeping tabs on the construction schedule of the clubhouse and were able to visit the site a few weeks before Christmas. The building is coming along nicely and we were quite pleased with the progress.

"However, in viewing the premises it occurred to us that the interior begged for a different touch. Something more feminine, more hospitable to conversation, study, and enjoyment than the setup of men's clubs."

A few of the ladies nodded. Several frowned, perhaps wondering where this was going.

"So after consulting with Stanford White, he suggested that we have Elsie de Wolfe design the interior of the club."

She paused. The reaction was slow in coming. Daisy assumed it was from shock. Maybe they should have discussed it with individual members before presenting it to the committee as a whole.

On cue, pandemonium broke out.

The gavel banged with precision. "Ladies, let us discuss this in an organized fashion, else we will miss lunch altogether."

The committee subsided.

Daisy sat back and watched in admiration. Bessie knew how to control her audience. Years of working among temperamental actors and playwrights had given her a perfect sense of how to build to a climax.

Several hands went up.

"The chair recognizes Mrs. Bull."

"Why does he want to turn us over to Miss de Wolfe? We hired him, and he should honor that agreement."

"And so he will. Though as we often discussed in the course of our work with him, many of us have expressed the desire to make the rooms more to women's needs. And in our last discussion, he brought up the idea that a woman would more closely be able to actualize our ideals. He's very aware of Miss de Wolfe's interest in French and Colonial design. They often exchange ideas. Have collaborated on several projects. And thinks she would be the obvious choice."

Sarah Hewitt stood. "I can attest to her skills; she did wonders with several of my rooms."

"And to mine," added a voice from the other side of the room.

Bessie had placed her claques in perfect position to sway the others.

Helen Barney stood. "It's all well and good for Elsie to help her friends. But we're talking about an entire building. One that must be above the pale."

Daisy had made the exact same argument when she first heard the scheme.

"The question is," Sarah said, "who will provide a more feminine look. As brilliant as Stanford White is, can he adapt his style to make it uniquely ours?"

"And . . ." Helen Whitney fairly popped out of her chair. "Manage it before the turn of the next century. He's just now beginning to look for furnishings for our house, and he started four years ago. We don't even have glass in the windows yet."

She sank back in her seat, and Daisy wondered if Bessie had enlisted her to the cause or whether she reacted out of pure frustration with Stanford.

"Which brings us to the question of scheduling," Bessie said. "Mr. White is in the middle of several large projects. The Colony Club would get Miss de Wolfe's full attention."

"I'm sure we all respect Miss de Wolfe," said Mary Dick, "but she's still an amateur."

"Only because she doesn't accept payment for her work," Sarah said.

"Well, I say it isn't time to rock the boat."

At which point opinions broke out around the room while Bessie sat back, content to let them work it out.

"But if he can't stay on schedule, we might never get a club."

"Which will play right into the Princeton Club's hands. Since they expect to buy us out before we even open."

"Yes," said another. "But she's an actress. What does she know about architecture? We need someone with reputation, with stature, respected in the world of architecture. Interiors are more than putting a vase here, a lamp there."

"Anyone who has seen my parlor," Sarah said, "will know she's more than that."

"And a woman, they'll laugh us out of town," rose another voice.

"Let them try," yelled several women.

"They're already laughing at us—"

"Just the other day—"

Bessie banged the gavel. Twice. "Mrs. Harriman is recognized."

The din subsided somewhat. "Ladies, let us discuss this rationally. And think of our aims. The whole purpose of the club is for women; we undoubtedly will ruffle some feathers."

Alva Belmont rose from her chair. "So what if we incur the wrath of those who would keep us idly at home? I say we vote yes for Elsie." She sat down quickly before Bessie's gavel came down again.

"You would, Alva Belmont—"

The reactions rose to a fever pitch.

"Ladies, ladies." Bessie banged the gavel. "Perhaps if you heard an endorsement from Mr. White himself."

She was answered by a resounding *yes* from the group.

"In that case, Mr. White, will you be so kind as to join us?"

All heads turned toward the door, including Daisy's. She cut a look at Bessie in pure admiration. The twinkle in Bessie's eye was as good as a wink. What a master.

Stanford strode toward the dais, his tailored suit exuding charm, masculinity, and authority. His limp was hardly noticeable today.

"Ladies," he began. "I can only say one thing to you. Give it to Elsie and let the girl alone. She knows more than any of us."

While the ladies were still recovering from that pronouncement, Bessie moved to hire Elsie for the job. Daisy and Anne Morgan seconded, as they both had agreed upon beforehand. And the measure passed.

Stanford took his leave and the ladies all hurried into their coats to join the other members for lunch and to be the first to deliver the news.

Daisy waited for Bessie to gather up an array of folders, papers, and her notes, none of which she had used.

"Props," Bessie said. "Makes you look like you're fully prepared."

"And were you?" Daisy trusted Bessie's judgment and Stanford's. But the resolution seemed to have passed very quickly with no time for the others to really consider their vote. And what if they'd voted no?

"Always. Plus Stanny agreed to assign Elsie an assistant who can render Elsie's ideas into a plan and keep him in the loop."

"Did the two of you plan his entrance?"

"But of course; timing is everything. And with that in mind, let us go, or they'll start lunch without us."

CHAPTER 15

February 1905

Since Christmas, Nora had been spending as much time as possible at the construction site while still putting in an appearance at the drafting room each day, even when she wasn't needed. She was afraid being out of sight too much might mean Mr. White would forget her when it was time to assign new projects.

She'd been working at McKim, Mead, and White for over nine months. There were hardly any rumblings or snide remarks from the men now and no longer a need to pack up her equipment whenever she left her desk. Mr. Nast was the only one holding on to some grudge that she didn't understand.

She was invigorated by the work and gaining incredible experience during the day. But when she was at home at night, with her own designs laid out before her, when she tried to apply what she'd learned on the job to improve her own work, impatience tripped her up.

She'd started on a new design during the Christmas holiday. Her first attempt at a tenement building. The first tenement law had been passed four years before and it seemed to Nora that things weren't moving fast enough to help those who most needed it now. She doubted MMW would ever stoop to designing a tenement building or a tuberculosis hospital. And she wondered if she was making the right choice.

She spent more than one night, when sleep refused to come,

worrying that by working on projects for pampered women and other rich clients, she was somehow failing her duty to Papa and Jimmy.

So in early February when Mr. White called her into his office, she felt a surge of hope. There had been talk of putting more draftsmen on the Pennsylvania Station project, which was moving at a snail's pace. She loved her time at the construction site, but when all was said and done, it was just another rich person's house.

As soon as she left the drafting room, she placed her hands behind her back, crossed her fingers, and prayed that this meeting would lead to something new and useful to the people who needed it most.

She was surprised to see George Douglas sitting in the office with Mr. White. She'd hardly seen him at all since they'd returned to work after the holidays. He was kept busy going from one site to the next, "like juggling knives," she'd heard Mr. Wojcik say one day. But he didn't explain what he meant.

White motioned her in and told her to sit down.

She sat, feeling suddenly anxious since he'd never asked her to sit before. There were no plans on his desk to give her. George looked serious. Had he complained about her for some reason? Oh, God, please don't say he was going to fire her. Her mind rolled through the past few weeks, searching for any misdemeanor she might be guilty of, but came up blank.

"I have a new assignment for you. Something very important."

She sat up straighter. At last. She needn't have worried. Her mind raced ahead, wondering if it would be a completely new project.

"I've been discussing the situation with George and he agrees that it will be good experience for you."

She merely perched on the edge of the chair. What could it be?

"I'm certain that the School of Applied Design taught you the importance of furnishings according to design. That as an architect you would be responsible for either buying or commissioning furniture for new construction or, in the case of renovations, to style the design to fit around the current furnishings."

Nora nodded slightly, suddenly not following his train of thought. She'd studied the styles and main features of each period. Visited a few mansions and office buildings on school trips.

"Excellent. I find that I'm a bit overextended in that particular area and I've asked Elsie de Wolfe to take over that part of the Colony Club design."

Elsie de Wolfe. The name sounded familiar. But Nora couldn't place her among any of the lady architects in town. He was turning over the Colony Club to another architect. Odd, but it would free her and George to work on other projects.

"You are to be Elsie's assistant." He smiled at her as if awaiting a response. As the doors to Nora's future slammed shut in front of her.

"And what will my duties be, sir?" she asked.

"Whatever she needs. For starters, the woman can't draw. So you'll have to render her ideas into readable plans and watercolors. And I'll be consulting every now and then to see how things are going."

So a copyist, not even an architect. And to someone he obviously didn't trust. On her own.

"And since I'm sure Elsie will often be traveling to collect the interior furnishings, you will have to be on hand to receive shipments, catalogue and store them. Other than that, she'll tell you what she needs. And you'll receive an extra stipend for your work from the Colony Club itself."

That at least was something—but not enough to accept this setback. She risked a glance at George but he just looked . . . She couldn't begin to read his expression. Why didn't he say something? Stick up for her? Tell Mr. White that she was more useful in the actual architectural parts? Not as a secretary for an architect who couldn't draw. How had this Wolfe woman even gotten the job?

"I'm sure Miss de Wolfe will gather a team of artists and craftsmen to work with her. They can be a temperamental lot, but George here thinks you can hold your own."

She cut a look to George, but he was watching Mr. White.

Mr. White slapped both palms on his desk and pushed to his feet. "Now I'm due to lunch at the University Club, but first thing tomorrow I will take you over to meet her. And, Bromley . . ." He took a moment to scrutinize her appearance. "First impressions."

What was wrong with the way she looked? Did he expect a walking dress and feathered hat? He'd be sorely disappointed.

Before she could even form words, George stood and motioned her toward the door. And Nora, furious but stunned into silence, stood up and left.

She heard the footsteps behind her as she stormed down the hall.

"Nora, wait."

Nora walked faster. Once again she'd been passed over—no, pawned off on a project they obviously didn't care about. All that talk about the virtues of being on-site. How could she have been taken in like this? They'd never intended to give her a chance. It was cruel to have given her hope.

"Nora!"

She had to get away. Not to the drafting room. They'd all have a good laugh soon enough. Nora, the doggie girl, was being farmed out to a designer who couldn't draw.

Something, either a growl or a sob, escaped her. She was almost past George's office when fingers clenched around her arm and she was yanked inside.

She turned on him. "What?"

"I know you're upset."

"You're a genius."

"If you'd stop and think, you'd see this as a great opportunity."

"To draw *her* designs because *she* can't? I'll be no better than one of those yappy little dogs that get a special room for themselves. I bet she has a yappy dog. She gets to have the ideas and I have to make them a reality."

"That's what you do every day," George said, his exasperation palpable. "And it's a big responsibility."

"Whoever heard of an architect who can't draw? All it takes is a straightedge and a pencil. I've never even heard of her, and trust me, I would have. I know of every working woman architect in town."

"She's not an architect."

That stopped her . . . momentarily. "What is she?"

"She's an actress."

Nora groaned. *Elsie de Wolfe.* Now she remembered where she'd heard the name. Lydia had pointed her out at the awards ceremony. Elsie de Wolfe flitting about in her gossamer dress, kissing everyone on both cheeks, gesturing flamboyantly. Yes, she remembered her.

"Evidently she's had some success in the field."

Finally she looked up at him. "Why are you doing this? Why won't he use me on any important projects? I'm just as good as the other draftsmen."

"Better than most of them," George agreed. "And this is important. I know you're anxious to build the next great generations of buildings for the betterment of mankind but—"

"Are you making fun of me?"

"Never."

"It's not real work. I don't mind drafting, that's important work. But copying her ideas into pretty rooms for a bunch of rich ladies? It's demeaning."

"Nora Bromley, I believe you're a snob."

A physical slap couldn't have stung her more.

"You're wrong," she spit back, tears pricking at her eyes.

He didn't answer. She'd thought he was different from the others.

"I am not a snob. How could I be? I don't have any hydro thingies, will never get a doggie playroom, I don't even have a dog. Nor will I ever be able to afford a fur coat or even a fur anything. You're wrong."

"Am I? Then you need to stop thinking some projects are better than others, have more right to be built than others. Rich people have a right to have what they want, and their money allows us to design and build things for people whose budgets don't always accommodate their need. Every Fifth Avenue mansion we design, every Pennsylvania Station, means we can afford to work for a little less for those unable to pay as much."

He pulled up a chair and nudged her into it. Pulled another up and sat facing her, leaning toward her in his earnestness, their knees almost touching. "These ladies may seem like frivolous pieces of fluff to you, but they actually care about things. They can be valuable allies when it comes to building things that we all care about. And they are willing sometimes to help pay for them."

"You don't understand."

He took both her hands in his. "Then tell me."

She shook her head. How could she? Her hands felt warm in his, safe.

"I can't—" She tried to pull away but he held fast.

"Then make me understand."

"Because I'm only here because my brother died and couldn't be. He wanted to make homes for people who can't afford mansions, but deserve a clean and healthy place to live." Like her family. If she couldn't do that, she would be betraying her brother's legacy and her papa's faith in her. "I promised him and Papa.

I *promised*." She bit her lip and gulped back the sob that banged in her chest.

He leaned toward her. "I'm sorry. I didn't realize."

She shook her head, unable to look at him. "It doesn't matter. I'll do what I have to do to keep working. But someday. Some—" She broke off, unable to form the words.

"It does matter," George said. "I believe in what you believe in. There are a lot of us who do. We're the next generation, Nora. Buildings will be completely different from the ones we know now. Fireproof and waterproof with heat and ventilation in even the lowliest apartments. Efficient and inspiring, not just imposing. Interiors that don't follow a formula but are useful and comfortable. They'll soar into the sky like—" He broke off.

Castles in the air, Nora finished for him. Jimmy would have liked him. But at the moment Nora didn't.

"No one will ever take me seriously."

"They already do. Do you really think that White would turn this over to someone he didn't trust? His reputation depends on your success."

She looked past him to his designs. Buildings that would soar.

"For what it's worth, I believe in you, too. You have a future in architecture. I know you do."

Nora took a shuddering breath. Tried to remember all the things Professor Gerhardt had said. It was proving harder than she imagined. "Okay, I'll keep my opinions to myself."

"That's my girl." He squeezed her hands, then looked down at them as if just now realizing what he was doing. He practically flung her hands away, stood up. "Forgive me. I got carried away." He took a step away from her.

"I know. It's what I like best about you," she said, and fled.

NORA RAN DOWN the hall, not to the drafting room, but to the elevator. When it came, she flung herself inside and leaned against the cage's wall, her emotions at war: disappointment, distrust, and the one little question that wiggled past the rest.

Had he just held her hand? He had. George Douglas had just held her hand. Hands. Both of them. She lifted them to see if there was any sign of being held. But they looked the same as before.

Maybe it wasn't a real hand-holding. More like a gesture to keep someone in place. Or to emphasize a point. It wasn't a real hand-holding.

The elevator stopped at the fourth floor and she got out. But if it wasn't a real hand-holding, why did she feel so . . . so . . . fizzy?

All three secretaries looked up when she burst into the room.

"What is it?" asked Higgie, sounding alarmed.

"Uh, I'm sorry," said Nora, already embarrassed about barging in unannounced. What if one of the bosses had been there? "I just had a—Oh, I don't know—"

"That's it," Lavinia exclaimed and stood up. "Are those men giving you trouble again? I swear I'll—"

Nora shook her head.

"One man?" asked Sadie.

Nora nodded. "Sort of."

"That awful Collin Nast?" guessed Lavinia.

"Mr. White. And George."

Higgie stood, looking suddenly formidable. "Well, ladies, in that case—Lavinia, put up the *Back in fifteen minutes* sign. Sadie, get the kettle boiling. Come on, Nora. We want to hear all about it."

Over tea and a package of biscuits they always seemed to have just opened, Nora told them about getting assigned to drawing for a decorator instead of architecture.

"What did George say?" asked Lavinia.

"That I was being a snob for not wanting to work with an actress who thinks she can design the interior of the Colony Club.

Some of us have had to work so hard just to get a start. I know I've been lucky, but to just decide you want to decorate houses without any training and be given the entire interior of the Colony Club. Ugh. I just want to do some good. I'm not a snob."

"Of course you aren't," Higgie said. "I don't know what's gotten into him. He's usually very polite."

"Which actress?" Sadie asked.

Nora shrugged. "He apologized, but . . ."

"But which actress?" Sadie pressed. "Someone we'd know?"

"Someone named Elsie de Wolfe."

"Elsie de Wolfe?" Sadie clutched both hands to her chest. "She's just the most glamorous thing in the theater these days. She orders all her gowns from Paris. She's just divine."

Lydia Rhodes had said pretty much the same thing about her at the awards ceremony. "I thought she was just flighty. Kissing everybody that came near her."

"You met her?"

"Not really."

"Too bad," sighed Sadie. Then, perking up, added, "But you will. You'll be working with her. You can pick up tips from her, and then tell us about them."

"Tips? From an actress?" Lavinia piped up. "Nothing you need to know."

Sadie made a face at her. "She's very cultured. She's been all over the world. I saw her in a play with Lionel Barrymore last year. Dreamy. She was good, too, but Barrymore, he was heavenly and so handsome."

"Ladies," interjected Higgie. "I believe we're here to discuss Nora's dilemma, not the merits of Lionel Barrymore or Miss de Wolfe."

"That's right," Lavinia added. "What do you want us to do?"

"Nothing," said Nora. "I just needed . . . I don't know."

"Some friends to listen," Higgie said. "You can count on us."

"Thank you." She'd meant to ask them about the hand-holding part, but decided against it. Friends or not, some things were just better kept to yourself.

DAISY HAD JUST returned with Ethel from walking in the park when she was surprised but not alarmed to see Miss Gleason hurrying toward them.

"Oh, dear, what's afoot?" Daisy asked, untying Ethel's bonnet and handing it and Ethel to the parlormaid.

"There is a . . . delegation waiting to see you. I put them in the library since Mr. Harriman is home early and reading the newspaper in the parlor."

"What kind of delegation? Couldn't you put them off?"

"I tried, but the Right Honorable Reverend Snyder said it was a matter of some urgency and that he would wait." She lowered her voice. "He has an entourage with him."

"Snyder. Hmm. I don't suppose he said what it was about?"

"He wouldn't say, but I caught a snatch of conversation as I left; I believe they are against the idea of a women's club."

Daisy sighed. "How many ways can one say, 'We're not an insurrection—we just want a place to visit and study and for out-of-town members to stay overnight'?"

"I'm sure you will think of as many arguments as it takes to change stubborn minds."

"Then I'd better see them."

"Shall I stay to take notes?"

"If you don't mind. To show them we take their concerns seriously . . . and we do. Though there is no cause for this hysteria, and I won't back down." Daisy straightened her shoulders and put on a pleasant smile, just enough to show them welcome, though she wished they were anywhere else. And went to the library.

She took in their ilk in one glance: two dowagers; a young man soberly dressed and carrying a Bible; a balding, sallow-skinned man with a paunch; and the reverend, wearing a clerical collar and a censorious attitude. She strode straight to the latter, holding out her hand. "My dear sir, what a pleasant surprise."

The reverend was a wiry man, with thinning hair pomaded in sparse strips over a shiny pate. He shied back, avoiding her handshake, and began abruptly, "I believe you know why I have come."

I don't even know who you are, thought Daisy. "I'm afraid I don't, but I see you've brought friends. Won't you all sit down?"

Having no choice but to act the gentleman, he waited for her to be seated, not behind the reading desk but in one of the occasional chairs where the group had assembled. Then he motioned for the others to be seated before joining them on a straight-back chair that Daisy had always hated.

When they were all in place, Miss Gleason sat primly behind the desk, her pen poised to take notes.

Her secretary was a gem among gems.

Daisy smiled at the clergyman and then at his friends.

Retrieving his manners, he introduced the two ladies, whose names Miss Gleason took down and Daisy promptly resigned to Kingdom Come. The younger Mr. Edwards, an evangelical minister visiting from out of town, and Mr. Koch, a minor official in Anthony Comstock's Society for the Suppression of Vice, which was enough to have Daisy boot him personally from the room. However, being a lady, she merely gritted her teeth and tried not to look at him.

"I am the Right Honorable Reverend Snyder, and I've seen from the *Tribune* today that you have not relinquished this idea of a women's club." He could barely enunciate the words, his lips were so tightly pursed.

Daisy merely smiled and hoped he choked on them.

"Indeed," she said. "Construction is proceeding nicely and we've recently hired a decorator. We already have four hundred members and are meeting weekly to discuss important events of the day."

"Instead of staying at home and attending to your husband and children, like a decent Christian woman," interjected one of the ladies.

"Not at all. We women, as you must know, work as many hours keeping our households running smoothly as a man on Wall Street or at the local grocery. And like men, we need a little relaxation time and refiring of the brain in order to keep in top form. We intend the Colony Club to be that place for women just as the Princeton Club or the University Club is for businessmen."

"An outrage," exclaimed the young firebrand with the Bible.

"On the contrary. It's a rejuvenating tonic to expand our minds and enjoy the opportunity to engage with other women and their ideas."

"You have morning calls for engaging with other women," countered one of the dowagers.

"Fifteen minutes of conversation about weather and fashion doesn't always satisfy the need for continuing education."

"Poppycock. It's just an excuse for neglecting your wifely duties."

"As a good Christian, I can truthfully say I have never neglected my wifely or motherly duty."

"Coming home this late? It's almost dinnertime."

"Yes, I admit my daughter and I are ready for our supper, but we were having such a good time in the park, we lost track of the hour. And Mr. Harriman is waiting in the parlor and we shall dine as soon as we're finished here."

"Hmmph," said the dowager.

"So you refuse to honor the wishes of the church and these fine people and desist from your plans." Reverend Snyder appeared to grow more colorless with each exchange.

"Well," said Daisy, "it's gone quite beyond my power to stop it, not that I would if I were able. The Colony Club will be a positive addition to the city. We have many plans to aid those in need, as well as . . ." Daisy hesitated, then thought, *Why not?* "Doing what we can to address the problems that so far neither the city government nor the religious institutions have been able—or willing—to resolve. Now, I'm certain that you wouldn't want to deprive my husband of his dinner any longer. Thank you so much for coming." She stood.

The reverend had no choice but to stand and, with a sharp nod to Daisy, herded his people out of the room, where the maid was waiting to show them out of the house.

As soon as the door closed, Daisy let out a relieved breath.

Miss Gleason shut her notebook. "I'll tell the staff to stop the next group at the stoop."

"No, it will only make them more determined. Thank you for staying. Now, hurry off to your own dinner. We'll finish any other outstanding business tomorrow."

Daisy waited for Miss Gleason to leave, then stopped by the wall mirror to tidy her hair and undo any vestiges of bad temper from her person before joining Bordie in the parlor.

"Are they gone?" came Bordie's voice from behind his copy of the *Times*.

"At last." Daisy sat down across from him.

"Are any of them still standing?"

"Of course, Bordie. Even though Reverend Snyder refused to shake hands as if I were some Jezebel right out of the Old Testament."

Bordie lowered his paper enough to grin at her before gruffly clearing his throat and saying, "Daisy, really," before disappearing behind the newsprint again.

"You know, sometimes I feel like for every step forward I take, I'm knocked two steps back."

This time Bordie's paper lowered just enough to show both eyebrows raising in disbelief. "You?" He put down the paper and patted the sofa beside him; she came to sit by his side.

"You just keep doing what you do. I have a profound faith in you, and your successes to date are undeniable. You just have to stand firm until the rest of the world catches up to you."

"Oh, Bordie," she said, resting her head on his shoulder. "You don't know how much I needed to hear that."

"Well, it's true, even when I'm trying to read the evening paper."

Daisy laughed, the path suddenly clear before her. "Go back to your news. I feel much better."

Amazing what the tiniest encouragement could do. And being a woman in uncharted territory, encouragement was hard to come by. She might just say a word of the same to that young architect, Nora Bromley, next time they met.

CHAPTER 16

The next morning Nora dressed in a clean and crisply ironed shirtwaist and her best skirt, but no long johns, and put on her normal work shoes in spite of the cold.

She didn't know quite what to expect and she didn't want to appear too scruffy for the actress. She'd brushed her hair to a shine and carefully plaited it, then rolled it into a coronet at the back of her head. It was the best she could do. To her mind, she looked very professional.

She brushed her only coat, and set out for McKim, Mead, and White.

Mr. White had not yet arrived so she took her place at her drafting table to wait. Fergus nodded when she walked in. As she walked past Collin Nast's table, he glanced up. "Heard you got a date with the boss," he said under his breath.

Nora ignored him, just slid onto her stool and began to gather up the things she would need. At ten, Mr. White stuck his head in the door, lifted his chin. Nora grabbed her coat and, double-checking her pockets, hurried to meet him.

"Eh, Bromley. Ready?"

She nodded and they took the elevator down to the street where a long red automobile sat at the curb. Nora hesitated when the chauffeur opened the back door.

"Well, get in, we don't have all day."

Nora swallowed. "I—"

"Let me help you, miss." The chauffeur took her elbow and practically shoveled her into the back. She scrambled to the far side of the lush leather cushion. She'd never been in an automobile before. Even the hansom cabs she and George sometimes took from the club site to the office were horse-drawn.

Mr. White climbed in beside her.

The engine cranked up, and, with a jerk that almost sent Nora flying, the automobile shot forward. Nora gripped her hands together as she tried not to imagine all the horrors that could happen on their way to Irving Place.

When they reached their destination a few minutes later—a red-brick three-storied corner house with white cornices and painted iron railings—Nora's fingers were white-knuckled. She climbed out of the auto and stood with quaking knees while Mr. White consulted with his driver.

Then Mr. White ushered her up the steps and rang the doorbell. The door was immediately opened by a young parlormaid.

"Morning, Mildred. Miss Marbury and Miss de Wolfe are expecting us."

"Yes, sir, they're in the dining room and ask that you join them there."

"Excellent." He shrugged out of his coat and handed it and his hat to the maid. Nora barely had time to unbutton hers before it, too, was whisked away, and Mr. White gestured for Nora to precede him, saying, "Bessie makes the best Turkish coffee in town."

Nora walked dutifully ahead but came to a stop in the archway of the most amazing room she had ever seen. Not the dark wainscoting or chair rails of normal dining rooms, no heavy mahogany table or china cabinets. All the woodwork, including the doors, was painted white like confectionary icing around green-striped walls. Fresh flowers adorned a delicate painted sideboard.

Two women sat at opposite ends of a white table.

The lady nearest them looked over her shoulder and lifted a delicate hand. "Stanny, it's been ages."

White strode over and kissed her outstretched hand. She hadn't even bothered to stand. She had to be Miss de Wolfe.

The woman at the far end was as stout and substantial as her companion was petite and fairylike.

Nora remembered her from the day the ladies had visited the site with Mrs. Harriman. Miss Marbury.

"Sit yourself down, Stanny. Miss Bromley, do sit down. Have you breakfasted? Coffee? Tea?"

White pulled out a chair for Nora to sit, which she did; no one except George had ever done that, and there was an awkward moment when nothing happened since she didn't know quite how to maneuver the chair back to the table.

"Heavens, Stanny," Miss Marbury said. "Leave the girl alone. She's perfectly capable of sitting down without your assistance. Welcome to our little house, my dear. I hope this will be the beginning of an excellent solution to the Colony Club. Don't you agree, Elsie?"

"Indeed," Miss de Wolfe said. "Stanny says you're quite the thing, Miss . . . ?" She lifted her eyebrows at Mr. White, who had poured himself a cup of coffee from the pot on the table.

"Uh, Bromley, Nora Bromley."

Nora ticked a smile at Miss de Wolfe.

"Miss Bromley. I'm sure we'll get along famously."

Nora squeezed out another smile; it hurt her cheeks. Surely they hadn't turned over the finishing of the Colony Club to this otherworldly creature.

"I'm certain you will," White said, half charm, half ultimatum.

"You know, my dear, Elsie designed this room," said Miss Marbury from her other side.

Nora's mouth was dry, but she managed, "It's . . ." The furniture was so light that it looked like it might float away except for the cloths and cushions that held it down. Light filtered into every corner.

"It is indeed," Miss Marbury continued as if she knew exactly what Nora was thinking. "Now, if you'll excuse me. I must get back to work. Enjoy yourselves."

She pushed her chair back and rose ponderously to her feet. She was wearing a wool morning dress with a white collar that reminded Nora of one of the teachers at the School of Applied Design. It looked incongruous in comparison to Miss de Wolfe, who managed to perch daintily on the straight-back dining chair like a nymph in one of the paintings at a museum.

"Yes, and we must work, too," Miss de Wolfe echoed and wafted from her chair. "I've prepared a place in the sunporch where we can set up. Stanny, bring your coffee. Miss Bromley and I have a busy morning ahead." She held out her hand and Nora sprang from her chair. Mr. White complained but he followed, bringing his coffee and snatching a piece of toast from the rack on his way past.

The sunporch was even more amazing than the dining room. Painted bright yellow with the same white-painted woodwork, with plush wicker chairs and love seats upholstered in fabric patterned with enormous chintz roses. Nora had never even imagined such a place.

Miss de Wolfe swept across the room to a wicker table where pencils, pastels, and several paper sketchbooks had been set out. Two delicate wicker tea chairs sat side by side facing the sunlight.

Nora tried to imagine her mother sitting here doing the mending, Rina with her schoolbooks. The patients at her hospital . . . She could see them, and it made her smile.

"So you like my little hideaway?"

"Very much," said Nora.

"It took some time for others to get used to. One doesn't expect an English cottage in a New York row house."

Mr. White chuckled, which startled Nora. This was a different side of the usually gruff man she had come to expect. "You do have a way with color, Elsie, my love."

Elsie trilled a laugh. "I've been studying the blueprints that Stanny sent over, but I confess, I can't make hide nor hair of them. Which lines are walls and which aren't."

Nora's momentary euphoria plummeted and crashed.

White stepped aside and, taking her cue, Nora went to stand beside Miss de Wolfe at the table.

"For instance, what are these lines here?"

Since Mr. White didn't volunteer an answer, Nora said that it was the first-floor entrance.

"Are these windows or doors?" Miss de Wolfe pointed to the short lines along the exterior wall.

"Windows. You can tell because there is a bar across the bottom. Doors are open."

"How clever."

"Yes," Nora said, determined to show patience.

"And I do know that the rectangles are the various rooms."

Nora nodded. Not always, but she would save that for another day. "All the rooms are labeled. The veranda, the parlor, the tearoom. These short lines in the middle are the stairs to the basement and to the other floors. This long narrow space is where the lavatories will be. And a second staircase."

"The strangers room," Miss de Wolfe said. "How mysterious. Shall we make it a seraglio?" She flashed a smile to Mr. White, who smiled in return.

"It's because it's a women's club and the strangers room is where you can meet friends who are not members," Nora explained. She almost added "like in a boardinghouse or women's hotel," but caught herself just in time. She doubted if Miss de Wolfe had ever seen the inside of such humble living environs.

"This little box at the top corner gives the basic dimensions. There are also accompanying spec sheets." Nora riffled through the pages on the table and found the sheets for the first floor. "These give specific measurements so that all interior additions fit within the specified parameters."

"You're so clever. I remember your design from the awards ceremony. Everyone was very impressed." The actress turned with a flourish. "Oh, Stanny, she's perfect." Just as quickly she turned back to Nora. "You can draw?"

"Yes."

"She's excellent," White assured her. "You just tell her what you want and she'll make it happen."

It was a preposterous thing to say. Nora couldn't make impossible things possible. And she wasn't certain that Miss de Wolfe even understood the notion of measurements. But she held her tongue, determined to make the best of the situation. There would be time to explain this later. Miss de Wolfe did have an eye for color and how to give a room a special feeling. Nora would give her that. Time would tell if she could actually design the inside of an entire building.

"I have some ideas already." Miss de Wolfe reached for the large sketch pad.

Mr. White took the opportunity to quietly slip out of the room.

GOOD HEAVENS, SHE *really can't draw*. Nora stared at the lopsided . . . urns? And were those boxes supposed to be mantels? There were several things that she couldn't distinguish at all. This was going to be impossible. How would she ever translate these things to reality?

She listened mutely while Elsie de Wolfe explained what she had in mind, as she turned one page after another of drawings that might as well be hieroglyphics.

"Don't look so stultified, my dear. Didn't Stanny tell you? I can't draw a lick, but I can see it in my mind. And I promise you my design will make the Colony Club the nonpareil among clubs. If they insist on seeing everything in advance, you'll just have to be my translator."

Two hours passed and Nora was bleary-eyed from sketching when Miss de Wolfe suddenly declared, "That's enough for today. I have appointments at several antiques dealers and have to arrange for my buying trip. We'll need an office and a storage warehouse. Bessie will absolutely have a fit if I bring one more objet d'art into the house. Tomorrow, same time? Ah, this is what I was meant for, Nora."

Minutes later Nora was back on the street, disoriented and alone. She had no idea where she was or how to get back to the drafting room or the club site, much less home. Which way was north? She'd lost all orientation in her frightening ride in Mr. White's automobile.

The front door opened and she cringed. What would Miss de Wolfe ask of her now?

But it was Miss Marbury, lumbering down the steps. "You'll have to forgive Elsie; her mind is so often in the clouds that she forgets the little necessaries that make life work." She pressed some coins into Nora's hand. "Take a cab back to wherever you need to be. As soon as the details are arranged with Mr. White, we'll talk about your per diem." With that, she bustled back up the steps and shut the door.

Bemused, Nora chose a direction and walked until she came to a trolley stop where she was directed across the street for the trip north. She decided to return to the architectural offices to report to Mr. White about their progress and perhaps he would explain to her just exactly what her duties would be and how much time she should spend with Miss de Wolfe. Then she would spend the rest of the afternoon deciphering her notes and turning Miss de Wolfe's designs into something recognizable.

But Mr. White wasn't in and neither was George. So Nora selected several sheets of paper and took them over to her drafting table to begin—and wait.

She'd been so intent on remembering all the things that Miss de Wolfe had said during the morning that she was startled by the snide remark from her tormentor, Collin Nast.

"Well, well, what have you and the boss been up to this morning? Has he finished with you already? Did he treat you to lunch?"

"What? Actually I haven't had lunch. I was too busy."

"I just bet you were."

It took Nora a second to understand what he was insinuating and she blushed hot.

"If he's finished with you, I might be interested. I'll even treat you to lunch."

"How dare—" Nora didn't get her sentence out before Fergus sprang from his stool and strode over to where Nast was sitting.

"Shut your filthy mouth, Nast."

"What are you so riled up for? I just asked her about lunch."

Fergus grabbed Nast by his lapels and yanked him off the stool. The stool fell back with a clatter.

"Fergus, no!" Nora grabbed his arm.

Fergus had pulled Nast up until the two men were face-to-face. "*I* know what you meant. The whole room heard it. And we won't stand for it. We're gentlemen here and if you can't be the same, maybe you should rethink your career."

"Fortunately, you have no say in the matter," Nast spit back. "She should never have been given a place here; she's nothing but trouble, as we've just witnessed."

"You're the trouble," said Fergus through gritted teeth, but he let go, adding a shove for good measure. Nast staggered, snatched up the stool, and, after glaring at Fergus, straightened his collar and sat down.

Sorry, mouthed Nora.

Fergus just shook his head and went back to work.

But later, when most of the draftsmen were taking an after-noon break and Nora was on her way downstairs to catch the secretaries up on her visit with "the actress," Fergus pulled her aside. His cheeks were flushed. "I'm sorry that you have to deal with that oaf. Really, Bromley, most of the men here are perfectly accepting of women as architects. And gentlemen, to boot. It's just a few closed-minded—"

"I know. Thanks for sticking up for me, but don't get yourself on Nast's bully list. I've dealt with guys like him all my life. He doesn't frighten me."

"Good for you, but watch your back. No one likes him; he's a teller of tales. I guess what he lacks in talent he thinks he can make up for by spying for the powers that be."

"I'll be careful."

"Look, Nora, I think you're doing groundbreaking work, and one day there will be women architects thick on the trees, and it will be because of you and a few others, but that's only if you survive the journey."

Nora smiled. "Why, Fergus, how did you get so wise?"

"Huh?"

"That's exactly what my old professor said." And something she'd been in danger of forgetting. "Just don't let my battle make it rougher for you."

"Nah. I, too, know how to handle guys like Nast. I suppose you're going down to take your break with the girls."

Nora nodded.

"Tell them hello for me."

Surprised, Nora said, "I certainly will."

ALL THREE SECRETARIES were sitting at the lunchroom table when Nora walked in.

Sadie and Lavinia looked up expectantly, while Higgie stood up to pour Nora a cup of coffee.

"How did it go? What was she like? Is she as glamorous up close as she is on the stage?"

Nora held up both hands against their questions.

Higgie put a cup in front of her and slid the ever-present plate of biscuits toward her. "Give Nora time to catch her breath." But she, too, sat down and looked expectantly at Nora.

"First of all, Fergus Finnegan said to say hello."

"He has a crush on Sadie," Lavinia said.

"He does not." Sadie blushed and slapped Lavinia's arm.

"See?" Lavinia said. "But enough about Fergie, tell us about Miss de Wolfe."

"Well . . ." Nora took a sip of coffee and put the mug on the table. "She's very beautiful . . . She's dainty, like a fairy-tale princess. Sometimes. But then, I don't know, she gets all dramatic when she's describing what she sees in her head? I mean, she's like . . ."

"An actress?" Sadie prompted.

Nora hadn't seen that many actresses, mainly the few times the Yiddish Theatre had put on plays in the park, none of which Nora understood and whose actors didn't act at all like Miss de Wolfe. "I guess."

"What was she wearing?"

Nora shrugged. "A dress?"

"Ugh," moaned Sadie. "Was it gossamer and ribbons, or shiny and rustled when she walked, or was it like one of those Chinese robes that you wrap around like a shawl?" Her eyes had grown wider with each suggestion, and they suddenly blinked. Breaking Nora's astonishment.

"It was a dress; it had flowers on it. She seems partial to flowers. Big pink and yellow flowers. Her dress matched the room."

"Huh?"

"The room where we worked was painted yellow. Let's see,

they were still at their coffee when we arrived and their dining room had green-striped wallpaper and the table and chairs were painted white. There were flowers in a big blue-and-white urn. It made me think of a picnic. The whole house was like being in a garden. It was beautiful."

Now Lavinia groaned. "But what about *her*?"

"She was nice enough. The other lady was a bit gruff, and quite fat. They looked a little funny together, like Jack Sprat and his wife. Except they are both ladies."

"So are you going to be working with her on the Colony Club?" asked Higgie.

"I don't really have a choice. She knows what she wants, but she can't illustrate any of it. Mr. White told me that's going to be my job."

"Well, they all say upstairs that you are a remarkable draftsman," Higgie said.

"They do?"

"Well, George Douglas does," Lavinia said. "But I'm sure everyone else thinks so, too."

"Not everybody," Nora said, putting down the cookie she'd just picked up. "That Collin Nast was making all sorts of snide comments to me when I returned. Fergus told him to shut up, then grabbed him by the collar."

"Bravo, Fergus," said Higgie. "That Nast fellow is so hateful. You keep clear of him if you can."

"I try, but he seems to go out of his way to attack me. And his desk is placed so that I have to pass him anytime I get up. I just don't want to get Fergus in trouble because of me."

Sadie sighed. "Oh, no, that wouldn't be good at all."

Lavinia rolled her eyes and leaned on her elbows toward Nora. "Tell us more about Miss de Wolfe."

Nora told them all she could remember. But what she remembered most was the house and the way it was furnished. "Miss de Wolfe mostly talked about color and the importance of everything being placed so that it brought the maximum amount of serenity. 'Because who wants to walk into an anxious room?'"

"She said that?" asked Lavinia.

Nora nodded. She'd never thought about serenity in regard to a room. It was one of those words that thinkers used. But sitting there in the lunchroom with the other three, she thought about her hospital and how the furnishings as well as the building itself could lend serenity to the life of the patients. It was a good word, *serenity*. She would have to remember it.

After the break she took the elevator upstairs, thinking *serenity*, and rolling the word silently on her tongue, knowing full well that as soon as she passed by Collin Nast's drafting table, her serenity would shatter.

She hadn't let on to Fergus and she hadn't mentioned to the secretaries just how disconcerting it had been. Was that what they all thought? It was too humiliating. All she wanted to do was be an architect. There were plenty of jobs for everyone. Why did it matter that she was a girl?

Why did men always have to spoil everything?

CHAPTER 17

On her second day as Miss de Wolfe's assistant, Nora went alone to the house on Irving Place. Miss Marbury informed her that the club had a spare office at the temporary building, and she and "dear Elsie" would be moving into it next week as soon as it was equipped with whatever office fixtures they deemed necessary.

She asked Nora what supplies she would need; when Nora hesitated, she said, "Don't be shy; Elsie certainly won't be. Tell me exactly what you'll need. Paper, paints, protractors, I'll have it fitted out completely. We don't want to scrimp; the ladies will be meeting right across the hall and are bound to pop in to see how things are progressing. Things will go smoothly if they are impressed. Make a list. I'll send it over to the supply store to be delivered. The office has a window, but not the best light, so perhaps a lamp—or two. She's in the sunroom," Miss Marbury said before turning away, and Nora made her way down the hall, which seemed even more cluttered than the day before, to the back of the house.

Miss de Wolfe was standing by the wicker desk. "Oh, you're here, come in."

Nora stepped into the room, remembering to make a detailed note of the actress-turned-decorator's attire so she would have something to tell the girls when she returned to the architectural office. A frock in light pink and peach, made of soft material that hung in folds with a curlicue pattern outlined by little holes that looked like hundreds of minute oculus windows. A fascinating technique. Nora was tempted to touch it, just for its interesting texture.

Her short jacket was made of flounces of the same material and trimmed in lace. Nora couldn't help but wonder what a day full of pencil-lead smudges would do to the front ruffles.

"I made some sketches," Miss de Wolfe said. And Nora realized she'd been staring.

Nora glanced at the desk where several sheets of scratchings awaited her. A vase? A potbellied stove? A tree, possibly?

"A fountain I saw in the back of Handy's Antique Statuary. It would be perfect for the veranda. I paid very careful attention to it. Because I didn't want to buy it outright until we have a place to store it. But I drew what I could and wrote down the rest of the details. There." She pointed to the top-right corner of her sketch. Nora took a moment to try to match the scribbling to the oblong figure on the sketch.

She frowned at the paper. She could sort of see it. But a fountain inside the clubhouse? "A fountain?"

"Yes, the sound of the water will be relaxing to the ladies." She threw out her hands in a graceful gesture that Nora guessed was meant to represent water.

"Water lines will have to be laid to supply and drain it," Nora said. "I'm not sure . . ."

"Put that on the list to tell Stanny."

Nora would ask Mr. Wojcik if it were possible or within budget. "Maybe if you described it to me while I draft it . . ."

So with Miss de Wolfe leaning over her shoulder and Nora with her pencil at the ready, slowly a fountain began to take shape. A bulbous base with flutes of diminishing widths as it reached the top, a frieze . . .

It took half an hour, but at last they had a recognizable rendering of Cupid.

"And how large is this fountain?" asked Nora.

"From the ground it comes to about here." Miss de Wolfe sliced the side of her hand across the top laces of her jacket. "But I think it will need a plinth, and plants, water plants . . ." She was gazing in the air now and for a split second Nora thought of Jimmy, his gaze focused somewhere far away, somewhere the others couldn't see.

"Miss de Wolfe?" she said, recalling the actress back to the here and now.

Her expression changed and she frowned at Nora. "Do you think you could call me Elsie? When no clients are around, at least." She sat down on the chintz sedan and brought the knuckles of one hand to her forehead.

"*Miss de Wolfe* reminds me of my acting days." She smiled slightly, as if remembering. Then she sat up abruptly, her mood changing as swiftly as her skirt's reaction to her change of position. "But that is all behind me now. Forgotten. This is my new life. And we shall be Elsie and Nora in the art room and Misses around everyone else. Except Bessie, of course. Now this one . . ."

Elsie pulled the paper forward. Nora's first thought was a potato with ears.

"A club chair. They will be for the reading room. Just as comfortable as the men's version, and in leather, I think, but not that hideous dark brown that says ancient history." She placed two delicate fingers to her lips. "Light, of course, but not ecru? Green. But a light green. *Le vert du printemps.* Subtle and relaxing. We'll have to have them made exclusively. Joseph Meeks might do. We must call and get an estimate."

Nora jotted down everything in her little notebook, sounding out the words she didn't understand, even *ob jay dar* and *vair duh pranton*. She'd have to ask Fergus if he knew what they were

when she got back to the drafting room. She wouldn't show her
ignorance to Miss de Wolfe any more than absolutely necessary.

She began drawing the chair, with Elsie directing. "The back
should be high enough to create a little privacy . . ." A light trill
of laughter. "But not so high as to make it impossible to overhear
the latest *on-dit*." Nora wrote down *ondee* with a question mark
beside it.

They worked like this all morning with Elsie giving directions
and Nora sketching and writing detailed instructions. She would
render them more neatly and in color when she was back at her
drafting table.

They'd just finished up an idea for wall sconces when Elsie stood abruptly. "That will do for today. I wanted to see the
construction site, but I have an appointment with a client to
redo her boudoir. She's leaning toward light blue, but I think
periwinkle would be perfect with her skin tone. I have to run
over and get a swatch before our meeting." She shook her head
in dismay while Nora ran through her mental color wheel to land
on periwinkle.

Miss Marbury was waiting for them in the foyer. "Don't leave
yet, my dears. If you want a working office, and a storage space
for the menagerie that is taking over our home, I must get a list
of what you need."

"But Bessie, I made a list last night."

"Yes, dear, but Miss Bromley hasn't, and since you'll be traveling, she'll be responsible for most of the drafting as well as the
day-to-day business; she needs to be well stocked."

What other kind of business was there? Nora wondered, suddenly seeing months of deciphering Miss de Wolfe's scribbles and
never seeing a real architectural assignment ever again. Then the
other part of the sentence dawned on her.

"Where are you going?" she blurted out.

"Well, I can't find furnishings sitting in an office on Madison Avenue. I'll start in London first . . . I have a few ideas . . . Yes, London, and the countryside, then France; I can segue that into our *vacance* at Trianon." She nodded to Bessie. "I'm sure the countryside there will be littered with objets d'art."

Bessie chuckled. "I can see I'd better secure a large storage space. A warehouse, perhaps. Why don't we all have a cup of coffee while you two discuss the various things you'll need."

Coffee—delicious, dark, and hot—was accompanied by sandwiches and pastries, and to her chagrin Nora's stomach growled just looking at them.

"Just as I suspected," Miss Marbury said. "They don't give you a minute to eat properly. You architects have one-track minds." She said this gruffly, but affectionately. "Now eat. And when we're done, we'll discuss your per diem."

Now that was a phrase Nora understood. She was to get a per diem, and if she was very careful she would be able to add even more to her savings. Nora gratefully and enthusiastically chose a sandwich that she ate while they discussed supply needs, and a half hour later, her list was complete and her stomach replete.

"I think we've covered everything you might need, Miss Bromley," Miss Marbury said as the maid took the dishes away. "And if you should—"

"Bessie," Miss de Wolfe said. "We're calling Nora, Nora, and she's calling us Bessie and Elsie. We'll be like one big happy family."

Bessie rumbled a resigned laugh.

Nora just sat there; it was as if she, like Alice, had unwittingly stumbled into Wonderland.

Nora returned to the Fifth Avenue office loaded down with notes and sketches and a parcel she suspected contained the leftover sandwiches.

She spent the afternoon translating Elsie's scribbles into objects, moldings, and bits of detail work, first in pencil, then in watercolor. She made sure to add a spec box even when there had been no specs given. Somehow she would have to instill in Elsie the importance of accurate measuring.

She took a tea break, even though she wasn't hungry, but she knew the secretaries would be dying to hear about Elsie, and for a change Nora had news—and sandwiches—to share.

"WE WERE HOPING you would show up," Higgie said, pouring Nora a cup of tea.

"And I brought sandwiches." Nora sat down. "They gave me lunch and sent me back with a care package."

"Ooh, yummy," said Sadie, looking inside the brown paper package. "With the crusts cut off, too."

Which was a big waste of food, if you asked Nora, but since no one did, she kept her opinion to herself. After the sandwiches were passed around, they all gave Nora their full attention.

She described Elsie's dress and the way the holes made the pattern.

"Eyelets," Lavinia informed them. Then, seeing their expressions, she continued, "A kind of cutwork in lace and fabric."

Nora sighed. Her knowledge of fabrics was basic. It wasn't that she had neglected that part of her studies, it was just that the actual building interested her more. Well, she would surely get an education working with Elsie. Maybe there was a silver lining to being banished to the ladies' club.

Nora slumped onto her elbows. "There's so much I don't know."

"You're just starting out," Higgie reminded her.

"And they're always saying words I don't know or understand. Even when they're talking about architecture. Today, Elsie—"

This earned her an "Ooh" from Lavinia. And a "So you're on first names now" from Sadie.

Higgie brought the other two back to the topic at hand. "Tell us some of the things she said."

Nora opened her notebook where she had meticulously copied down everything the best she could.

"For one, she said that the club would be a 'non-payroll' among other clubs."

"We know about payrolls, that's for sure," said Lavinia.

"I don't think she was talking about money. And she said it in a nasally voice."

Nora looked at the three frowning faces.

"Beats me," Sadie said.

"Me too," said Lavinia. "But it's probably French. 'Cause they all"—she held up a limp wrist and said in a stuck-up voice—"'visit the Continent' all the time after they get finished in Paris."

"Huh," said Sadie, "Paris would have finished me if I had to talk in French all day."

"Pay them no mind," said Higgie. "Say it again."

"Non-payroll," Nora repeated, stressing the last syllable the way Elsie had.

"Non-payroll." Higgie rolled the word around a couple of times. "Non-payroll among clubs," she mumbled to herself. "Payroll, non-pay . . . nonpareil!" she exclaimed.

"That's it," said Nora. "Non-para . . . paray . . ."

"Nonpareil. It just means way better than everything else."

"Nonpareil," repeated Nora.

"You'll get the hang of it."

"It seems impossible."

"Look," Higgie said. "You just keep writing down the words and bring them here and we'll figure out what they mean and how to pronounce them."

"Yeah," Sadie said. "Then you'll be just as good as them."

"I am just as good, just not in French."

Higgie nodded. "And we'll make sure you're good enough in French, too. We'll all help."

"Not me," said Sadie. "I can say *pardon moi* and *merci*, but that's about it."

"But Higgie knows French," Lavinia informed them.

"No kidding?" Sadie said. "Higgie, where did you learn French?"

Higgie shook her head. "I know a few words in a lot of languages, but I do know some working French, and I'm fluent in shorthand."

Nora didn't even know shorthand.

"And for what I don't know, I'll bring in my French dictionary."

That impressed them all.

"So you just bring us the word and we'll figure out the rest. Deal?"

"Deal," said Nora. "Thank you."

"It'll be fun," Sadie said. "We can all learn. It'll impress the fellas."

"One fella in particular?" Lavinia chided.

Sadie blushed. "Maybe."

THE NEXT FEW days of work fell into a pattern. Each morning Nora would take her sketches to Irving Place, where more things appeared magically every day.

Every afternoon, Elsie would go off on her *objay* hunt and Nora would return to Fifth Avenue to translate her sketches into renderings, which she kept in a folder to be later catalogued in an inventory book. Something she'd learned to do at the School of Design.

When she finished, she would go downstairs for tea with the secretaries.

Higgie made rectangles of paper with the French word on one side and the meaning on the other. They all dutifully recited the word and memorized the meaning just like they were in school again.

One night they left work together and stopped at a small café that catered to working girls and had a dinner of soup and bread.

Then, at the end of the week, a note was waiting for Nora to go directly to an address on Madison Avenue the following morning. A look at the address meant it must be close to the construction site, and when she stepped off the trolley she realized it was just two doors south of it. That would be convenient.

She was tempted to stop and say hello to Mr. Wojcik and the crew, but decided not to be late on her first day at the new office. Besides, being so close would give her plenty of opportunity to see them—and George—more often.

She hadn't seen much of him since baring her soul in his workroom the day she'd been given this job. She couldn't help but wonder what he thought of her. If he still thought she was stubborn, immature, and spineless. Why on earth had she broken down that way? And in front of George, of all people.

She pushed the thought away and strode purposefully up the steps to the new office. She tried the knob. The door opened to a man sitting just inside.

"Yes, ma'am?" He was kindly looking, with a curling mustache that made him look like he wore a permanent smile.

"I'm Nora Bromley?"

"Ah, yes, the lady architect. You go straight down the hall. It's the door on the right, across from the assembly room."

"Thank you."

She recognized some of the objects placed along the wall. Bessie had wasted no time moving out Elsie's purchases. Hopefully not into Elsie and Nora's office.

The door was open. Elsie and Bessie were inside, deep in discussion.

Nora knocked lightly on the doorjamb. They both turned and beckoned her in.

She only managed a few steps before she stopped.

If a heavenly choir had burst into song, Nora wouldn't have been surprised. It was wonderful. A large rectangular room, painted white, with a window on one side, large enough to let in the light, and a new drafting table beneath it.

"I had one of the men from Stanny's fit it out. It should have everything you need." Bessie pointed to a set of drawers, then pulled one open. "Instruments here. Paper and notebooks. And so on. Anything else you need, just tell George Douglas at the site.

"I had them put your drafting table by the window. We thought you should have the light since you'll be spending a lot of your time here. Elsie's is over there." She pointed to a smaller desk across the room. "The two of you should be able to rub along fairly well, I should think."

"Yes, absolutely," Nora managed, overcome with the largesse of it all. The need to say more was interrupted by a loud grumbling and grunting coming from the hallway. A minute later, three men shuffled by carrying a huge object covered in a canvas tarp.

"My fountain," exclaimed Elsie, and rushed out to oversee.

Bessie looked toward heaven. "I've rented a storeroom down the hall while I look for a full-size warehouse nearby. You'll need to sign for and catalogue each item as it comes in, and keep track of its location. Elsie is bound to hire a stable of artists and craftsmen, so you'll need to coordinate those. When things get in full gear, we'll bring in a secretary to take care of the paperwork. Can you manage until then?"

Nora didn't really have a choice. "Of course."

"Good. I have to run. A meeting with Charles Frohman in half an hour. The man never lets up. Toodles. Tell Elsie I'll see her this evening. We have the Bellingham dinner." And with that, she was gone.

The room suddenly seemed much bigger.

Nora began taking out her sketches, delegating one drawer for them and another for her own implements, even though there were new ones already in a drawer. She ran her hands over the wood of the drafting table. Took a deep breath. This was hers for the duration.

Nora couldn't believe it; no more Collin Nast making ugly jokes, no more disappearing protractors and straightedges. She sat down on the stool in front of the drafting table. It was the perfect size, and it tilted at several different angles.

And maybe being close to the site, she would get some actual architectural hours in as well.

Elsie swooped in several minutes later. The one thing Nora had learned about Elsie was she never did things like other people—she never just entered a room or asked a question. Every move was graceful, yet grand, every statement or question nuanced with meaning.

And she was always on the go.

"I would like to see the room my fountain will go in. Shall we go?"

"Go where?"

"To the site, of course. I must breathe in the air. Get a sense of its personality."

She'd get plenty of air, Nora thought. The exterior walls were up and some of the load-bearing walls inside, but there was no heating. It looked like Nora might need her long johns again.

"I'm not certain it's convenient for us to go. I haven't been there for a couple of weeks and I don't know what they're working on today."

"It doesn't matter, we'll be as quiet as mice. Bessie said she first met you when you were up a scaffolding. How delicious."

Nora didn't know how the men would feel about Miss de Wolfe breezing through anytime she liked. Especially if she decided to climb up the scaffolding.

She was beginning to like Elsie. Even though she acted like some fairy creature, she was really quite smart. And the things that she said about decorating made sense. But it was different and bound to cause a stir, especially among the men working on the site.

They would see right away that Elsie knew nothing about construction or actual building. Though they, in turn, probably never had a thought about what happened to the interior once they finished their part of the building. Nora just hoped they didn't dismiss her as a silly woman. Especially since Nora had worked so hard to win them over.

Mr. White had treated Elsie with respect, though he did flirt with her. Theirs was a different world Nora would never understand. More likely the men would fall over themselves to be nice to Elsie. She was an actress, after all. And everyone knew how men liked actresses.

Maybe even here Nora would be the odd man out. She gathered up papers and pencil and the one straightedge that had made its way out of her pockets so far and followed Elsie out. She hadn't even had time to take off her coat.

CHAPTER 18

I'm not sure this is a good idea," Nora explained, hurrying after Elsie, whose fur coat was billowing behind her.

Elsie didn't seem to hear.

"A building site can be dangerous. It's customary to have a visit cleared in advance."

"Oh, pooh," Elsie said good-naturedly. "I'm the designer. I need to feel the ambiance, the flow, the sense of it."

"I understand, but the interior walls aren't up yet." At least not on the upper floors, and the basement level was a maze of pipes, electrical tubing, and heating ducts, and was dark as a cave. Nora had only seen it from a spot safely on the temporary stairs.

Truth be told, she'd love to see the progress they'd made while she'd been drawing pictures of vases, armoires, and furniture for Elsie. And now with talk about cataloguing and coordination, she might never get back.

She was nothing more than a lowly paid secretary who could draw a straight line. And now she would show up at the site in her years-old coat next to Elsie's silk and fur.

It was humiliating.

When they reached the entrance to the club site, the temporary door was shut, the arched transom covered by a plank of wood.

But instead of going inside, Elsie walked out into the street.

"Miss de Wolfe! Elsie—" Nora warned.

Elsie waved her away. She stared up at the facade as traffic moved around her. She suddenly threw up her arms. "Isn't it glorious?"

It was, but not worth being trampled by horses or crushed by automobiles.

Finally, much to Nora's relief, Elsie returned to the sidewalk unscathed and pulled the door open.

Nora followed her inside, then jumped back as Elsie twirled in a graceful pirouette, her arms outstretched and the hem of her fur coat brushing the floor. Nora wouldn't have been surprised to hear applause.

"Can you see it?" asked Elsie, not really asking Nora, but confirming her own expectations.

Actually, Nora *could* see it. Not in the same way as Elsie, with fountains and exotic vases, but as five floors of interior walls, plumbing, electricity. All constructed with the latest methods. And she had to admit, it was pretty spectacular.

Several carpenters who were standing nearby were the first to notice them. Suddenly arrested in motion, they gaped at the two newcomers. Across the room, workers stopped and stared. Nora could see George and Mr. Wojcik with one of the welders through the open door of the construction office.

All three men looked up. George frowned, which changed to a look of surprise, and at last a smile.

Nora smiled back, but he wasn't looking at her. He was looking at Elsie.

He groped for his jacket that lay across the back of a wooden chair and quickly slipped it on as he came forward. "May I help you?"

"Good afternoon. I'm Elsie de Wolfe . . ." She paused, waiting for acknowledgment to register.

"Of course. Miss de Wolfe. *Enchanté.*" He leaned over her extended hand.

Nora resisted, barely, rolling her eyes.

Elsie opened her hands, indicating the space around them. "I'd love to view our new clubhouse."

George glanced at Nora. She gave him a hint of a shrug and left him to it.

Mr. Wojcik stepped out of the office and strode up to stand behind Nora.

"I'd be delighted to show you," George said. "Though you must be careful, a construction site can be a dangerous place."

"I shall hold on to your arm."

That did it. Nora rolled her eyes.

Someone snorted. Most likely Mr. Wojcik, since she seemed to be the only one who heard it.

George and Elsie started off. Nora turned to greet Mr. Wojcik, but they'd barely said hello before Elsie's "Nora!" pierced the reunion.

"Excuse me." Nora hurried away.

When she reached Elsie and George, they were standing in the main area and George was pointing to where the terrace would be.

"Nora, that's exactly where my fountain will go, close to the back wall . . ."

Nora flipped open her notebook and wrote it down. By the time she'd done a quick sketch with a note to check the dimensions and the placement of the closest water conduit, the other two had moved on.

She hurried after them.

They had stopped at the set of rudimentary stairs leading down to the basement.

"But I *must* see the pool," Elsie was saying. "Stanny has told me all about it. I'm leaving for a buying trip soon and must make sure that I know exactly what to get."

Buying trip already? She'd only just started to set up shop. Nothing was organized. Nora hadn't even rendered her a schemata with accurate dimensions.

Mr. Wojcik strode up at that moment and, seeing Nora's look of dismay, said, "Not sure the lady—ladies—oughta be going down there right now."

"But I must," implored Elsie, hands clasped like a heroine right out of a melodrama.

The men exchanged looks. George appeared indecisive for about two seconds, then he reached over and unhooked the chain. He picked up a heavy flashlight that hung by a rope. "We have limited lighting down there. We can't venture far." He took Elsie's arm. "Careful now, watch your step."

Mr. Wojcik shook his head and motioned for Nora to follow. She heard the chain clank in place as soon as she was on the stairs.

The very *dark* stairs, she noticed, with the only light bouncing ahead of the two people in front of her.

She sighed, and felt her way after them. It wasn't her first trip to the basement. But with the flashlight casting shadows against the girders and beams, Nora couldn't repress a shiver.

They stopped at the pool, heads together, as George explained that it was finished but had been covered for safety.

Nora tiptoed behind them. "I'm sorry, I didn't catch that."

They both jumped and turned toward her, the light casting their faces into high relief. It gave Nora a fright.

"Oh, there you are," said Elsie. George seemed to have lost his voice.

"I was just saying to George . . ." She drew out his name like an accordion. "Stanny wrote me copious notes on the pool. And we are *très sympathique*."

Nora didn't bother to write the first part—Mr. White had left her the same notes—but she took the time to sound out *tray simp a teek*, and wrote it down.

"It is to be in the Greek style with lattice overhead. Entwined with grapevines. I shall hide thousands of little lights in glass grapes. Oh, yes, I like that. Nora, we must have ample electricity."

Nora tucked her head. She didn't remember any mention of thousands of little lights.

"And mirrors," Elsie added, "along the walls." She peered into the darkness. "To illuminate and expand the brilliance. A nonpareil among pools."

Another nonpareil, Nora thought, but now that she knew what it meant she didn't bother to write it down. Promises were great, but for Nora, she would just wait and see.

George just stood there like an oaf.

When Elsie had imagined her lights to her heart's content, they went back upstairs, this time Nora leading the way. She didn't need a flashlight, but she was extra careful not to trip. That would be too embarrassing.

Mr. Wojcik was waiting to let them out.

"And now the ballroom. I must see that before we go."

"The assembly room," Nora corrected, but no one was listening. George and Elsie forged ahead. Mr. Wojcik winked, offered Nora his elbow, which she took, and they clomped up the stairs to the second floor together.

"Delightful," Elsie said, when they were all standing in the assembly room. "Just the right size, with an overhead gallery?"

"Yes," said George. "It will be . . ."

But Elsie had gone ahead. "And French windows. The drapes . . ." She trailed off. Then whirled suddenly to face them. "And candelabra sconces between each window. *Louis Seize*. At least two dozen, maybe four."

Mr. Wojcik broke in. "They'll have to be converted to electricity, ma'am."

"Very well."

"Beggin' your pardon, but it's an expensive process."

"Well, I'll work it out with Stanny. We can always get them made to order. I know several artists who would gladly construct them to my measurements. I can see it now."

"But they wouldn't be authentic," Nora pointed out.

"What do we care for authenticity if a copy does just as beautifully? We'll not be slaves to the past, no marble, no gilt, no dark paneling, just bright and clean and modern."

Nora winced and bent her head over her notebook, her cheeks flaming. George had wanted her to take this job. Well, now he was seeing her in her subservient role. And to think, she'd just begun to like the dramatic Elsie. Today reminded her just how the hierarchy lay.

Elsie finally agreed that they'd seen enough for one day. With many *merci*s and *au revoir*s to George and the men, and a gracious hand held out to Mr. Wojcik, Elsie took her leave. George saw them to the street, and Nora and Elsie made their way back to their office, Elsie declaring she was *aux anges* and Nora plain old hopping mad.

She managed to make it all the way down the sidewalk without looking back. Was George still watching them?

But as they entered the building, she did risk a quick glance up the street. George still stood there watching them and looking befuddled.

Well, good, he should be. Making a fool of himself over an actress. Didn't he know she treated all men that way? "*Id ee oh,*" she muttered, proud of herself for remembering what it meant.

NO SOONER HAD they returned to the office than Elsie, who had been rhapsodizing all the way back about the glories to come, announced, "Well, I must run, dining at the Bellinghams' tonight."

Once Elsie was gone, Nora huffed a sigh, returned her coat to the peg, and sat down at her desk. But instead of copying her notes from the site visit, Nora stared out the window. She had to admit, Elsie's ideas, though fanciful, did have a certain rationale to them. It would cost a fortune, though she supposed that didn't really matter overmuch to the rich ladies for whom the club was being built.

She had no doubt it would be beautiful.

Still, it was hard not to let a bit of resentment niggle its way into her heart. Why did a few have so much when so many did without? It didn't seem fair. "Especially when you are one of the many," she muttered to herself.

She turned from the window, looked at the blank wall beside her desk. Maybe she would bring her copy of her hospital design to put on the wall to remind her that there were other projects besides the Colony Club waiting for her—if she played her cards right.

"Are you busy?"

Nora jumped at his voice.

George poked his head in the door. He was wearing a woolen winter coat and held a homburg between his fingers.

It took her a moment to recover. "If you're looking for Miss de Wolfe, I'm afraid she had other engagements and has left for the day."

He burst out laughing.

Not the reaction she'd been expecting or had hoped for.

"Are you going to invite me in?"

"Certainly." She gestured him inside.

He stepped in and glanced around the room.

"Nice setup."

"Miss Marbury arranged for it."

"And much warmer than the one we have."

She didn't think that warranted an answer, so she didn't give one.

"Oh, come on, Nora, what's up?"

"I'm sure I don't know what you mean."

His smile wavered a bit. "You hardly said a word when I was taking the decorator around, and now you're acting like someone's secretary."

"I *am* someone's secretary."

His expression changed. "That's it, isn't it? You're still mad about being assigned this project."

"Am not."

"Then come have tea with me. Mrs. Tova has been asking where you are."

She meant to decline, but her stomach growled, and Mrs. Tova made splendid pies.

"Come on. My treat."

"You didn't pay her last time."

"She has a generous heart. Where's your coat?"

He looked around, found it on a peg behind the door, and snatched it off. She watched as he held it out for her to put on and her resolve withered. It was the polite thing to do—any gentleman would do the same, but for some reason the fact that it was George made her feel embarrassed.

"Don't make fun of me."

"I wouldn't dare." He gave the coat a little shake. She gave in and turned for him to slip it over her shoulders.

"All right, I'll have tea."

"That's my girl."

She darted a glance at him. It sounded like something a father would say. George Douglas wasn't that much older than she was.

"You're paying."

"Of course, didn't I say? My treat."

"I mean, really, to Mrs. Tova."

"I'll insist. Though she'll put up a fight." His smile broke her willpower and made her feel a little silly. She'd been mad at George for paying so much attention to Elsie, fawning over a woman who must be twice his age, no matter how young she tried to act. And Nora suddenly realized that the anger she was feeling toward them both wasn't anger at all, but jealousy.

She closed her eyes, let out a long breath. *Nora Bromley, act your age. This is strictly professional.* "Shall we go?"

She walked out of the office, then stopped when George followed her. "I wonder if I'm supposed to lock up or something."

"We'll ask the porter."

The porter assured them he would lock up and off they went.

Out in the air again, Nora's hunger ratcheted up a notch.

Mrs. Tova hurried out to meet them. "I'd quite given you up. Hello, Nora, we've missed you—haven't we, Georgie?"

George grimaced.

Nora grinned. "I've been . . . busy."

"Too busy to eat? You have to keep your strength up if you're going to keep this ragtag bunch of construction workers in order."

"Thank you, Mrs. Tova," said George, looking chagrined. "Didn't you say you were making lamb stew today?"

Mrs. Tova winked at Nora and hurried away.

"What was that all about?"

"Nothing. She likes you."

"I like her, too," Nora said, and they lapsed into an awkward silence.

Finally George leaned forward. "What were you doing at the site today?"

"I told her it wasn't a convenient time to bother you."

"That's not what I mean."

"Then what do you mean?"

"You ran around three steps behind us like you were the paid help."

"I am the paid help."

"You know what I mean."

"No, I don't. I've been gotten out of the drafting room and put on lackey duty. No more distracting the draftsmen."

"That is such bull—and you know it."

"Really? You saw what my duties were. Candelabra. *Yes, ma'am.* Twinkly lights. *Got it.* Can you feel the *ambi-antz*? Well, actually I could, and it was all concrete and steel and plumbing and electrical wiring. Not twinkly lights."

"Oh, Nora, grow up."

That stung. Her eyes pricked. She'd grown up years ago. First when her brother died, then her father, when everything fell apart except for her chance to fulfill her promise to them and save her family. Now she was stuck off somewhere—a wonderful somewhere, she had to admit—just so the men wouldn't have to deal with her. And she was failing everything.

"I shouldn't have come." She started to rise, but he reached across the table and pushed her back down.

"I know this isn't what you wanted to be working on, but most people don't get to choose their projects. We all wanted to work on Grand Central, and look how that turned out—the extra draftsmen they hired for the competition have been let go. You're still here. A credit to you, but also to luck that you were in the right place at the right time."

"Lucky to be copying down notes about twinkly lights and candelabras while Miss de Wolfe flits about like a fairy making castles in the air."

Castles in the air. In the real world, imagination died and castles disappeared. Nora would never be seduced by that kind of thinking again.

"It's going to be a constant struggle for you, Nora, for any woman trying to break into this business. But if you succumb this soon, where will you be?"

Nora looked away, not wanting to face his question or her own insecurities.

George took her hand the same way he had that day in his office. "It's important to know how to coordinate the interiors.

All that talk about her fountains and mantels and sconces. It may sound silly, but her ideas are sound.

"Unless we are born into society or wealth like White and the others, most of us never get enough education in that aspect of architecture. You have an opportunity to learn from her. And she will be dependent on you to make sure her creativity fits to specs or they'll go on the trash heap, and we'll all be in big trouble. Especially Mr. White.

"We're all depending on you to make this work. And if you do, you'll know exactly what to do for the next project. And while she's off on buying trips, you'll have more time at the site and to work on your own projects. I assume you have been?"

She hadn't been. She'd been so angry at Elsie, George, Mr. White, her family for not being patient, her roommates for being sloppy—everyone, including herself.

"Your job is to make sure everything fits and has the proper outlets, and to talk her out of things that won't work."

"But I want to be working on buildings."

"Then work on your hospital, or a school, or whatever interests you, so you'll be ready when the time comes. God knows you wouldn't have that opportunity if you were working in the drafting room or the field all day."

The barb hit home, and she knew he wasn't just talking about her. "Oh, George, is that what's happening? You're stuck running around keeping all these projects working when you could be building your own?"

"Nora, you have to have clients to commission your designs. Hopefully one day, I will have built enough of a reputation with McKim, Mead, and White that I will attract my own commissions. And so will you."

"Here it is, nice and hot." Mrs. Tova's voice broke into the conversation and their hands sprang apart as if they'd touched the hot bowls of stew.

Mrs. Tova beamed at both of them. "I will bring bread. Eat, eat."

And they ate, until Nora was stuffed and feeling warm and slightly sleepy. But it was getting late and she had to get back to the fourth floor and Higgie's French flash cards. And try not to let on that she'd had tea with George. That would raise some eyebrows, whether deservedly or not. What would they think? Nora didn't even know what to think. Or how she felt.

CHAPTER 19

I'm off to Europe next week," Elsie announced as she burst into their office one morning in March.

Nora looked up from her rendering of Elsie's latest idea about lamps for the overnight guest rooms, as yet barely framed and plumbed. But whenever Elsie had an idea, she wanted to explore it immediately.

"Europe?" Nora asked.

"Yes, next week. I must have more material to work with. I have exactly the chairs in mind for the tearoom. But I haven't seen them anywhere in New York. I'm sure I can find them at one of the antiquarian stores in London. Or if not . . ." She rummaged through the notebook they kept on Elsie's writing desk. "I know just the woodworkers who can construct them for me."

She glided across the room and looked over Nora's shoulder at several iterations of reading lamps.

"Light," Elsie said, spreading her arms, her sleeves brushing the top of Nora's head. "Why is it when you feel like reading a book, you have to sit in the most uncomfortable chair in the room and twist into contortions until the lamplight falls on the page?"

Nora had finally learned to take these frequent questions as rhetorical and merely waited for Elsie to answer this one.

"I'll choose the same lamps for each room, designed specifically for reading. And placed over the bed so that after a long day of traveling or shopping, you can put your feet up, stretch out, and enjoy an hour or so of reading while comfortably propped up with pillows. Why don't men think of these things?"

Another rhetorical question. They always came fast when Elsie had latched on to an idea. Nora sometimes imagined all of Elsie's ideas floating around in her brain, hovering in different places until they found the best place to settle, at which point she would rattle off the idea for Nora to copy down and re-create.

Nora was getting better at it, though Elsie was also becoming more prolific. And now she was going to Europe, leaving an entire club to be designed.

"I just talked to George and Mr. Wojcik about framing the veranda walls with trellises, light green, the columns, too, all clad in trellis work in the French style."

A horror to dust, thought Nora, putting the lamp designs aside and replacing them with a fresh sheet of drawing paper.

"The panels should run parallel to the ground with square openings. Except behind the fountain. Those will be diamonds."

Elsie turned slowly as if looking at the walls of the veranda and not the already crowded space of their temporary office. "And . . . a polygon border where the cornices will go . . . And vines . . ." She trailed off and Nora jotted down *vines* at the edge of the page. They had more than a year before they needed to worry about plants.

"You must keep an eye on the installation of the trellises or they'll erect them like a New England bean patch."

Nora couldn't begin to imagine what it all might be costing. She never heard anyone discussing money, except George and Mr. Wojcik. She thanked her lucky stars that she didn't have to deal with requisitioning the funds to pay for all these brilliant ideas. Though she supposed she should learn that aspect of architecture, too. She remembered George mentioning that he was going to Columbia to study business.

"While I'm gone, you'll be in charge. I'll send things back and you must write them all down. But now I'll need you to draw up the floor plans with everything named so I can refer to them while I'm abroad.

"While I'm gone you'll also have to make certain that everything delivered is the correct piece and is intact. Send anything broken or damaged back to be replaced. Once you sketch and catalogue the piece, send it to the warehouse space Bessie rented and note where it's stored so we can find it when we need it. It isn't too far from here. Soon it will be spring and you'll be glad not to be cooped up here or at the site all day."

Nora gritted her teeth as she saw her own work drifting away in a plethora of paperwork. This was a job for a secretary, not an architect. She'd thought she'd finally earned a real place alongside the men. But this sure felt like she was being shoved aside again.

Two days later, a typewriter and a telephone appeared in the office, neither of which Nora had any intention of using. For another week, she and Elsie spent hours poring over blueprints, making lists, and taking unscheduled walks to the site, where Mr. Wojcik or George would patiently explain things that would work or wouldn't, then see them on their way.

Several times Nora was summoned to Irving Place with renderings and plans in tow to find Mr. White and Elsie discussing some aspect of the design.

Since she was spending so much time away from the drafting room, she hadn't seen Mr. White much over the winter and was shocked by the change in his appearance. Mr. White did not look well and wore an air of distraction. But he efficiently led Elsie through the vagaries of design, and though she sometimes pouted, she took his advice.

The following week, Elsie boarded a ship to London and the office grew quiet. Nora took a day to reorganize the whirlwind Elsie had left behind. The next morning, she gathered up all her work from her room at the Parker Hotel and transferred it to her office.

The first telegrams from Elsie arrived while she was still on the ship, followed by several more every week with orders and questions. Each one needed to be signed for, noted, and filed with the changes she wanted implemented, an explanation of some item she thought would be perfect for somewhere, or names of artists she'd hired for special projects, whom Nora must contact to "liaise" with. A word Higgie later told her was French and meant "to communicate with." She sent instructions for those artists only to rescind them a few days later when Elsie changed her mind.

Nora came in early and left late and soon her office became more like a home than a place of work.

Outside the office, the ladies came and went, always looking like they just stepped out of a fashion plate. It seemed they were always at the assembly room meeting about something. Lectures and talks and sometimes card playing. When there was music, Nora would tiptoe across the hall to listen. She learned about books, current events, heard her first classical music concert.

It was almost like the club was their home away from home. Which Nora guessed was the whole point. To have a place where they could be themselves and not worry about other things.

Only they did.

And Nora was astounded.

The ladies weren't just enjoying themselves. They were educating themselves. And Nora felt a stab of envy, and allowed herself just a moment to imagine being dressed in finery, invited to card parties and balls and listening to lectures about everything under the sun.

One night Nora was frowning over how to adapt a blueprint of an apartment building to make it affordable for those who lived in the unhealthy, miasmic buildings of the tenements when a burst of applause sounded from across the hall.

It was an evening speech by some woman who had formed a union of some kind. The ladies had been talking about it for several days.

Nora doubled down on her concentration.

Another burst of applause.

Nora got up to close the door against the noise, but as she reached it, someone yelled out from the audience. She'd never heard any shouting from the club members. As far as she knew, society ladies never raised their voices.

But when it happened again, it was so unusual that Nora stepped into the hallway to listen.

The door to the assembly room was shut but since she knew the speaker would be at the far end, she cracked open the door and peeked inside. A small woman, whose face barely appeared over the podium, raised her hands in the air. "The conditions are criminal. Greed of the landlords and the factory owners is causing an intolerable working environment."

There were murmurs through the audience where every seat was filled.

"Most of those people never know the heat that this room enjoys, or the light and air that are afforded by these huge windows.

"The women who work in the garment factories, some no older than twelve, work twelve- and fourteen-hour days, shoulder to shoulder in double rows where they haven't even room to stretch out their legs. The windows are nailed shut to prevent the soot from the street settling on the fabric. And consequently the air is fetid and unhealthy, causing disease, loss of hope, and, even more likely, tragedy.

"Recently a false scream of 'Fire' caused a stampede at one of these death traps; several women were injured in the panic to get out. The aisles were so narrow that when one person fell, the entire row behind her went down like dominoes. It was a miracle that no one was killed. But mark my words, it is only a matter of time if something isn't done."

But what could be done? Nora wondered.

As she thought it, Mrs. Harriman rose from her seat. "How can this be remedied? Especially since the owners are bound to balk at the cost."

It was like she'd read Nora's mind.

"First, a simple reconfiguration of the workspace. Increasing the distance between the machines by a mere six inches on each side increases efficiency by creating enough space to work without constant cramping. What you lose in workspaces you gain in productivity. Which is why women garment workers need a union."

Nora raced back to her office to get her notebook and was back again to hear the word "cross ventilation."

Nora wrote quickly, her mind racing. It was the same as in any good building: traffic flow, fresh air, all the things she'd incorporated into her hospital and her attempts at a school and apartment buildings. And now a garment factory.

She was lost in ideas when applause brought an end to the lecture. Nora longed to stay and talk to the speaker, but she didn't dare. She was not a member; she shouldn't even be here. She looked up to see Mrs. Harriman looking back at her. In a panic, Nora fled across the hall and into her office, closing the door behind her.

She sat perfectly still waiting for a knock on the door and the chastisement that would follow. A reminder to remember her place.

Outside the door, the ladies gathered their wraps, and talking excitedly, they left the building. Gradually all became quiet and Nora pulled out a fresh sheet of drawing paper, her mind alive with the things she heard from the lecturer. It would be so simple to make what she was describing safer, more comfortable, and more efficient.

She drew out a rectangle and looked at it long and hard before she began to sketch: windows, oversized, with plenty of light, with sashes so they could open and screens fitted to the openings to prevent insects and soot from coming inside. Windows on each side of the room would create cross-ventilation except on the most sluggish of days. In winter, a simple ventilation conduit down the center of the room could bring heat. It would take some outlay of money, but it would easily be made up when the workers were not slowed down by numb fingers or swooning from the heat. She lost herself and her sense of time in the possibilities.

When the knock finally came, it was the porter telling her he was closing the building for the night.

THE NEXT MORNING Nora came in early to organize her work for the Colony Club, but she was also excited to get back to her drawing from the night before. She'd drawn it in the euphoria of a new idea, and she wondered if it would stand up in the daylight. She'd placed it on the wall next to her hospital and the other buildings she was working on. As soon as she'd hung up her coat, she went to the wall to study it.

Rudimentary, but definitely workable.

Satisfied for now, she began to tackle the cataloguing of new items and finishing up the detailed drawings she'd made of each. She was hardly aware of the sound of workmen clearing away the chairs from last evening's meeting and replacing them with large round tables for the luncheon at noon.

Nora was concentrating so intently it took a moment for her to realize someone was knocking at the door. Then the door opened a bit and a head peered inside.

Mrs. Harriman. Nora stood, steeling herself for the inevitable reprimand from listening to the lecture the night before.

"Good morning. Are you busy? Should I come back later?"

"No, please." Nora gestured her inside, flustered by her friendliness.

"I just stopped in to see how you're faring," Mrs. Harriman said. She was always so neat, Nora thought, and unconsciously smoothed down her skirt. Today she was wearing a visiting dress with a chevron pattern of navy blue and cream with a wide collar that softened her straight nose and lips.

Mrs. Harriman took a moment to look around the room. "You look very much in charge. Do you have everything you need?"

"Yes, ma'am."

Mrs. Harriman smiled. It lit her face. "Miss Bromley, no need to call me *ma'am*. We're all professionals here."

Nora's breath whooshed out, but Mrs. Harriman didn't seem to notice. She'd walked over to the wall of Nora's sketches.

"I saw you listening to the lecture last night."

"Yes, I'm sorry. I shouldn't have."

She turned toward Nora. "Why on earth not?"

"I'm not a member, I'm just a . . . a . . ."

"One of the architects who is making our club a reality. I'd say that gives you a certain cachet."

"Is that a good thing?"

"An excellent thing." She turned back to the wall and continued to peruse the plans there. "I've seen your hospital design before, and it's just as impressive as it was the night it won the award. But this new one is based on what you heard last night, isn't it?"

"Yes," Nora said, forgetting her anxiety. "When you asked how the problems could be remedied. It's what I wanted to ask, too, so I made notes and have been playing with some ideas on how to make workplaces safer, more comfortable, and efficient. One doesn't have to cancel out the other."

"No, it doesn't," Mrs. Harriman said. "You keep working on it, maybe one day soon we'll get someone to listen. In the meantime . . ." She crooked her finger for Nora to follow her.

She led her across the hall to a narrow door in between the double doors that led to the assembly room. She opened it to reveal a narrow staircase. "It leads to the musicians' gallery, which we never use. You can sit and hear the lectures without being seen. How about that?"

"Oh, yes, I don't know how to thank you."

"Nora, one of the purposes of the Colony Club is to educate, ourselves and others. We consider it our duty. And I want you to take advantage of what you can learn here."

Nora nodded. She couldn't think of words good enough to describe how much that meant to her.

"Now I must run. Giving a luncheon when there's no kitchen is a feat. But we're attracting too many members to continue to take advantage of someone's personal dining room."

She started to leave, then stopped in the doorway. "You have a bright future ahead of you. Don't let anyone try to talk you out of it."

And with that she was gone. And Nora recited Daisy's words to herself over and over until they were ingrained in her very soul.

THE LUNCHEON WAS well attended, with a full four courses prefaced by a spirited general meeting where a letter the board had received from the ladies of the Temperance League was read, asking the club members to pledge themselves as a nondrinking and nonsmoking organization and with an invitation to join their society.

As far as Daisy was concerned, though there wasn't a designated "smoking room" à la the men's clubs, she didn't think they should police a member who might light up during her afternoon coffee. And as far as spirits were concerned, no one could possibly hold dinner parties and soirees without a decent selection of wines. Besides, once they started bending to outside groups with special interests and banning one thing, it would never stop until they had nothing.

"Over my dead, dehydrated body," Bessie had exclaimed to Daisy before standing up from the luncheon table and suggesting they postpone consideration of the letter until a later meeting since the soup was getting cold.

The motion easily carried.

But afterward as they sat chatting over a second cup of coffee while the hired staff cleared the dishes and began removing the tables and chairs, a Western Union boy entered the room. "Telegram for Miss Marbury."

Bessie sighed and lifted her hand, fingers pinched together so that the boy slipped the paper between them. He touched his finger to his hat and retreated.

Daisy raised her eyebrows.

"I tip them by the week," Bessie explained. "Elsie has already sent ten telegrams and she's been in London less than three weeks. She's shipping all sorts of stuff back before she even checks with Nora, poor child."

"She only received five thousand in seed money."

Bessie chortled. "That has never stopped Elsie, but don't be concerned. She will be given carte blanche just like Stanny would have been. There is money in the account enough to carry the decorating. And if we run low, we'll just have to find a few more patrons."

"Why doesn't she send them directly to the warehouse?"

"She feels they need to keep track of everything. And she's

right. Though God knows Nora is already here all the time, except when she's at the site. We should probably think about getting the assistant an assistant. It's a lot of responsibility for an untried girl."

"She's bright and dedicated," said Daisy. "But I think she'd rather be designing her own buildings than keeping track of Elsie's shopping sprees."

"As well she should. She's talented. Stanny says she's the best draftsman he's had in years, and then ruined it all by saying 'if only she wasn't a woman.'"

"Well, I hope he hasn't banished her here just so he won't have to deal with her and the friction her presence might cause with the draftsmen."

Bessie arched an eyebrow. "It's not Nora Bromley that he doesn't want to deal with. It's us as a group, and, truth be told, we'll be more likely to get this club open in the next decade with Elsie and Nora at the helm. Poor Helen Whitney blurted out the other night that she would have bought an already constructed house if she'd known it was going to take this long. You can imagine the reactions of horror that got."

"I shudder to think," Daisy said.

"I don't think we need worry. Soon we'll be leaving the whole future of architecture in Nora's hands, and others like her."

"I just hope we're not derailing her progress. She's in a man-eat-man business."

"Every profession is a man-eat-man business for women," said Bessie. "But think of all the future clients she's grooming here. The ladies seem to like her, and if we could only dress her up a bit, I'm sure she would have no trouble holding her own." Bessie shuddered. "I imagine her going back every night to the boardinghouse or wherever she lives, washing and ironing out her shirtwaist until it's as thin as a wafer."

"Which reminds me," Daisy said. "I told her she could listen to the lectures if she stays out of sight."

"You'll make a progressive of her yet," Bessie said. "She'll earn her salary on this job."

"Do you know what she's being paid?"

"Not a clue, though I'll check with Stanny. I know she's getting paid piecemeal by the company and by Stanny when working exclusively for him, like with the Colony Club. I've taken a per diem for her out of Elsie's budget, but we may have to supplement her salary.

"Stanny is badly in debt, Daisy, it's getting dire. I say this to you purely confidentially for the sake of the club's finances. And not for sharing."

"I would never. But is it as bad as that?"

"Worse," said Bessie, and drained her cup.

CHAPTER 20

April 18, 1963
Washington, D.C.

"Looking back on those days, it's amazing we got anything done. Between nonstop socializing during the season, the trips abroad and summers away, our lives were full of disruptions and distractions. On a certain date we'd drop whatever we were doing and leave for the Continent. We'd return at the beginning of summer with new wardrobes and our heads filled with art, enduring the city's heat only long enough to change wardrobes and take off to Newport or one of the other resorts.

"It was a different time, and we depended so much on other people getting the work done for us. I think if we had realized what a precarious place that put us in without a master on board to finalize everything, we might have pulled out of the deal and settled for someone else. Stanford was spending most of his time on buying trips to Europe and visiting friends and enjoying life as if he didn't have a care—or a responsibility—in life. But even at his most exasperating, Stanford was a genius who never scrimped or cut corners.

"So like every year before and after, we left the summer of 1905, content to let others do the work and make the decisions: Stanford's young assistant to oversee the construction site, one young girl to manage the entirety of the club's interior.

"I look back on that time now with a certain embarrassment of how blasé we were about something that meant so much to us all. Having seen so much happen in the world since then makes me truly grateful for those two young people and all the workmen who sweated through the summer for our future endeavors.

"That summer was particularly sans souci, but by September when people began drifting back to the city to prepare for the festivities of the season, there was one thing uppermost in our minds: to finish the clubhouse so that we could have a fall opening the following year.

"The first thing I planned to do when I returned from Newport was to go to the assembly room and seek out Nora. With Elsie still in Europe, spending several times the amount of our original budget, I was anxious to make sure everything was in order and ready to go full steam ahead on her return. But there was still the regatta and the national championship at the Newport Tennis Club to be attended, and the end of August seemed so far away . . ."

Nora brushed her sleeve across her forehead to keep the sweat from running into her eyes or dropping on the drafting paper. Summer was upon them, and the heat and humidity scraped at everyone's tempers. Tools slipped from sweaty hands. Splinters festered more quickly, light heads and tepid drinking water led the men to take longer lunch breaks and even longer visits to the local tavern in the afternoon.

Nora made the rounds each day: her office, the site, office, site. Twice a week she reported to the MMW offices in case they got any ideas of moving her out while she was working elsewhere. On those evenings after everyone had left for the day,

Nora met the secretaries downstairs for Higgie's French lesson. Afterward, they would often stroll through Madison Square Park, eating rapidly melting ice cream cones and laughing over the latest company gossip. Sometimes they would take supper in one of the small canteens along Twenty-third Street. And Nora began to realize that she had friends at last.

Sunday dinners resumed at Louise and Donner's, though only once a month, which Nora thought they were all grateful for. The baby had moved into Mama and Rina's room permanently, and Nora felt the full weight of her responsibilities.

Each visit, she begged Rina to hang on just for another year. By then, if all went well, she would have a secure income and they could be together again. After dinner she'd make the trip back to her room at the Parker Hotel with their future weighing heavily on her heart, and she'd fall into bed, knowing that the heat would keep her from sleeping, but not being able to sit or stand for another moment.

The Colony Club transformed from a shell of concrete, brick, and steel to a lovely Colonial Revival building. Inside, the interior walls went up. The upper floors were installed. Doors, windows, and alcoves were finished and outlets for electricity and water were ready to be connected.

Nora organized fabric swatches, paint and wallpaper samples until her eyes blurred. Relayed messages to and from Elsie to artists and craftsmen whom she'd hired for specific purposes. The number of artists in her workshop grew until managing their mail and telegrams alone became nearly a full-time job. At least three times a week, a statue or mantel or whatnot would arrive that Nora signed for, catalogued, sketched, measured, then repacked to send on to the warehouse. Occasionally she would snatch a few minutes to work on her own designs.

And sometimes she even saw George.

Then almost without warning the weather turned, not quite

so hot, nor so humid, and with the weather came the ladies of the Colony Club.

So Nora wasn't totally surprised when, one night, Mrs. Harriman knocked on the office door. She was dressed for the evening in a rose-colored gown trimmed with lace and gold fleur-de-lis.

Nora jumped to her feet, aware of her own appearance, her skirt and shirtwaist covered with sawdust from the latest arrival. Her hair unkempt and flying about her face. "Welcome back, Mrs. Harriman."

"It's wonderful to be back. I don't want to interrupt your work," she said. "We were just driving by on our way to dinner and I had an idea."

Oh, heavens, not any more changes.

She had to snatch her attention back to what Mrs. Harriman was saying. ". . . have asked me to speak along with some others on the state of tenements and tuberculosis in the city. Of course, I'm not an expert, but they wanted someone from the private sector. Dr. Jamison will also be speaking. And Mr. Almirall, the architect chosen to build a new tuberculosis hospital on Staten Island."

Mrs. Harriman rummaged in her evening purse and drew out two large paper tickets. "I have these for the lecture. I thought perhaps you and a friend might like to attend."

Nora automatically looked down at her skirt and graying shirtwaist. It was an automatic response and one that embarrassed her.

"There will be people from all walks of life there. It's not a dress affair," Mrs. Harriman said without a hint of condescension. "I think your ideas will mesh with what Dr. Jamison and I will talk about. And you're bound to learn something from the architect whether you agree with him or not. You're the future of so many things. I hope you'll come." She placed the tickets on Nora's drawing desk and said good evening.

When she was gone, Nora picked up the tickets. "New

Hope for the Eradication of Tuberculosis." Dr. Ernest Jamison, Mrs. Florence J. Harriman, and Raymond F. Almirall. She'd like to go, but she wouldn't go by herself. And who would she ask?

For a moment she thought to ask George; he was an architect and would be interested, but she didn't know how to go about it. Or if it would be too forward. So when she met with the secretaries for their French lesson, she asked if one of them would like to go.

Sadie shivered. "Too depressing. And it's on a Friday night."

"And what would you be doing on a Friday night that's so important?" asked Lavinia.

Sadie shrugged one shoulder. "Wouldn't you like to know?"

"Don't tell me Fergus finally asked you to the pictures."

"Well, he did, sort of. He said sometime would I like to maybe go . . . so I'm keeping my Friday nights open until he asks me."

Lavinia sighed and shook her head. "Thanks, Nora, but it doesn't really sound like something I want to hear."

Nora tried not to show her disappointment. She'd been hoping that one of them might be interested.

"Actually, I would like to hear what they have to say," Higgie said. "And I just happen to have this Friday free."

Sadie rolled her eyes. "You always have Friday nights free. You never go anywhere."

"And we know for a fact," Lavinia added, "that several of the guys upstairs have asked you out."

"Maybe I'm waiting for the man of my dreams," Higgie said.

Lavinia and Sadie both groaned. "Better look harder or you might have to settle for just all right."

"Or wind up an old maid," Sadie added with a shudder.

"Hey, where's your spirit of the modern-day woman? It's the man of my dreams or a successful career as bookkeeper-secretary for a famous architectural firm." She smiled smugly. "Or maybe even both."

"Still, I wouldn't wait too long," Lavinia said.

It was decided. Friday after work, Nora and Higgie set off from the McKim, Mead, and White offices to take the trolley downtown to Cooper Union.

Nora was shocked at the rush of fondness and nostalgia she felt entering the Great Hall, the rows of hard, closely packed seats, everyone pushing through the doors as soon as they opened and scrambling to choose a seat so as not to get stuck behind one of the vaulted columns that would obstruct their view of the speaker.

Nora presented their tickets and the usher led them down near the front where a section was cordoned off for special guests. Nora and Higgie exchanged looks and sat down.

Nora was suddenly nervous; she glanced around at other special guests, mostly men in dark suits and beards. Professional men. A handful of women, several of whom were expensively dressed, patrons perhaps. Others who wore capes denoting their nursing professions.

"This is quite a crowd," Higgie said, looking around.

"I hope you won't be bored," Nora whispered.

"I don't think so. I like learning everything."

Nora was always surprised when Higgie would mention some odd fact, or something from the newspaper or that she knew a little French. Higgie didn't speak much about herself or her family. Actually, none of the secretaries did, and that was fine with Nora. They all had to earn their own way. It was best they didn't compare.

Her thoughts were interrupted as three people, one of them Mrs. Harriman, walked onto the stage and took their seats. They were followed by another man who stood behind the podium.

"Good evening and welcome. I'm James Tully, Commissioner of Charities, and I'm pleased to introduce our speakers. As you know, our fine city has been plagued by an insidious disease, which we've been attempting to address. We're fortunate to present three speakers this evening . . . Mrs. Florence J. Harriman . . ."

Nora sat up straighter and nudged Higgie.

". . . who will give us an overview and a projection of the state of the disease in our crowded tenements. Dr. Jamison, who will present the latest techniques in tuberculosis diagnosis and treatment. And Mr. Raymond Almirall, who has been chosen to design the newest sanitarium in our pursuit of eradicating this dread disease. So without further ado, I give you Mrs. Harriman."

Daisy walked to the podium, nodding graciously to Mr. Tully. "Good evening. It is gratifying to see so many of you here." She paused, looking over the crowd.

"In the last year alone, the United States saw the deaths of over two hundred thousand citizens from tuberculosis."

She leaned forward over the podium. Nora swore the audience moved closer to her, mesmerized as she wove a story of hardship and despair, the efforts to clean up the tenements where most of the cases existed. "We have made inroads thanks to people like you, and physicians like Dr. Jamison and architects like Mr. Almirall and other young architects who are right now studying to build in a manner that is most efficacious for everyone."

She caught Nora's eye, and Nora's heart swelled.

Higgie leaned toward Nora and nudged her in the ribs. "She's talking about you, Nora."

Nora nodded, blinking back tears.

Mrs. Harriman returned to her seat, Nora wondering how she had ever thought her a silly socialite with only her own comfort to worry about.

Dr. Jamison took her place and talked about his recent experiences conferring with German doctors, other advancements in the medical sphere, and how early treatment could lead to cures, which shot a stab of grief through Nora's heart. If Jimmy could have just lasted longer.

"And this evening I'm excited to announce that the new hospital proposal, the New York City sanitarium for consumptives, to be built on Staten Island, has been passed."

Finally the architect, Mr. Almirall, took the stage.

Nora pulled her thoughts back from regret and sadness. The doctor wasn't that old, in his thirties, maybe, but he spoke with authority and enthusiasm. He'd barely begun before she groped for her notebook and pencil, and began taking notes.

"Mrs. Harriman and Dr. Jamison have enlightened you all about the need for good air, sanitary conditions, and adequate medical treatment. Building an edifice to accomplish these things is where I come in. To begin with, the ward buildings will be built in an arc, which is designed to furnish the maximum sun exposure . . ."

Nora wrote as fast as she could.

". . . each of the three pavilions planned will accommodate approximately one hundred patients . . .

"The entire roof will be a garden where ambulatory patients can . . ."

Nora's hand was cramping by the time the architect finished and Mr. Tully ended the lecture.

Nora gathered up her things. "I think we should thank Mrs. Harriman for the tickets."

"By all means," Higgie said. "That was fascinating."

Mrs. Harriman was standing in a cluster of people in front of the stage. She saw Nora and Higgie approach and motioned them over.

Nora introduced Higgie.

"Thank you so much, Mrs. Harriman," said Higgie. "It was such an enlightening talk."

"So glad you enjoyed it." She turned to the other two presenters. "May I introduce Miss Higgins and Miss Nora Bromley, one of the architects on the new Colony Club."

Nora smiled, feeling a little daunted being introduced to the man who was going to design and build the largest tuberculosis sanitarium in the country.

"Nora won the School of Applied Design award for her design of a tuberculosis hospital."

"Indeed?" said the architect with a lift of his thin eyebrows.

Nora swallowed. "Yes. But on a much smaller scale. I'm still studying. And what I learned tonight was invaluable."

He smiled.

"It was on a smaller scale," Mrs. Harriman said, "but incorporated many of the same features as the new Sea View Hospital. She'll be the next generation of forward-thinking architects."

Nora couldn't believe how flattering Mrs. Harriman was being. She had really seen what Nora had been attempting in her design; most people didn't bother to look that closely.

Mrs. Harriman turned to Higgie. "And are you studying architecture, too?"

"No, I'm the bookkeeper for McKim, Mead, and White. That's where Nora and I met."

"Did I hear someone mention bookkeeper?"

It was Dr. Jamison, who turned from the person he'd been talking to and flashed a smile at Mrs. Harriman and then at Higgie.

Higgie blushed. "Yes, a simple job, but a necessary one."

"Indeed," said the doctor, whose smile created a dimple in one cheek.

"It's a difficult job," Nora broke in. "She organizes timesheets and salaries for over fifty architects and draftsmen. And keeps the office organized and efficient."

Higgie just stood there, blushing. Nora had never seen Higgie blush.

Dr. Jamison's smile broadened and another dimple appeared on the opposite cheek.

"That is an excellent report," he said. "I for one believe that it is the bookkeepers and secretaries of the world who make the difference in how a business is run. Invaluable, especially to the medical profession."

"My father was a research librarian at Columbia College," Higgie said. It was the first time she'd ever mentioned her father. And Nora couldn't help but wonder why he hadn't encouraged her to go to college rather than secretarial school. "I was in charge of keeping his notes in order. It was good training."

"And are you interested in medicine?"

Nora left them to it, and returned her attention to Mr. Almirall, who was explaining how the sanitarium would be accessed and the problem of humidity.

Mrs. Harriman excused herself to speak to some other attendees.

It was several minutes before the architect gave his excuses of a later engagement and left.

Nora turned back to find Higgie still in conversation with Dr. Jamison. Just the two of them. Feeling guilty about having left her friend to fend for herself, Nora hurried over.

"Sorry, I was listening to Mr. Almirall. Are you ready to go?"

"Yes, of course," Higgie said, almost sounding like her normal self, though her color was still flushed.

"It's been a pleasure, Miss Higgins," Dr. Jamison said. "And if you ever decide to leave your post and would consider organizing the medical world, please let me know." And in a rapid sleight of hand, he extracted a card from his jacket pocket and handed it to Higgie.

Higgie frowned at it for a moment, then took it. "It was nice meeting you."

She turned away and she and Nora started across the room.

Suddenly Dr. Jamison reappeared at their side. "Perhaps I could call on you one day to discuss this further."

Higgie blinked, then managed, "That would be . . . fine," and she hustled Nora toward the door.

"Good heavens," Nora said when they were on the street and waiting for the trolley. "I had no idea you were interested in medicine."

Higgie sighed. "Neither did I." The trolley came and there was no more talk of doctors or architects that night.

BY MORNING, NORA'S brain was reeling with ways to improve her design. She wouldn't try to make it larger. She wasn't convinced that huge facilities were the answer to everyone's needs. But Mr. Almirall had made accommodations for a roof garden, possibly high enough for cleaner, less humid air.

Nora began to think about air filtration. Something she knew nothing about. But she bet George or Mr. Wojcik would.

She went to her office early and took her hospital plan down from the wall, carefully rolling it into a cardboard tube, and carried it up the avenue to the clubhouse site.

"Nora!" George said, striding quickly to the door to greet her. At least she hoped it was a greeting. He seemed agitated.

"Is this an inconvenient time?"

"Not at all. I was wondering where you've been; we haven't seen you on the site recently."

"I've been here, but not when you've been here."

"I've been spending a lot of time over at the Madison Square site."

"How is it going?"

"Nothing new, just a question of keeping everything on schedule. What have you been doing?"

"Accepting deliveries, cataloguing them, and sending them to the warehouse."

"We're a dull pair."

Nora noticed the dark circles under his eyes. Doing double duty for Mr. White while Mr. White was on a buying trip. She'd never realized what a large amount of time decorating interiors demanded. Or the number of trips to Europe it would entail. Of course, all these were rich clients who only wanted the best. She bet Mr. Almirall never scoured Europe for the best bedpans and wheelchairs. Or perhaps he did. She was trying to learn not to show her own lack of experience.

She realized that George was just watching her, a question on his face. And she'd been daydreaming. "Actually, I came for some advice, but if you're too busy . . ."

"Depends on what it is. Any more mantels that are too large for the space?"

"One, but I intercepted it and sent it as a gift to Mr. White for the Payne Whitney mansion."

"Playing fast and loose with the club's money?"

"Of course not—Mrs. Whitney happened to see it when it came in and decided she wanted it. I just made a note of it. She and Miss Morgan took care of the sale. Miss Morgan's the club treasurer . . ."

George flicked her cheek. "I was teasing you."

"Oh."

"So what can I do for you?"

"I'm not sure, but Mrs. Harriman gave me tickets to a talk last night where this architect, Mr. Almirall, talked about building a new sanitarium."

"Sea View. I read about it in the paper."

"Oh. Well, I didn't think the location was ideal. I mean, it's lots of land so that is good, but the air is not the best, so I was wondering about air filtration. I mean, I know about charcoal masks for individuals, but is there a way to filter entire ventilation systems? I mean . . ." She paused to extract her hospital plan and unrolled it on a nearby workbench. "Could a charcoal 'mask' be placed over the entrance ducts to a building and have it vented to all the rooms? If you could do that for an entire building, you could have sanitariums right here in New York City."

George pulled a mechanical pencil from his shirt pocket and pointed to the design. "The easy answer is I don't know. I suppose you could take one of the new Carrier systems . . ."

They worked for a good half hour, heads together, and Nora thought about how she missed collaborating. She'd always dreamed of a place of her own, but with Elsie out of town, and having the new office all to herself, she missed the camaraderie of other architects and the secretaries, and . . . George to consult with.

He looked up. "What are you smiling at?"

Nora shrugged. "Just happy, I guess."

He laughed. "Me too. Somehow, things are just not the same without you poking around and asking questions."

"You're the one who said I should poke around and ask questions."

"Did I? Sometimes my brilliance surprises even me."

"I don't understand. Am I being annoying?"

"Not at all. You always have a unique perception of everything. Things seem a little monochromatic when you're not around."

Monochromatic? Did that mean he liked her a little?

CHAPTER 21

Nora was sitting in her office one morning, studying a bill for a black lacquered bedroom set Elsie had ordered from one of her many craftsmen. She reluctantly added it to the spindle that she would present to Miss Morgan the following day.

Each reckoning day, Nora would cringe while Miss Morgan looked over the receipts from the week. The cost of the interiors was skyrocketing. But each week the treasurer of the Colony Club took the bills with a smile and a thank-you and carried them away. Never once did she complain to Nora about the seemingly exorbitant expenses. Perhaps rich women never had to worry about expenses.

Nora reached for her sketchbook, hoping to get a few minutes to experiment with some design features of her apartment building, when the door flew open and Elsie burst into the room.

"I'm home!" Elsie looked radiant in a sleek fall coat. "Nora, how I've missed you." Elsie swept over to Nora, who was just rising from her chair, and took her by the shoulders to kiss the air near both of Nora's cheeks.

She hardly alit for a second before she slipped out of her coat and draped it over the one empty chair. Then she spun around in a swirl of teal-and-black silk. "Everything is so organized, and what's this?" She went over to the display crib Nora had asked George to requisition for her that now held watercolor and pen-and-ink renderings of the catalogued items.

Nora began to explain the function of the crib, but Elsie had already moved back to the door.

Surely she wasn't leaving already.

But she merely stepped into the hallway, motioned to some-one out of sight, and called, "Bring it in here for now. Careful, I didn't bring that all the way from Paris for you to destroy it in the halls of the Colony Club."

She stepped aside to let two beefy carters haul in a wooden crate that filled the entire corner of the room. They dropped it to the floor and left without a word, only to be replaced by another man carrying a stack of fabric swatches at least two feet high.

"I was going to have everything delivered directly to the ware-house. But I absolutely must see if these fabrics work. Come along. I'm dying to see what's happened since I've been gone."

"What's in the crate?" Nora asked.

"A veeery expensive wall painting from Zuber and Cie. I don't know quite where to put it, but it's wonderful. Tell me that they've finished at least some of the rooms."

"Yes," said Nora. "The first and most of the second floors have walls. The gymnasium and assembly room are finished except for the floors, which will go in last. They're working on the res-taurant floor now."

"Excellent." Elsie took a deep breath as if she were breathing in country air. "It's so good to be back. When I'm in France I feel like I never want to leave, then I come here and feel just the same way. And you can't know how freeing it is not to have to go to the theater night after night." She smiled mischievously. "Except to watch Bessie's plays, of course. She's very excited about this new one. *Peter Pan*. I'm sure it will be a success, Bessie is always successful. But so shall we be. Are you ready?"

Elsie reached for her coat. Nora snatched a sketchbook from the stack on the worktable, stuffed several mechanical pencils, a straightedge, and gum eraser into her skirt pocket, and decided against wearing her coat. Best just to be a working architect in a shirtwaist and skirt than to look like a pauper in a hand-me-down coat.

Elsie was already at the door, but she threw a look over her shoulder. "Bring those samples with you."

Nora scooped up the stack of fabric squares, staggered under the weight, then hurried after her.

When they reached the site, Elsie stood frowning at the heavy temporary door. "When will they put in the real door?"

"Finished windows and doors will go in once the major construction is complete."

"We're only a year away from the opening."

"They'll be installed in time," Nora assured her. Since Elsie hadn't moved, Nora shifted the stack of samples to one arm and shouldered the door open. Elsie swept inside.

Mr. Wojcik and George appeared from the back of the space and hurried forward to greet Elsie. The other men working in the area stopped to watch.

Like bees to honey, Nora thought as Elsie waited regally for her minions to bow before her. Nora shook herself. No use being mad at Elsie because she was so attractive to men.

Nora risked a glance at George but he was totally enchanted; even Mr. Wojcik had a goofy smile on his face and he was probably fifty. He should know better.

Elsie let them fawn for a couple of minutes, then started down the hall, followed by her entourage of two, followed by Nora balancing her notebook and the stack of samples in one arm while she fished her pencil from her pocket.

Elsie stopped suddenly. "Green over there, and Wedgwood blue for the walls, Nora."

Nora was looking around for a place to put her stack when it was lifted from her arms.

"Looks like you need an assistant," George said.

Nora started, flushed that she'd been having mean thoughts

about him when here he was being nice. It was kind of annoying and kind of sweet.

"The one on the top, Nora."

Nora snatched the top swatch. And found a wall to hold it up to while she waited for Elsie's decision.

Elsie cocked her head one way, then the other. "Maybe. I'll know better when the real lights are installed."

She turned and resumed her journey, which Nora expected was to the trellis room.

Nora tried to take the stack of samples from George but he held on. "You take notes, I'll hold the goods." He gave her such an understanding, amused smile that her stomach did a little flip-flop.

Fortunately the trellis walls were finished, the columns were clad, and Nora caught a glimpse of the water pipes at the far end.

"The fountain fits perfectly," Nora said, cutting off any potential changes that Elsie might have in mind.

"Yes," Elsie said dreamily. She looked around the room, saying nothing, but seeing whatever she saw. And Nora took that as a good sign.

They were taken upstairs where they peeked into the gymnasium, and then stepped into the assembly room.

"Oh, that reminds me," Elsie said, looking up at the ceiling high above their heads. "I need you to go to Cooper Union and copy the chandelier in their assembly room. I'm going to adapt it to our assembly hall. It will be perfect with a few tweaks. Now, who can I get to cast . . ." She wandered away; Nora followed, scribbling in her notebook as she walked.

Several stops and sample comparisons later, the men's adoration had changed into impatience. Mr. Wojcik was the first to excuse himself, and hurried back to work. Which left George. Nora took pity on him and suggested they return to the office and discuss what they had planned from seeing the rooms.

Elsie was amenable, so Nora took her stack of samples and swatches back and George walked them to the exit.

"Thank you," Nora said.

"Anytime," said George and closed the door behind her.

NORA SPENT THE next few weeks traveling from her office to the warehouse, from Cooper Union to the bronze caster, artists, and craftsmen, and working with Elsie on the interior presentation renderings to be shown at the first club meeting after the New Year.

The weather grew colder as fall slipped into winter. The temporary club site was constantly in use. Dinners, lectures, concerts, afternoon teas. Nora could understand the ladies' impatience for the new clubhouse. They were quickly outgrowing the assembly room, and someone was always complaining about not having a restaurant on-site.

But they soon would, Nora wanted to remind them. Of course, she would never volunteer an opinion, since they were already pressing her for information, trying to sneak peeks at the drawings, and feeling free to give advice about works in progress.

Several times Mr. White joined them to confer with Elsie and advise Nora, and though he often had to sit during their sessions as his hip was giving him problems, Nora flourished under his supervision.

By December, they had put together four of the major rooms, Nora and Mr. White doing the watercolors, Elsie describing what would go where and pulling samples of wallpaper and swatches of fabric to accompany each painting.

It was all quite beautiful, Nora thought, though she'd never seen decor put together in such a way except in the Irving Place house.

She liked it. The whole color scheme and the lightness of it made her smile. She just hoped it had the same effect on the ladies. The trellis room looked like a wonderful summer garden. All the rooms so far were beautiful in their simplicity.

Nora was surprised and pleased when she was presented with an extra paycheck from the Colony Club for her added duties. If she continued to work for them like this through the next year when the club opened, she should be able to move her mother and Rina into an apartment.

Christmas was approaching, and for the first time in her life Nora had so many people she wanted to give presents to that she knew she couldn't afford them all. So she decided to draw something special for each one. Every night after her work was finished for the club, she sat at her worktable and drew illustrations of the club, or portraits, or just funny little scenes, then affixed them to cardboard cards, writing *Happy Holidays* and the name of each recipient in her best hand.

The Friday before Christmas, Higgie declared an early day to celebrate the season before they all parted until the following week. Nora stopped by Mrs. Tova's, who had promised to save some raspberry sponge roll for Nora to take to a party with the secretaries. In return, Nora gave Mrs. Tova a picture of the café's exterior.

No one was in the business office, but she could hear laughter from the lunchroom and she hurried to join her friends. She found them wearing festive paper crowns, sitting around the table laden with sweets and a bottle of cider.

"We were about to give you up," said Sadie.

Nora added her sponge roll to the other sweets and accepted a paper crown from Lavinia. They toasted the season and each other and all felt a bit giddy though the cider wasn't hard. It was their joy in each other, Nora decided.

They gorged on all the sweets, and laughed and made extravagant wishes for presents, then opened the little gifts they had made for each other. Higgie had crocheted fobs for their watches. Sadie had embroidered each a handkerchief with their initials. And Lavinia had written out a recipe for skin cream on festive cards that she decorated with yarn. Nora had drawn pen-and-ink portraits of each and backed them with cardboard. They all exclaimed how like they were.

"If you could have anything, anything at all, what would it be?" Sadie prompted.

"A million dollars," Lavinia volunteered. "So I wouldn't have to work. Though I like working here with all of you."

"What about you, Nora?"

"A house, a really nice house."

"That's an odd thing," said Sadie. "Coming from an architect. You can build one. Now, me, I want a handsome, rich husband."

"Surprise, surprise," Lavinia said.

Higgie glanced at the wall clock and grabbed her coat. "I'm sorry," she said. "I have to go."

"But it's still early and there's more cider." Sadie held up the bottle.

"Sorry."

The other three looked at her.

"Oh, oh, oh," said Sadie. "Don't tell me, you have a date to-night?"

"Maybe," Higgie said. "I really have to go. Merry Christmas. Merry, merry Christmas." She shrugged into her coat, patted her hair, and hurried out the door, leaving the other three staring after her.

"Wow," said Lavinia. "She's never run out like that before."

Sadie frowned, her brows knitting together. "I wonder . . . what if she does have a date?" She made a beeline for the window that overlooked the street.

It took only a second for Nora and Lavinia to follow her. They all peered down to the sidewalk below. A minute later they saw Higgie step out the office door. They all pressed their noses closer to the pane, but Higgie just turned to the left and hurried away, like she did every night to catch the corner trolley going downtown.

"I guess we'll never know," Lavinia said.

"It's probably nothing," Sadie added. "Wishful thinking."

They lingered a few minutes longer, then Nora offered to stay and clean up. After hugs and wishes for a happy Christmas, Sadie and Lavinia left. Nora sat down. She was in no hurry to get back to her room at the Parker. Her roommates weren't leaving until tomorrow for their two days off. She sighed, crumpled up the wrappings, tossed them in the trash, and finally put on her coat and went downstairs.

George was leaning against the wall next to the door, but he saw her and straightened up. "Mrs. Tova said you would be here with the secretaries. And I just saw Miss Higgins leave, then the other two. They said you were still upstairs. Do you mind that I waited?"

Nora shook her head. She'd made something for George; it was in her coat pocket, but she had already decided not to give it to him. "Is something wrong?"

"No. I just wanted to say goodbye."

"Goodbye?" Nora took a step back, alarmed. "Are you leaving?"

"Just until the New Year. I'm visiting my parents for the holidays. It's been several years since I've seen them. They put their collective feet down this year."

It occurred to Nora that just like with the secretaries, she didn't know anything about him, outside of his work. "Do they live far?"

"Just Westchester."

Nora shook her head. She supposed everyone knew about places that she'd never heard of.

"It's an hour away by train. Listen. There's Christmas music in Madison Square. I thought maybe you'd like to walk over and hear a bit . . . if you're not in a hurry," he added.

Nora shook her head. "I'm not."

It was only a few blocks to the square. Nora could hear the oompah-pah of the music when they were still a block away.

They stopped at the park entrance, where peddlers and food vendors crowded the sidewalk. The smell of fresh-cut evergreens filled the air around them. George bought them pretzels and they strolled beneath the trees, oblivious to the cold, standing close to ward off the wind that occasionally whipped past them. They passed another cluster of holiday vendors, and on impulse George bought a red woolen scarf.

Nora was surprised when he lifted it over her head. "So I can always see you coming." He laughed and tied it around her neck. They continued on their way, Nora suddenly feeling a warmth that she suspected had more to do with George than her new scarf.

The little memento she'd made for him was nestled in her coat pocket, but she couldn't decide whether to give it to him or not. It seemed so forward and yet didn't he deserve to know how much she appreciated him, along with Mrs. Tova and the secretaries?

"What would you do if you could do anything in the world?"

His question caught her off guard even though she'd been sharing her thoughts with the secretaries just a few minutes before.

"What I'm doing now, only I would do it faster."

George laughed. She'd never known someone who laughed so easily. "How could you go any faster? The men on-site are amazed at your energy . . . I am, too."

"I'm saving to get a place where my mother and younger sister and I can live together." She clamped down on the end of that sentence. What had possessed her to tell him that? No one wanted to hear hardship stories. And she certainly didn't want anyone, especially George, knowing how she really lived.

"Where do they live now, if I may ask?"

"In Brooklyn with my older sister. She needs help with her growing family."

"Ah," said George in a way that made her afraid he could see behind the words of her answer.

"What would you do?" she asked.

"Well, one day I want to have my own architectural firm. Build modern buildings. With emphasis put on function as well as on aesthetic . . . Well, you've seen some of my designs in my office."

She nodded. "When do you think you'll do it?"

"Once I've built enough of a reputation and have a few potential clients lined up. I'm not going to be one of those people who goes off on his own too soon only to have to come back and start all over again."

Somewhere during that explanation, he'd slipped her hand through his elbow. "You must be freezing. And I'm a cad for keeping you out so long. Besides, the band has stopped playing."

Nora looked up and listened. He was right. She hadn't even noticed. They began walking back to the street.

"Which way is home?"

"What?"

"I'll walk you home. Which way do we go?"

"Oh, no, that isn't necessary. I'll take the trolley across town. Look. There's one coming now."

"Then I'll accompany you."

"No—thank you."

The trolley clanged to a stop. "Thank you for my scarf. Thank you for helping me to see new things." She pulled away, slipped the packet from her pocket, and shoved it into his hands. "Merry Christmas."

She turned to go, but he pulled her back, planted a quick kiss on her cheek, and lifted her up the trolley steps. "Merry Christmas!"

She turned for a last look as the trolley pulled away. His head was bent. He was opening her present right there on the sidewalk.

Since Christmas Eve fell on a Sunday that year, Louise had decided that their regular Sunday dinner would suffice for a family get-together. So that morning, Nora packed up her few gifts plus a jar of Mama's favorite pickles and a loaf of rye bread, tied her new red scarf around her neck for courage, and caught the trolley to the bridge.

All the night before, as she lay in bed, Nora had tried to remember the moment George had kissed her cheek. But the memory quickly faded into sleep and this morning as the trolley rattled over the bridge to Brooklyn, it disappeared altogether.

Swallowing down a sense of dread of what might wait inside, Nora rang the doorbell. Rina answered, but not with her usual enthusiasm. Whether happy or sad, Rina was always full of vitality, but today, she just looked petulant.

The baby was wailing from another room, and Rina turned and hurried away, leaving Nora to make her way inside.

She stepped into the parlor, where Little Don was running around yelling at the top of his lungs, while Donner sat with his newspaper in his regular chair. Nora went straight to the kitchen to deliver the bread and pickles to Mama, who was bent over a roast turkey. It didn't look large enough to feed all of them, and Nora wished she hadn't come.

Mama saw Nora and hurried toward her, arms open for a hug. Nora could feel the bones in Mama's back; she was working too hard. Not eating enough. She looked drawn, but Nora smiled and blinked away tears.

"Nora, I've missed you. Merry Christmas."

"You too, Mama," Nora managed to whisper past a searing throat.

Even though she loved Mama's cooking, she ate just enough to be polite. Saving the rest for everyone else. Nora was still sending money to Louise every month. There was no reason for this stinginess.

After dinner, Donner didn't even make an attempt to join in the festivities, just plucked his jacket off a peg—Nora noticed that his jacket looked new—and left the house. The rest of them opened presents, while Little Don sat in Mama's lap sucking his thumb and Louise scowled.

To her discredit, Nora couldn't wait to get away. She couldn't stand to see Mama and Rina living this way when Louise had promised Papa to take care of them . . . Mama was little more than a servant and Rina was eclipsing from lack of attention. Nora had to figure out how to get them away.

She left as soon as she could; Rina followed her to the door.

"Why won't you let me live with you?" she hissed through clenched teeth. "You don't know what it's like. Haven't you made enough money to get us out yet? Mama is wasting away, I have no friends. I couldn't bring them to the house if I did. Mama and I have to share our room with both children. I can't even go anywhere because Mama needs me to help out here. I'd be better off working at the factory."

"You're not going to work until you finish school. And that's final. You promised Papa."

"Well, you promised to take care of us and I never even see you."

"Just a little longer, I promise. Please, just be patient."

"I'm tired of being patient." She pulled away and ran back into the house. The memory of the look she shot Nora before she slipped back inside lasted a lot longer than the memory of George's kiss.

CHAPTER 22

New Year's Eve, 1905
Manhattan

"Happy New Year!" Elsie raised her glass to the friends and admirers who flocked around her: her old theater chums, her new patrons from the Fifth Avenue set. She'd chosen Rector's for her celebration because it brought both facets of her life together. Always popular with the Broadway set, Rector's had a taste of the Plaza about it, only with more drama—and more lobster.

As for herself, she was decked out in a Paris confection she'd been saving for the New Year celebration, the new era of Elsie de Wolfe. Expensive enough to turn old-money heads with just enough flash to excite the literary and theater set.

Her guests mingled shoulder to shoulder with those they might not otherwise ever behold. And from what she could see, they were all making quite a go of it.

Tonight was *her* triumph. Elsie the indestructible. She'd left a successful theater career for an even more challenging and fulfilling profession. So what if that headline was only surface deep? She had at least had the good sense to get out before the decline, unlike poor Delilah Gamlen, who stood a few feet away, clinging to a painfully small group of admirers.

Elsie wondered if they noticed that Del had been putting on weight and her makeup was applied a little too thickly. The observation didn't give Elsie a rush of glee, but a profound sadness mixed with overwhelming relief. And she praised the gods—and Bessie—for giving her this second chance.

Dear Bessie. Everything she touched seemed to turn to gold. Good reviews, box office sales, extended performances. She was standing across the room, with Anne, of course, and Charles Frohman, probably hatching a new hit play over champagne and chocolates.

But tonight it was Elsie who was on the top of the world. She'd found what she was really good at. Thanks in part to Bessie.

She caught Bessie's eye and smiled. Bessie excused herself and started over, followed by Anne. Tonight Elsie didn't even begrudge Anne or the amount of Bessie's attention she demanded.

It had been touch-and-go at first, culminating when the two of them had hied off to Anne's country estate the day after Christmas. Though Elsie could hardly believe that J. P. would allow Bessie in the door, some sort of armistice must have been struck between the two power brokers of Anne's future.

Left behind, Elsie might have languished, but fortunately, within the hour, she was back at work at her Colony Club, going over the final designs they would be presenting within the week to the decoration committee.

The renderings were spectacular. Just as she saw them in her head. Of course, to give credit where credit was due, Stanny and Nora, her hardworking assistant, had done the actual paintings, but the ideas were all Elsie's. Stanny hadn't even made suggestions. She'd invited him for dinner tonight but as usual he was already engaged. Which probably meant he was out carousing with the reprobates he seemed to prefer these days. Which was doing him no good, either for his health or his reputation. By all accounts, they were a predatory bunch. Even though they were discreet, word had a way of getting out. Elsie only hoped that none of it was true.

Bessie and Anne finally made their way to her through the crowd.

Bessie leaned closer to be heard. "You look radiant, my dear."

"Oh, Bessie, I feel like I've finally found my milieu. I've received so many offers to decorate homes that I've had cards made up."

"You'll need to get a proper office soon," Bessie said. "And a showroom where you can highlight the artists and antique dealers you already have at your fingertips."

"Yes," Elsie said. "I'll be a great success."

"Not just a success, my dear. You'll be the mother of American interior design."

NORA STOOD IN the assembly room before the first club meeting of the new year, perusing the five presentation pieces, double-checking that the proper sample swatches and detail drawings were placed by each selection.

Working with Elsie and being so directly involved in the process of furnishing rooms, Nora had gained a new perspective about the work. Rather than frivolous and lightweight, she saw it as a synthesis of form and function. Pleasing to the eye and inviting to the body. As a building of any kind should be.

And as much as she had resented it at the time, she had to admit that the experience had been an excellent opportunity to understand aspects of architecture that she would have missed in the drafting room. Exactly what George told her would happen.

She wouldn't be part of the presentation this morning. Still, she had dressed in her tidiest working attire. She'd briefly considered wearing her best dress, but she didn't want anyone to think she was trying to rise above her station as a hired architect. But what was her station? Mrs. Harriman had said they were all professionals. Though Mrs. Harriman didn't have to work for a living. Bessie did, Elsie did; actually many of the single ladies did.

They all treated Mr. White like he was one of them. And she supposed he was. They even showed deference to George, though perhaps he, too, came from a rich family. There was a lot she didn't know about the workings of society, even after almost a year of working among them. She just knew that she would never be one of them. Which didn't really matter. Her profession would define her existence.

And that was fine. Because she was an architect.

"Nora, what on earth are you doing standing there with your head in the clouds?"

Nora jumped at Elsie's voice. Her head *had* been in the clouds.

"I was just taking a last look."

"They look divine. I hope Stanny uses you for all his projects."

Nora smiled. Working for Mr. White would mean financial security. And yet . . . *Patience*, she reminded herself.

Voices sounded from the hall.

"They're coming," Nora said superfluously.

Elsie consulted her watch. "They're early."

As she said the words, Bessie and Mrs. Harriman walked into the room. Nora moved to the side to make a quick departure.

"Nora," Daisy said. "How was your Christmas?"

"Very nice, thank you." If you looked past the mess she'd had to clean up from her roommates and the depressing day she'd spent in Brooklyn, she'd had a whole day to incorporate her newly discovered ideas into her own designs.

"I hope Elsie and Stanford gave you a few days off."

"Heaven forbid," Elsie said. "We live for the work, don't we, Nora?"

"We do." Nora could attest to that fullheartedly. The work, for her, at least, was everything.

"Well, it certainly looks like you've been busy," Mrs. Harriman said, indicating the row of easels.

They were interrupted by the arrival of several other ladies, members of the decorating committee, the twelve women who would bestow their judgment today.

Nora started to slip away.

"Aren't you staying?" Mrs. Harriman asked.

Nora glanced at Elsie. She hadn't mentioned to Nora that she would be needed.

"That's not necessary," Elsie said. "You've been working all morning. Have a cup of tea."

Not necessary . . . Not that Nora wanted to stay for the meeting. She wasn't really comfortable around the ladies. Even though most of them were perfectly nice and she did want to hear their opinions. And she would.

She said goodbye and passed several other ladies entering the room. When she was certain all had arrived, she took her notebook and pencil, just in case anyone had a suggestion, and slipped up the narrow stairs to the musicians' gallery to listen in.

She sat in the chair she'd pulled over near the rail and peeked quickly over the edge to see Bessie at the front of the room and the backs of twelve heads. Then she leaned back where she couldn't be seen from below. Heard Bessie call the meeting to order. Then Elsie's brief introduction, and then the first picture. "This is what I call the trellis room. As you can see . . ."

"What on earth is a trellis doing all over the walls?" asked one lady, clearly upset. They weren't even giving Elsie a chance to explain things.

"It will be relaxing to have your tea and conversation in a surrounding that is *like* a garden. From the fountain to the tiles, to these tables and wonderful octagon-backed chairs."

"But tearooms are always—"

The rest of her sentence was cut off as other voices rose to give their opinions.

Nora gave up trying not to be seen. She peered over the railing.

Elsie looked small and gossamer standing alone in front of this formidable group. Nora wished she'd insisted on staying to lend her support.

"Ladies!" Bessie banged the gavel on the table. The ladies subsided. "Let us listen and learn before espousing our own opinions."

"I've been overseeing the decor of my home for nearly four decades, and I think I know what a room should look like."

Nora couldn't tell who had spoken. A large-brimmed black hat with feathers and some kind of bird with its wings spread covered the speaker's face.

Nora stared at Elsie, trying to tell her to stand firm, but she needn't have bothered.

Elsie just smiled graciously at her audience.

Mrs. Harriman hadn't said a word throughout the exchange. Nora scooted over to get a look at her face. Like always, her expression was thoughtful and benign and didn't give anything away. But Nora wondered what she was thinking. If she was suddenly worried that they'd chosen the wrong decorator.

They hadn't, and Nora longed to go down and convince them of that. She'd started out just like them, questioning Elsie's abilities. Her ideas had been odd and unusual then, but they made perfect sense now.

Elsie patiently waited for the ladies to subside, then said, "I have no doubt that we all have ideas about how a club should look. But think about it for a moment. Do you want just another men's club? Brown chairs, brown wainscoting, brown carpeting. Why, I can almost smell the stale cigars."

Someone tittered.

Another said, "Never in our club."

"You're thinking that trellises are just strips of wood, forming a plain lattice as any garden walk would have. But the French take these same strips and follow all sorts of beautiful patterns with such skill, they were an inspiration for this room. If you'll look closer . . ." The row of women leaned forward; several got up to peruse the sketch at arm's length.

"On days like this . . ." Elsie continued, "when the weather is cold and the wind is raging, you step into the club, take off your outerwear, and voila! You're in the trellis room, a winter garden. Warm and bright and comfortable, where you can sit alone with a good book or chat with friends."

Slowly, curiosity began to overtake skepticism.

Elsie moved on to the rendering of the guest rooms, each furnished with a simple four-poster bed with side table and lamp, a small chaise longue, and a dressing table with a mirror. Elsie had barely begun to describe it when the opinions began again.

Nora sighed. It was going to be a long morning at this rate.

"It's too plain. Barely more than a servant's room. The bed is plain, the dressing table is plain."

"Bedrooms should be lush and feminine," another lady agreed.

"Feminine?" asked Elsie. "When a woman reaches her hotel after a day's journey by train or motorcar, what does she want most?"

"A cocktail," called out one of the ladies.

That did get some laughter.

"True, but as to her room, I do not believe that she cares one iota whether or not her bed is of gilded wood with cupids perched on the four corners, or if the drapes fall in classic folds from ceiling to floor. Or if the painting of an Old Master hangs on the wall. What she wants first of all is a good bath, which is right through this connecting door." She made a graceful gesture to the far side of the rendering at the outline of a door. "And a comfortable chair or chaise where she can put her feet up for a few minutes before going out again. Ribbons and tassels and paintings by Grand Masters don't add to our comfort."

"But what are those pear-shaped things over the dressing table?"

"Lights," said Elsie. "How many times have you tried to dress for the evening and you can barely find your earlobes for lack of lighting? It comes, I'm sorry to say, from men doing the decor.

These lights will shine right where you need them for dressing your hair and face. No more hit-and-miss in the dark."

"I've said that for years," said Mrs. Perkins. "Bully for you, Elsie. I like it."

Nora sat spellbound as Elsie wove her web and drew them in.

"And when we dress to go out, or the next morning, the lights can be properly arranged so that we can sit at the table and get some idea of how we're going to look when we face our friends and society.

"Ceiling lights and lamps halfway across the room can't tell a woman where a dab of powder should go, or if her coiffure needs a little attention. What is the signature of an Old Master in comparison to that?"

Nods and murmurs. Elsie would have them eating out of her hand like seals at the zoo before she was finished.

"The sufferings women have endured from this form of martyrdom would fill volumes and have gone on too long."

"Hooray," yelled Sarah Hewitt.

Elsie bowed slightly in acknowledgment. "Too long our homes have been designed without our comfort in mind. The Colony Club will change that. A new look, for a new age."

Applause. A couple of the women shook their heads, but the room was Elsie's.

"I assure you, you will have a club that caters to your comfort and your needs, leaving you free to participate in endeavors that interest you."

Elsie executed another practiced nod. Nora wouldn't have been surprised if she'd fallen into a full-blown curtsy. The room erupted in polite, but enthusiastic, applause.

The motion to accept was voted on and passed and Nora took the opportunity to sneak back to her office, where she waited just inside the door to listen as they all gathered their coats and left.

Then waited impatiently for Elsie to return, which she did a few minutes later, with a relieved, "Whew," as she closed the door and leaned against it.

"You were splendid," Nora said in a gush of admiration.

"You heard?"

"I was in the musicians' gallery."

"Je pense que c'est le succés brilliante!"

Nora concurred. Higgie's French lessons must have been paying off, because she understood completely.

"I thought that lady in the bird hat was going to fight you."

"I knew she'd come around."

"How?"

"I'll tell you a secret. One that every good actress, salesman, or politician knows. Instead of giving people what they think they want, give them what they ought to have, and teach them to want it."

Nora blinked, then recited Elsie's words in her head so that she wouldn't forget them.

"Don't look so serious, my dear. I was an ugly child born in an ugly age."

"But you're beautiful," Nora protested.

"Changing myself was a great accomplishment. I project beauty and therefore am seen as such. But changing this age in which we live, there is a real challenge." She trilled a laugh. "They've been living with this oppressive Victorian idea of decor and decorum for so long, they think they're experts on everything. It's just never occurred to them there might be something better.

"In that world, they *are* experts. And afraid of anything different or new. But things will change. They will change. And I will be the one who changes them."

CHAPTER 23

April 18, 1963
Washington, D.C.

"It had taken us so long to get started, now we were terribly anxious to have it finished.

"With the designs agreed on, Elsie left early that spring for one final buying trip before taking her usual summer vacation at Trianon. She'd long ago overspent her budget. But we were feeling generous and excited and spared her no expense. And from the renderings we'd seen, I knew it was going to be exactly what she had envisioned.

"By the time I left for Newport that summer, the construction was pretty much completed. The windows had been installed as well as the doors. The floors were laid in the late spring and covered with heavy canvas tarps until the finishing touches were applied and it was time to move in the furniture.

"We had engaged a housekeeper from London and she was due to arrive in the fall to take charge of housekeeping and hiring additional staff. Mr. Wheatland, from the University Club, had agreed to be our superintendent.

"Bessie designed the club's coat of arms and Elsie sent back a score of blue-and-buff staff uniforms to reflect its colors.

"We had cupboards filled with monogrammed linens ready for the restaurant and guest rooms, and with Nora

*overseeing the delivery and storage of decor, I had no
qualms about the club being able to open its doors in late
fall. A dream would finally be realized, a club for women
to nourish great ideas, embrace educational advances, and
support social movements. It would be grand.*

"And then in June, the unthinkable happened."

June 1906

"Murder!" Nora heard the newsboy's strident cry as she hurried down the street to work. The morning sun was already hot and she was perspiring, but she couldn't slow down. She was running late. The newsboy's cries grew louder. It must be something important to raise such an outcry.

It wasn't until she neared the corner that she began to make out the rest of the words. "Famous architect dead! Thaw kills White at the theater. Get your papers here! Stanford White murdered!"

Nora jolted to a stop. That wasn't right. It couldn't be. She began to run toward the young boy and his stack of papers, blindly groping in her pockets for a nickel. Managed to come up with a coin of some kind; thrust it at the newsboy and yanked a copy of the *New-York Tribune* from him. Then hurried over to prop herself against the wall to read words she refused to believe.

*Shoots Him at Madison Square Roof Garden Opening—
Architect Dies Instantly. Slayer's Wife Sees the Tragedy.*

The words blurred before her. Nora wiped her sleeve across her eyes. "Stanford White, the well known architect, a member of the firm McKim, Mead & White, was murdered last night by Harry K. Thaw, of Pittsburg, member of the well known family. . . . White died almost instantly."

Nora shook her head. This was a mistake. It must be a mistake. He couldn't be dead. It must be a different Stanford White. ". . . one thousand persons present, and a panic followed the shooting. . . ." Nora's teeth began to chatter in spite of the heat. "Thaw was as cool as though nothing. . . . . he blamed White for ruining his domestic life and being the cause of his unhappiness with his wife, who before her marriage was the well known artists' model and chorus girl, Evelyn Nesbit. . . . A white sheet was placed over the body. . . ."

It couldn't be true. Clutching the newspaper, Nora ran for the trolley stop, looked up the street, but there was no trolley in sight.

She couldn't wait; she stepped off the curb, a horse neighed in her ear, the carter yelled obscenities at her. She didn't stop, didn't even look, just crossed the street, at first walking, then running all the way to McKim, Mead, and White. Only, now White was gone.

Gone.

Nora arrived at the building with her hair flying and a stitch in her side. Then she saw the horde of people surrounding the entrance to the McKim, Mead, and White building.

The crowd was so thick she couldn't see the entrance. She took several deep breaths, then threw herself into the swarm of bodies, fighting her way to the front door. The doorman on the other side of the glass recognized her and opened the door just enough to let her slip through. The crowd of reporters immediately pressed back toward the door.

"There's hardly anyone up there, miss. The bank can't even open its doors. McKim called in this morning, said the firm was closed until further notice and to send everyone home."

"Is that all? Did he say when they were going to reopen? Isn't anyone here?"

"Mr. McKim said not to let anyone up. I sent the secretaries home, but some of the draftsmen had already arrived and they're still up there. But you'd best go home, miss. You don't want to get involved in that rowdy crowd out there. They're hungry for smut. And they'll do anything to get it. Go on home now."

How could she explain to him—this was home. "I have to— I'll only be a minute."

Nora ran to the elevator, past several bank employees who had collected in the foyer and were peering out at the crowd.

The ride to the fifth floor seemed interminable. When at last the door opened, she rushed out into an empty reception area. She stopped to listen but hearing no sound, she hurried to the drafting room and pushed the doors open.

A group of about ten men stood huddled together, talking in low voices. The first one to look up was Collin Nast. He was frowning. When he glanced her way, the frown turned to a scowl.

"What are you doing here?"

"I work here, remember?" Nora snapped back, her shock and horror turning to anger. She'd thought she would find answers here. How could her employer, her mentor, be dead? What could he possibly have done to deserve this? Some man named Thaw. She hadn't stopped to read the whole article she was still clutching to her chest.

She'd run here without thinking, as if her being at the office could make it all go away. She would find him sitting at his desk all rumpled from a night out on the town, his brilliant ideas just waiting to find their way through his still-drunken stupor to make the beautiful buildings he was famous for.

But looking at Nast's contorted face, she knew even if she went back to his office, he wouldn't be there. Stanford White was dead. He would never amaze them with a new design. The world would be a bleaker place.

And what were they to do without him? What would Nora do? The realization made her stagger back.

"Don't you dare faint," snarled Nast.

"I never faint." Skirting the group, she made her way back to her drafting table. *Her* drafting table. Without him, would they keep her on? She had just started several details for the Madison Square church apse for George. Surely they would need to be finished. And there was the Colony Club.

She barely glanced at the men. They had gone back to their mutterings like she'd never been there. And maybe to them, she never had.

The group broke up. One of the other men called out to her, "We're leaving—if you don't want to be locked in, you'd better come now." Several others were already walking toward the door. Nora quickly filled her pockets with the few things she hadn't moved to the Colony Club and, still clutching her newspaper, hurried after them. For a second she considered running to George's office to salvage his work, but surely he had a key and could get in later, when the curiosity seekers had dispersed.

Her skirts had barely cleared the doorway before Nast slammed the door shut and locked it, and Nora wondered vaguely why it was he who had the key. No one even liked him, certainly not George. She didn't know about the bosses.

She was rushed into the elevator and the first group rode down, where they waited in the lobby for the second group so they could all get out together. The bank employees had cleared out or gone into the bank. Only the architects were left.

Then the doorman unlocked the door and they pushed their way out.

Shouts for information rose up around them, the reporters pushing and shoving to get closer to the group. "Is it true that . . . ? What about Nesbit? Did White ever bring her here?"

Four of the draftsmen managed to break through the group, but they were pursued down the street by the reporters who hadn't managed to get a prime spot.

Their escape left an open view to several cameras set on tripods. Another few hand-held cameras hid the faces of the men who wielded them.

Nora was buffeted between two draftsmen. Behind her, Nast pushed them forward.

"What about White's private upstairs office? Is it true that he used it for clandestine activities? Did he bring Nesbit there? Any other women?"

"Why don't you ask her?" Nast's voice broke past Nora's ear and sliced into the crowd.

All eyes turned on Nora. Cameras went off as she stared in surprise.

"I work here!" she cried, but her voice was lost in the swell of questions and pushing and shoving.

"She's his 'personal' assistant!" Nast yelled.

"I am not." She got no further; the reporters surged forward and several more draftsmen took the opportunity to get away. Nora tried to follow, but she was pushed back as questions and insinuations were pelted at her.

"I just work here! I'm a draftsman just like the others," Nora cried. If they bothered to look at her, they would realize she was not the kind of woman who might interest any rich man. She was a lowly employee. But they were carried along on their own excitement.

And from somewhere, a distant police whistle shrilled through the pandemonium. The reporters ignored it as long as they could; Nora ducked her head and butted through the remaining newspapermen.

Then a hand clamped around her arm and snatched her from the crowd. Her feet flew out from under her and she fell forward. They were going to trample her or tear her limb from limb, and all she could do was clutch at her newspaper as her world spun out of control.

She was being held on her feet, guided down the sidewalk away from the noise.

She tried to wrench free but her head was spinning. The heat, the murder—Mr. White was dead. A sob escaped from deep inside her.

"It's all right. You're okay. Stop fighting me."

She stopped as his words made their way to her understanding. "George?"

"Yes, who did you think? Open your eyes."

She blinked against the sun. He was just a black shadow, then slowly he came into focus. "George!"

The sound of pounding feet behind them. A shrill whistle, this time not a policeman but a human whistle, and she was being trundled into a . . . taxi. One of the new motorcars. Before she could remonstrate, they were headed uptown, and she started to shake.

George pulled her closer. "What the hell happened out there?"

"Didn't you hear? Mr. White is—"

"Yes. I've been in a conference with the two partners since dawn. All they're interested in is avoiding a scandal. A little late for that."

George's voice sounded so bitter, so unlike him, that a chill ran down her spine.

"I didn't—It isn't true. The things Nast said—I have to get to work."

"I have to get to breakfast and so do you." A few minutes later, he hustled her into Mrs. Tova's café. It was crowded; George didn't stop but trundled her through the dining room and into the kitchen.

Mrs. Tova glanced up in surprise, took one look at them, and hurried them into a back room with a long rectangular table and two benches. "Where we workers eat. But it's quiet." And she disappeared.

George sat Nora down, wrestled the newspaper she still held in a death grip out of her hand, and placed it on the table.

"I don't understand." She touched the crumpled newspaper. Tried to smooth it so she could read, but the words swam before her eyes. "What's going to happen?" And she started to cry.

George sat down beside her and put his arm around her shoulders. "Nora. You have to stay strong. There are rough times ahead and it will take everything we have to get through it."

"Because Mr. White is dead?"

He sighed, his chest heaving against her shoulder. "Yes, but also because of what will come out because of it. It's complicated," he said before she could ask him more.

Mrs. Tova returned with a platter of eggs and toast and ham.

George scooted away from Nora.

Nora tried to smile her thanks, but the smell of the food was making her feel sick.

Mrs. Tova just nodded and left them to it.

George filled her plate.

"I can't."

"You don't have a choice. We'll all need all our strength in the days to come."

She picked up her fork. "Why?"

But even though she pressed him to explain, he refused to say more.

ELSIE CARRIED THE telegram out to the villa's terrace where Bessie was reading the script of her latest acquisition.

"Stanny's dead."

Bessie looked up, frowned against the sunlight. "What on earth are you saying?"

"Stanny's dead. Murdered." Elsie waved the telegram at Bessie. "That awful Harry Thaw shot him at the roof garden theater."

Bessie held out her hand; Elsie swept down the steps and across the paving stones to drop the telegram in her hand, before lowering herself onto a chaise. *Like Sarah Bernhardt*, she thought, and sat up. This was serious. It was real. Stanny was dead.

"Good God," said Bessie. "Accused of ruining Harry's wife? Thaw taken into custody." She lowered the telegram until it rested across her stomach. "This is madness."

"Sheer madness." Elsie sighed. "I mean, Evey was a pretty little thing, but certainly not worth dying for."

"Harry Thaw is off his rocker. His mother should have had him committed years ago." Bessie picked up the telegram again. Scowled at it. "Poor Stanny. I suppose I should send one of the servants down to the tobacconist's to get a copy of the international paper. Find out the full story." She shook her head. "Stanny, dead. And in such an ignominious fashion."

"It will be the talk of the town."

"Scandal of the season, at least. And if there's a trial . . ."

DAISY'S KNEES SIMPLY gave out beneath her when Bordie brought the paper from the city on Tuesday afternoon. She'd just returned home from watching a tennis match at the Newport Tennis Club and he was waiting for her in the parlor. She was surprised.

"You're here on a weekday and so soon," she said. "I'm delighted. I'd told the cook that I would be dining at the Belmonts'. Shall I—"

"Daisy, my dear. You haven't heard?"

"Heard what? Has something happened?"

"Stanford White was shot last night."

"Shot? I didn't know he hunted."

"Not a hunting accident. At the Madison Square Garden roof theater."

"I don't understand."

"Harry Thaw accused him of wrecking his marriage and shot him."

"That reprobate! Is he badly injured?"

"I'm afraid he's dead."

That was when her knees gave out. Fortunately there was a chair nearby.

Her first thought was for Stanford's wife. Her second was to ask what exactly had happened.

Bordie read directly from the paper he'd been holding. It was a horrible story; an unhinged Harry Thaw had approached Stanford's table during the intermission of *Mam'zelle Champagne*. "If it's any consolation, they say he died instantly. But, Daisy . . . there's bound to be a scandal."

Daisy nodded slightly. "Stanford wasn't known for his discretion, it's true."

"What I mean is . . ."

He didn't have to finish; the implications came to her in one fell swoop. "Oh, dear. Do you think I should go back to town? The clubhouse was near completion when we left, but there is still much to be done. Who is in charge now? Young George Douglas? Heaven only knows what has been dumped on his shoulders, poor man. And with Elsie in France. I wonder if she knows."

"If she doesn't, I'm sure she will soon," Bordie said. "You said the girl who is assisting her is a gem, so I wouldn't worry there, and I wouldn't rush back to the city. There's absolutely nothing you can do. Besides . . ." He hesitated, then added, "It might be best to let things blow over before jumping into the fray."

"Yes, of course. You're absolutely right. I'll telephone Nora tomorrow. There's a telephone at the assembly room office. Bessie insisted we install one. I'll tell Nora to carry on and let her know that the club will make sure that she's continued to be paid, since I'm not certain exactly where her paycheck has been coming from. If it's been directly from Stanford, well, things might be tied up for a while."

Bordie leaned over, took her hand, and kissed it. "My dear, you are the mistress of understatement."

CHAPTER 24

Nora spent the rest of the morning at the site, lost in a blur of sadness, confusion accented by shots of the searing pain of loss. Her mentor was gone. Killed by a madman, defiled by the newspapers, who said awful things about what he had done to a young woman. It broke her heart to hear him so maligned, someone who created such beauty.

What would happen to all the projects now? What would happen to all the draftsmen? And most importantly, what would happen to her?

And that was when she finally had to admit that what she was feeling was more than grief, or sadness. It was anger. She was angry, furious that he'd died. Deserted her. He'd been her promise of a future in architecture. She had no assumptions that McKim or Mead would keep her on. They didn't want her in the first place.

Later that afternoon, George gave her a key to the site. "I may not be around as much as I have been lately. Someone besides Mr. Wojcik should have a key. Since you're right next door, would you mind taking charge in case one of the delivery people needs to get in and Mr. Wojcik is not around? Keep it safe; don't loan it out. And don't let any of the ladies talk you into letting them take a peek. And make sure to lock up when you leave. Will you do that? We'll all have to be doing double duty until things calm down."

Nora took the key, wondered where she should keep it, then decided it would be safest in her extra-deep pockets. When she got back to her office she would pin it with one of the large safety pins they used to hold the samples together.

That night when she finally returned to her room, Lucy and Connie were both sitting on Lucy's bed, a newspaper spread out before them. Their heads snapped up, their expressions curious and much too eager for Nora's liking.

"Isn't this the guy you work for?" Lucy asked, holding up one edge of the paper.

Nora nodded.

"He's a pervert," said Connie.

Nora gritted her teeth. It was futile to try to defend Mr. White. She had read three different newspapers that day, and even the straitlaced ones like the *Times* printed enough for her to realize that Mr. White was a very immoral man.

"I just worked there," Nora said, feeling like a traitor.

"Did he ever try it on with you?"

Nora shook her head. She took her toothbrush and towel and went down the hall to get ready for bed. Hopefully they would have lost interest before she got back.

But even though she took her time, they were still sitting on the bed, poring over the article.

"You know," Lucy began, "a girl can't be too careful with her reputation."

"I know," Nora said.

"Are you going to quit?"

Not your business, thought Nora. "I'm working on a project."

"You should leave."

"I have to finish this project. Besides, he's dead; what harm can he do now?"

She climbed into bed and turned her back to them, squeezed her eyes shut, trying to ignore their insinuations. She had no idea what was to come.

NORA'S EYES WERE swollen shut the next morning; she must have been crying in her sleep. And she was bone-tired. She didn't get out of bed until Lucy and Connie left for work. Then she washed and dressed and went to McKim, Mead, and . . .

She took the Twenty-third Street trolley crosstown to Fifth Avenue, but when she stepped down to the sidewalk, she hesitated. Which way did she go? Should she walk down the two blocks to the drafting room? She had no reason to go there. She'd moved most of her things to the club office. They might not even be open for business yet. She missed Higgie, Sadie, and Lavinia, but she was too tired to make the trip just to find the office deserted.

Instead she turned left and cut through the park to Madison Avenue and the uptown trolley.

It was slightly cooler under the trees, the leaves rustling with an occasional breeze. But Nora wasn't thinking about the heat or the park; she was thinking of the buildings that surrounded it. The church, not yet completed. She might have gone in to say a prayer, if she knew what kind of prayer to say. She walked past without slowing down, heading for the northern corner, drawn like a moth to a flame, to one of his finest buildings—the scene of his death.

When she reached the corner of the square, she didn't cross the street, just looked up at the tower, the arches, the brickwork. His masterpiece, Madison Square Garden, where there on the flat roof that she couldn't see from where she stood, Harry Thaw had shot and killed him. It didn't seem real.

Several people were already there gawking, pointing at the roof and accusing him of all sorts of things. She wouldn't believe the things they were saying about him. He'd made the world more beautiful. She just didn't understand. She stood until the others moved away and the tears dried on her cheeks, then she crossed the street and took the trolley uptown to the Colony Club.

George wasn't there, but Mr. Wojcik was, and as soon as he

saw her, he pulled her aside. He held his finger up and reached over to an open newspaper, this time the *Evening Journal*, a gossipy, sordid rag. He shook it out, then folded it over. "Is this you?"

He pointed to a spot on the paper, a grainy photo of the draftsmen outside the doors of the Fifth Avenue building. And there in the middle was Nora. She pulled it from his grasp and saw the lede line. "Who is this mystery woman? Another victim of White's private quarters upstairs? Read all about it on page six."

She tried to open the newspaper but her hands were shaking too badly.

"Don't," Mr. Wojcik said. "It is all . . ." Lost for words, he spit on the tarp covering the hardwood floor. "But people will talk. Don't listen to them."

At that moment the door opened and George strode in. He, too, was holding the paper. "Oh," he said, drawing up sharp. "I was hoping you hadn't seen it yet. Absolute garbage."

"What am I to do?" said Nora. "Can I make them take it back?"

"Best to just sit tight and ignore it. It will pass. No one reads this Hearst rag anyway."

"You and Mr. Wojcik do."

George heaved a sigh. "Some other news will take its place in a day or two and it will be forgotten. But your family . . ."

Nora gasped. "Donner reads the *Journal*. My sister's husband. My mother might see this." And Louise would have a fit.

"I need to warn them. But I can't, there's a shipment of bedroom lamps arriving today. Maybe they won't see it."

Neither George nor Mr. Wojcik looked convinced.

"How did this happen?" George asked.

"It was when we were all leaving yesterday morning. Nast pointed me out."

"Collin Nast?" George said. "Why didn't you tell me?"

"He's always horrible. I didn't think anything of it. I knew they took a photo but they were taking lots." She sank onto a nearby sawhorse. "Maybe they won't recognize me. What does the article say?"

"A 'bystander' said you were White's personal assistant and your name was Nora."

Nora covered her face with her hands. "Why would he do that? Why does he hate me? I've never done anything to him."

"You're a woman. That's enough for some pea-brained men. Plus you're better than he is."

"Where is he?" growled Mr. Wojcik. "I will teach him some manners."

"No!" Nora and George cried at once.

"Thank you, Mr. Wojcik, but I'm sure it will blow over, as George said."

"I think it's best if all of us just get back to work," George said. "If there are any repercussions, we'll deal with them in good time."

"If you're sure," Nora said, trying to feel a little more optimistic.

"You'll see. Now, don't you have a delivery to see to, and the electricians need to start on the wiring of the ballroom sconces. Before you know it, Miss de Wolfe will be back and ready to arrange the furniture. But for now, I have to get to the Payne Whitney site."

Nora had been so upset with the murder and her own problems that she hadn't noticed the circles under George's eyes, or the paleness of his skin. And she realized in a moment of clarity that he'd been working overtime for longer than just the last day. He'd been picking up the slack for Mr. White for a while now.

"Thank you, both of you," Nora said, trying to shower both men with heartfelt gratitude. They had both been so good to her, patient with her while she asked a million questions and demanded to be shown the smallest construction event.

She'd selfishly taken advantage of them in order to further her own desires and hadn't thought of anyone else. Hopefully

George was right and this blight of a photograph would be forgotten with the next headline. And promising herself she would be more considerate going forward, she walked down the avenue to begin her day.

The day went smoothly; a few ladies who happened to be in town met to play several rubbers of bridge and gossip about the "terrible news of Stanny's death." They greeted her with a smile. Evidently none of them read the *Journal*. For which Nora was thankful.

She returned to her room that evening thinking that perhaps George was right; already the evening papers were touting a new indiscretion by the famous architect.

But her brief respite of hope exploded when she found both roommates once again sitting on Lucy's bed, another newspaper spread out on the covers before them.

Nora didn't even have to guess what paper it was.

"Nora Bromley, your picture is in the paper," Lucy said.

"I saw. None of it—"

"Were you really his personal assistant?" Connie asked. "How could you?"

"I wasn't. I was just hired—"

"He paid you? I can't believe you would do such a thing."

"I drew architectural plans. I'm Elsie de Wolfe's assistant on a building project. I hardly ever saw him."

"Well, it says here that you were often called away to his private office, where he took young girls to have his way with them."

"I don't know anything about a private office. The only office I ever saw was in the hallway with everyone else's office."

Their looks said they didn't believe her. They also said they wanted to hear every lascivious detail.

"Sorry to disappoint, but you'll have to look elsewhere for your fallen woman."

"Hmph," said Connie. "Where there's smoke, there's fire."

Nora didn't deign to answer. Just grabbed her toothbrush and towel. Announced that she was taking a bath, though it was really too early for bed, and hurried down the hall to the bathroom. She took her time and there was more than one knock on the door asking if she was about done.

When she at last came back to the room, Lucy and Connie were gone. But they'd left the paper open to the same page they had been reading.

Nora hadn't been able to take a good look at the photograph, before Mr. Wojcik had taken the paper away and carried it with him when he climbed the stairs to the second floor.

She'd been afraid to stop at a newsstand on her way home, in case she was recognized.

She listened for any sounds of footsteps in the hallway, then went over to take a look. It was an ordinary photo, people leaving a workplace. Except that she was the only female in a sea of men. And she was in the center of the picture and her expression showed all the shock and sadness that she was feeling.

Only the prurient mind of a reporter could make it any more than it was. And he did. Beyond his "Who is this mystery woman?" he managed to cast aspersions on her reason for being there, whether she had been upstairs all night . . . even though Mr. White hadn't been. That should have stopped his pen right there. But he was just getting started. At first calling her petite and plainly dressed, hardly more than a child, he finished off with "just the kind of innocent the hedonistic White would love to spoil."

Nora's cheeks burned; so did her stomach. It made her sound stupid as well as immoral. "What did he teach her? Certainly not architecture." Why ask a stupid question if he was just going to answer it in the most malicious way? To sell papers, of course. People loved smut, didn't care if it was true or not. But she never thought she would ever be the subject of such evil intent.

She'd never even had a sweetheart. She'd been too busy fulfilling her promise to her family. What must George and Mr. Wojcik and all the others think of her? Even if they didn't believe it, just to have read those words . . . She'd never be able to look them in the eye again.

Please, please let this be the only paper to print such lies. And please let it be over by tomorrow.

The next morning, she breathed a sigh of relief when she saw photos of Evelyn Nesbit, the actress whose husband had shot Mr. White, plastered across all the front pages. Wondering if they'd said the same awful things about her, Nora bought a copy of the *Journal* and one of the *Tribune*.

The news seller didn't even look at her twice. That was a good sign.

She took the trolley to the Colony Club office. Locked the door behind her and opened the *Journal*. It wasn't over after all. She'd merely been moved to the second page, her face cut out of the group photo and set in a line with several other potential "companions" of Stanford White, most of whom were chorus girls or artists' models.

She picked up the *Tribune*. Took a minute to look at the poor girl who was today's headlines. *Evelyn Nesbit.* Small, with dark hair and a pale complexion, she didn't look much older than Nora. But she did look a bit like her.

For a second Nora could only stare. The similarities were too close to be comfortable. But Evelyn was beautiful; Nora wasn't. Only her mother ever told her she was. Still, people might think— Well, she couldn't help what people might think. She quickly folded the paper, folded it again, and crushed it into a ball before throwing it in the wastepaper basket. Took it out again and tore it into strips until there was nothing recognizable about it.

She knew it wouldn't change anything. She could tear every paper printed into strips and it wouldn't erase the disgust she

felt. Since her first day at McKim, Mead, and White, she'd refused to listen to the comments the men had said about her or
even about Mr. White. Now she was learning they might be true
about him, but not about her, though not everyone would believe her. *Where there's smoke, there's fire.*

Well, she didn't care what everyone thought. She would
just keep working and not let it bother her. Hadn't George said
it would blow over when another scandal took its place? But it
would still be there, just below the surface, ready to erupt. People would judge her, no matter what she said or did.

And her friends?

Did she have any? Certainly not her roommates; they had already decided.

Sadie, Lavinia, and Higgie? If she did have friends, it was
the three secretaries. But she hadn't seen them since before
Mr. White had been killed. What were they thinking? She
couldn't even find out. They were friends at the office, but they
never talked about their home lives much, and she didn't know
where any of them lived.

The ladies of the club? They would never be her friends, but
they had always been congenial, friendly. They would reject her
now, even though none of it was true. It wouldn't matter whether
they believed it or not. It would hurt their reputation to be associated with anyone associated with Stanford White. Reputation
was everything for most of them. It hadn't taken long for Nora
to figure that out.

What if they fired her? Would she still be paid for her work
there?

Bile rose in her throat; she swallowed it. She wasn't hungry
but she couldn't remember the last time she'd eaten. She would
go by the office on her way home. If the girls were there, she
could at least try to explain.

The last delivery arrived just after six. She checked the contents. Two heavy rolls of Oriental carpets. Too late to send them to the warehouse, and the back room was filled to capacity. So she left them leaning against the office wall, crowding the space with several other bolts of fabric too delicate for the warehouse.

Nora couldn't help but take it as a bad omen, as if she was gradually being pushed out of her last refuge.

She'd deliberated all day about going out to Brooklyn immediately to stave off any bad news, or to wait until Sunday dinner and hope that it had "blown over," as George said it would. Or that they had never seen the photo at all.

But if they had . . . she needed to explain it right away before Louise blew it out of proportion and added it to her bag of complaints about Nora.

As soon as she finished work, she knew she couldn't put off the inevitable any longer. Her trip to see the secretaries would have to wait. She took the trolley to Brooklyn.

It was the longest trip of her life, jostled and shoved by riders all anxious to get home. The ride seemed interminable and yet Nora found herself standing on the stoop of Louise's apartment building way too soon. She should have stopped, had a cool drink. Her blouse was wet with perspiration.

She passed her hand over her face and down her neck, then wiped it on the back of her skirt, straightened her collar, and knocked on the door to the apartment. Stepped back when the door opened.

"Nora!" Rina broke into a smile. Then her eyes widened and her face fell.

They had seen the photo.

"Rina! Who is that?"

Louise.

Rina just stood there as if Louise's voice had turned her to stone.

Nora swallowed. Better to get it over with. She eased past Rina. And stepped inside.

She was barely through the door before Louise started screaming, "How dare you come here!"

"I guess you saw the newspaper," Nora said, trying to stay calm. She could feel Rina slip in behind her and close the door.

"Seen it? Everyone's seen it. I can't even face the neighbors."

Nora didn't know she ever bothered to go out, but she bit her tongue to hold in the temptation to strike back.

Louise turned away, grabbed a folded newspaper off the nearest table, and shook it in Nora's face.

Not only had she seen it, she'd kept it at hand, probably waiting for this occasion. Nora was half aware of Mama in the bedroom doorway, Little Don clinging to her dark skirts.

"Louise, stay calm, please, none of it is true."

"How do we know that? You, who would do anything to help yourself. The company you surround yourself with. Ach. Your precious boss murdered by a jealous husband. He was a pervert, everybody says so. And there you are, next to him every day. You've shamed our family."

"Louise, no," Mama said feebly from the doorway. Why wouldn't she come closer?

"You're not listening," said Nora. "I didn't do anything but work in a room with a hundred other people; none of them were Mr. White." She wouldn't tell Louise that all of them were men.

"Don't mention that name! I don't want you in my house! Get out. And don't come back."

Rina sprang forward. Nora managed to grab her as she passed.

Rina struggled beneath her grasp. "That's not fair!"

"Louise, she's your sister," Mama implored, easing herself and the boy into the room, but Louise paid no attention. Mama started to cry, silently, as if her tears might disturb them.

"You contaminate my children just by walking in the door.

Rina would have been better off working at a factory than going out in the world you inhabit!"

Nora swayed. Had Louise lost her mind with the last pregnancy?

"Shut up! Just shut up!" Rina screamed. "You've always hated us. Well, I hate you more!"

"Rina!" Nora warned, but Rina pulled away and rushed into the bedroom, knocking against Little Don, who started wailing.

"See what you've done!" Louise grabbed the boy and swung him to her hip.

"I'll go. I won't come here again. You and your children are safe from my bad influences." *And my money*, she added to herself. She turned to her mother, who said nothing but stumbled forward and grasped Nora with frail, trembling arms.

"I love you, Mama. None of this is true. I'm not evil; I didn't know about any of this. I didn't do anything but work hard to become an architect. Like I promised. Tell Rina . . . Just tell her."

She slipped from her mother's grip and ran out into the sultry evening. She was shaking, too overwhelmed with despair to think where she was or where she was going. She ran past the trolley stop, down the hill, past the neighborhood stores. She was at the bridge before she realized it had begun to rain.

CHAPTER 25

June 1906
Newport

Daisy looked up from her book when the parlor door opened. "Bordie, you're home early. Things too boring for you at the reading room?" Daisy smiled fondly at her husband. She was well aware that little reading was done at the reading room. Mainly it served the same function for the gentlemen of Newport as the tearoom did for their wives. If you discounted the cigars, spirits, and racing tips.

"I saw something that was troubling."

"About Stanford? I've decided to steer clear of the news."

Bordie, who had been in the act of unfolding the newspaper he'd been carrying, looked up. "I fully concur . . . except for this." He shook the paper and refolded it to a different page.

"Here is today's *Journal* from the city. I may be mistaken, but isn't this the girl who is working on your club?" He handed her the newspaper and pointed to a photo. "There."

Daisy sat up and took the proffered paper. Peered at it. A grainy group of men and one small young woman. Daisy held it closer, gripped the edges.

"What is this?"

Bordie's lips tightened.

"Is it so very bad?" Daisy began to scan the article.

"Someone in the group accused her of being more than the architect's assistant."

"More?" Daisy blinked. "Meaning . . . Oh, stuff and nonsense. That poor girl works herself to the bone from morning to night. She wouldn't have time for anything else even if she was tempted. Which is also absurd. Though she's a lovely little creature."

"Just like Stanford liked them."

"Please. I'd rather not know." Of course, she already knew. Even women dropped their insular protection at times. They knew White carried on in improper ways. They didn't delve too deeply. It was not a place one wanted to spend time.

"Well, I won't believe it of her. She's levelheaded. And even if Stanford attempted to seduce her—she may be pretty and young, but she's tough as nails. No, I won't believe it." She dropped the paper on the side table. "Why on earth are you even reading that filthy rag?"

"Because it's all the talk down at the reading room. I thought I should come warn you. The men are grumbling about their wives' names being associated with the man in the papers."

"Well," Daisy said. "They can relax. We are no longer associated with him. He's dead. He was our architect, for heaven's sake."

"Yes, dear, I just thought that forewarned would be forearmed, and I expect you'll be visited by more than one disgruntled lady on their morning calls tomorrow."

Daisy sighed. "I'll handle them if I must."

"I have no doubt you will, but, Daisy, there may be worse to come."

"What do you mean? You don't think there's any truth in these accusations about Nora, do you?"

Bordie cleared his throat.

"Bordie?"

"Actually, I don't, and hopefully this conjecture will pass into obscurity before anything comes of it. But there are bets being taken, I'm sorry to say. Not me, I wouldn't trifle with someone's life that way. But you should be prepared."

Daisy's fingers came to her cheek. "And we've left the poor child alone to finish all aspects of the building and furnishings, while dealing with Stanford's . . . I don't even know what to call them."

"Best not to try," Bordie said, sitting down beside her.

"What were we thinking, leaving town so near the opening? Bessie, Anne, and Elsie in France, me in Newport as if we didn't have a care in the world. Do you think I should go back?"

"To do what?"

"To make certain Nora's okay and that George Douglas is keeping things moving."

"Doesn't the office have a telephone? Why don't you telephone before you go hieing back to the city? It may blow over fairly quickly."

"Do you think it will affect the opening of the club?"

"I don't see why. It sounds like George Douglas is on the ball."

"That's not what I meant."

"The scandal, you mean. Well, as for that, we'll just have to wait and see."

BY THE TIME Nora got off the trolley at Twenty-third Street, the rain was driving at angles across the street. It didn't matter; she was already wet; what was a little more? She ducked her head and hurried toward the Parker. Her throat was thick, her tears mingling with the raindrops until she didn't know which was which. How could Louise be so cruel? Surely she knew Nora better than that. And Mama just stood there. Why hadn't she stuck up for Nora? Did she think her guilty, too?

Only Rina, in her hotheaded way, took Nora's side. Which Nora loved her for, but worried about what Louise would do to punish her in the future.

Nora tripped up the steps to the hotel entrance, her stomach sour with hunger and disappointment. Her family had cast her off. She pushed open the door, stood for a minute inside, dripping on the carpet, then headed for the stairs.

"Miss Bromley?"

Nora looked up to find the desk boy holding out an envelope. Nora took it. "What is this?"

"It's—it's from the management, I'm afraid."

Nora frowned, not understanding. She tore it open, revealing several coins. She glanced up at him.

The desk clerk chewed on his lip.

There was a folded note, which she pulled out. *To Miss Nora Bromley. You are hereby evicted from this hotel. To begin immediately. The remaining rent for the month is enclosed within. The hotel staff will see you out by the end of day.*

She read it again as the words gradually sank in. Still she didn't believe it. She looked toward the boy.

"They can't do this. I haven't done anything wrong. I'm paid up."

He just stood there looking miserable. "Someone complained."

And she bet she knew who. "Thank you."

She marched to the stairs, climbed the three flights to her room. Her room no more. But when she reached the landing, she stopped and leaned back against the wall to gather her strength. How could they expect her to leave by tonight? Where would she go? Her fingers clenched into fists involuntarily. It didn't matter; if they wanted her out, she would leave. And go . . . somewhere. Somewhere . . .

She pushed away from the wall, but her knees gave out and she gripped the stair rail to keep from falling. She took several long breaths, then crossed to her room. Opened the door.

Lucy and Connie were both there, both with their coats on. She'd obviously caught them before they could escape from having to admit their perfidy.

"We're sorry," Lucy said, before Nora even spoke. "But we

have our own reputations—" Nora struck out her hand to silence her, and Lucy gulped back the next word.

"We packed for you," Connie said. "We're awfully sorry."

They would be, if they had torn, folded, or damaged in any way any of the things she had not yet transferred to the office. Then she noticed the suitcase on the bed, next to a sack stuffed full and her portfolio bulging at the seams.

And suddenly she was too overwhelmed to even look at what was inside.

She pulled up every vestige of strength, crossed to the bed, and took one brief look around the room, to make sure they hadn't missed anything. They hadn't. The only thing Nora could do was leave. She hoisted the bag, the suitcase, and the portfolio—everything she owned in the world—and struggled to the door.

"Good luck," said Connie.

Nora didn't stop, but banged through the door. Lucy ran after her.

"Where will you go?"

"You should have thought of that before you had me thrown out." Nora lifted her head as best she could and half carried, half dragged her things to the stairs.

When she heard the door close behind her, she heaved a shuddering sigh, then dragged everything down the stairs to the first floor.

The desk boy saw her coming and ran over to hold the door. As if he couldn't get rid of her fast enough. She stepped out in the rain. Stopped on the sidewalk.

Where *would* she go? She probably had enough cash for a room at the YMCA, if they would even take her in the state she was in. It was close to eleven. She might just make it to the office before the doorman closed for the night. She could sleep in her office until the next morning and then decide what to do. At least she would be dry and safe.

But she couldn't walk. She hoisted her belongings and trudged to the corner where she got on the first trolley going east. When she at last stood outside the temporary quarters of the Colony Club, the building was dark. Heart racing, she stumbled up the two steps to the shallow alcove and tried the knob; it was locked. She banged on the door, waited, banged again. It went unanswered.

And all the hard work, the scrimping, the saving, the long hours, the abuse she'd taken, all crashed down on her at once. She'd been a fool to think she would ever be an architect. The world was cruel to those who had nothing. It was even crueler to those who tried to rise above their place. Slowly she slid down to sit on the steps, her belongings scattered about her, the hem of her skirt soaking up the rain.

She could just stay where she was. It wasn't so very long until morning, then she could . . . could . . . She shivered. How had she come to this?

Only a few days ago, everything seemed possible. But in an instant, like the prick of a soap bubble, it was gone. Her hopes, her determination, her future.

She closed her eyes. Just rest for a while. Something sharp was sticking in her thigh. The protractor in her skirt pocket. She didn't really care, except the pain was keeping her awake. She slid her hand in the pocket, pushed the protractor away, and touched something else.

Her fingers wrapped around it automatically. It was a key. The key George had given to her. She hadn't had to use it yet. She would use it now. Get dry, make herself presentable, and leave before anyone arrived in the morning.

Clasping the key in numb fingers, she gathered up her things and hurried up the street to the Colony Club site.

The door opened easily, like it had been waiting for her. She dropped her things, and quickly locked herself in.

It was blessedly dry inside, and now that she was safe, she

felt cold, but not frightened. She wouldn't turn on the lights. Someone might notice. She felt her way toward the construction office. There she turned on the desk lamp and shone it into the corner. No one would see it from the outside.

She dragged her things into the cramped space. Pushed the portfolio to one side and opened her suitcase. She knew there was water laid on in the first-floor lavatories. She groped her way down the hall in the dark, where she quickly washed her face and hands and changed into dry clothes. The energy it took left her lightheaded and tired beyond belief. Maybe just a little sleep, an hour or so before dawn. She swayed as she pulled her old winter coat from the bottom of the suitcase and threw it on the floor for her bed.

But as she started to collapse onto it, her eye caught sight of a little metal frame propped on the communal desk. It was the sketch she'd made of George for Christmas. He'd kept it out where he could see it. She lifted it from the desk and, clasping the cheap tin frame, she lay down on the coat, curled into a ball, and fell asleep.

June 1906
Versailles, Villa Trianon

I t was a delightful morning, Elsie thought, as she watched Anne pour coffee into the Dresden teacups—trimmed with simple scalloped edges and adorned with a spray of flowers that echoed the garden without competing with it. The set had called to her from among the garish wares in the flea market just the week before.

Just delightful. Even with Anne there. Elsie was quite getting used to her, and even inured to seeing those beautiful Poiret and Worth gowns that sat so unflatteringly on her large frame. It was unfortunate. No regimen of exercise and dieting would ever show them to good advantage. She'd soon be off to Switzerland to do the "cure" as she did every summer, and nothing would change.

"It's beyond me," Bessie declared as she tossed down the latest edition of the *International Herald Tribune* and reached for a muffin. "How Stanny, so charming and generous, so distingué, could let himself be the victim of a *crime passionelle*."

"I suspect because the perpetrator was that idiot Harry Thaw," cut in Elsie. "Everyone knew he was not fit for society. And it doesn't speak much for Evey either." Elsie didn't care about Evey. She was angry at Stanny. He'd talked her into leaving the stage to design and then had the temerity to get himself killed, leaving her mid–new career and on her own.

"How could he do this?"

Anne looked shocked.

Bessie just reached over and took Elsie's hand in hers. "It's a bit of a setback, but you've survived setbacks before. This one will be no different."

Dear Bessie, she always knew what to say. How to handle every situation. Elsie would overcome this. Just like she overcame everything that stood in her way. With Bessie's help, of course.

She owed her so much. And if she had to put up with Anne to make things work, it was a price she was willing to pay.

"Do you think the club's reputation will be sullied because of this?" Anne asked, worry creasing the space between her thick eyebrows.

"Absolutely not," Elsie said. "It's probably best that everyone is out of town. The scandal is bound to pass before it's time for us to make the final push." Elsie was not called the best-dressed actress on the Rialto for nothing. She knew that dressing the part was half the battle. And she knew how to make things work. She would make the Colony Club the best-dressed club in the city. And not have to depend on Stanford White to do it.

CHAPTER 26

Nora heard a voice calling to her from the dark. She huddled tighter, tried to ignore it. Then the shaking began. Gentle at first, then again and again.

"Miss, miss, are you all right?"

She blinked her eyes open. Mr. Wojcik's face peered at her like a balloon just out of reach.

"George! It's Miss Bromley! Here on the floor."

And then Nora remembered. She pushed to a sitting position. She'd meant to leave before anyone arrived and sneak back to her own office.

But she'd slept like the dead.

She tried to stand, but her legs were stiff, her back ached from sleeping on the hard floor.

She tried to straighten her skirts, but George appeared in the doorway, frowning. "What the—?" He stepped inside. "Are you hurt? What are you doing here?"

"I'm—I'm sorry," she stammered. "It was late and I couldn't get in and then I remembered the key."

"But why?"

Nora's lip trembled. She was too ashamed to explain.

George knelt down beside her. "What's happened?"

Nora shivered, remembering the night before. Her clothes were dry, but now there was a pain in her stomach. And she suddenly felt too weak to stand.

"Wojcik, go around to Mrs. Tova's and ask her for a pot of coffee and some rolls."

Mr. Wojcik grunted and hurried away.

"Come on, Bromley, pull yourself together. Whatever happened, you're safe here." He took both her arms and pulled her to her feet, guided her to the nearest wooden chair.

She tried to smooth her hair, but between the rain and sleeping rough, it was hopeless.

"Go into the lavatories and wash your face; you'll feel better."

Nora nodded, though she couldn't make herself look at him. She walked stiffly to the door, held on to the jamb long enough to steady herself, then walked down to the lavatories, where she washed her face and hands, and tidied her hair as best she could. She would do better later when she was down in her own office, where the facilities were finished and offered every amenity to the ladies of the club.

When she was feeling steadier, she returned to the office to try to explain why she was there.

The first thing she noticed was that someone, George, had tidied up after her. Her coat was hanging on a hook on the wooden beam. Her stomach flipped over when she saw that the sketch she'd made of him had been returned to its place on the drawing table. Her cheeks flamed. And she quickly looked away.

George didn't ask any more questions, and they sat in an uncomfortable silence until the sound of heavy footsteps heralded Mr. Wojcik's return.

He placed a bag and a heavy tin pot of steaming coffee on the desk. From the bag, he pulled three mugs and several large rolls stuffed with a cold meat and butter.

George poured coffee into a mug and handed it to Nora. She took the cup gratefully, noticed that the back of his hand was scraped, and felt a sting of indignation that he was still having to do manual labor along with everything else. Mr. Wojcik held out one of the sandwiches.

But Nora couldn't seem to let go of the mug that she clenched in both hands.

He put the sandwich at her elbow.

"Now, miss, you tell us what's happened."

So Nora told them, stammering out some parts and bravely plowing through the most hurtful part. About being turned away by her own family, then her hotel. "I hoped that the assembly room would still be open, but everyone was gone. Then I remembered the key. I'll have to find a place, but who will . . ." And to her horror, she broke down. "Everybody thinks I'm one of his women. And I'm not."

"Lordy," said Mr. Wojcik. "'Course you're not. Everyone knows *that*."

"They don't. I have no place to go."

"You have a little money saved, don't you?" George asked.

Nora nodded. "But that's for my mother and sister to have a place of their own."

"Well, considering they kicked you out—" A look from George stopped Mr. Wojcik mid-sentence.

"It wasn't their fault; it was my older sister. They live with her."

"Well, never mind," George said. "Eat that sandwich. I have an idea."

"What?"

"Eat."

So Nora ate and discovered that she was hungry. When every crumb was gone and her mug was empty, George said, "Come on."

"Where?" asked Nora.

"To the McKim and Mead office."

Nora shrank back. "I can't."

"Don't worry. McKim and Mead are both lying low. You're not going back there after today. You'll work at the Colony Club for the foreseeable future."

This was the last straw. "They've fired me, haven't they?" she said, the weight of her own words dragging her down to the worst kind of despair.

"Not yet. But they're old-fashioned, unimaginative. Mr. White was the genius in that firm."

Nora held up her hand. "Don't. Don't try to make it better. I'll have to find a new job. I knew they didn't want me. I did everything I could to make sure they had no reason to fire me. But it didn't matter, did it? Who will hire me now?"

"It wasn't your fault. You have a job on the Colony Club. When it's finished, we'll worry about the next one. Is this all your stuff?"

Nora nodded.

He shook his head. "We'll send for it later."

Mr. Wojcik was left in charge of her possessions and Nora and George took a cab to Twenty-fifth Street.

The crowd outside had dwindled to two bored-looking reporters slouching by the newsstand.

George whisked her inside before they had time to react. They rode up in the elevator, Nora pressing against the back as if she could disappear. But it stopped at the fourth floor.

"No, what must they think?"

"Not what you think."

He pulled her out of the elevator and into the office.

Sadie, Lavinia, and Higgie looked up, then jumped from their seats and hurried toward Nora.

"We've been so worried," Lavinia said. "The nerve of those reporters and that so-and-so Nast. Everybody knows he's the one who told the reporters all that nonsense about you."

"You should sue him for libel," Sadie said.

"As for the reporters," Lavinia added, "Higgie poured a bucket of water down on their heads. That cooled their ardor for a story right quick, I can tell you. They've been keeping their distance ever since."

But too late to help Nora.

Higgie didn't look contrite. "They asked for it," she said calmly. It made Nora smile a little.

"That's all well and good," George said. "But we have a small problem."

Nora hung her head. "I got kicked out of my room."

"At the women's hotel?"

She nodded.

"No matter," said George, brushing her lack of a future aside without a care. "I thought maybe one of you ladies might have some suggestions of where she should look for a new place."

"Someplace that won't ask for a reference," Lavinia said and winced. "I already have two roommates or I'd sneak you in."

Sadie bit her lip. "I still live at home. What about the Y or the Martha Washington Hotel? Or else you could . . ." She shrugged.

"For heaven's sake," Higgie said. "Come stay with me until you get settled."

"I couldn't. Thank you. But you'll be tainted by associating with me."

"Oh, pish, as if I care what those gossipmongers write."

"Good. That's settled," George said.

"No, George, it isn't. I can't. I'll think of something. Someplace where they haven't read the papers."

"It was one grainy photo in one trashy newspaper," Higgie said. "Buck up now. We girls are made of sterner stuff."

There was a knock at the door. Nora shrank back, as Sadie and Lavinia scrambled back to their desks.

The door opened and Fergus walked in. He broke into a wide grin.

"Bromley, where have you been keeping? The guys were all asking about you."

"Yes, Fergus?" George said. "You needed something?"

"Oh, yeah. McKim sent over a couple of men to clean out *his* private office. They've finished going through all the . . . you know." He looked around at the others and lowered his voice. "You've never seen such things. They want to know where to take them."

George scoffed. "Hell, I don't know. McKim gave the order, take them to him. Miss Higgins will give you his address."

Higgie gave George a stern look, but wrote out an address.

"We'll need to pay the carter."

George sighed, pulled his wallet from his trouser pocket, counted out several bills, and held them out to Fergus. "A few extra to keep their mouths shut."

Fergus started to take them, frowned, then peered more closely at George's outstretched hand. "Ha! So that's it. We were all wondering how—"

"Fergus! This should be enough," George said, thrusting the bills into Fergie's hand, then shoving his wallet back into his pocket. "If they want more, have McKim make up the difference."

"Gladly. And bully for you." Fergus touched his fingers to his forehead. "Ladies." He hurried out.

"Are they moving all his plans already?" asked Nora, trying to follow the conversation but failing. "I still have sketches for the church to turn in."

"Not plans," George said. "Let's—"

"So it's true!" Sadie exclaimed.

"Never you mind," said Higgie. "The less we know, the better."

Nora turned to George. "What did they move?"

"He had some papers, and, uh, things of . . . of . . ."

"Pornography," Higgie said.

Nora slumped. "Was he so very bad?"

"Worse," George said. "But he was a genius as an architect." And he sounded as if his heart was breaking.

"Well." Higgie slapped her palms on her desk. "I declare work over. Nora, where are your things? We'll take them to your new digs."

"Higgie, I really appreciate it, but I couldn't. You might get kicked out, too. Just for bringing me to your room."

"No one would dare."

"Really, I can't. George, tell her."

"George, stay out of it," Higgie said. "I won't take no for an answer. Actually, I owe Nora a favor."

"Me?"

"Yes, but we'll discuss it later. Cover your typewriters, girls, we're taking the afternoon off."

Newport

As soon as Daisy finished breakfast and saw Bordie off to a day of yachting, she asked Miss Gleason to put in a call to the club office in New York. There was no answer, but she wasn't too worried. Nora was kept busy running between the warehouse and the office and the site. She might not have even seen the photograph yet. Daisy would catch up to her at some point. Make certain that things were still running smoothly, though she couldn't imagine why they wouldn't be.

Nora was very competent for such a young girl, and so was George. Though with Stanford gone, there would be no one to turn to if Elsie needed guidance. The thought of all the rooms still to be decorated before the opening was daunting.

But there was no reason to worry, until there was.

Hopefully, Stanford's scandalous death would fill the headlines for a few days, be milked by the sensationalist press for a few days more, and by the time they all returned to the city, it would barely be talked of. Which reminded her . . . Would there be a memorial service? Bordie would go if she asked him to.

Perhaps they could avoid the fallout while they enjoyed the summer in Newport.

Wishful thinking that didn't last beyond the first morning call.

The first to arrive was Lillian Stevens, quickly followed by Helen Whitney before the door had even closed.

"I'm sure you've heard the news," Helen began as soon as she sat down.

"It's a disaster," Lillian said. "Albert would absolutely give me no details. Thank goodness for the servants; Dulcie, our parlormaid, sneaked a copy of the *Tribune* up to me after breakfast."

"It does look pretty bad," Helen agreed. "And he hadn't even finished my house."

Lillian clapped her lace-gloved hands to her cheeks. "A disaster, I tell you. We'll have to postpone the opening."

"Postpone what?" Alva Belmont asked, sweeping past the maid and into the room.

"The opening of the club, of course. We can't have our name associated with scandal. Not of this magnitude, at least."

"Absolutely not," countered Alva. "Just because Stanny took an inopportune time to get himself killed—"

"Alva, how can you say such things?" Daisy motioned for Alva to be seated and waited for the excitement to calm.

"It's going to be even worse than before," Lillian said. "Our reputations will be in shambles. Just this morning Albert had the gall to chastise me at the breakfast table. Shaking his paper at me like a street urchin and avowing that this was what came from letting women decide things like clubs for themselves." She hmphed disgustedly. "As if we were no better than Evelyn Nesbit."

"Lillian, she was just a child when Mr. White, um, knew her," said Helen.

"Little you know. No better than she should be. Where was the girl's mother to let something like that happen to her child?"

Alva rolled her eyes. "As far as Evelyn Nesbit is concerned, she wouldn't be in this fix now if it hadn't been for her mother. She wasn't alone in the world. Her mother was pulling the strings from the moment she met Stanny, and probably still is, as we speak. The woman is a ruthless manipulator. She'll see that Evey comes out of this just fine."

"Alva, really, where do you hear such things?"

"There's no need to take any measures at this point," Daisy interceded. "We have two months before any of us return to the city. Let us wait and see what the atmosphere is then. After that, we can discuss the best way to proceed."

Though if it were up to Daisy alone, she wouldn't let their opening be postponed because of one man's indiscretions, even if he was their architect.

"Well, I don't . . ."

"Daisy's right," said Alva. "It's too soon to know how this will evolve. Especially because most of the coverage is by the *Journal* and a couple other sensationalist papers. You know they can't be trusted with real news."

"True," said Helen.

"In that case," said Lillian, "did you hear what happened at the Rensselaers' operatic evening last night?"

They were all eager to change the conversation, and for the next few minutes they delighted in the latest misdemeanors of the summer residents.

Daisy listened and reacted while she wondered if there was any way to prevent this scandal from growing too big to handle.

The subject of Stanford's death was only brought up briefly as the ladies left. "I am of the firm belief we will feel the repercussions of this," said Lillian. "Bessie and Elsie are the only women I know who manage to flirt with fire and come out unscathed."

"And so will the ladies of the Colony Club," Daisy assured them as she showed them all out. "We must stand together and continue as we mean to go. We'll open in the fall as planned."

But when they were finally gone, Daisy sank back against the door and acknowledged to herself what she'd refused to in front of her visitors. If things didn't blow over quickly, they would be in a pickle.

WITH THE PROMISE of having Nora's belongings sent to the address Higgie had written down, George put Nora and Higgie into a taxi, one of the new gasoline ones, the novelty of which took Nora's thoughts from her predicament until they arrived at West Tenth Street.

She pressed Higgie's arm. "I don't think this is a good idea. You have to think about yourself."

"I am," said Higgie. "You don't know how lonely it is living with no one to talk to but my aunt, who's always so busy—"

"You live with your aunt?" exclaimed Nora. "Oh, no. I couldn't. What will she think?"

Higgie paid the cabbie and got out, pulling Nora along with her. "Well, let's go find out, shall we?"

"She lives with you in your room at the boardinghouse?" This would be worse than rooming with Lucy and Connie at the hotel.

"It's just here." Higgie led her up the steps to a small brownstone with glistening French windows. She rang the bell.

After a couple of minutes, it opened. "Good heavens, Caroline, what are you doing home so early?"

"Lunch, perhaps?"

Nora was so astonished, she didn't move. Higgie's name was Caroline? This tall, dark woman, dressed in severe black, was Higgie's aunt?

"Come on in and meet my last living relative on earth, Aunt Sorcha."

"She exaggerates," the woman said. "I'm sure we must have one or two others, somewhere. And you are?"

"Nora," Higgie supplied, which was a good thing, because Nora was too stupefied to answer.

"Well, you better come in. Welcome to our humble abode."

Nora stepped inside as it slowly dawned on her. This wasn't a boardinghouse, this was a home. Maybe they took in boarders.

"I can pay," Nora blurted.

The woman squinted at her, picked up a pince-nez on a cord pinned to her blouse, and leaned closer. "For what?"

"Nora," said Higgie gently. "This is my house. I didn't tell you because I didn't want to scare you away. It's small but it's comfortable, and we need some company besides ourselves, don't we, Aunt?"

Nora's lungs were beginning to hurt; she let out her breath. "The whole house?"

"It was left to me by my father."

"But you have to work." Nora clapped her hand over her mouth. "Pardon me. I didn't mean . . ."

"Does that seem strange to you? Would you stop being an architect if you suddenly didn't have to work?"

"Of course not."

"I like to work. I have a talent for figures and organization. Before my father died, I kept house and organized his financial records. After he died, I went to work for McKim, Mead, and White. Well, I couldn't very well sit around here being sad and letting the world go by. And they were sorely in need of someone with my qualifications. Besides, a little extra cash is always nice."

"Lunch," said Aunt Sorcha and turned to walk down a dark corridor.

Over thick crusty slices of ham pie and greens, Higgie explained to her aunt about Nora's predicament, while Nora hung her head and blushed with shame over being placed, even wrongly, in such a scandal.

But the only thing the aunt said was, "Typical of these sensationalist rags. Hearst is the worst of them all. He should be made to eat his words—literally."

Higgie nodded and smiled at Nora. "A bluestocking *and* a progressive. Now if you're finished, I'll show you to your room and maybe you'd like a hot bath. And some clean clothes."

Nora was suddenly aware of how she must look: her clothes slept in, her hair uncombed. "I'm . . ."

"Yes, yes," said the aunt. "Take the day to reclaim your right to be you. Tomorrow is another day, and you'll be back out there with a vengeance. Don't let them kick you down. They will, you know. You just have to get back up and keep going." With that, she started clearing the table.

Nora followed Higgie up the stairs. "Aunt Sorcha never lets anyone give up. She's indefatigable. She even got arrested a few times for protesting various iniquities. I hope that doesn't put you off."

"No," Nora managed, shocked, but not at all put off.

At the top of the stairs, Higgie opened a door into a bright room, with a bed in the center covered in a chenille spread and flanked by delicate side tables with lamps. A window looked out onto a tree.

"This will be your room. I hope you like it."

Nora just stared, not quite comprehending.

"Mine is just next door. We have to share a bath. Oh, not with Aunt Sorcha; she's upstairs."

Nora just shook her head.

"What? Don't you like it?" It wasn't the question, but the disappointment in Higgie's voice that made Nora look up.

"It's beautiful, but . . ." Tears filled her eyes.

"What? You can tell me."

"It's just . . . I never had a room to myself before."

"Never?"

"Never."

"Oh. Well, you do now. I'll run your bath. There's lots of hot water, take as long as you like." And she hurried away. "Do you like lavender or lily of the valley?" Higgie called from the next room.

Nora stripped out of her clothes and climbed into the tub. It was the most luxurious thing in the world. Not extravagant like the fixtures the Colony Club would have. But to Nora, with the smell of lavender wafting around her, it was like being in heaven.

She washed her body, washed her hair, then when her fingers were shriveled and the water began to cool, she climbed out and wrapped herself in a big white towel.

There was no one in her room, but the clothes she'd been wearing had been taken away. Her other clothes had been delivered and put away in the wardrobe. She sat at a dressing table before an oval mirror, combing her hair until it was free of tangles, then braided it into a decent bun at her nape. And in a moment of sheer relief and hope, she took her Sunday-best dress from the wardrobe and wore it downstairs to join Higgie and her aunt.

CHAPTER 27

Nora, Higgie, and Aunt Sorcha sat around the dining table over a big pot of chicken and dumplings.

"We usually eat in the kitchen," Higgie informed her.

Nora was glad that they weren't eating there now. As it was, she couldn't help but make the comparison of this relaxed, companionable meal with the last uncomfortable dinner she'd had with her own family.

"Well, miss, we'd eat out here more often if we received more visitors," Aunt Sorcha said, then glanced at Nora. "But now that there are three of us . . ."

"Oh, I'm not—" Nora began.

"True," said Aunt Sorcha. "Caroline has told me all about it. Consider yourself one of the household now."

After pressing large dessert bowls of fruit on them, Aunt Sorcha quickly washed the dishes and announced that she had a meeting to attend. "I suggest you two get to bed early. Though I expect you'll be gabbing into the wee hours. I'll lock up when I return."

And off she went.

Nora was nodding on her feet, but instead of going upstairs, Higgie motioned her to the cozy parlor, where they sat on a long camelback sofa. Higgie tucked her knees up and leaned back against the rolled arm.

"I'm sure I must be an imposition," Nora blurted. "I don't know why George brought me to you. I'll try to find someplace to live. I'll pay my share here until I do. I really appreciate it and I'm so . . ."

"Don't you?"

Nora stopped. "Don't I what?"

"Know why George brought you to me? Well, actually to the two of us?"

Nora shook her head.

"Because he knew he could trust us."

Nora was confused.

"To take care of you, ninny."

"I can take care of myself," Nora said without much conviction. She hadn't been doing a very good job of it lately.

"Of course you can, we all can. The point is we shouldn't have to, and we don't have to. But isn't it nice to know someone cares about how you fare?"

Nora nodded. "You and Sadie and Lavinia have become my best friends."

"And George?"

"He's been very open-minded and helpful."

"We noticed."

"But he shouldn't have imposed on you."

"Aunt and I are delighted to have you here. I especially hope you'll like staying here. I love Aunt Sorcha to pieces but she usually goes out after dinner and it gets dull having no one to talk to while she's out making the world a better place.

"Really. It will be fun," Higgie assured her. "Unless you don't think you'll be comfortable here?"

"How could I not be?" Nora said, and in spite of her best effort, tears sprang to her eyes.

Higgie pulled a handkerchief from her waistband and handed it to Nora, waited for Nora to dry her eyes, then asked, "Do you play cards?"

"Gin rummy, but I'd like to learn other games."

"And jigsaws—do you like puzzles?"

Nora nodded. She wasn't sure whether she did or not. She could barely remember her childhood when life was fine and they didn't know the hardship that was to come.

"But Higgie, I'll pay my fair share."

"Absolutely not. I told you I owed you one."

"But what? I don't remember anything."

"Remember you asked me to the talk on tuberculosis?"

Nora nodded.

"And I got to talking with Dr. Jamison?"

"I remember."

"He asked if I would be willing to give him some pointers on bookkeeping. He's opening his own clinic. I said I'd be happy to. And, well, he came over one evening and we worked out a method for keeping track of patients and cross-referencing their care . . ." Higgie looked away. "Actually, he's visited several times and once he invited me to tea."

"That's lovely," Nora said. "But I didn't do anything. You did."

"You got me away from my drab existence and inspired me to do something worthwhile for a change. I mean outside of keeping the books for the architectural firm."

"You like him?"

"I do," Higgie said.

"I'm glad. I hope you can help him get set up."

"And make him famous and rich," Higgie added. "Then maybe he will build your hospital."

Nora laughed. "That is a lovely dream."

"Well, it might come true. Please say you'll stay."

"Okay. But do you have an empty jar?"

"Like a mason jar? Yes."

"May I have it?"

"Sure." Higgie frowned but went to get one.

While she was gone, Nora took out several dollars that she'd secreted behind her belt. When Higgie returned with the jar and handed it to her, Nora stuffed the money into it. "You don't want me to pay, but I've seen what anger money causes. I'll just put it in here, so if Aunt Sorcha ever needs it . . ."

"And if I refuse to take it?"

"Then I will have to find another place to live."

Higgie shook her head. "You're a hard nut to crack, Nora Bromley. You can put your money in the jar, but I have every hope that one day you'll trust people to be your true friends."

The next morning when Nora and Higgie came downstairs, Aunt Sorcha had their breakfast waiting for them. Oatmeal with raisins and brown sugar. A delicacy that overwhelmed Nora. They left for work with containers of leftover ham pie, an apple, and flasks of tea.

They took the trolley uptown. Higgie got off at Twenty-first and Nora continued on to Thirty-first. But instead of going directly to the assembly room office, Nora stopped by the Colony Club site to thank George and Mr. Wojcik for helping her.

Dressed in a crisply starched shirtwaist, her skirt brushed until it looked new—all thanks to Aunt Sorcha—and her hair done with special care, she stepped into the new club, and stopped in amazement.

The interior actually looked like a club. Most of the construction equipment had disappeared. The walls were bare and clean and ready for a coat of paint or wallpaper. Most of the metal shavings and sawdust had been swept away. It must have taken days for this to get to such a pristine state, but with the murder and the unraveling of her life, Nora had let it happen without her. She'd slept on the office floor surrounded by darkness never realizing that just outside the door, her dreams were coming true.

The sound of distant hammering led her to the trellis room, where several carpenters were putting the finishing touches on the fountain base. George was observing them, hands thrust into his pockets.

Nora stood watching, amazed at the building, at the progress, and at her part, small as it was, in the making of it. And she would do more as soon as Elsie returned and they began installing the furniture and decor. She could already see it. The little wooden tables and chairs would be perfect for this room. Like being in a garden in winter.

Elsie had been right all along.

George turned and caught her eye, surprise turning to a smile as he strode toward her.

And all the humiliation of being found sleeping like a vagrant on the office floor washed over her.

"You look wonderful," George said. "I mean . . . you look well rested. I hope you're comfortable at Miss Higgins's."

Nora nodded. For a moment . . . "Yes, thank you. And thank you for helping me yesterday."

"Oh, that; my pleasure." He turned to view the trellis room. "We're making good progress, don't you think?"

"Yes, I do. Well, I'd better get over to the assembly room. I'm sure more things have been delivered while I was . . . uh . . . away."

"Of course. Maybe we . . . Well, come over any time to check on things."

"Thanks, and tell Mr. Wojcik thank you."

"I will."

Nora turned to go.

"And Nora. You really do look wonderful today."

"Thanks." She managed not to smile until she was out the door and hurrying down the sidewalk.

AS THE DAYS passed, deliveries of decor accelerated. Each morning Aunt Sorcha would send Higgie and Nora off after a hearty breakfast. Every evening when they returned, Nora exhausted from coordinating the flow of goods and Higgie exhausted from the panic that had turned the architectural firm into chaos, Aunt Sorcha would have dinner ready.

Each week, Higgie brought Nora's paycheck home since they had all decided that it would be better for Nora to stay away from McKim and Mead, even though they were mostly out of town.

The news about Mr. White's murder ebbed and flowed, but Nora wasn't bothered by reporters again. The wife of Harry Thaw was giving them enough scandal to keep them in print for ages. The summer passed and Nora forgot about looking for another place to live.

At first Nora missed her family and felt guilty that she'd somehow failed them. She'd written to tell her mother and Rina of her move, and had received one letter in return. Her mother apologized, assured her that they didn't think she had done anything wrong and that she was a good daughter, but she finished with the admonition not to write again, as Louise had threatened to destroy the letters. "You must forgive her, dear Nora, she has had a difficult life."

They had all had difficult lives, Nora thought unsympathetically. Many people had worse than her family. Rather than moping around and complaining, they did something about it. There were even other people organizing to help them have a better life. Rina hadn't added anything to the letter, which could only mean she was still angry. Nora didn't blame her. She was just a child—or should be.

Nora wondered what her mother would think about her new living situation. At the beginning of each week, Nora put money in the mason jar for her room and board, and left it on the kitchen counter. Each day when she returned from work, the jar had been returned to the cabinet. The jar was never emptied.

Aunt Sorcha and Higgie absolutely refused to spend it. It

wasn't as if they were rich and could afford to support another person. They were just generous. Something Nora realized she needed to learn. She'd been scrimping and saving for so long, she didn't know how to so easily give more than she received.

At night Nora and Higgie did jigsaws. Sometimes Higgie would work on her tatting while Nora chose a book from Mr. Higgins's superlative library and curled up in the big comfy chair. Sometimes they just talked about "girl things," according to Higgie.

The summer fell into a steady rhythm. Every morning they would catch the trolley together for the ride to their respective offices. And Nora found herself missing not just Sadie and Lavinia, but the drafting room, even with Collin Nast in it. Before the murder, she had begun to earn respect from her colleagues. Some had even become friendly. And she worried about what they might think of her now.

But then she would forget everything when she arrived at the site and something new and amazing caught her attention as the building transformed more and more into the Colony Club. The cornices and woodwork had been installed. The walls were primed for paint and wallpaper. All waiting for Elsie's return.

"We can't wait any longer to hang the ceiling over the swimming pool," Mr. Wojcik informed them one day. "Tomorrow it gets installed, no more waiting."

Everyone that day stopped their work to go downstairs to watch. Nora took the morning away from her burgeoning inventory to watch the trellis arbor carefully raised piece by piece over the swimming pool just like Mr. White had described it. When the last section had been tied off at the proper height, the electricity was connected, and above them, hundreds of tiny lights winked from grapes of clear blown glass.

Fit for Grecian goddesses, Nora thought. And tried not to imagine Miss Morgan or Miss Marbury or quite a few of the others garbed in bathing costumes.

"All the trappings of a pagan orgy," Mr. Wojcik whispered to George.

George laughed. "The ladies will love it."

There weren't too many meetings since almost everyone was still out of town for the summer. But Nora was not lacking in her introductions to new ideas. There were nights when Nora and Higgie helped make signs for Aunt Sorcha to take when she left to go out marching and meeting for causes that Nora had already begun to learn about from the Colony Club lectures. And while they painted, they discussed a myriad of topics, the future of medicine and the modernization of working conditions. Unions, housing, and even women getting the vote, which was a particular hobbyhorse for Aunt Sorcha.

Nora often wished she could introduce her to the Colony Club ladies; she would be a powerhouse among them. But it was an exclusive club, no matter what their great works were. Besides, as Sorcha pointed out the one time Nora mentioned it, "There are more organizations out there than a person could ever join. The way to resolve problems is from all angles."

On the nights when Aunt Sorcha was home they would play cards or dominoes. Some nights Dr. Jamison would join them for dinner and a rubber of canasta, for which Nora was showing some aptitude. There were even a few times when Aunt Sorcha, busy with a speech she was writing, insisted they invite George to make a fourth. Those were the really fun nights where concentration on the game soon devolved into laughter and good-natured claims of foul, until Aunt Sorcha's return startled them into complete silence. She'd look over the group while they held still, then say brightly, "Carry on." And went off to make them all tea.

It was fairly clear to Nora that there was more to Higgie and the doctor's friendship than playing cards and bookkeeping. Even though Higgie would deny it, saying that she could never leave

Aunt Sorcha. "She's taken care of Papa and me since my mother died years ago. I couldn't repay her by leaving her to live alone."

"I'd hardly call her alone," Nora said. "She's out almost every night with one group or another. And besides, I'm here." Nora bit down on her words. "Not that I could ever take your place, but she would have someone nearby if she needed help with something."

"But what about you?" Higgie asked.

"What about me? I have my work so far. And when this project is over, I'll get another one . . . somehow. I doubt if I'll be able to stay at McKim, Mead, and Whi—" She stopped. There was no more White. And yet he seemed to live in every room of the new Colony Club.

"Oh, I know that, I have every confidence in you. But there are other things . . . other people, maybe?"

"I doubt my family . . ."

Higgie shook her head. "I wasn't thinking of your family, Nora."

"But I am."

"I know. I hope they appreciate you for it." And that ended the conversation.

ONE AFTERNOON WHEN Nora was overseeing the delivery of twenty cartons of dining linens to the fifth-floor restaurant, George strode into the room. He turned an expert eye on the proceedings and pulled her aside.

"Almost finished?"

"I hope so."

"Well, let somebody else finish. Mrs. Tova has been asking where you are. She demanded I bring you to tea today."

Nora looked back at her boxes—not exactly what she'd planned for her career in architecture, but Elsie would be back any week now. "But I have—"

"To come with me," George finished for her. "Where's your hat?"

"Oh, George, I don't wear a hat on work days."

She quickly asked one of the staff to finish unpacking and verifying as George steered her toward the doorway.

Mrs. Tova greeted Nora as if she were a long-lost relative, talking animatedly about everything and piling pastries and sandwiches on plates.

"Ah, it's about time. You are too busy to come and see me?"

"I've been swamped," Nora said. "I'm sorry."

"No matter. You are here now. And now we can properly celebrate."

"What are we celebrating?" Nora asked.

"Your very own Saint George."

George groaned. "I think you might have wandered into blasphemy, Mrs. Tova."

"No, no, no. It is true."

"What?" Nora asked, intrigued.

Mrs. Tova crooked her finger for Nora to move closer. "It is a secret." She crooked her finger again.

Nora moved closer. "About what?"

"Of how that no-good Nast fellow got a black eye."

"You've never even met the man," George protested.

"Bah. Our Georgie fixed his wagon right fine." She beamed at George, who looked uncomfortable. "After that newspaper said all those things, he went right over there and gave him two black eyes."

"One," George mumbled and frowned at her.

"George?" Nora asked, surprised. She didn't believe it. He was so calm all the time.

"I lost my temper," George admitted.

"Protecting your honor, he was." Mrs. Tova nodded sharply, giving George her blessing.

George was busy fumbling with his napkin.

"He was a lion," called one of the men at a table across the room.

"George the lionhearted!" his companion agreed, and they both lifted their tea mugs toward George, laughing heartily.

George just ducked his head and frowned at Mrs. Tova. "A secret, huh?"

"Oh, my pigeon pies are in the oven." She bustled off.

"Did you really give Collin Nast a black eye for what he said about me?"

George nodded. "If you must know, yes. And I'd do it again," he said, then stuffed a jelly tart into his mouth to end the conversation.

"That's how you bruised your knuckles? I thought it was from the job. Thank you." She didn't know what else to say, but she basked in the glow of feeling that someone would do that for her.

Neither of them mentioned it again, but as he was walking her back to the assembly room, he took her arm. "I've been thinking lately . . ."

She turned to him, scrutinized his face. "You sound very serious."

"I am. I've been thinking about the future."

Oh, God, what now? Was he going to pull her off the Colony Club project? Had her reputation become as bad as that?

"We're so busy now; can't we worry about the future later?" Besides, she was already worried about her future. Petrified. She only kept her wits about her by staying busy and not thinking about anything except the job at hand. And she couldn't lose this job, too.

He smiled down at her. "You're right. One thing at a time." He slipped her arm in his. "Well, now, do you think they finished counting the tablecloths while you were gone?"

Nora shrugged. "I sure hope so." And at that moment she

hoped a lot of things: that she'd stay employed, that she would one day build her hospital and all the other buildings that lived in her head. That all her new friends would prove to be lasting friends. That her family would welcome her back one day . . .

"What?" George asked, breaking into her thoughts.

"Nothing," said Nora, reeling as the most traitorous thought she'd ever had caught her unawares. She wanted to be happy.

CHAPTER 28

Elsie and Bessie lay side by side on deck chairs aboard the SS *Cedric* as they sailed for New York. They'd been at sea for four glorious days. The weather had been mild, the passengers congenial, and it was heaven being aboard ship, just the two of them.

Just like the old days. Anne wouldn't return to the city for another few weeks.

Bessie had spent the last few days with her head in a stack of new plays she was considering. Sometimes they read scenes together to see how the language flowed. But mostly Elsie strolled the deck or sat on the deck chairs to sketch an idea she had and which was so poorly executed it could only be understood by her. And sometimes mystified even Elsie.

She turned her head to watch her companion. Bessie was getting older—they both were. She'd begun dyeing her hair.

"How's the new play?"

"It will be a hit," Bessie said, without looking up from the manuscript.

"You don't seem to be that enthused. You've been on that same page for several minutes now."

Bessie closed the manuscript. "I was thinking about Stanny."

Elsie nodded. "We're all going to miss him."

"They're going to crucify him in the trial."

"Do you think so?"

"No doubt. The Thaws and their money? Harry is a violent

man, madly jealous and crazy as a loon. But the family money will bury Stanny under a barrage of god-knows-what. It's already started; Evelyn prancing around for the papers, acting like Little Miss Innocent. It's detestable."

"She's quite the good actress. I noticed that the first time we met her." Elsie hadn't much liked her then. She bit back a surge of resentment. "What a waste of a talent, to descend to these cheap theatrics, while that useless rat of a husband extinguishes the life of a great architect."

"And will most likely go free for it." Bessie jabbed her hand in the air.

A steward magically appeared at her side.

"Two champagne cocktails."

The man bowed and strode away.

"Mark my words, before this is over, Stanny will be the monster and Thaw and Evelyn will be the victims. But regardless of what the Thaw family spends, no one will come out of this unscathed. Not even Harry, eventually."

Elsie hoped Bessie was wrong but she had no misconceptions about what money could buy. It wasn't like the news in France had been all that enlightening or even continuous. But what there was hadn't been kind. They had even mentioned the Colony Club in conjunction with Stanny's name.

And Elsie felt a stab of nerves, the kind that one felt before the opening of an untried play. More than a case of butterflies, but a rush of excitement accompanied by dread, praying that it would be a success. Only this time, the curtain would be opening on the rest of her life.

Elsie had landed several more clients among their guests in Versailles. Had future projects lined up once the Colony Club opened.

If she still had a future after Stanny's fall from grace.

Of course she would, she reassured herself. Men were notorious for their peccadilloes. Stanny wasn't the worst of the lot. It was the way of the world. The world of men. Well, they could have their world. As long as it didn't mess up hers.

NORA WAS PORING over the lists of items to be moved into the new building when the office door opened and Elsie's voice trilled, "Nora, my dear! I was sure I'd find you here hard at work."

Nora whirled around. "Welcome back," she said, delighted to see her and just a little relieved. "How was your trip? I think you'll be pleased with the work done while you were gone."

"I'm sure I will. I knew I could rely on you to keep all those men on their toes."

"Well, we did have a—a setback."

"Yes, Stanny. A tragedy. That's why we owe him a spectacular success."

"The papers are—"

"Never mind them." Elsie stopped to rummage in a tapestry bag. She pulled out a small paper bag. "Here is a *petite cadeau pour toi*."

A present. Nora didn't know quite how to react.

Elsie took the problem out of her hands. She opened the bag and slid two nacre hair combs into Nora's hands.

Nora's breath caught. They were beautiful, but much too dear for someone like Nora.

"Don't you like them? I saw them and thought they would be perfect with your lusciously dark hair."

"They're beautiful," Nora managed.

"Well, let me put them in for you." Elsie stood back and ran a practiced eye over Nora's head. "You should really have a swept-up hairstyle, but we'll make do for today." She turned Nora one way and another, then slid one of the combs above her coil of braid at the crown of her head. Cocked her head, considering, and placed the other at the side. "Perfect!"

She rummaged in her bag again, pulled out a hand mirror that she held out for Nora to see.

Nora unconsciously touched her hair.

Elsie lifted Nora's chin with her forefinger. "You're beautiful, Nora. Let others see that. Now let's go see this beautiful building."

NORA AND ELSIE stood just inside the white marble vestibule, the hallway stretching before them like an invitation into Wonderland. And Nora tried to see it as Elsie was seeing it. So much had been transformed since she'd left for Europe. It was all there before them, chronicled within these finished walls. The problems overcome, readjustments made, the setbacks, the excitement, the frustrations, the heartache, the pride of a job well done.

Could Elsie see that? Or did she just see an empty vessel to be filled with her own ideas?

That was the last thought Nora had before she was swept along on Elsie's enthusiasm, down the hall. Elsie stopped at the door to the reading room, its walls painted in a pale bluish green. "Perfect, just like sitting beneath the sky."

Across the main hall to the veranda, now completely clad in green diamond-shaped trellises. Nora could see the plumbing sticking out from a semicircle of stone that would house the Cupid fountain that had been waiting in storage for over a year.

"Where is everyone?" Elsie asked, looking around.

"Most of the construction crew have gone on to other projects. The few carpenters left are upstairs with the woodworkers, finishing the sleeping apartments. The restaurant is stocked with linens and cutlery and the kitchen is nearly finished. There is a crew waiting to begin moving things from the warehouse, when you're ready for them."

"Call them in. I'm ready!" Elsie proclaimed and made a graceful pirouette as if she were surrounded by an audience.

"I've written up several plans on how to proceed if you'd like to look at them," Nora said. "What was the construction office is now the Colony Club business office. They've already moved in. But Mrs. Harriman said we could use the other reception room, the strangers room, for our—your office, which will put us on-site, and she'll be able to release use of the office in the other space."

"Excellent," said Elsie. "When can we get started?"

"I'll have the office moved tomorrow."

"Even more excellent. Now where is the man in charge?"

On cue, George and Mr. Wojcik walked through the front door. They immediately checked on the threshold before collecting themselves and striding toward the two women.

"Miss de Wolfe," said George. "Welcome home."

Mr. Wojcik nodded. "Ma'am."

Elsie acknowledged them both with a graceful gesture that wrapped them both around her little finger.

Nora wished she could be more like that herself. It certainly made some things easier.

"Nora and I have been visiting the first floor. We'll move our office over tomorrow and be ready to begin furnishing on the following Monday." Before either man could protest, she added, "If that's amenable with you. Nora says you're ready but I don't want to mess up your very busy schedule."

"But of course—just let us know what you need," said George.

Nora had a hard time not rolling her eyes.

"Excellent." Elsie started for the door.

George grabbed Nora's arm as she followed.

Great. Now he was going to complain. But he merely looked at her hair. "I haven't seen those before."

"What?"

"Those hair things. They're new."

Nora realized he was talking about her hair combs. "They're a present from Miss de Wolfe."

"They're pretty. You should have nice things."

"Thanks, I—"

"Nora?" Elsie called from the doorway, and Nora hurried to catch up.

ELSIE AND NORA moved their office into the new building the following day. The newly hired domestic staff was hard at work, organizing silver and dinnerware, stacking sheets and linens. Others folded towels for the bedrooms, gymnasium, and swimming pool. Teams of men moved furniture up the stairs and over floors, still covered in tarps.

Things began to progress in earnest. Between trying to organize their office, coordinate schedules, and keep track of Elsie's burgeoning changes, Nora was giddy with trying to make everything happen.

Elsie, on the other hand, just seemed to snap her fingers and the exact person she needed would appear at her side. Everyone was working indefatigably, and work was progressing steadily, but there was still much to do.

The death of Stanford White had caused various setbacks, and the ladies ceased talking about a fall opening. They chose a new date in March that would allow the building to be completed without rushing. But in actuality, as Nora learned from Elsie and Bessie, they were hoping the worst of the scandal would have passed by then.

Mrs. Harriman moved into the business office, along with Anne Morgan and the club secretary, Mrs. Damrosch, and several others. She asked Elsie if she could furnish the parlor and tearoom at the back of the building for the home and building committee meetings, as they were in continual conferences with the housekeeper and general manager.

On Monday, the furniture for the tearoom, parlor, and reading room arrived, along with a steady stream of art, statuary, and fabrics, bringing artists, sculptors, and seamstresses with it.

The installation was going so well that Nora began to think they might have smooth sailing ahead.

Then the house committee arrived for their first meeting.

"Cabbage roses!" shrieked Mrs. Canfield, as if a mouse had just run across her toes. "They're awful! What was she thinking?" Her outrage reverberated throughout the hall all the way to the strangers room, where Nora was working on the reading room plan. She hurried out to see what was happening. She met Elsie running down the stairs from the second floor and they both ran to the back parlor.

Several committee members were there and they had plenty to say.

"It's so . . . so plain. Did she forget half the furniture? This does not reflect the serious nature and purpose of the club. This is New York City, not some country cottage!"

"Well, I think it's charming," said Mary Dick.

"Sometimes I question your taste in fabric, Mary."

"But it is certainly more conducive to sitting and chatting," argued Maud Bull, settling into an upholstered armchair. "Very comfortable."

"I like it," pronounced Mrs. Harriman, who had followed Nora to the altercation. "Why don't we give it a try before we make a final judgment?"

"Good idea," said one of the members. "Do we have a quorum?"

Mrs. Harriman smiled at Elsie and Nora and went back to her office.

"They certainly do have a lot of opinions," Nora said.

"And most of them bad," Elsie added.

ONE DAY GEORGE and Nora were discussing a minor adjustment in the gymnasium storage space when Mr. Wojcik stormed in. "She wants to change the wallpaper!"

They both looked up.

The ladies must have been at it again, Nora thought. "Don't worry, Mr. Wojcik. Elsie—Miss de Wolfe will take care of it."

"No, miss, it's Miss de Wolfe that wants to change the wallpaper."

Nora practically ran from the room, followed closely by the two men.

They found Elsie standing in the foyer, arms akimbo and staring in the direction of the front door.

"It's all wrong," Elsie announced. "I thought it would accentuate the marble and be a perfect prologue, but the colors are not true to the idea." No one said a word. It seemed like the entire building fell silent. "I was *wrong*, I admit it. This is just ugly. We'll have to start again. Take it down, Mr. Wojcik."

George and Mr. Wojcik exchanged looks. Mr. Wojcik mumbled something that sounded like "raving mad" before he nodded. "Yes, ma'am."

The paperers arrived the next day, covered the floor and the woodwork, removed the wallpaper, and reprimed the walls. Two days later new wallpaper was installed.

Elsie took one look, said, "*This* is what I meant," and wandered away.

DURING THE NEXT few weeks, load after load of furniture and tables, paintings and lamps were delivered to the site. Droves of young men came to apply for work. In the kitchen, sous chefs and busboys were given instructions. A maintenance team was assigned duties. But they hit a snag when it came to the uniformed house men. With a line of hopeful men of all heights and shapes waiting to apply, they discovered Elsie had ordered all the uniforms in only one size. So a dozen young men were hired not for their expertise but for the size of their trousers.

Everything was coming together. The rooms filled with furniture laid out to plan, drawn by Nora to Elsie's specifications. The interest in Stanford White's murder began to wane as Bessie said it would. And everyone began looking forward to the holidays.

At the beginning of each day, Nora would walk through the rooms, making notes of the things that had been finished, and what was left to be done.

Then one day she noticed that several chairs had been moved. She knew Elsie hadn't changed her mind. She was adamant about every little detail. And though it could be maddening, Nora respected her for it. She moved the chairs back to their original positions.

Several days later it happened again, this time in the tearoom. But there had been a committee meeting the day before; perhaps they had moved the seats by necessity and hadn't put them back. Nora rearranged them to the original layout.

No matter how closely Nora oversaw the placement of each chair, chaise, table, or lamp, the configurations changed overnight.

"Are you moving the furniture around?" she asked Elsie one morning.

"No, why would I?"

"I thought it might be the workmen," said Nora. "But now I'm not sure."

"We can't have people actually using the rooms before the Grand Opening. Everything will look lived-in for the reviewers."

They asked Mrs. Harriman to send out a letter, asking the ladies to curtail their visits except for the tearoom and parlor for scheduled meetings.

They hoped that would be the end of it. But one morning Nora arrived at the club to a reverberating shriek. She didn't even stop at the office but rushed toward the sound, to find Elsie standing in the middle of the reading room, hands clenched into fists at her sides. "They're doing this on purpose. I'll have their heads!"

Nora just stared. They'd spent the entire day before putting the finishing touches on the reading room, exactly as Elsie envisioned it, down to the books on the shelves.

This morning the room had been completely rearranged, the chairs pushed into tight groups; one of the settees from the main lounge had been moved into the room, shoving two high-backed chairs into the corner to make space for it. It seemed that the pieces had gotten up and traded places overnight.

"Where's Bessie?" Elsie stormed out of the room, Nora following at her heels.

They found Bessie in the assembly room, overseeing the hanging of the coat of arms she had designed specifically for the club.

"You have to do something," Elsie demanded.

"Certainly, my dear," Bessie said.

"They've moved the furniture again. I'll have to completely rearrange the reading room back to the original. It will take hours. How am I expected to get this finished if they keep changing it while I'm gone?"

"A legitimate question," Bessie agreed. "I'll call a meeting of the home committee, if you'll be so good as to address them."

"My pleasure," Elsie growled and stormed out of the room.

Bessie smiled at Nora and turned back to the workman who was still standing on the ladder holding the heavy frame against the wall.

"A little higher on the right, I think . . ." Bessie said.

The next day all twelve members of the house committee met in the back parlor.

"It has been brought to my attention," Elsie said, "that certain of you have taken it upon yourselves to rearrange the furniture. While I appreciate your enthusiasm, if we are to be able to open on schedule, I must ask you to refrain from adding your special touches to the rooms."

There was some grumbling. Elsie stood her ground. "Please,

ladies. I just ask one thing: that you please leave everything as it is until our Grand Opening. After that you may do anything you wish with the furnishings." She nodded graciously and left the room, pausing as she passed Nora, who was lingering by the door. "They can stack them in the middle of the floor, light a fire, and dance widdershins around them, naked for all I care."

Alarmed at the idea, Nora rushed after her. "You don't mean that."

"Of course not. They'll gradually come around, end up thinking it was all their idea, and love every piece exactly where and how I placed it."

THANKSGIVING CAME AND went and Nora began to think of her family. She'd been so busy, she hadn't even had time to catch a moment for a clandestine meeting with Rina. But her bank account was beginning to look healthy and she wondered how long it would be before her mother and Rina could find a place of their own.

Their own. The idea startled Nora. She meant *our* own. As much as she loved living with Higgie and Aunt Sorcha, she couldn't take advantage of their hospitality for much longer. She would miss them when the time came. Then chastised herself for the thought. Her family needed her. She couldn't forget that.

One night at the beginning of December, Nora and Higgie were sitting by the fire, Higgie working out a budget for Dr. Jamison, and Nora nodding over her book on Roman art. Aunt Sorcha came in from the library and announced that she'd like to invite Nora's mother and younger sister to Christmas dinner.

"I don't know why I didn't think of it for Thanksgiving, except that we were all so busy. But we'll make up for that at Christmas. We'll have a feast, see if Dr. Jamison has plans, and George Douglas, too. And anyone else you girls would like to invite."

Nora wrote the letter to Mama that night with a shaking hand. What if they refused to come, made excuses that they couldn't leave the children or that Louise needed them? Well, Nora needed them, too. Still, she wouldn't get her hopes up. *Please let me know soonest. Love, Nora.*

She put the letter in the post the very next morning.

Much to her surprise, Mama and Rina accepted. And Mama included a thank-you to Aunt Sorcha for her thoughtfulness.

Suddenly there was more Christmas spirit and less angst over the scandal of the century. Aunt Sorcha was busy feeding the poor down on Varick Street, but she still found time to make fruitcakes and fancy breads that Nora had never seen before.

Nora insisted they use the money in the mason jar for the Christmas feast. For days Nora left the house with the sweet aroma of rising dough filling the air and came home at night tired to the bone to find soup or stew warm on the oven.

"I think I must be getting fat, the way you feed me," she told Aunt Sorcha one night.

"A little flesh never hurt a girl, and you came to us mere skin and bones."

Two days before Christmas they went down to the corner and bought a Christmas tree. A luxury indeed. They trimmed it with old glass ornaments and chains of cranberries and popcorn that they also ate until they were stuffed.

All the while Higgie seemed to glow with happiness. Nora thought it might have something to do with Dr. Jamison. But no matter how much she cajoled, Higgie wouldn't say a word.

On Christmas Day, Nora dressed in her Sunday best, the same dress she'd worn for the last two Christmases. But Aunt Sorcha helped her do her hair on the top of her head and placed the nacre combs to the most effect, then found a ribbon to tie around Nora's waist. By the time she had finished, Nora was feeling quite up-to-date.

When the doorbell rang, Nora was the first to answer it. Mama and Rina stood huddled together, tentative, until Nora pulled them inside.

Aunt Sorcha came running from the kitchen to greet them.

"Forgive my apron." She helped them off with their coats.

Rina turned to hug Nora.

"How do you like the new dress Mama sewed for me?" Rina glanced at Nora's old dress and bit her lip.

"Don't you look spiffy," Nora said brightly.

"She looks quite the young lady," their mother said.

"She does, and it's a perfect color for you. Now come meet Higgie and see our tree."

Mama and Aunt Sorcha hit it off though they couldn't be more unalike. The bluestocking and the seamstress. Rina was fascinated by the books in the library, and spent much of her time poring through their contents.

By the time the doctor arrived, followed shortly by George, it was like they'd all known each other forever.

Dinner was "spectacular," according to Rina, and they all ate until they couldn't eat any more.

"I would like to make a special Christmas toast," Dr. Jamison said.

They all raised their glasses. "To good friends and family, to the spirit of the holiday, and to Miss Caroline Higgins, who has graciously accepted my proposal of marriage."

This caused a call for another round of punch and they were all quite merry when Mama insisted it was time to take their leave.

Aunt Sorcha sent them home with a bundle of leftovers and made them promise to come to Sunday dinner the following week. George and Dr. Jamison offered to escort them to the trolley stop, and with a final burst of "Merry Christmas and happy holidays," the house settled into a sated silence.

It was sad to see Mama and Rina leave. And yet Nora also felt content. And excited for Higgie's engagement.

"You'll stay here for a while at least, won't you?" Higgie asked as they sat in Nora's room getting ready for bed. "I mean, we won't be getting married for a while, but I don't want to leave Aunt Sorcha alone. She's taken care of me all my life."

"I won't leave as long as she wants me here."

"Thank you, Nora. You know, even with all the trouble Mr. White caused, I have to thank him for bringing us together. I've always wanted a sister." She squeezed Nora's hand. Then turned away to energetically brush her hair.

But before Higgie left for her own room, Aunt Sorcha stuck her head in the door. "Tomorrow you and Higgie and I are going shopping. You'll both get new dresses, and Nora, you will get a new coat. And before you argue, we'll use the money in the mason jar."

"I don't think there's enough to buy dresses and coats," said Nora. "Maybe at the secondhand clothing vendor."

"Absolutely not. A new coat, warm and well-made, will last a lifetime," she said as if reading an advertisement. "Besides, there's a sale on."

CHAPTER 29

1963
Washington, D.C.

Daisy's eyelids fluttered. It was past her naptime surely, but she was almost at the end of her tale. Well, this leg of it, anyway, and the young journalist Meg had been so attentive and eager for every detail.

Daisy shifted in her chair and looked at the girl across from her; she hardly seemed tired at all.

"Some years," began Daisy, "you can't wait to end. Nineteen-oh-six was that kind of year. We'd made wonderful progress with the club, years of work and hope and believing to suddenly be brought down by the untimely death of Stanford White. We were still mourning our friend. Despite the things that were being said about him, the things one read in the papers, he was our friend. He'd built us a beautiful building for our club and I just couldn't bear to turn completely against him.

"We all breathed a sigh of relief as the clock struck twelve and noisemakers sounded and champagne overflowed and we said goodbye to a year we couldn't get rid of fast enough. We may have been quit of it, but it still reared its ugly head and threatened the very existence of our hard-earned club.

"It was a different time, not like today when scandals come and go so quickly, when indiscretions are brushed

aside or ignored. Or derided, but without the accompanying paralysis you feel when you see society as you know it begin to show its underbelly. No one was ready for that.

"Stanford White, a man applauded for his immense talent, for his congeniality, for his charity, well-liked and well-respected. Suddenly everything he'd touched was tainted. And it seemed everyone feared they would be tainted by his very existence.

"It was the final throes of the Victorian Age, an age that prided itself on piety and morality, outwardly, at least. One was not to look too deeply beneath that fragile facade, where dark underpinnings simmered, breeding fear of change and threatening the very foundations of society. The few times it surfaced publicly for all to see, it was impossible to ignore, made people wonder, ask impertinent—no, dangerous questions.

"Stanford's murder brought out all those fears. Men who had known him for years, maybe even participated in some of the excesses he was accused of, removed themselves from his sphere. Pretended not to have known him all that well or had never known him at all.

"Husbands forbade wives to discuss him. Afraid of the stain that might attach to them merely for admitting they'd been his friend, associate, acquaintance. I think that was the year I learned just what men, and women, would do to protect themselves. Preachers railed against licentious behavior that they saw as running rampant in society; they increased their attacks against the Colony Club, not even open yet, the notion of a women's club being an example of perverse behavior that should be torn out before it was allowed to take hold. It became a kind of mass hysteria. Or a plague that might be catching.

"McKim and Mead merely left town, making infrequent

appearances at the business while the drafting room practically ran itself and poor George Douglas and a few other senior architects tried to hold things together.

"Several intimates fled society completely. Some even fled the country. Business associates found themselves shunned; a school where Evelyn Nesbit had studied as a girl had to declare bankruptcy when parents began to withdraw their daughters just for its association. And unfortunately, being the last commission he worked on, the Colony Club received its share of the disdain.

"Harry Thaw's trial opened on January 23, 1907, and we held our breaths and hoped that it wouldn't bring us down, too."

January 1907
Manhattan

"Liar!" Bessie slapped the *Times* down on the dining table. "That little hussy, trying to look like Little Miss Innocent. It makes me sick. The viper."

Elsie was looking at a very similar photo in her copy of the *Tribune* of Evelyn Nesbit, dressed like a schoolgirl, the plain dress and lacy white collar and childish expression. She looked absolutely ridiculous with her hair pulled back and held with a big bow, sorrowful child eyes looking out from her beautiful, betraying face.

"Does she expect people to believe her 'Poor me, I didn't know what was happening' act?" asked Bessie.

Before Elsie could even swallow her mouthful of coffee, Bessie continued, "I can tell you one thing, if Evey didn't know what was happening to begin with, her mother certainly did, and she's made a fortune off Stanny ever since."

"Well, she certainly knows what she's doing now," said Elsie, just as outraged. "I suppose that's what this meeting with the men's advisory committee is all about."

"Why else would they call a meeting? They're getting cold feet."

"They can't. We're almost ready to open." Elsie didn't know how Bessie could be so calm. Elsie's new life, her new career, her reason for being was in danger of being extinguished. She'd thrown everything she had into this new venture. How could she ever start again?

Bessie put the paper aside. "Don't worry, my dear, that was part of the bargain; they wouldn't interfere. We'll see this through, but if I ever meet up with Stanny in whatever afterlife there might be, I'm going to box his ears for causing us such trouble."

NORA STOOD AT the window of her office in the strangers room. Ever since the trial began, a group of angry protesters—mostly outraged preachers and politicians, a few zealous members from Anthony Comstock's despised Society for the Supression of Vice, and the occasional woman whose fervor overtook her sense of decorum—had congregated outside the Colony Club building. They had been there every day, sometimes parading up and down the sidewalk, sometimes milling about, sometimes just staring at the building as if they could see inside. They yelled threats of damnation at those who came to work each day. Accosted every passerby to warn them of the devil's work being carried out inside.

"Men with too much time on their hands," George said, coming to stand beside her.

"Is it happening at McKim and Mead, too?"

"Not so much. The bosses are playing it safe. McKim is lying low. He's convinced it's the end of their firm. That the business will never recover."

"And will it?"

"I don't know," George said pensively. "But . . ."

She wanted to ask him, *But what? What about me? Am I out of a job?* But he didn't continue, and he looked so tired she didn't want to worry him more.

"Things are up in the air, especially about White's finances. We'll get paid for what we're working on now. I insisted that they pay you for the work you did, but after that, I don't know. Stanford had a budget for the club, though I don't think any of us will see that. The man was bankrupt."

"What will become of the club? We've all worked so hard. Mrs. Harriman said the men's advisory committee is asking for a meeting this morning. Do you know what they want?"

"I didn't even know there was a men's committee."

"Elsie said they put up the initial money, mainly husbands and fathers, but on the condition that once the club was up and running it would support itself."

"Well, if it's any consolation, they're not the only ones suffering because of the trial. People are so ready to throw blame on others. Look at those people outside. They don't know any of you, or even what the club is about. But one newspaper, one preacher or lady moralist decides that something is bad, and everyone jumps on the bandwagon."

"The club has to survive," Nora said, surprised at the heat in her voice. "It's beautiful and they do so many good things. I've seen that while I was here. They're needed. Their work is too important to be brought down by someone else's scandal."

George smiled. "You've certainly changed your ideas about them."

"I was ignorant before. But surely it won't come to that."

George shrugged. "Things have gone bust for less."

"Will you be okay?"

"Actually, I wanted to—"

"Oh, look, here come Elsie and Bessie." Nora laughed more

out of surprise than humor. Bessie had just cracked her umbrella over the head of one pushy sign carrier.

Nora rushed to let them in.

"A pox on those busybodies," pronounced Bessie. "We came for war! Where are they meeting?"

"Mrs. Harriman and the other ladies are already in the assembly room," Nora said. "But only a handful of the committee have braved the picket line to attend so far."

"That's not a good sign," said Bessie. "I hope we have a quorum."

"A quorum?" blurted Nora. "What are you going to vote on?"

The door opened and several other women poured inside.

"I have half a mind to call out the dogs," Alva Belmont said. "Too bad they're all in the country."

Bessie nodded at Alva and the others. "Thank heavens you came and brought our bravest and most outspoken members. I have a feeling we're going to need to stand together."

"Don't worry about us," said Emmie Winthrop. "Not even J. P. Morgan is going to take my squash courts away. Ladies, shall we go?"

They all tramped down the hallway.

"Fingers crossed," Elsie said, before following the others.

Nora crossed her fingers and didn't let them go for another half hour at least.

DAISY WAS BESIDE herself by the time the door to the assembly room opened and Bessie and Elsie finally arrived. Anne had appeared an hour ago, furious with her father, and on the verge of tears. "He'll try to close us down if he can. He thinks we're doomed to fail. And there's nothing that he hates more than financial failure. And all because of this stupid trial. And when he sees those people outside . . . Ugh!"

"I'm certain we can come to a mutual agreement," said Daisy

calmly, masking the roiling of her stomach at the thought of losing their club. Their right to assemble, their special place to grow and learn and make a difference. And before it even opened.

Well, they would survive. Even if they had to start all over, they would continue. It was too important a service to succumb to external circumstances. Already they had become active in several progressive movements and were just beginning to see the fruits of their labor. There was so much more to do.

Bessie and Elsie strode across the floor, bringing an entourage of three. At least they now made a quorum if a vote was called.

"Well, we're here. Where are the men?"

"Not yet arrived."

Bessie pulled a face. "Afraid to cross the picket line, eh?"

"Oh, Bessie, don't," Anne said, her eyes bright with unshed tears.

"Hold firm, my dear. We will prevail."

"I hope you're right," Daisy said. She'd cudgeled her brains for days trying to find an argument that would sway the men's advisory board that they could make the Colony Club a self-supporting entity. But as Bordie had pointed out, the trial of the century, as the papers had taken to calling it, was sucking the life out of everyone.

"But I have total faith in you," he said, then ruined it by adding, "If anyone can get out of this mess, it's you."

Bessie shrugged out of her coat. Anne and Elsie both reached for it, but Elsie won out.

Bessie continued toward the front of the room where a dozen or so women were seated, all wearing worried expressions.

"Ladies, we are going to have a fight on our hands. I expect you all to stay strong. That little hussy, Evelyn Nesbit, is giving the performance of a lifetime, but if J. P. and the other men on the advisory committee think these theatrics will close us down, we'll show them a performance they won't forget."

"Bessie!" Anne pleaded.

"Don't worry, Anne, no fisticuffs or blue language."

"But the scandal!" Maud Bull sighed.

"Maud, my dear, as long as there are men on earth, there will be scandals in the newspapers. If we caved to every scandal, we'd never get anything done."

"Maybe if we wait six months or so, it will all blow over."

"There will just be a new scandal to take its place."

"I suggest we put any notion of postponing the opening aside right now," said Daisy, her calm tone belying her dry mouth.

She'd barely finished her sentence before the double doors opened and three men entered. Delegates from the advisory board. J. P. Morgan led the way, accompanied by Charles Barney, who immediately looked for his wife, who was sitting across the room scowling at him like thunder. Frank Polk walked on his far side, trying to avoid his wife completely.

Daisy pulled herself together and went to greet them. She wished Bordie were here. He was quite good at reading other men, especially when it came to finances, which Daisy surmised was the sticking point of this meeting as much as the possibility of scandal that might be attached to the club.

J. P. took the lead and got right to the point. "Through no fault of your own, circumstances have made it difficult to further endorse the continuance of the Colony Club." Several gasps, but before anyone could dispute his words, he continued, "As you know, the Princeton Club has long been interested in buying this property."

"Never!" yelled Alva. Mary Dick tried to hush her, but Alva continued, undaunted. "They've made fun of us since we began. They've just been waiting—"

"Like jackals," someone supplied. Daisy couldn't see whom.

"Like jackals," Alva continued. "To let us do all the work, then reap the spoils of our labor. I said no then, and I say no now."

"Ladies, let Mr. Morgan present his argument," Daisy said, her own fury threatening to boil over. How dare he expect them to give in so easily. And to the Princeton Club.

J. P. drew himself up, looking even more formidable than usual. "It's just unfortunate timing that Mr. White is so closely linked to this club, which is why—"

"Are the Payne Whitneys selling their house that isn't even finished yet?"

"We are not!" came a voice from the back. Helen Whitney must have slipped in at the last minute.

"And what about the Madison Square church? Are they closing their doors?"

"Ladies, they are in different positions than the Colony Club," J. P. argued.

"Only because they're not a women's club."

"Well, I'm sorry to say that's partially true."

"The Princeton Club isn't afraid of being stigmatized by the fact that Stanford White is the architect?" Bessie asked.

"It is different for men, Miss Marbury."

"We are well aware of that!" said Alva, which earned her a disdainful look from J. P.

Daisy stood. "Then let them buy Mr. White's house on Twenty-first. I hear it's going to be for sale."

"Mrs. Harriman, Daisy," J. P. adjured. "You know we have supported the club all along, but this exceeds all bounds. We are only concerned for your safety and reputations."

"And for *your* finances," Alva snapped back, before Daisy could answer.

J. P. motioned to Barney, who handed him a sheet of paper. "We have looked at the numbers. You've already exceeded costs for the furnishing of the club."

"I believe you gave carte blanche on that item," Anne said quietly. She was not only J. P.'s daughter, she was also the club treasurer.

"And so we did, and it looks"—he cleared his throat—"lovely. However, continuing to run in the red is not an option. As you well know."

"We do not intend to run in the red," Daisy said, cutting in. "However, we must open first to prove it."

"The advisory committee has considered and we strongly suggest—no . . . strongly *advise* you to consider the proposition from the Princeton Club."

"That hardly seems fair, to judge us before we begin," Bessie said icily.

"Miss Marbury. You may know the theatrical business better than any of us, but this club is bound to falter."

"And if it does, we'll recover," said Anne, standing up next to Bessie.

Daisy closed her eyes. The last thing they needed was to turn father against daughter, or vice versa. Or worse, to set him off, just by seeing Anne and Bessie stand against him.

But J. P. merely passed over his youngest daughter and continued, "The papers have already been drawn up; you won't get a better offer. And you could easily end up in bankruptcy like several businesses have already just because of their association with White. Just like White himself." He stretched out his hand and Mr. Polk placed a sheaf of papers in it.

"Here is the contract. Have your lawyer look it over; discuss it among yourselves, if you feel that is necessary. But don't linger. If this trial lags on, the Princeton Club may reconsider and withdraw its offer."

All eyes in the room turned to Daisy.

She took a deep breath. Did she take it and pretend to be willing to compromise? She had no intention of selling the club. But she was not the only one involved. They had all worked hard; they were all depending on her. They might lose a few members. Well, if they did, she would get new members. It might be safer to cut their losses, but there were times you had to stand firm in spite of everything. This was one of those times.

J. P. still held the contract toward her. Not a woman in the room moved. They were all focused on the papers in J. P.'s hand. The air stood completely still and so did the air in Daisy's lungs.

She collected her wits. She and Bordie might not be as rich as some of the men and women in this room, but they were determined and honest and loyal. And they knew how to make a budget work.

"We thank you for your advice . . . and we'll appreciate your continued support in whatever we decide."

"I think," J. P. broke in, "that we have decided the best course of action is to sell."

"Sir, your committee promised not to interfere in the running of the club," Daisy reminded him, as calmly as her racing heart would allow.

"I think we're a little beyond that now. You can't even open to members with that mob outside."

"Nonetheless . . ."

She couldn't say it. *We will take your advice under consideration.* She wouldn't consider it. But she took the contract from him. It was a slim sheaf of only four or five sheets. As if they didn't even need to bother with the wherefores and wherebys, which was the attitude of most of male society. And Daisy Harriman, the coolheaded, compromising, never-show-hysterics Daisy Harriman, took the pages in both hands and calmly tore them in half.

"You may tell the Princeton Club we will not be selling."

J. P. looked as thunderous as she'd ever seen him; the other two committee members looked just as displeased. She hoped to heaven she hadn't jeopardized Bordie's career in banking. But she'd done what she had to do.

From somewhere behind her someone clapped, and then another until the room filled with the applause of Manhattan's first-ever women's club.

"I hope you won't live to regret this day."

"I hope we won't, and I sincerely hope you will continue to see us through whatever may come as you have seen us through so much thus far."

"Humph," he said, and, evidently feeling there was nothing more to say, the men's delegation left the room.

Daisy turned to the other women, who sat watching her expectantly and perhaps a little apprehensively. "Thank you all for coming. I think we're all agreed about continuing."

She was met with a resounding cheer.

But as soon as they had gone, she took Bessie and Elsie aside.

"Well," Daisy said. "That is that. I believe we need a plan."

IF THERE WAS ever a time Nora missed her little hidey-hole above the rented assembly room, it was today. She and George hovered near the closed door, but could make out little of what was said. But when applause broke out, they hightailed it back to Nora's office, leaving the door only slightly ajar.

They heard more than saw the men's committee stride by and out the front door, where they were greeted by renewed chanting on the street. Nora and George raced to the window in time to see the men climb into a carriage.

"Going to *their* club, no doubt," George said dryly.

"I wonder what happened."

They weren't to know. A few minutes later, as the other women dispersed, Bessie, Elsie, Anne, and Mrs. Harriman went into their office and closed the door. They didn't emerge for the longest time and when they did, they immediately left the building, going in their own carriages or automobiles to parts unknown by Nora or anyone else she asked.

As THE REPORTING of the trial grew more lurid, the handful of picketers outside the door of the Colony Club grew. George took to meeting Nora on the corner to escort her through the crowd to the door.

She told him it wasn't necessary. After her first confrontation with the photographers the day after Mr. White's death, she'd determined not to let anything stop her from doing what she needed to do. In work or in life.

But he insisted and she accepted; and she had to admit that between George's presence and her new winter coat, she felt as if she could face down the world.

The weather was cold but sunny, and the crowd and the signs grew, until they had to push their way unceremoniously through the milling protesters. One day two men actually tried to bar their way. But the door opened and they slipped inside.

"This can't go on much longer," Daisy said. "The women are afraid to come."

"Just be patient," Elsie told her. "Things will change."

And then one day, things did change. Though not because of Elsie. It began to snow. A slicing, biting kind of snow. One by one, then in groups, picketers drifted away, their ardor cooled. It snowed for several days and the crowd continued to dwindle as the temperature dropped. Whatever snow had managed to melt during the afternoon froze over during the night, making traversing the pavement treacherous. And just as the ice began to melt and they prepared themselves for another onslaught of angry protesters, the temperature dropped again. And it all froze over once more.

"If this is Elsie's plan—'wait for the snow'—I have to say, I don't think that will do the trick," George said one day as he sat on the edge of the desk, watching Nora finish the last details to a plinth he needed for another project.

He'd been spending more and more time at the Colony Club office rather than his own at McKim and Mead. But when she asked him about it, he just changed the subject. He became such a fixture that Nora cleaned off a space at her worktable for him. And when one day Fergus showed up with a roll of plans for him to look at, she knew things must be bad.

"What's going on?" Nora asked.

"Nothing . . . yet," George said, and sent Fergus on his way.

"I'm not going to be able to come back when this is over, am I?"

George shook his head. "I'm afraid not."

Nora knew that. She'd known it for a while. But hearing George say it made her stomach—and her hope—plummet.

"But don't worry, Nora."

How could she not? "Will you give me a good reference at least?"

"What? I can't give you a reference. I'm just a cog in the machine."

"No, you're not. You're the one overseeing all the projects."

"I don't have a name."

"Sure you do. Everybody has a name."

"I mean, nobody knows it."

"But—"

They were interrupted at that moment when Elsie burst into the room.

"I've never been so happy to see bad weather in my life. And take a look at this." She pulled a magazine out of her tapestry bag and placed it on the desk between George and Nora.

"*Harper's Bazaar*. You can't get much more established than this." She riffled through several pages and read, "'Roundly out-ranking every other woman's club house in the country—even of two continents, the Colony Club of New York. . . .' Et cetera, et cetera . . ."

She skimmed the page with her forefinger. "Ah! '. . . a stamp of approval by Miss Elsie de Wolfe, the actress lately turned pro-fessional importer of objet d'arts, has been entrusted with the interior decorating and furnishings.'

"It does mention Stanny, but only once. It goes on to describe everything in detail. For eight whole pages. Eight. People will be beside themselves to see inside." She looked up at George and Nora through her eyelashes. "But they won't be able to. It's a private club."

Nora smiled, but she didn't see how an article in a ladies' mag-azine was going to help stem the antipathy to their club.

"Oh, don't you see?" Elsie said, catching Nora's expression. "It only mentions poor Stanny once. And there are other articles to follow. We'll turn the tide of public opinion, you see if we don't.

"Bessie and I have arranged the whole thing. The two of us together can convince people of anything. I knew all those years of acting were for something. And now I know it was to ad-vance my true calling as an interior decorator. The first woman in America."

"But how?" asked Nora.

"My dear. We're having a Grand Opening, inviting everyone who's anyone. Is Daisy here yet?" She snatched up the magazine and swept out of the room just as she had swept in.

"Heavens," George said. "Is she always like that?"

"Often," Nora said. "But she's usually right, about design, and about how to get things done." She quirked her mouth. "She sure had you and Mr. Wojcik eating out of her hand."

"She did not."

Nora gave him a look.

"Well, you have to admit, she does know how to get your attention. But what do you think she means about a Grand Opening?"

"I have no idea, but whatever it is, I'm certain it will be grand."

"In that case, how about lunch? Mrs. Tova is making steak-and-kidney pie."

CHAPTER 30

After the *Harper's* article, other articles began appearing in newspapers and magazines, and every one began with "Miss Elsie de Wolfe" followed by descriptions of the Colony Club. Stanford White's name appeared seldomly and only in passing. Mrs. Harriman explained to Nora that it was a clever strategy by Bessie and Elsie to divert interest to the retired actress and away from Stanford White, so people wouldn't associate them with the disgraced architect. Nora understood, but it hurt a bit for her to see him cast aside, regardless of how licentious his private life had been.

She read the newspapers, kept up with the trial. She didn't want to believe the things that were said about him by the Thaw woman. Nora couldn't bring herself to call her by name. And the way Elsie and Bessie talked about her, Nora felt no need to throw her an ounce of sympathy. But the papers certainly did.

"Crocodile tears," Bessie proclaimed with disgust when she caught Nora shaking her head over an article on the trial. "They should forbid the sob sisters from attending. They've absolutely turned the story around to suit their readers. Now you listen to me, Nora Bromley. Don't believe everything you read in the papers." She snorted and strode toward the door, but turned before she left. "It's a sad tale. But Stanny's tragedy will become our triumph."

"That's terrible."

"Yes. But he would expect us to survive. And for his building to be used and enjoyed. And it will survive, for Stanny's sake, and for ours."

Once the decision had been made to go ahead with the Grand Opening, almost everyone dove in with enthusiasm.

"Just thought I'd help," Helen Barney said one day after she expertly folded a hundred napkins into a complex design. "I learned it from my nanny when I had the chicken pox as a girl. It's a very calming pastime."

Nora moved from floor to floor, overseeing the final touches. The bedrooms were finished, all with simple beds, a chaise longue, a writing table, and adequate lighting for both reading and primping. On the fifth floor, the restaurant was prepared for dining. Small tables with shield-back chairs were set with white linen, all embroidered with the initials of the Colony Club.

Even the staff quarters on the mezzanine floor were neat as a pin, though they would not be part of the tour that Elsie would present on the evening of the Grand Opening.

Mrs. Harriman sent out stacks of invitations and was delighted at the acceptances she received.

The group of protesters had for some reason lost interest and dwindled to almost nothing about the same time last-minute hammering ceased.

"Moved on to another scandal," George said.

Nora hoped so. She'd been invited to attend, though she thought it might be more a case of her being available if something dire happened.

Of course her Sunday-best dress was nowhere near what the others would be wearing. Even the newspaper and magazine journalists would be wearing their finest, since only the crème de la crème of that profession was invited. None of them would be taking clandestine photographs and causing trouble.

And then the big night arrived.

ELSIE LOOKED OVER the main lounge where the guests would gather for a few words from Daisy and Anne. The waiters were standing by, all wearing their buff-and-blue uniforms that accentuated the decor perfectly.

She took a deep breath. As for herself, Elsie felt rather resplendent in her new evening gown, sent especially by Poiret for the evening. The fire was crackling in the fireplace at the far end of the lounge and she was relieved to see that the chimney didn't smoke the tiniest bit.

Bessie made her way toward her, carrying two champagne coupes, her gown of beads and sequins sparkling in the light.

"I thought you might need this."

Elsie took one of the coupes. "I do." She held it to the light. "I think they're rather nice, these glasses, don't you?"

"You are the expert on glassware. I just like the champagne. To you, my dear." And Bessie lifted her glass to Elsie.

Elsie felt a rush of triumph, gratitude, and stage fright all rolled into one. She owed Bessie more than she could express.

"And to you, and to Stanny," said Elsie.

"You're going to be a success, my dear. Ah, there's Daisy. And she's brought Bordie. Good, though after tonight, he'll have to come in the private door with the rest of the men." She trundled away to greet them.

Elsie handed her glass to a nearby waiter, who stood at the ready. The champagne just took the edge off, but she didn't want to be too relaxed. She was ready to embark on the most important role of her life. She was ready. The moment was here. The outer doors opened and the guests began to pour in.

Elsie met and greeted everyone, but didn't say too much. *Build the allure, make them eager, promise them the experience that will change their lives.* It was all theater, really, presentation, manipulation. Sometimes you had to work with an inferior play, make the best of things, but tonight was the pinnacle of excellence, a grand simple building, with furnishings like they had never seen.

After tonight, interiors would never go back to the doom and gloom of the last century. And Elsie de Wolfe would be there ready to guide her new clients into the new epoch.

Across the room, Daisy greeted the guests, her voice rising over the hum of conversation and gently guiding it to silence.

Her welcoming speech was brief. Elsie had been a little concerned about Daisy. She was so very formal and not the most dramatic speaker, but she kept her part short and, after a meaningful pause, finished with: "And now, I present the Colony Club and its interior designer, Miss Elsie de Wolfe."

Daisy gestured to Elsie. Elsie lifted both arms, the silk of her sleeves billowing, and her audience turned as if she were the conductor and they the instruments.

"Good evening, friends. Please join me on a tour of the largest and most beautiful women's club in America, and perhaps the world." She bowed slightly and guided them to the stairs and down to the marble swimming pool.

The gasps of awe behind her lifted her, and she basked in the glow of the fairy lights hidden among the arbored ceiling and reflecting off the walls of Venetian glass. It was a fairyland of mystical Oriental splendor.

Elsie knew just when to break the mood and led them seamlessly through changing rooms, saunas, and masseuse cubicles, then back up the stairs to the first floor.

And so it went through the reading room, parlor, and trellis room. To the second floor, where much was made of the running track, while Elsie enthused about the health benefits of exercise.

On to the assembly room, her wall sconces lighting the room like an army of elegant sentinels, the small panes of the full windows reflecting their light.

Here was her future. Her audience, hanging on to every word, awaiting her gift to them. Elsie's heart overflowed with emotion, and when she blinked away tears, she was astonished that she hadn't even needed menthol to make her eyes glisten.

NORA TAGGED ALONG behind the others, being discreet, nervous and yet excited to see their work through others' eyes. Elsie spun her magic and for the first time, Nora wished she'd seen her onstage. But mostly she was just nervous that something would go wrong, though she didn't know what. Everything had been checked and double-checked; drapes tied back with perfect knots; pictures hung securely . . .

And Nora had been a part of it. This moment of pride was immediately followed by the panic that had begun to beset her in quiet moments. She took a deep breath and stole away, the festive mood suddenly deserting her as she neared her office in the strangers room, where she was no longer a stranger. Yet, knowing soon she would have to move out.

Where would she go now? She'd have to start looking for a new position. At least she wouldn't be alone in the rain and homeless, this time. Higgie and Aunt Sorcha had become a second family to her.

She opened the office door and found George leaning over her desk looking at some plans.

"What are you doing here?"

He jumped and turned around. "Standing by, in case you . . . You know, these are really good."

"What?"

"These are yours, right? The factory design?"

"Shirtwaist factory. I did those after that Miss Lemlich's talk. She's a garment worker. And the things she said . . . I meant to do more, but things got so busy here." She was surprised by a yawn. She was suddenly so tired.

"Well, maybe you'll have more time to work on your own projects now that the club is finished."

"Where?" She hadn't meant to sound so brittle, but suddenly alone in her office with George, the immensity of the future was overwhelming.

"Well, be patient. Something will turn up."

Nora rolled her eyes, mainly to stay awake. She sank into her desk chair.

"Like I said, I may have a proposal."

Nora's stomach dropped. "A proposal?" Professor Gerhardt's advice about women in architecture echoed in her mind. One way that women could get ahead was to work for their architect husbands, until the needs of the family became too pressing. But not for Nora. Not even with someone who she—She swallowed a big, unhappy knot in her throat. She had a promise to fulfill. *No, no, thank you. I'm an architect. And I'm going to stay that way.*

George frowned. "A business opportunity . . . maybe."

"In architecture?"

George nodded, his face blank. "Like I said. Maybe."

"WELL," SAID DAISY, accepting another coupe of champagne. "I think that went swimmingly."

"Yes, indeed," Bordie agreed. "You ladies are on the road to success."

The ladies in question, about seven of them, committee members, who were the last to leave, all raised their glasses.

"We'll drink to that," said Bessie and drained her glass.

"We pulled it off," said Elsie. "And hardly anyone mentioned Stanny. Though it does seem a shame; he would have enjoyed the kudos tonight immensely."

"True," Bessie said. "But he will someday get his due, when this horror is over and the world can see him for the talent he was."

"Will that really ever happen?" asked Nora, who was standing at the edge of the group.

"Oh, yes," said Bessie. "There will always be a bigger scandal just waiting to take today's biggest scandal off the front page. And soon people will forget why it was such a big deal. It's the way of the world, as Congreve reminds us. Of that you can be sure."

"And will you go back to the architectural firm now that the club is completed?" Daisy asked Nora.

"They don't want me back. They never wanted me in the first place. Only Mr. White did. He's the one who hired me."

"The only forward thinker in the group," Bessie said.

"Well, don't despair," Elsie said. "I'll be opening my own interior decoration business soon, and I'm sure we'll have enough business to offer you a place."

"Thank you, but—"

"Elsie, you are relentless," said Daisy. "Poor Nora is practically dead on her feet. I, for one, need a good night's sleep before worrying about the future and I bet she does, too. We open tomorrow for the members. Our first official day. You and Nora can discuss things then." She smiled at the young architect, dressed in simple percale with two beautiful combs in her hair. She was talented; she needed a future in architecture, not as a shadow to Elsie's growing demand as a decorator.

Nora should be designing her hospitals, schools, factories. The girl obviously needed a salary, but Daisy hated to think of her giving up her dream just to keep herself and her family afloat. It was the story of so many young women. Not being able to afford to accept an opportunity if they were lucky enough to get one.

Best for everyone to sleep on it.

"Thank you all for the work you've done. Tomorrow the real work begins. Come, Nora. Let's get your coat and send you home." Daisy walked the girl down the hall to the strangers room.

She helped Nora into her coat. The girl really was physically exhausted, and probably frightened and confused. The rest of them had been celebrating without a thought about those who would move on. Those who had laid the brick, built the walls, installed the electricity. And those who had nursed them through everything.

"Thank you," Nora said in a small voice. And Daisy remembered the first day she'd met her, scrambling over the scaffolding, bold and determined and undaunted. Daisy hated to think that those attributes had been beaten out of her all because of the stupid scandal.

Daisy walked her outside where the Harriman driver waited in Bordie's new automobile, and realized she didn't even have the girl's address.

Once that was taken care of, she put Nora inside and leaned in after her.

"I know this must be a difficult time for you. And I don't want to sway you one way or another, but I've seen your designs, heard your ideas, watched you work indefatigably for someone else's success. Don't sell yourself short. Don't be afraid to go after what you want."

"I want to be an architect."

"Then go after your dream, fulfill your promise."

"I'm not sure I know how. Not now."

"I completely understand, my dear. We all feel that way sometimes. I must have felt that way a hundred times since I had the idea of a women's club. Felt that way more times than not during the last few months.

"Each of us has their own destiny to follow. I have faith in me and I have faith in you. And you have friends." She smiled; the girl could hardly keep her eyes open. She might not even remember what Daisy had just said. And really, who was Daisy to give advice to someone in such different circumstances from her own?

"Good night. See you tomorrow."

Daisy stood a long time watching the car drive away, so long that she was shivering by the time Bordie came out to see what was keeping her. "I sent Nora home in the car," she said on a yawn.

"Of course you did. Come back inside. I assume it's coming back for us?"

"Of course."

"Do you think there are any sandwiches left?"

THE NEXT DAY a theater sandwich board appeared in the foyer, announcing the four Tuesday meetings for the month and that the Colony Club doors were now open for its members. Ladies poured in from morning until evening, having tea and gossiping, quietly reading the newspapers and periodicals in the reading room, chatting in the main lounge, their voices sometimes rising as a point was being made. They played cards in the parlor. They talked about the latest French fashions, the latest strike by the coal miners, and a group around Alva Belmont nearly came to fisticuffs over women's right to vote.

It was getting on toward evening and the ladies showed no signs of leaving. Nora returned to the strangers room and began collecting her materials and supplies.

"Can I come in?"

"George, where did you come from?"

"McKim and Mead. I came to pick up our plans and stuff."

"Oh." Nora turned back to what she was doing. She couldn't look at him. He was going back to work, work where he belonged, where he could climb the ladder of success. And she . . . she would straighten up her things and . . .

"Did you give Elsie an answer yet?"

She shook her head.

"Do you want to take it?"

"I don't know; she pays well."

"But do you want to do wallpaper and latticework for the rest of your life?"

"You know I don't, but right now it's my only option."

"Not necessarily."

"McKim and Mead won't take me back. You said so. The only résumé I have is connected to Mr. White."

"Look at me."

She shook her head. She didn't know what he was going to say but she was afraid of what it might be.

He turned her chair around with her still in it.

"Remember last night, I told you I might have a proposal." He held up his hand, preventing her response. "A business proposal. I've given McKim and Mead my notice. Fergus Finnegan and I are opening our own architectural firm. We've discussed this, and we want you to come in as a partner, if you're interested. It will be slow going at first. We have to build up a clientele, but between the three of us, that shouldn't be a problem. Just slow.

"We have different skills, skills that will complement and aid the others. Fergie is a draftsman, understands plumbing, electrical, all that stuff. I want to concentrate on big buildings for the future, and you have your hospital and schools. We can all build houses, and you can draw better than both of us together.

"It won't pay nearly as much as Elsie would, but you'd be doing what you love, right? Fergie's brother has a few feet of storefront that he doesn't need at the moment and we can set up shop cheap.

"We'll split everything three ways. We just have to be patient. What do you think? You might get a job with another firm, but with us, you'll be able to spend time with the designs you most want to do. We'll enter contests, do what we have to do to drum up clients. It won't be easy. But—Why don't you say something?"

"Because you've been running on so, I haven't had a chance." Actually her heart was bursting. They might fail, but . . .

"You don't want me just for my watercolors?"

"No, though they are very good."

"I'd be a full partner?"

"Yes."

"With my name on the sign out front?"

"When we get one. Yes, Finnegan, Douglas, and Bromley."

He saw her look and explained, "We tried all kinds of name arrangements, and this sounds the best."

Nora nodded. "You promise?"

"Yes. Even if some day I make another kind of proposal and you say yes, it will always say 'Bromley' on the sign outside."

The words she'd been waiting to hear for so long. She was an architect. "Bromley" on the sign. *We made it, Papa, Jimmy. We made it.* "In that case, I accept."

"Great! Let's go tell Mrs. Harriman and the others." He pulled her out of her seat and down the hall, where they found Mrs. Harriman, Anne, and Elsie looking over the activities. It was getting late and the ladies still showed no signs of leaving.

"Ah, Nora, George. Still working?"

"We just came to tell you that Nora has accepted a position as partner in Finnegan, Douglas, and Bromley."

"Ah, you're striking out on your own?"

George nodded, animated as much as Nora had ever seen him. "It's a new century; the future is ripe for new kinds of buildings. New attitudes toward design, as Miss de Wolfe has proven."

Elsie bent her head demurely, a gesture bound to floor any man who was close by, but Nora could tell Elsie was pleased. "I'll expect all three of you to be available to consult on my projects as the need arises."

"Of course," Nora said. "It has been such an honor and an

education. Thank you all." Her throat tightened and she blinked hard to overcome the swell of emotion inside her.

"That is splendid," Mrs. Harriman said. "I know we'll see great things from you both. And you both have connections here. I know several people interested in your ideas for hospitals and apartment buildings, and I imagine with your backgrounds you'll be called on for a variety of commissions."

"And I expect you to give me advice on a lounge for military families that I'm interested in fitting out in Brooklyn," Anne Morgan added.

AND A HOSPITAL, thought Daisy. She, too, would make sure that opportunities came Nora's way. And not just Nora. There were other projects that needed support, inequities to be tackled. A city, a country, a world to make better. The Colony Club was just the beginning.

As they stood there, Mrs. Perkins, a matriarch of society who had been supportive throughout the process, and the mother of several important men in the city government, came toward them, hands extended. "Daisy, I want to thank you. I have waited for this evening my entire life. I have just telephoned home and told them not to wait dinner for me. I'll be dining at my club tonight." She laughed delightedly. "Whoever thought this moment would ever come?"

"I did," said Daisy. "I never doubted it in the least."

CHAPTER 31

November 1909
Manhattan

Nora reached for a piece of toast without looking up from the plans that were folded next to her breakfast plate. She needed to find another two feet to include a book-return chute for the new library design.

At the other side of the table, George's head was bent over his copy of the *Times*.

"Huh," he said.

Nora made a quick note on the edge of the blueprint. "What's the 'huh' about?"

"The ladies of the Colony Club are in the news again."

"Oh?" Nora put down her pencil and gave him her full attention. "What is it this time?"

"Seems they're not content just to donate to the cause, they've taken to marching alongside the striking women garment workers." He smiled, then read, "'Dressed in their finest hats and mink coats, they placed themselves between the marchers and the policemen and hired thugs, thinking they were less likely to arrest and beat the female strikers with respectable women among them.'"

"Bully for them," said Nora. "If I had a mink coat, I would join them."

George dipped an eyebrow at her from across the table.

Nora suppressed a grin. "Maybe my new tweed would do?"

"I think you're doing quite enough without getting yourself arrested. You just leave the ladies to do what they do best and you do what you do best. Like Aunt Sorcha, a brigade unto herself, always says, the way to resolve problems is from all angles.

"And yours is to finish the prospectus for the new library on West Broadway. If we get the bid, we'll insist they keep a special shelf for every book written about the strike of 1909—when someone gets around to writing about it."

"You sound like you think the strike will succeed," said Nora.

"Well, it should, at least to some degree, and you shouldn't be so impatient for the world to change."

"I know, 'brick by brick,'" Nora said. "As *you* always say when I want things to happen faster."

"Hopeless advice on my part, I'm afraid. But listen to this. The press is calling them the Mink Brigade." He chuckled. "I don't think they mean it in a complimentary way."

"Well, I like it," Nora said. "These newspaper people don't have a clue as to the power of Daisy and her Mink Brigade.

"Which reminds me, I'll be back late tonight. I'll finish the final library plans and leave them with Fergie, but then I have to meet Anne Morgan at the Brooklyn Navy Yard. To think that until Anne came along, the navy didn't even bother to feed the men who serve our country. They had to go off the base to buy their lunch from food carts. And stand on the street just to visit their families."

"So you've told me."

"The newspapers can scoff all they want at what they call the Mink Brigade. But thanks to Anne—"

"And you."

"—the navy is about to have a refitted space to serve a thousand men and their families. And this is just the beginning. Anne intends to establish the same program on more bases."

"And hopefully hires you for them all."

Nora pushed her chair back and looked fondly at her partner in life and work. "I'll always be happy to consult, but first there's an apartment complex and a hospital wing renovation to finish. And"—she picked up her blueprint—"fingers crossed, this library to build."

George finished his coffee. "Lest I be considered the slacker in this family, I'll accompany you down to the office and get to work. Oh, I almost forgot, Aunt Sorcha and your mother have invited us to have Thanksgiving dinner with them."

He followed Nora to the hall, then held out her winter coat for her. She turned into him, slipped her arms into the sleeves, and stretched up to kiss his cheek.

"I appoint you as official supporter of the Tweed Brigade. Shall we get to work?"

April 18, 1963
Washington, D.C.

"And that's how we established the Colony Club," Daisy said. "It's still in existence, you know."

The young reporter sighed. "And from there you embarked on an eminent career. Social reformer, union organizer, suffragist, diplomat, political activist."

"I've had a very meaningful life, for which I'm grateful."

"But what about the others? Did your paths cross again?"

"Oh, yes. We all stayed in touch through the club. Enlisted others and have had much success in the causes we supported.

"Elsie was so successful with the Colony Club that it established her reputation in New York, and it soon spread.

As Bessie predicted, she became known as the mother of American interior decoration, though Elsie I'm sure would prefer to be known as the queen."

"And Nora?"

"She built her hospital; several, in fact. Finnegan, Douglas, and Bromley became known for their civic buildings, as well as a number of schools and affordable apartment buildings. They used the newest and safest materials and designs. She and George got married, as we all knew they would. And true to his word, he kept 'Bromley' in the firm's name even after she became a Douglas.

"We used to exchange cards every Christmas. George died just a few years back. Nora's children bring her to visit me every once in a while. So many of my friends are gone: Elsie, Bessie, Anne, and my dear Bordie and sweet Ethel. But they still live on in a way."

"In your heart?"

"Oh, yes, but in something even more substantial."

Daisy looked up at the citation so recently bestowed on her. "By their energy, skill, and dedication to so many causes, and through the lives they changed, they are all very much alive."

AUTHOR'S NOTE

Writing historical fiction is sometimes a daunting as well as exciting venture. You attempt to be as accurate as possible, while knowing that you're also writing fiction, which demands a different set of parameters. A story or scene with many historical figures participating may have to be whittled down to a number that a reader can remember. Sometimes characters have to be consolidated. That's why authors rely on the Author's Note to be fair and honest with our readers.

For example, many of the women at the original Newport meeting and the subsequent early meetings didn't figure largely into this particular story, so a decision had to be made. To learn more about those women left out of my story, I refer the reader to Daisy Harriman's memoir, *From Pinafores to Politics*.

On the other hand, some important historical characters who were absent became recurring characters in this story and after consultation with my editor we decided to add them to the original meeting.

Of the three main point of view characters, two were real historical figures.

Daisy Harriman is, of course, well-known today. At the time when she had the idea of a women's social club, she was a thirty-two-year-old wife, mother, and socialite. The Colony Club was one of her first forays into her work as a reformer, organizer, and diplomat, for which she earned the first Citation of Merit for Distinguished Service Award. Active in women's suffrage, food purity, child labor laws, working conditions, and tuberculosis treatment (she eventually donated the Harrimans' Mount Kisco estate to be used as a tuberculosis sanitarium), she was also active at the federal level and served as U.S. Minister to Norway.

Elsie de Wolfe was indeed known as the best-dressed actress of the Rialto, the name for the theater district when it was clustered around Union Square before migrating to Forty-second Street. And though not an extremely talented actress, she did, according to all who knew her, have an exacting eye for style. She is known as America's first interior decorator. Until this time interiors were usually designed by the architect. The Colony Club was Elsie's first big commission and from there her career in design flourished. She owed much of both of her successes to her companion for twenty years, Bessie Marbury.

Bessie was one of the most powerful theatrical agents of the time. Among her clients were Oscar Wilde, Victorien Sardou, J. M. Barrie, among others. She was a formidable planner and was instrumental in the forming of the Colony Club and in inducing Stanford White to design the clubhouse.

Stanford White is perhaps remembered these days more because of his murder at the rooftop theater of Madison Square Garden and the subsequent sensationalist trial than his architecture. Unfortunately many of his works have since been demolished.

Much has been written about this aspect of his life, but what was interesting to me was how his fall affected so many people. And how the mere association with the world-famous, suddenly disgraced architect could be detrimental to even the most tangential relationships. Something that with our instant news sources today we can all relate to.

My third point of view character, Nora, is entirely fictitious, but she had many good models to inspire her—and me. There were successful female architects at this time (Alice Hand, Mary Gannon, Faye Kellogg, Louise Bethune, etc.). In 1900, only thirty-nine American women had graduated from formal four-year architectural programs. And though a degree in architecture wasn't necessary, it was important to have a good apprenticeship, which was difficult to come by for women.

I never found that McKim, Mead, and White ever employed an in-house female architect, though White employed a large network of independent artists, many of whom were women. Nora, if she'd had a studio from which to work, would have become one of those independent contractors.

The original clubhouse is still standing and is the home of the American Academy of Dramatic Arts. The Colony Club itself is still in existence, though they moved to more spacious accommodations shortly after the original clubhouse was finished.

In the course of my research, as always, I found primary sources to be of immense benefit. Especially the New York newspapers that as well as reporting daily on the news, both local and world, also give us day-to-day insight on fashion, entertainment, art, politics, and the prices of everything from lingerie to automobiles.

For those interested in further reading, I suggest:

Ladies and Not So Gentle Women—Alfred Allan Lewis
Gilded Suffragettes—Johanna Neuman
From Pinafores to Politics—Florence J. H. Harriman
Stanford White's New York—David Garrad Lowe
The House in Good Taste—Elsie de Wolfe
Elsie de Wolfe: A Life in Style—Jane S. Smith
My Crystal Ball: Reminiscences of a Busy Life—Elisabeth Marbury
Triumvirate: McKim, Mead & White—Mosette Broderick
Mrs. Astor's New York—Eric Hombergger

ACKNOWLEDGMENTS

Writing and publishing a novel is never a completely solitary occupation. It takes many hands and minds to bring a book from an idea to the reader. Sometimes it takes a village, sometimes it takes a club. Thanks to my club on this one.

To Gail Freeman, who lets me talk and pace and then says "that one" and has an uncanny ability to find one little fact that makes my ramblings fall into place.

To Lois Winston for her clearheadedness when I'm at my muddiest. And to both for being my good friends.

To my local librarians who have my ordered books ready when I walk in the door. I couldn't do it without you.

To designer Elsie Lyons and retoucher Wendy at Windyveil Design for their wonderful cover art.

And especially to my editor, Tessa Woodward, whose love of literature inspires me every time, and to my indefatigable agent, Kevan Lyon; her energy and belief in her authors seem boundless.

And to the whole William Morrow team that made *The Colony Club* an actuality, I thank you.

ABOUT THE AUTHOR

Shelley Noble is the *New York Times* and *USA Today* bestselling author of eighteen novels of historical fiction, historical mystery, and contemporary women's fiction, including *The Tiffany Girls*, *A Secret Never Told*, and *Whisper Beach*.

A former professor, professional dancer, and choreographer, she now lives in New Jersey halfway between the shore, where she loves visiting lighthouses and vintage carousels, and New York City, where she delights in the architecture, the theater, and ferreting out the old stories behind the new.